Henry Cholmondeley-Pennell

The Angler-Naturalist

A popular history of British fresh-water fish, with a plain explanation of the

rudiments of ichthyology

Henry Cholmondeley-Pennell

The Angler-Naturalist
A popular history of British fresh-water fish, with a plain explanation of the rudiments of ichthyology

ISBN/EAN: 9783337391270

Printed in Europe, USA, Canada, Australia, Japan

Cover: Foto ©Andreas Hilbeck / pixelio.de

More available books at **www.hansebooks.com**

THE ANGLER-NATURALIST:

A POPULAR HISTORY

OF

BRITISH FRESH-WATER FISH,

WITH

A PLAIN EXPLANATION

OF

THE RUDIMENTS OF ICHTHYOLOGY.

BY

H. CHOLMONDELEY PENNELL,

AUTHOR OF "HOW TO SPIN FOR PIKE," ETC. ETC.

ILLUSTRATED BY UPWARDS OF 150 WOOD ENGRAVINGS.

LONDON:

JOHN VAN VOORST, PATERNOSTER ROW.

MDCCCLXIII.

TO

HENRY RALPH FRANCIS, ESQ., M.A.,

JUDGE, NEW ENGLAND,

ONE OF THE MOST ACCOMPLISHED OF LIVING ANGLERS,

THIS VOLUME

IS AFFECTIONATELY INSCRIBED

BY HIS PUPIL IN THE GENTLE CRAFT,

THE AUTHOR.

No work on Natural History has hitherto been published adapted to the special requirements of Anglers and others who may wish to possess, in a compendious form, a fair general outline of Ichthyology, with some account of the Fresh-water Fish of the British Islands and the distinctions by which they may be most easily recognized.

This *desideratum* it is the object of the present volume to supply.

To materials drawn from the writings and private correspondence of eminent naturalists and sportsmen have been added the results of much personal experience; and it is hoped that the practical form in which the subject has been arranged, divested of all avoidable technicalities, may induce lovers of fishing to acquire the rudiments at least of the science a knowledge of which is so indispensable to the full enjoyment of their sport.

Particular attention has been given to the history of the Pike, and the various Salmon and Trout species, as being preeminently the game fish of the country, and, in the case of the Salmon, as representing in a national point of view an important article of food.

To Mr. Frank Buckland, Sir J. Emerson Tennent, and Dr. Albert Günther, of the British Museum, the Author is desirous of recording his sincere thanks for the kind assistance he has received in the preparation of this work.

Weybridge,
   July 1, 1863.

Mr. Van Voorst having kindly placed the illustrations of the late Mr. Yarrell's magnificent "History of British Fishes" at the Author's disposal, they have been gladly made use of in the great majority of instances throughout the following pages.

Most of these engravings were executed under Mr. Yarrell's immediate superintendence during a lengthened term of observation; and it was felt, therefore, that it would be difficult, if not impossible, to supply equally perfect and reliable designs within any available period.

THE

ANGLER-NATURALIST.

PART I

CHAPTER I.

INTRODUCTORY REMARKS.

THE age in which we live is emphatically one of *use*. Utilitarianism, in its best as well as in its worst sense, has struck deep root into the national soil, and in nothing is more strongly shown than in the prevailing character of our literature, in which, if we except the standard three-volumed novel, fiction may be said to have given place to fact, poetry to prose, and the *belles lettres* generally to works of a *quasi* moral, political, or scientific character. Amongst the latter, essays on Natural History more or less popularized have been conspicuous for the very favourable reception accorded them by the public; but of these none have been specially devoted to Ichthyology *, whilst

* From the Greek, *ichthys*, a fish, and *logos*, a treatise.

B

for the most part what has been written has appeared in a detached or fragmentary form,—the information furnished being either too scanty and incomplete, or too diffuse and overlaid with technicalities to suit the requirements of the uninitiated. Thus it results that the "science of fish" is still far from being as widely understood and appreciated as amongst a nation of sportsmen might have been naturally expected; and the young student would probably find himself not a little perplexed in attempting to arrive, unaided, at any clear general conception of a subject which, if stripped of needless difficulties and plainly set before him, he could have mastered with perfect ease.

To the angler the value of even a moderate acquaintance with ichthyology cannot be exaggerated. Not only is it of the greatest practical use, by the insight which it gives him into the habits, food, spawning-seasons, &c., of the several fish—and consequently into the best means of taking them—but it also doubles the pleasures of success. The most insignificant captures have to the naturalist an interest of their own, apart from their mere weight in ounces. He is able to identify the various species he meets with (many of which would otherwise pass unrecognized), to distinguish their sexes, ages, and conditions, and to read with an intelligent eye the wonders of this marvellous and beautiful page of Nature. In spite of the advance of Fish-science of late years, there are still many moot points and disputed theories connected with it which require elucidation, and possibly new varieties of fish yet to be discovered; and it may often be within the power of the angler-naturalist to observe and accurately describe characteristics and peculiarities of the highest interest to science. Notwithstanding, however, these inducements, it is astonishing how many there are, calling themselves sportsmen, who are content to remain all their lives simply Killers of fish—of the habits, idiosyncrasies, and even of the very names of which they are too often ignorant. Nor let it be supposed that this is a mere figure of speech: many species, particularly of the Salmon and Carp families, are only distinguishable by minute, though well-defined, differences, imperceptible to the uneducated observer; and it is perhaps not too much to assert that a very large proportion of the former are chronicled by their captors under names with which they have no connexion whatever.

This observation is even in some degree applicable to old and experienced fishermen. " Names are the representatives of things; if a man does not know the names of things in the water, he may sit by it all his lifetime without gaining much information for himself, and absolutely none that he can convey to others. The alphabet of science is its technicalities; and consequently the unlearned sitter by the water is in an exactly similar position to the man who attempts to study a book without having first learned his A B C."

To their credit be it spoken, however, there are very many who aspire to better things, and who have endeavoured really to qualify themselves for the name of Anglers of the first angling nation in the world. England is, indeed, preeminently the land of the rod and line—the fisherman's paradise. There is no other country where the gentle craft is so thoroughly understood and appreciated, and where everything around unites to make a man an angler, and to keep him so. Is he a bottom-fisher? here he may wander by the margin of ever-gliding streams, knee-deep in meadow-sweet, or, with tranquil mind, muse away life "in the green gleam of dewy-tassel'd trees." Is he a troller? in England he will find broad meres and stately rivers that might ravish the soul of a Nobbes. A fly-fisher? by the rush of a Dove, or a Coquet, he will be mated with trout and the goddess of scenery—

"Shut in—left alone—with himself, and perfection of water."

Yes, England is the paradise of the angler; and to England, as Badham has gracefully expressed it, "in after-life, wherever he may have travelled and fished in the mean while, he will be delighted to return, and re-visit the scenes of his angling boyhood—the banks of each well-known stream, the unchanged lake, the paternal pond, and the boat of 'auld lang syne' rising two inches in the boat-house to greet him—that dear old boat to which he used furtively to creep, and, loosing her rusty and trusty chain from its moorings, confide his mistress's name and the earliest efforts of his Muse, or else, in some bright August day,

"' When showers were short and weather mild . . . .
Would sit all day, with patient skill,
Attentive to the trembling quill.'"

The mere sight of a fishing-line in after-life is often-times sufficient, without the aid of other accessories, to awake pleasant memories of the past. "Quels souvenirs touchants cette ligne peut rappeler!" writes Lacépède: and if there must always be a touch of melancholy blending with these pleasant associations—associations which the chances of life, or of death, may perhaps make it impossible that we should ever renew—depend upon it, it is not the melancholy that "corrodes," but rather the tender senti-ment which soothes the heart where it rests, and leaves its owner a kindlier and a better man.

But I am forgetting my utilitarian motto. To all true anglers, then, I venture to submit these pages; and I would say to them, grudge not a few hours, or even days, to a pursuit which will assuredly repay you fiftyfold by years of after-gratification.

CHAPTER II.

GENERAL OUTLINES OF ICHTHYOLOGY.

ORGANIZATION OF FISH.—BREATHING-APPARATUS.—TEMPERATURE
OF BLOOD.—SIGHT.—HEARING.—FEELING.—SMELL.—TASTE.—
AFFECTIONS.—ORGANS OF DIGESTION.—THE BRAIN.—THE SWIM-
BLADDER.—SEXUAL DISTINCTIONS.—ORGANS OF REPRODUCTION.
—SCALES: FORMATION AND USES.—MODE OF PROPULSION.—
BONES.—FINS.—TEETH.

FISHES form the fourth or lowest class of vertebrate
animals (*i. e.* animals possessing a back-bone) in the great
systematic division of the Animal Kingdom ; and from the
fact that the salt waters alone occupy more than seven-
tenths of the globe's entire surface, and are in all probability inhabited, stratum super stratum, as far as, or even
further down than the rays of the sun can penetrate, it will
readily be conceived that they are not only the most numerous of all vertebrate animals, but must infinitely exceed in
numbers the whole of the other three classes of the same
grand division.

What may be the precise depth of these ocean fields
at which life ceases and the profound of darkness and
death begins, we have no direct means of ascertaining. It
necessarily varies, however, with the latitude, being greater
as the rays of the sun are more direct, and less as their
obliquity increases, and it probably also varies with the
nature of the bottom.

Duly to apprehend the various *plans* on which fish are constructed requires a thorough acquaintance with piscine organization in all its forms; and even a condensed treatise on such a subject would necessarily occupy a volume. In the present outline, therefore, the general characteristics and most remarkable features only are brought before the reader, his attention being more particularly directed to those organs upon the modifications of which the *classification* of the various families and species, especially of fresh-water fish, is based.

Fishes are, in scientific phraseology, " *Oviparous Vertebrata*—that is, vertebrate animals bringing forth eggs— with a double circulation, and respiring through the medium of water."

In common with other animals of the same division, they possess a *continuous longitudinal nervous axis*, commonly called the ' spinal marrow,' situated in the centre of the spine, and composed of four parallel columns, one pair of which receive the *nerves of sensation*, coming from the surface of the body, and the other pair form the roots of the *nerves of volition*, or *action*, in connexion with the muscles governing the movements of the fish. The *vertebræ*, or joints of the spine, forming the backbone, in which this nervous axis lies, are in many fishes wholly gristly, or cartilaginous, but in others more or less bony.

The term ' spinal column ' includes both the nervous axis, or spinal marrow, and its envelope.

By an enlargement of the anterior*, or more forward, end of the nervous axis, the *brain* is formed, with which the nerves of smell, sight, taste, and hearing are connected.

Immediately under the spinal column, and divided from each other by thin membranes, are situated the organs of respiration, circulation, digestion, excretion, and also, when it exists, the air- or swim-bladder†. This type of structure is common to all vertebrate animals; but the peculiar attribute of Fishes is, that in them the function of respiration, or oxygenation of the blood, is performed through the medium of *water*, not merely temporarily, but during the continuance of life.

Breathing-apparatus.

For this purpose they have, on each side of the neck, gills (*branchiæ* ‡), consisting of arches of bone, to which the filaments, or spongy portions, of the gills are attached, and which have their surfaces covered by a tissue of innumerable blood-vessels. There are five of these branchial, or gill-, arches in fish, of which four support gills, the fifth being appropriated to the 'dentiferous pharyngeal arch,' a bony arch in the throat, bearing teeth. In breathing, the water is taken in at the mouth, and, after passing through the gills, is allowed to escape behind by the gill-openings. In its passage through the gills and gill-fila-

---

* *Anterior*—used to signify the part nearest the nose of a fish,— which is sometimes also named *proximal*, the Latin for 'nearest.'

† Sometimes called the 'hydrostatic organ.'   ‡ Latin for 'gills.'

ments, the water imparts to the latter the oxygen of the air which it contains, and receives carbon in return, as in the lungs of an air-breathing animal: the gills do not *decompose* the water, so as to derive oxygen from it, but merely *separate the oxygen from the common air contained in the water*; hence, if water is deprived of this air, or impregnated with unwholesome gases, fish cannot exist in it.

The blood is propelled to the gills by the heart, which thus answers to the right ventricle of warm-blooded animals; and from the gills it is sent to an arterial trunk, lying immediately under the back-bone, which is the left, or systemic, ventricle of the heart, and which sends the blood throughout the body of the fish.

The gills of fish possess the power of imbibing oxygen not only from that portion of air which is mixed with the water, but also directly from the atmospheric air itself; and this process may frequently be observed in a vivarium, or other receptacle for fish, where the water is foul, or not changed sufficiently often. I recently witnessed a remarkable example in the case of a stock-pond newly constructed, into which the fish had been put before the water had properly cleared. In this instance the whole shoal, amounting in all to some hundreds, consisting of various species, remained for long periods together with their mouths partially out of water, for the purpose of breathing. It has also been observed that when fish confined in a limited space are prevented by any means from taking in air at the surface, they die much sooner than others which

are allowed to do so. The great majority of fishes, however, cannot continue to breathe in atmospheric air *alone*
beyond a very limited period, as, without the aid of fluid,
the gill-filaments shortly become stuck together, when of
course the air cannot pass between them, and they lose
the power of imbibing oxygen. Hence the gasping of
fishes out of water, which is the *effort of Nature to separate the gill-filaments.*

Temperature of Blood.

The consumption of oxygen in all fishes is comparatively
small, which may be the cause of the cold nature of their
blood; and the temperature of the bodies of fish that swim
near the bottom is seldom more than two or three degrees
higher than that of the water at its surface*. In surface-
swimmers a temperature of 10° Fahr. above that of the
water has been occasionally found; and it may be received
as a general law, that those fish which swim near the surface
have a high standard of respiration (and therefore of temperature), die rapidly on being taken out of water, and
have flesh prone to quick decomposition,—and *vice versá.*

---

* A very ingenious application of this principle has lately been
made, by the invention of a machine for re-oxygenating the water in
bait-kettles, vivaria, &c. The apparatus is composed of a tube formed
in the shape of the letter T, to the perpendicular of which an india-
rubber air-ball, or a pair of bellows, is attached. The transverse portion
of the tube is pierced full of minute holes, which, being placed in the
kettle, the air, upon pressure of the ball, is forced out into the water,
which is thus made fit for respiration.

Two better examples of these laws could not perhaps be given than those of the Bleak, a surface-swimmer, and the Tench, a ground-swimmer. Amongst sea-fish, Mackerels, Salmon, and Herrings may be quoted as instances of the former law, and Eels, Flat-fish, and Skate of its converse.

Fish are sometimes designated "surface-swimmers," "midwater-swimmers," or "ground-swimmers," according to the part of the water which they naturally inhabit.

With a low standard of respiration, and tenacity of life, is connected the extraordinary power exhibited by some species of sustaining extremes of high and low temperature. The Gold-fish lives and thrives in water as high as 85° Fahr. Fishes exist in the hot springs and baths of various countries, ranging from 113° to 120°; and in South America Humboldt saw fish thrown up alive, and apparently in health, from the bottom of a volcano, along with water and heated vapour which raised the thermometer to 210°, or two degrees below the boiling-point.

On the other hand, in parts of Europe and North America, Perch and Eels, and several species of Carp, are not uncommonly frozen and thawed again, and even transported from place to place in a frozen state, without injury to life.

Sight.

The eyes of fish occupy entirely different positions in the different species,—in some, such as the Skate, being placed high up, near the top of the head, and in others, as the Pike, lower down on the side of the head (the more frequent situation)—their position, however, being always adjusted to suit the habits of the particular fish. The external surface of the eye itself is nearly flat, but the lens is spherical—a structure which, in a dense medium, affords the greatest power of vision at short or moderate distances, rather than a very long sight. When water is clear and undisturbed, however, the sight of fishes is very acute; and for this reason it is that a ruffled water is always preferable to a smooth one for purposes of fishing. I believe myself that the sight of fish in clear water is longer than is generally supposed. Standing by the side of a Scotch loch in bright calm weather, I have frequently remarked a Pike basking at from fifteen to twenty-five yards from the shore, and could plainly perceive that the observation was mutual. The fish, after fixedly regarding me for a few moments, has generally backed slowly away into the deep water, disappearing so motionlessly—if I may use the expression—that the eye was hardly conscious of its retreat until it became aware that it had vanished. Moreover, it is well known that a basking Chub will sink upon the flitting of a swallow across the river; that in ponds where Carp are habitually fed by visitors, the former will follow the latter about for the expected *largesse*; and that instances have been authenticated—in several cases under my own observation, elsewhere detailed—in which fish evidently recognized their keepers, as well by sight as by sound: thus clearly leading to the inference that, *when we can see the fish, the fish can see us.*

By all means, therefore, let the fisherman study to keep as far away from the water, and as much out of sight as possible. This is the first of the two golden rules for successful angling.

Hearing.

Much has been written at different times by clever anatomists * on the subject of the sense of hearing in fish, some denying its existence entirely, and others asserting it in a greater or less degree,—the former basing their arguments mainly on the absence, in most species, of any external auricular orifice, and the latter upon the internal structure of the head, and practical experiment.

The probabilities of the question would appear to be with those who maintain the existence of the sense, for these reasons :—

1. Because all fish, though generally wanting the Eustachian tube, and tympanal bones, have internal ears, or sacs which, if they do not answer the purpose of hearing, certainly cannot be proved to answer any other. 2. Because water, though the denser medium, is necessarily more or less impressible by the waves of air, or sound, and a vibration of the one, therefore, cannot but cause a corresponding vibration of the other,—water, moreover, receiving the vibration of the ground. And 3. Because

* See *Physiological Researches,* by Prof. Breschet (Paris); *Dissertation on the Organ of Hearing in Man, Reptiles, and Fish,* Geoffroy ; *Structure and Physiology of Fishes,* Monro ; and the works of Cuvier, Valenciennes, Hunter, and others.

every fisherman knows, as a matter of experience, not only that fish can, and do, hear loud noises, but that they are constantly frightened away from his neighbourhood by them.

Instances in confirmation of this might be adduced *ad infinitum*; I will merely quote one or two mentioned by Mr. Yarrell. The Chinese, who breed large quantities of gold-fish, call them with a whistle to receive their food. Sir Joseph Banks used to collect his fish by sounding a bell; and Carew, the historian of Cornwall, brought his grey mullet together to be fed by making a noise with two sticks. Several other anecdotes bearing upon this subject will be found in the course of the volume.

To keep perfectly quiet, then, should be the angler's second golden rule.

Feeling.

The rigid nature of the scaly covering in the generality of fish renders it probable that they possess but little external sense of touch. Many of their members are more independent of each other than those of warm-blooded animals; they seem less connected with common centres, " in this respect," as Mr. Kirby says, " rather resembling vegetables "*. Some of their parts, such as the fins, if mutilated, can be reproduced; and, indeed, a fish, like a reptile, may be cut and almost dismembered without appearing to suffer materially. Thus, the shark from which a harpoon has just dragged a portion of its flesh pursues

* Bridgewater Treatises.

its prey without any apparent loss of appetite or energy. All anglers are well acquainted with the fact that a pike will constantly take a fresh bait immediately after escaping from the hook, and often with the broken tackle still imbedded in his jaws. Mr. Stoddart * even mentions a case in which this occurred after the fish had been for some time in his basket, from which however it escaped, and was instantly taken a second time. I have myself hooked the same pike with the spoon-bait three times within as many minutes; and an incident, elsewhere referred to, which occurred to me before several witnesses, where a perch was actually caught *with its own eye*, would appear to remove any doubts that may remain on the subject.

It must not be inferred, however, that fish are wholly destitute of the organs of feeling, which, indeed, are essential to a certain extent for their self-preservation. The lips in many species are soft and pulpy; the mouths of others are provided with barbules, or *cirri*,—sometimes called 'barbels,' or ' beards,'—largely supplied with nerves, and acting, doubtless, as delicate organs of touch, for detecting the nature of the substances with which they come in contact. A remarkable instance is observable in the Gurnards, which may be said to be provided with long, flexible, and sensitive fingers, to compensate for their bony lips. It is an almost universal rule, that ' bearded ' fish obtain their food close to the ground; and these feelers appear to be given, as a valuable equivalent, to species which, restricted

* Angler's Companion.

by instinct to feeding near the bottom of water that is often turbid and deep, must necessarily experience more or less imperfect vision from the deficiency of light.

Fishes are subject to comparatively few diseases, probably owing to the even temperature of the medium in which they exist. They are, however, very liable to external and internal parasites, which (with the exception of those peculiar to the Salmon) generally attach themselves to sick or wounded fish.

Smell.

The sense of smell is considered by most comparative anatomists to be very perfect. The nerves of smell are large, and the extent of the membranes over which they expand so considerable, that in a shark 25 feet long it has been calculated at from 12 to 13 square feet. The discrimination shown by fish in the selection and rejection of their ordinary food, and the preference stated to be exhibited for certain scented oils, &c., have been adduced as arguments in favour of their acuteness of smell; and there is no question that sharks will pick out and follow a vessel having slaves on board—a circumstance difficult to be accounted for, except on the supposition that they discover the nature of their cargo by scent.

The nostrils, which are simple cavities near the end of the muzzle, divided by a membrane, are generally pierced with two holes, but both openings lead to the same common canal.

Taste.

The sense of taste in fish is probably low, as a great part of the tongue is bony, and frequently furnished with teeth, placed there for the purpose of prehension. Obliged necessarily to open and close the jaws in respiring, they cannot long retain food in the mouth when quite shut, and the substance, if of small size, must be swallowed quickly and without much mastication. It has been thought possible, from the bony nature of the tongue and the shape of the teeth, which are calculated to assist in conveying food to the back of the mouth, that the sense of taste may reside in the soft, fleshy portions of the throat. A low sense of taste generally, however, would appear to be inferred from the fact that fish are often unable to distinguish poisonous substances, and are accordingly frequently destroyed wholesale by poachers. The sense of taste is more developed in the herbivorous than in the carnivorous fishes.

Affections.

Under certain circumstances fish have been known to exhibit a very decided affection for members both of their own and of other species. Such affection, however, has been most commonly observed to exist between fishes of the same species, but of opposite sexes, at the time of spawning.

Organs of Digestion.

The intestines of fish generally are short, and the diges-

tive process very rapid—so rapid, in fact, in some of the
carnivorous species as to have been compared to the action
of fire. I have mentioned elsewhere the case of a pike
taken with a large eel sticking in his throat half swallowed, the head-portion being already semidigested, whilst
the tail, still alive and struggling, protruded from his
jaws. The digestive process is most rapid, and the intestines shortest, in those species which live principally, or
wholly, on animal food; and the intestines are considerably longer, and the digestion proportionably slower, in
those which feed on vegetable substances. The same principle is observable amongst other classes of the Animal
Kingdom.

In some species, such for instance as the Grey Mullet
and the Gillaroo Trout, which swallow their prey whole,
the walls of the stomach are thickened, so as to afford increased muscular power; and in such species the stomach
has a considerable resemblance to the gizzard of a bird.
The intestines and stomach differ materially in different
families.

The kidneys are situated under and against the spine.

The Brain.

The brain of fishes, which is exceedingly small in proportion to their size, is formed by an enlargement of the
extremity of the nervous axis, or spinal marrow, and is
disposed as in reptiles, with the addition of 'nodes' or
'ganglions' at the base of the nerves of smell. The pro-

portionate weight of brain in a Pike, as compared with its body, is as 1 to 1300; in the Shark, as 1 to 2500; and in the Tunny—a remarkably stupid fish—but as 1 to 3700.

The Swimming- (or Air-) Bladder.

Inhabiting an element which is of very nearly the same specific gravity as their own bodies, fishes have no weight to bear, but have merely to propel themselves through the water; and their form, structure, and organs of motion are all adapted to this one purpose, according to the requirements of each species. Many families have, however, under the spine, in the abdomen, an air- or 'swimming'-bladder, varying in shape in various species, which they can expand or contract at pleasure; and this is believed to be for the purpose of enabling them to alter their specific gravity to suit the densities, at different depths, of the water in which they desire to swim or suspend themselves. Many species, notwithstanding, though wanting this apparatus, have very nearly the same habits as those which are possessed of it; and in some of these latter there is no external passage by which the air in the bladder can be inspired or expressed.

The contents of these bladders have been found upon analysis to consist sometimes of pure nitrogen, sometimes of almost pure oxygen, sometimes of oxygen, nitrogen, and carbonic acid combined in varying proportions, but rarely of common atmospheric air. Some bladders are composed of a single chamber or cavity; others of two chambers, and a few of three. Swimming-bladders are more general amongst fresh- than amongst salt-water fish. The whole subject is still, however, involved in considerable obscurity; but an interesting chapter upon it will be found in Mr. Yarrell's work on British Fishes *. The annexed woodcut exhibits a section of the air-bladder of the common Carp, with a probe introduced between the two chambers.

Sexual Distinctions.

If we omit one or two species, there are no very obvious external signs by which the sexes of fish can be identified (except when in spawn, as hereafter explained). The distinguishing peculiarities, however, which, with a little practice, will be found sufficient guides, are as follows :—

In the males, the respiratory organs, or gills, are *larger* than in the females, and, on the other hand, the abdomen or stomach is *smaller*. The males may therefore be known from the females by their somewhat sharper or more pointed muzzles, by the greater length of the gill-covers, and by the body, from the back-fin downwards, being *less deep* as compared with the whole length of the fish.

* 3rd edit., vol. ii.

Organs of Reproduction.

The productiveness of fish—a productiveness compared to which that of every other living creature appears insignificant—is limitless as the seas through which they are destined to range. The young produced by one Cod-fish at a single deposit have been found to number little short of four millions, and those of a Flounder to exceed one hundred and forty thousand.

With but one or two exceptions, fishes, as before stated, are oviparous, 'bringing forth eggs;' and the organs for this purpose are of the simplest possible description. As the spawning-season approaches, two elongated lobes, or rolls, of roe are formed between the ribs and the intestinal canal, one on each side of the body : these, in the female, are called *hard roe* whilst in the fish, and *spawn* after being deposited; and in the male, *milt*, or *soft roe*, in both cases. The membranes or bags in which these lobes of roe are confined are, in the female, sacs, and in the male, glands, termed *milts*. The lobes of roe in the female consist of a vast number of separate grains, called *ova*, or eggs, partially glued together, and enclosed in the bag or sac reaching to the side of the anal aperture, through which egress is permitted at the proper time. In the male the lobes of roe are smaller than in the female, and present the appearance of whitish fat; they remain firm until the actual spawning-season, when they become gradually fluid, and are ultimately voided in small portions at a time, on the abdomen of the fish being slightly pressed.

At the spawning-time, which differs in almost every species, the fish repair, some to the gravelly shallows or weedy banks of rivers, and others to the sandy bays of the sea. This is sometimes called "going to hill," or "roading." The female then deposits her eggs, in portions at a time, and the male presses his milt out over them; *and without this impregnation, no vivification, or hatching, can take place* *; the eggs could never arrive at maturity—in other words, would be addled. The female is in some instances attended by two males, one on each side, so as to secure the impregnation of the greatest amount of spawn, the range of the milt being immensely increased by diffusion in water. After this process the eggs are left amongst the gravel, or sticking to weeds or other substances, the glutinous nature of each egg supplying the means of adhesion; and when the time (which constantly varies) for the hatching of the egg arrives, the young fish breaks the capsule, or shell, which has become very thin, and escapes.

The growth of the fry is rapid in proportion to the

---

* A few unimportant exceptions to this rule exist. According to Cuvier, some species of the genus *Serranus* have each lobe of roe made up half of hard, and half of soft roe, and these have been considered as being capable of producing fertile eggs without the assistance of a second fish. This may, however, very possibly be considered as a malformation rather than a natural structure. Perch, Mackerel, Carp, Cod, and some others have been occasionally found with a lobe of soft roe on one side, and a lobe of hard roe on the other; and in these cases it is probable that the fish are prolific alone.

size of the parent fish, or the ultimate size attained by the species.

Artificial production—by impregnating the eggs taken from the female fish, with the milt taken from the male—is now extensively practised, especially at Huningue near Strasbourg, Perth in Scotland, Galway in Ireland, and Hampton on Thames, by the Angling-Preservation Society of that river, and promises to become a most important subject with reference to the re-stocking of our exhausted salmon fisheries. Mr. Buckland, the first of English pisciculturists, has recently exhibited, in the window of the " Field " newspaper office, a beautifully constructed apparatus for the artificial hatching of eggs, in which, by the use of glass boxes, the whole process has been clearly observable. Large quantities of the ova, both of salmon and trout, have been brought to maturity in this ingenious contrivance.

There are a few exceptions to the rule of fishes being oviparous. Amongst the Sharks and Rays one or two species are viviparous, and produce their young alive and complete in all respects. In those fishes which belong to the cartilaginous series, the sexual parts are more highly organized and complicated in their structure than those of bony fishes, resembling, in fact, the sexual organs in reptiles.

A few other fishes, again, such as the Dog-fish and some of the Rays or Skates, bring forth their young enclosed in horny cases, two examples of which are here introduced, a portion of one side of the cases being removed to show the young fish within.

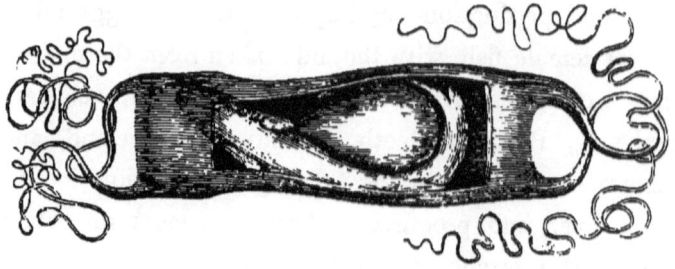

'Case' of young of Dog-fish.

Their empty shells, known by the names of "Mermaids' purses," "Skate-barrows," &c., are frequently picked up on the sea-shore, and will be familiar to most of us, though very possibly we may not have been acquainted with their origin.

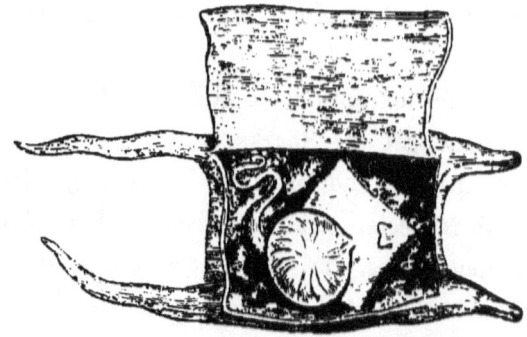

'Case' of young of Skate.

Scales : formation and uses.

The scales of fish, which are productions of the skin, exhibit considerable uniformity of arrangement. The lines in which each series of scales are placed cross each other nearly vertically, showing a figure resembling the letter X, or a sort of double cone, the scale in the centre forming the apex of each cone. Each scale is attached to the skin by its anterior, or more forward, edge, which fits into a sort of pocket, or 'follicle'; but the manner in which the scales overlap each other is variable.

The scales on different parts of the body are of different sizes; and those down the side, forming the *lateral line*, are pierced through in the centre with openings, to allow the escape of a fluid which lubricates the skin beneath. Examples of these are annexed.

Scale from lateral line of Basse.   Scale from lateral line of Ruffe.

The heads of most fish also possess these openings (or muciferous orifices, as they are termed) usually in greater numbers than the other parts of the body; and this distribution is one of the most beautiful arrangements of Nature. The mucus or slime by which the scales of fish are as it were varnished, or waterproofed, being exuded from the pores of the head, is necessarily carried backwards by the current—or, in still water, by the progressive motion of the fish—and spreads itself over the whole surface of the body. The lubricating fluid is most abundant in fish with small scales, such as the Eels. Occasionally the scales are entirely covered by a soft thick cuticle, so as to be detected only by close examination.

There are four denominations of scales, named by M. Agassiz—*Cycloid, Ctenoid, Ganoid,* and *Placoid*; (from the Greek words *eidos,* signifying resemblance, and *cyclos,* a circle, *cteis,* a comb or rake, *ganos,* brilliancy, and *plax,* a flat, level surface). The first two of these include all the most common forms of scales, and are marked with circular or concentric lines, discernible through a microscope, each line denoting a successive stage of growth by the addition of a fresh layer—the smallest, or top layer, having been first produced, and the others added underneath*. In the Cycloids these circular lines are smooth; whilst in the Ctenoids they are furnished with minute spiny points, or teeth, which, however, usually wear off on the disc of the scale, and remain only on the posterior margin, as shown in figure No. 2.

(1.) Cycloid scale from back ot Carp-Bream.   (2.) Ctenoid scale from lateral line of Perch.

The Ganoids have a hard, shining, enamelled surface, and

* By steeping in water, the several layers or laminæ of which scales are formed can be separated with a delicate penknife ; and by means of

other peculiarities, and are found in some families of salt-water fish.   The Placoids, which lack the hard enamel of the Ganoids, are scattered over the Rays and Sharks and one or two other groups.

Mode of Propulsion.

The principal organ of motion in fishes is the tail, assisted by the simultaneous action of the fins.   Progression is effected by the tail striking obliquely right and left against the water; for which purpose the spine is constructed to bend sideways, or laterally, instead of upwards and downwards as in most other vertebrate animals.

Bones.

To begin with the spine.   The number of vertebræ composing the spinal column varies greatly—from 16, for instance, in the Sun-fish, (and fewer in other species,) to 162 in the Conger Eel, and upwards of 230 in the Electric Eel.   The shapes of the vertebræ also vary, though commonly their *centra*, or bodies, are more or less narrowed in the middle like an hour-glass.   The ends are cup-shaped, and the cups filled with a bag of gelatine enclosed in a strong membrane, which, being united round the rims, forms a very elastic joint.

The annexed engraving will show the names and posi-

these, according to some authorities, the age of fish may be accurately ascertained—each layer representing one year's growth.

tions of the several bones of which the head of a Perch is composed.

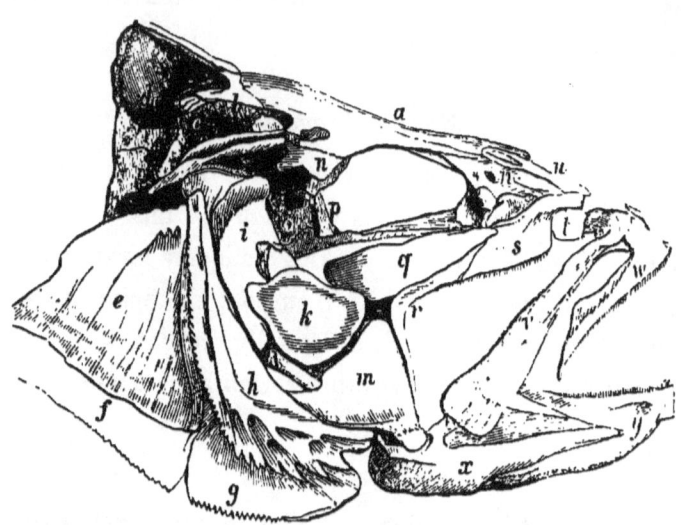

a. Principal frontal bone.
b. Parietal.
c. Inter-occipital, or par-occipital.
d. Inter-parietal, or super-occipital.
e. Operculum.
f. Sub-operculum.
g. Inter-operculum.
h. Pre-operculum.
i. Temporal, or epi-tympanic.
k. Tympanal, or pre-tympanic.
l. Sympletic, or meso-tympanic.
m. Jugal, or hypo-tympanic.
n. Posterior frontal, or post-frontal.
n*. Anterior frontal, or pre-frontal.

o. Great ala, or ali-sphenoid.
p. Sphenoid.
q. Internal pterygoid, or ento-pterygoid.
r. Transverse, or pterygoid.
s. Palatal, or palatine bone (bone of palate).
t. Vomer.
u. Nasal.
v. Superior maxillary, or maxillary.
w. Inter-maxillary, or pre-maxillary.
x. Articular portion, and
y. Dental portion of the lower jaw, or inferior maxillary bone.

The head in various species differs much in form, but in general consists of the same number of bones as in other vertebrate animals, viz. a frontal of six pieces, parietals of three, occipitals of five, sphenoid of five, and two of each temporal bone.

Of these the most important to the naturalist are the bones forming the gills, *e, f,* and *g*—and those constituting the jaws, *r, s, t, v, w, x, y.*

Amongst the latter the *inter-* or *pre-maxillary* * (*w*) forms in most fishes the edge of the front of the upper jaw, having the *maxillary* (*v*) behind it. The situation of the *palatine*† bones (*s*) is in the roof of the mouth, one on each side of the *vomer*‡ (*t*) ; and in the Perch both these bones and the *pterygoid* (*r*) carry teeth. The lower jaw, except in the cartilaginous fishes, has generally two bones in each side : a further reference to these bones will be found under the division " Teeth." The bones to which the fins are attached will be more conveniently noticed in the remarks on the latter organs.

The relative positions of the bones composing the gill-covers, or *opercula* §, will perhaps be more easily distinguished by a reference to the accompanying diagram of the head of a Trout, in which

* So named from the Latin *maxilla,* a jaw.
† *Palatine* bones, or bones forming the palate.
‡ *Vomer,* so called from a fancied resemblance to a *ploughshare,* for which the name given is the Latin.
§ *Opercula,* from the Latin *operculum,* a lid or cover.

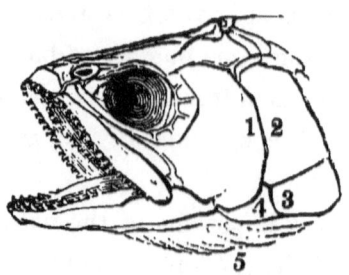

1. represents the *pre-operculum*, or fore gill-cover.
2. The *operculum*, or gill-cover proper.
3. The *sub-operculum*, or under gill-cover.
4. The *inter-operculum*, or intermediate gill-cover, and
5. The *branchiostegous* rays, or gill-rays.

The gill-covers, it will thus be seen, consist of four pieces each :—the *pre-operculum*, or fore gill-cover, 1; the *operculum*, or gill-cover proper, 2; the *sub-operculum*, or under gill-cover, 3; and the *inter-operculum*, or intermediate gill-cover, 4. The three last of these are articulated, or jointed on, to the temporal bone (*i* in head of Perch), and play upon the *pre-operculum* (a *fixed* bone), 1; and by the opening and shutting of these gill-covers respiration is carried on. When a line or division is observable anterior to, or in front of, the fore gill-cover, it marks the boundary of the cheek.

The *branchiostegous* * rays, or gill-rays, marked 5, form a bony fan-like appendage, or fringe, to the lower margin of the gill-covers, to which they are attached.

* Branchiostegous rays—from the Greek *branchia*, gills, and *stegein*, to cover.

The *form* of the gill-covers is of great importance, together with the fins and teeth, in deciding the classification of fish, and in some cases, as in the *Salmonidæ,* constitutes one of the principal means of identifying different species of the same genus.

Fins.

In considering the structure of fish, fins occupy a very prominent place, not only as organs of motion, but as affording, by their texture, position, and number, materials for distinguishing orders, families, and genera. The membranes of the fins are usually thin and more or less transparent, and are supported by slender bony processes, or props, called *fin-rays,* some of which are composed of single pieces, pointed at the end, designated *spinous rays,* from their resemblance to spines and thorns; and others of a number of separate pieces united by joints, and called, from their pliant nature, *soft* or *flexible rays.* Upon this difference in structure the two leading divisions of bony fishes are founded.

The numbers of fin-rays differ entirely in various species, and, occasionally, in different individuals of the same species.

The names of the fins are derived from the parts of the body to which they are most commonly attached, and a reference to the annexed diagram will assist in impressing these upon the memory of the reader.

They are :—

1. The *Pectoral**, or breast-fins, A (so called from their being placed on the breast or shoulder of the fish).

2. The *Dorsal*, or back-fins, E E.

3. The *Ventral* fins, B (named from their position on the belly).

4. The *Anal* fin, C (placed close behind the anal aperture).

5. The *Caudal*, or tail-fin, D.

(F marks the lateral, or side, line.)

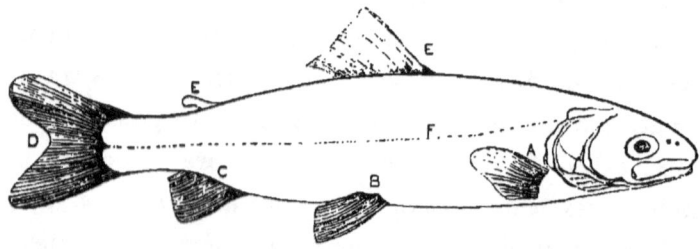

This list includes the *names* of all the different kinds of fins possessed by any fish, though the *numbers* and arrangements of them vary in almost every family,—some fish, such as the Salmon for instance, having two dorsal fins—and others, as the Eel, lacking the ventrals altogether. But of fresh-water fish inhabiting British lakes and rivers, all except the Lampreys and Eels possess the whole of the above complement of fins.

Of these, the pectorals are considered to answer to arms or fore legs in other animals, and the ventrals to the hinder

---

* These names are derived from the Latin *pectus*, the breast; *dorsum*, the back; *venter*, the belly; *anus*, the vent; *cauda*, the tail.

legs'; and by means of the former several of the spiny-finned species are enabled to progress upon dry land, and even to travel considerable distances from one pool to another *. The pectorals are supported by two bones behind the gills, one on each side, which are sometimes imbedded in the muscles, and sometimes connected with the spine, but more generally attached to the bones of the head.

The ventrals are commonly attached to the sides of the belly.

Teeth.

Closely connected with the fins and gills, as furnishing marks by which the *subgenera* of Fishes may frequently be distinguished, are the Teeth, which are so permanent in their characters as to be well worthy of particular attention. The teeth in various species differ materially in situation, number, and form : many species are almost, if not wholly, toothless; whilst others possess them on all the bones which assist in forming the cavity of the mouth and throat. They are found on the *inter-maxillaries*, the *maxillaries*, the lower jaw, the *vomer*, the palate, the tongue, the gill-arches, and even on the bones of the throat, or *pharynx*, behind these. This latter is particularly the case in the herbivorous fishes.

Sometimes the teeth are uniform in shape on the various bones of a single mouth; in other cases they are of different patterns. The most usual form in carnivorous

* An account of these fishes will be found in the Chapter on Pike.

fishes is that of a slender elongated cone, slightly curved inwards to assist in holding a struggling prey*; in herbivorous fish the form is commonly that of a short rounded tubercle with a flat crown, adapted for crushing. Sometimes the teeth are so small and numerous, more especially in insect-eaters, as to have the appearance of the hairs of a brush; and occasionally they are thin and flat, with a cutting edge. By these characteristics the habits and food of fishes may usually be as readily discovered as those of graminivorous and carnivorous animals by the same means.

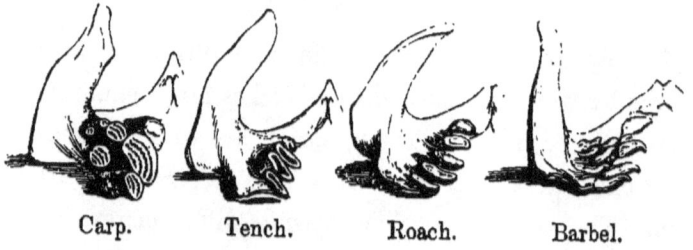

Carp.   Tench.   Roach.   Barbel.

The woodcut represents one-half of the " throat-teeth," looking from behind, in the Carp, Tench, Roach, and

---

* Teeth of this shape are termed *acicular*; if stouter, *subulate*; if teeth are hair-like, and short and densely crowded, they are said to be *villiform*; if longer and equally slender, *ciliiform*; if stronger and stiffer, *setiform*, or *brush-like*; if still coarser and curved, *card-like*; when much shorter than the latter they become *raduliform*, or *rasp-like*. Conical teeth longer and stronger than the others on the jaw are named *canines*; and those with broad flat crowns, *molars*, which is the name given to the large flat teeth of the Carp, shown in the engraving. These names take their origin from the Latin words *acicula*, a small needle; *subula*, an awl; *villus*, a fleece; *cilium*, an eyelash; *seta*, a bristle or brush; *radula*, a scraper; *canis*, a dog; *mola*, a mill.

Barbel.   These teeth are situated on a bone of the throat, named the left pharyngeal bone.

The teeth are named according to the bone upon which they are placed, as *inter-maxillary* teeth, *maxillary*, *vomerine*, *palatine*, &c.; and the engraving here introduced exhibits a front view of the mouth in the common Trout, which is chosen as displaying the most complete series of teeth amongst the Salmon family.

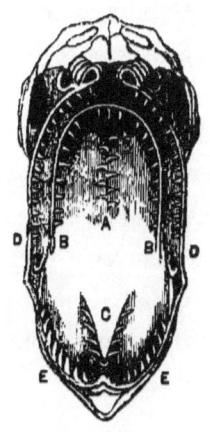

A, Teeth on *vomer*, or central bone in the roof of the mouth.
B B, Teeth on right and left *palatine* bones.
c, Row of hooked teeth on each side of the tongue.
D D, Teeth on *superior maxillary*, or maxillary bones.
E E, Teeth on lower jaw, or *inferior maxillary* bones.

CHAPTER III.

GENERAL CLASSIFICATION OF FISH.

FISHES are divided into

> Series,
> Orders,
> Families,
> Genera, and
> Species.

[Sometimes, for the sake of convenience, Families are further separated into Divisions or Subdivisions, and Genera into Subgenera.]

The two grand series of fishes consist of, (1) those possessing bony skeletons, which are called *True*, or *Bony*, *fishes*; and (2) those which have skeletons of cartilage or gristle, which are called *Cartilaginous fishes*, or *Chondropterygii*. The latter also want some bones of the jaws, and have other peculiarities.

The TRUE, or BONY, FISHES are divided into six Orders, viz. :—

Order I. ACANTHOPTERYGII, or *Spiny-finned Fishes*. (From Gr. *acantha*, a spine, and *pterygion*, a fin.)—In this Order the first portion of the back-fin, or first back-fin when there are two, always has spinous rays or supports—which are also found in the anal and ventral fins. This Order has no great divisions, but contains fifteen Families.

[The MALACOPTERYGII, or Soft-finned Fishes (from the Greek *malacos*, soft, and *pterygion*, a fin), furnish three Orders, founded upon the *position of the ventral fins*: viz.—]

Order II. MALACOPTERYGII ABDOMINALES, or *Abdominal Soft-finned Fishes*. (From Lat. *abdomen*, the belly.) —So called from the ventral fins being attached to the abdomen, behind the pectorals, without being jointed on to the shoulder-bones. It includes five Families, in which are the greater number of our fresh-water fishes.

Order III. MALACOPTERYGII SUB-BRACHIATI, or *Soft-finned Fishes with lower arms*. (From Lat. *sub*, under, and *brachium*, an arm.)—Named from their having the ventral fins under the pectorals, thus giving the idea of lower arms. In this Order, which consists of three Families, the pelvis is suspended to the shoulder-bones.

Order IV. MALACOPTERYGII APODES, or *Soft-finned Fishes without feet*. (From Gr. *α* privative, and *pous*, a foot.)—Have *no ventral fins*, which, being supposed to represent feet, have thus by their absence given the designation of "Footless." Has only a single Family.

Order V. LOPHOBRANCHII, *Fishes with their gills in tufts*. (From Gr. *lophos*, a tuft, and *branchia*, gills.)—

This arrangement of the gills is peculiar to this Order, which, moreover, have the gill-covers entirely closed behind, with the exception of a single small hole. Only one Family.

Order VI. PLECTOGNATHI, or *Fishes with soldered jaws.* (From Gr. *plekein,* to bind, and *gnathos,* a jaw.)— This Order has no true ventral fins. Many of its characteristics resemble those of the Cartilaginous fishes. The chief peculiarity is, the *maxillary* bone being soldered to the side of the *inter-maxillary,* which constitutes the upper jaw—in other words, the jaw-bones being soldered together. Two families.

The CARTILAGINOUS FISHES, or CHONDRO-PTERYGII (from Gr. *chondros,* cartilage, and *pterygion,* a fin), consist of two Orders, viz. :—

Order I. CHONDROPTERYGII BRANCHIIS LIBERIS, or *Cartilaginous Fishes with free gills.* (From Lat. *branchiæ,* gills, and *liber,* free.)—The fishes forming this Order have a single wide opening in their gills, and a gill-cover as in the Bony Fishes; but no gill-rays. The Order contains two Families.

Order II. CHONDROPTERYGII BRANCHIIS FIXIS, or *Cartilaginous Fishes with fixed gills.* (From Lat. *branchiæ,* gills, and *fixus,* fixed.)—These fish have their gills fixed at the outer edge, with a separate opening through which the water from each gill escapes. They have also small cartilaginous arches suspended in the muscles opposite the gills, which may be called gill-ribs. They form two Families.

The foregoing eight Orders are again subdivided into Families, Genera, Species, &c., as already stated.

The following List exhibits in a tabular form the classification above explained, with the addition of the names of the various Families :—

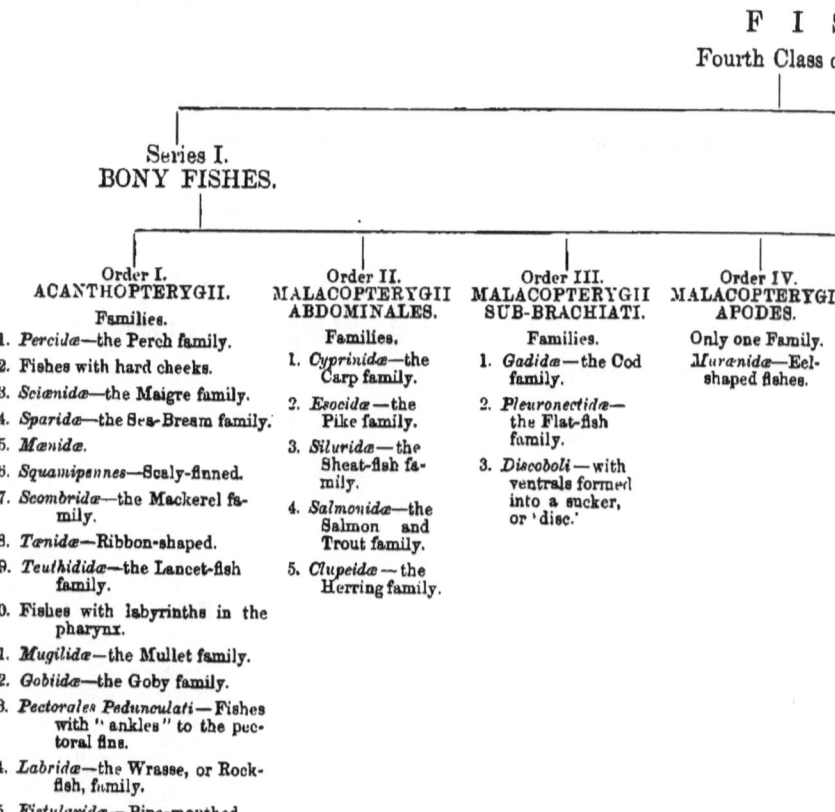

F I S

Fourth Class of

Series I.
BONY FISHES.

Order I. ACANTHOPTERYGII.	Order II. MALACOPTERYGII ABDOMINALES.	Order III. MALACOPTERYGII SUB-BRACHIATI.	Order IV. MALACOPTERYGII APODES.
Families.	Families.	Families.	Only one Family.
1. *Percidæ*—the Perch family.	1. *Cyprinidæ*—the Carp family.	1. *Gadidæ*—the Cod family.	*Murænidæ*—Eel-shaped fishes.
2. Fishes with hard cheeks.	2. *Esocidæ*—the Pike family.	2. *Pleuronectidæ*—the Flat-fish family.	
3. *Sciænidæ*—the Maigre family.	3. *Siluridæ*—the Sheat-fish family.	3. *Discoboli*—with ventrals formed into a sucker, or 'disc.'	
4. *Sparidæ*—the Sea-Bream family.	4. *Salmonidæ*—the Salmon and Trout family.		
5. *Mænidæ.*	5. *Clupeidæ*—the Herring family.		
6. *Squamipennes*—Scaly-finned.			
7. *Scombridæ*—the Mackerel family.			
8. *Tænidæ*—Ribbon-shaped.			
9. *Teuthididæ*—the Lancet-fish family.			
10. Fishes with labyrinths in the pharynx.			
11. *Mugilidæ*—the Mullet family.			
12. *Gobiidæ*—the Goby family.			
13. *Pectorales Pedunculati*—Fishes with "ankles" to the pectoral fins.			
14. *Labridæ*—the Wrasse, or Rock-fish, family.			
15. *Fistularidæ*—Pipe-mouthed fishes.			

NOTE.—It will probably assist the reader's memory to observe that when the name of a Family is of that Family always ends in *idæ*, from the Greek word *eidos*, signifying "resemblance,"—as, for example, and that where the name is founded on peculiarity of structure or habit, the Family name describes that

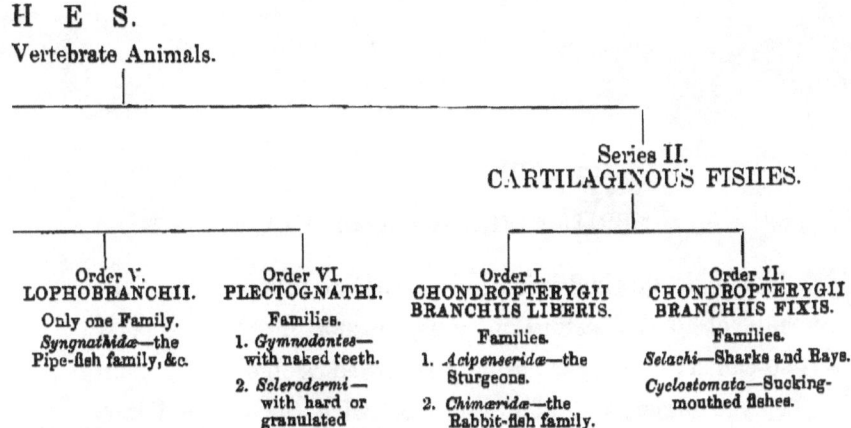

H E S.
Vertebrate Animals.

Series II.
CARTILAGINOUS FISHES.

Order V.
LOPHOBRANCHII.
Only one Family.
Syngnathidæ—the
Pipe-fish family, &c.

Order VI.
PLECTOGNATHI.
Families.
1. *Gymnodontes*—
with naked teeth.
2. *Sclerodermi*—
with hard or
granulated
skin.

Order I.
CHONDROPTERYGII
BRANCHIIS LIBERIS.
Families.
1. *Acipenseridæ*—the
Sturgeons.
2. *Chimæridæ*—the
Rabbit-fish family.

Order II.
CHONDROPTERYGII
BRANCHIIS FIXIS.
Families.
Selachi—Sharks and Rays.
Cyclostomata—Sucking-
mouthed fishes.

derived from that of a particular species (which is considered therefore as its *type*), the technical name in the *Percidæ*, of which the *Perch* is the type—the *Salmonidæ*, of which the *Salmon* is the type, &c.; habit or structure, as *Gymnodontes*—with *naked teeth*, &c.

PART II.

CHAPTER IV.

BRITISH FRESH-WATER FISH.

It was my original intention to confine this portion of the subject to the history of game, or sporting, fish, properly so called; that is, fish usually regarded as objects of pursuit by the angler, and affording sport with the rod and line. On further reflection, however, it appeared to me that this distinction would render the book less complete as a work of reference to the general reader, whilst amongst anglers themselves not a few might very likely be disposed to take exception to *my* exceptions. Some, for example, would probably account Bobbing for Eels a "sport:" I don't. Others might be inclined to look with an eye of favour upon the setting of Lampern-pots, or regard the poking under boulders for stranded and stertorous Bullheads as a highly attractive method of sporting: I can only say—I don't. Again, it would have been a bad compliment to my fair countrywomen, many of whom display such prowess in the ensnarement of Thames Gudgeon, to deny these the title of 'game fish'; nor could I have omitted without a pang the plucky little Sticklebacks, for whose capture the ragged

London urchins, with their rush rods and pin hooks, exhibit a skill and patience that might put more pretentious rivals to the blush.

On the whole, therefore, I deemed it advisable to adopt the more complete form of arrangement; and in the following pages will accordingly be found a notice of every generally known species of fresh-water fish inhabiting the British Islands.

A few observations upon the classification of these, although in some sense a repetition, may probably assist in impressing it upon the memory of the reader.

With one exception then—that of the Lamprey Family, which are *Cartilaginous**—the whole of our fresh-water species belong to the 1st, or Bony, Series* of Fish. Of these again the Perch and Bullhead Families are classed in the 1st Order of that Series (*Acanthopterygii**, 'spiny-finned' fishes),—the Burbot in the 3rd Order, *Malacopterygii subbrachiati*,—the Eels in the 4th Order (" footless soft-finned fishes," or soft-finned fishes lacking ventral fins *),—and all the others, including the great Carp, Salmon, and Pike Families, in the 2nd Order (*Malacopterygii abdominales**, or "soft-finned fishes having the ventral fins on the abdomen"). So that, in short, excepting the Lampreys, *the whole of our fresh-water fish are included in four Orders and embraced in seven Families*, as detailed in the annexed Table.

In this list, which includes the technical names of the

* A full description of the distinguishing characteristics of the various Series and Orders will be found at pages 36–39.

several fish, the *first* of such names indicates in each case the *Genus* to which the species belongs,—as *Perca*, the Perch genus, *Acerina*, the Ruffe genus, *Cyprinus*, the Carp genus, &c.

CLASSIFICATION OF BRITISH FRESH-WATER FISH.

1st Series. TRUE, OR BONY, FISH.

Order I. SPINY-FINNED FISH *.
    Family 1. Perches—PERCIDÆ.
        Species.
            Perch. (*Perca fluviatilis.*)
            Ruffe, or Pope. (*Acerina vulgaris.*)

    Family 2. FISH WITH HARD CHEEKS.
        Species.
            Bullhead, or Miller's Thumb. (*Cottus gobio.*)
            Rough-tailed Stickleback. (*Gasterosteus trachurus.*)
            Half-armed Stickleback. (*Gasterosteus semiarmatus.*)
            Smooth-tailed Stickleback. (*Gasterosteus leiurus.*)
            Short-spined Stickleback. (*Gasterosteus brachycentrus.*)
            Four-spined Stickleback. (*Gasterosteus spinulosus.*)
            Ten-spined Stickleback. (*Gasterosteus pungitius.*)

Order II. SOFT-FINNED FISH with ventral fins on the belly †.
    Family 1. Carps—CYPRINIDÆ.
        Species.
            Common Carp. (*Cyprinus carpio.*)
            Crucian, or German, Carp. (*Cyprinus carassius.*)
            Prussian, or Gibel, Carp. (*Cyprinus gibelio.*)
            Gold Carp. (*Cyprinus auratus.*)
            Barbel. (*Barbus vulgaris.*)
            Gudgeon. (*Gobio fluviatilis.*)

---

      * *Acanthopterygii* (see p. 36).
      † *Malacopterygii abdominales* (see p. 37).

Tench. (*Tinca vulgaris.*)
Bream, or Carp Bream. (*Abramis brama.*)
White Bream, or Bream-flat. (*Abramis blicca.*)
Pomeranian Bream. (*Abramis Buggenhagii.*)
Dace. (*Leuciscus vulgaris.*)
Roach. (*Leuciscus rutilus.*)
Dobule Roach. (*Leuciscus dobula.*)
Chub. (*Leuciscus cephalus.*)
Ide. (*Leuciscus idus.*)
Graining. (*Leuciscus Lancastriensis.*)
Red-eye, or Rudd. (*Leuciscus erythrophthalmus.*)
Azurine. (*Leuciscus cæruleus.*)
Bleak. (*Leuciscus alburnus.*)
Minnow. (*Leuciscus phoxinus.*)
Loach. (*Cobitis barbatula.*)
Spined Loach, or Groundling. (*Cobitis tænia.*)

Family 2. Pikes—ESOCIDÆ.
  Species.
    Common Pike, or Jack. (*Esox lucius.*)

Family 4. Salmon and Trout—SALMONIDÆ.
  Species.
    Salmon. (*Salmo salar.*)
    Bull Trout. (Grey Trout, Sewin, or Roundtail.) (*Salmo eriox.*)
    Salmon Trout. (*Salmo trutta.*)
    Common Trout. (*Salmo fario.*)
    Great Lake Trout. (*Salmo ferox.*)
    Loch Leven Trout. (*Salmo Levenensis.*)
    Charrs.
    Grayling. (*Thymallus vulgaris.*)
    Gwyniad. (*Coregonus Pennanti.*)
    Powan. (*Coregonus Cepedei.*)
    Pollan. (*Coregonus pollan.*)
    Vendace or Vendis. (*Coregonus Willughbii.*)

Order III. SOFT-FINNED FISH having lower arms *.
    Family 1. Cod—GADIDÆ.
        Species.
            Burbot, or Eel-pout. (*Lota vulgaris.*)

Order IV. SOFT-FINNED FISH lacking ventral fins †.
    Family 1. Eels—MURÆNIDÆ.
        Species.
            Sharp-nosed Eel. (*Anguilla acutirostris.*)
            Broad-nosed Eel. (*Anguilla latirostris.*)
            Snig. (*Anguilla mediorostris.*)

2nd Series. CARTILAGINOUS FISH ‡.

Order II. FISH WITH FIXED GILLS §.
    Fam. 1. Fish with mouth formed into a sucker—CYCLOSTOMATA.
        Species.
            Lamprey, or Sea Lamprey. (*Petromyzon marinus.*)
            Lampern, or River Lamprey. (*Petromyzon fluviatilis.*)
            Fringed-lipped Lampern. (*Petromyzon Planeri.*)

To give a practical example of this classification :—The Common Perch is a *species* of the *Genus Perca,* of the *Family* of the *Percidæ,* of the *Order Acanthopterygii,* belonging to the *True* or *Bony Series* of Fish ; or, in other words, is the 1st species, of the 1st Genus, of the 1st Family, of the 1st Order, of the 1st Series.

Space does not here admit of an account of the various structural differences, more or less important, upon which the several genera and species are founded; but they will be given in detail in the course of the volume, under the history of each fish. A few suggestions, however, for enabling the

---

* *Malacopterygii sub-brachiati* (p. 37). † *Malacopterygii apodes* (p. 37).
‡ *Chondropterygii* (p. 38). § *Chondropterygii branchiis fixis* (p. 38).

sportsman more readily to identify his fish, and for the treatment of any supposed new species or varieties, may probably not be considered superfluous.

First, then, upon the capture of any such specimen the best and simplest course is immediately *to preserve it*, according to the directions given in the Appendix, when it can be examined and pronounced upon at leisure, —dried or stuffed fish being comparatively useless for scientific purposes. If, however, from any cause this should be impracticable, the next best thing is a correct description in writing; and to give this with sufficient accuracy to make it of value to science—to render it, in short, such that a naturalist shall be justified in pronouncing with certainty thereon—all that is required is the clear comprehension of a few simple facts, and the power of recording them in an intelligible form.

The first point for observation is the *nature* of the fins— whether generally soft and flexible as in the Salmon and Carp, or hard and spiny as in the Perch : upon this it depends in which of the two principal Divisions of Bony Fishes —*Acanthopterygii*, or *Malacopterygii* *—the species should be placed. This distinction is so obvious and remarkable, that when once mentioned it cannot be overlooked by the least careful observer ; and as to one or other of these divisions belongs every fish, without exception, of which the sportsman takes cognizance, its importance is evident.

The spiny-finned fishes contain fifteen Families, but no

* See page 36.

great subordinate divisions : the soft-finned fishes on the contrary are divided into three strongly marked Orders founded upon the position, or absence, of the *ventral fins*; and to the first of these—*Malacopterygii abdominales*—the whole of our soft-finned *sporting* fishes belong.

Having decided, then, in which of these two principal divisions any fish is to be classed, it remains only to determine its family and species. As regards the former no difficulty whatever can be experienced, there being only four families in all to which it can belong, and these being clearly recognizable by the most obvious signs. To commence with the Spiny-finned fishes :—As *all* the sporting fish of this Order belong to one Family, the *Percidæ*—of which the Perch is the type—no mistake can possibly occur as to these. The Soft-finned fishes are embraced in three Families : the *Cyprinidæ*, of which the Carp is the type; the *Esocidæ*, of which the Pike is the type ; and the *Salmonidæ*, of which the Salmon is the type.

In regard to these Families, again, no difficulty can be found, every species of the Salmon possessing the peculiar characteristic of *two back-fins*, and no other species in the same Order more than *one*,—the Pike, of which we have only a single variety, being totally dissimilar from every other family,—and *the remaining species without exception belonging to the* Cyprinidæ, *or Carp Family.*

To decide with certainty, however, between different *genera*, or different species of the same *genus*, requires more minute observation and comparison, according to the characteristics which will be found appended to each. The points upon which such minor distinctions depend, and which will consequently be those to be particularly observed and noted, are,—

(1) The *shape of the body*, which can be best ascertained by placing the fish straight on a sheet of white paper, and, when it has stiffened, carefully tracing the outline with a pencil.

(2) The relative position of the *fins*; and their form, more especially as regards the back and tail fins *—whether forked, concave, square, or convex. To show the importance of the latter point—the *shape* of the tail-fin—it may be mentioned that upon this, next to the form of the gill-covers, ichthyologists have relied in distinguishing the Bull-trout from the true Salmon,—the tail-fin of the former being convex, and that of the latter more or less concave, in proportion to the age of the fish.

(3) The form of the head and *gill-covers* †, and their length from the tip of the muzzle to the hinder margin, as compared with that of the whole body, measuring from the tip of the muzzle to the extremity of the tail, where it joins the tail-fin; and the relative position to the eye, and to the lateral line, of a straight line drawn from the upper front teeth to the lower posterior angle of the *operculum* ‡.

* *Vide* cut showing the names of the fins, page 32.
† See page 30, and diagram of the various parts of the gill-cover.
‡ See cut at page 52.

D

(4) The nature of the *teeth**, and the names, if possible, of the *bones* on which they are placed †.

(5) The colouring of the body and fins of the fish, when first caught. The size of the scales, and the number forming the lateral line.

(6) The number of *fin-rays*, or supports, in each fin : these, in the tail-fin, are counted from the first long ray outside, either above or below; and in the other fins in all cases from the first ray nearest the head of the fish. The fin-rays are denoted, as in the following pages, by placing the initial letter of the name of the fin before the numeral expressing the number of rays it contains—as D. (for ' Dorsal ') 9 : P. (for ' Pectoral ') 15 : &c. Take for example the fin-rays of the Gudgeon, which are particularly simple:—

$$D. 9 : P. 15 : V. 8 : A. 7 : C. 19\tfrac{3}{8} \ddagger.$$

Occasionally there are short incumbent rays on the base of the tail-fin, above and below, and these are frequently omitted from the reckoning; when they are mentioned, it is in general in the shape of a *fraction* placed after the number of full-length rays, the numerator denoting those above the fin, and the denominator those below it, as in the example. When there is more than one dorsal

* See page 35.

† See illustrations of the mouth of the Trout, p. 35, and bones of the jaw, &c., p. 28.

‡ *Vide* cut showing names and position of fins, p. 32. (D. Dorsal, or back-fin—P. Pectoral, or breast-fin—V. Ventral, or belly-fin—A. Anal fin—C. Caudal, or tail-fin.)

fin, the rays are enumerated with a line between them, thus—

$$D.\ 9-12:$$

the first numeral having reference to the first, or more forward, fin.

In the *Acanthopterygii* with two dorsals, as in the Perch, the first is usually wholly spinous, and this is indicated, as in the last case, by a line between the two numbers; when, however, there is but one dorsal, of which the fore part only is spinous, the sign + is placed between the spinous and the soft rays. This is also the rule in regard to other fins partly spiny and partly soft: thus—

(Fin-rays of Perch) D. 15−1+13 : P. 14 : V. 1+5 : A. 2+8 : C. 17.

Some of the soft-finned fish have an occasional spinous ray; and when this is the case their position, &c. should be fully described—a perpendicular line *after such spinous ray* being drawn in the ray-formulary. Take the fin-rays of the common Carp for example,—

$$D.\ 4\ |\ 19:\ P.\ 17:\ V.\ 9:\ A.\ 3\ |\ 5:\ C.\ 19.$$

In this instance the 4th dorsal and 3rd anal fin rays are spinous.

The *form of the gill-covers* has been mentioned as one of the points to be most relied on, more particularly in the Salmon family, for distinguishing one species from another; for whilst, owing to circumstances of food, water, or climate, different individuals of the same species will often differ widely from each other, and from their original type (in so far at least as regards those externals which most readily strike an uneducated eye), the peculiarities of structure of the gill-cover, apparently of little moment, may, from their importance and permanence, not unfrequently indicate totally distinct and immutable species.

Almost all the really distinct species of the *Salmonidæ* are distinguished from one another principally by the form of the head and the formation of the gills, in the first degree, and by the dental system in the second,—any permanent and unvarying difference in these, coupled with variations of colour, form, habit, or the like, which might otherwise be deemed casual, being held to constitute a distinct species.

An example of this difference in the form of the gill-cover will be seen in the annexed engraving, in which the right-hand figure represents the gill-cover of the Sea- or Salmon-Trout, the central one that of the Bull-Trout, and the figure on the left hand that of the True Salmon.

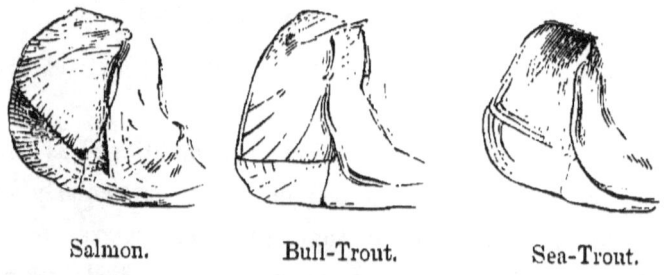

Salmon.   Bull-Trout.   Sea-Trout.

On comparing these figures, it will at once be evident that the hinder margin of the whole gill-cover in the true

Salmon forms nearly a semicircle, whilst that of the Bull-Trout approaches more nearly a right angle, and both differ entirely from the same parts in the gill-cover of the Sea-Trout. A remarkable result of these differences is, that a straight line drawn backwards from the front-teeth of the upper jaw (the mouth being closed) to the lower posterior angle of the *operculum* will, in the three fishes, run at a totally different angle to the lateral line of the body, and will occupy an entirely different position in respect of the eye. There is likewise a difference in the arrangement of the teeth.

TRISTOMA COCCINEUM.

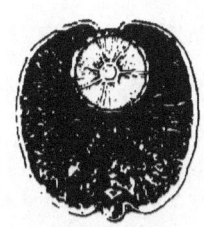 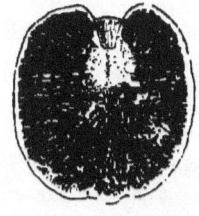

A PARASITE SOMETIMES ATTACHED TO SEA-FISH.

CHAPTER V.

Series I. *BONY FISHES.*   Family *PERCIDÆ* †.
Order 1. *ACANTHOPTERYGII* *.   Genus *PERCA* ‡.

THE PERCH.

(*Perca fluviatilis* ‡.)

Characteristics common to all the Perch Family.—Fin-rays partly spinous and partly flexible. Body oblong, and covered with hard or rough scales. Bones of the gill-covers variously armed at the edges with notches or spinous points. Most of the species composing this Family have the ventral fins under the pectoral.

THE Perch has been taken by Cuvier as the type of his first *genus,* distinguished by having two separate back-fins and other minor peculiarities, and I therefore commence this portion of the subject with the history of that species. The other fish will follow one another in their order of

---

* Fish with some fin-rays spiny, the others flexible. (See p. 36.)

† The Family of the Perches.

‡ *Perca,* the Perch; *fluviatilis,* of the river, Lat.

succession according to the classification of the same author, which is likewise, with some trifling exceptions, that
adopted by Yarrell in his ' History of British Fishes.'

Although the researches of recent ichthyologists have
led to the suggestion of various modifications in this
system, such modifications are still to a certain extent
matters of individual opinion on the part of eminent men,
and necessarily lack that general sanction and assent which
only time can give, and which have been hitherto accorded
to Cuvier's arrangement. The latter is, moreover, complete as a whole; and therefore, whilst by no means
ignoring the discoveries of contemporary science so far
as regards individual species, characteristics, &c., I have
avoided as far as possible any deviations from the system of
classification referred to, which might have tended to con-
fuse the subject to the mind of the general reader. But
to return :—

The common Perch (*Perca fluviatilis*) is very generally
distributed over almost the whole of Europe and Great
Britain, and is a well-known inhabitant of our English
lakes and rivers from the Tweed to the Land's End. In
Wales it is a somewhat local fish, and confined principally
to stagnant waters; in Ireland more widely diffused, though
still in distribution rather unequal; in Scotland very general south of the Frith of Forth, and comparatively rare to
the north of it, ceasing entirely amongst the innumerable
waters of Sutherland and Ross, or, where observed, owing
its introduction to very recent times.

Of the British Perch, so far as my experience extends, the Thames produces the best, in the matter of quality; Windermere and Slapton Ley, the greatest show as to quantity; and the Kennet, from Hungerford to Reading, the finest specimens for general size and weight. In this latter river, near Kintbury, Mr. Francis Hughes and myself took on one occasion several dozen Perch averaging more than a full pound weight each, and the largest fish considerably exceeded 2 lbs. The numbers of Perch existing in Windermere, and Slapton Ley, Devonshire, are almost incredible; but their size is insignificant, rarely passing a few inches, and more commonly being still smaller.

The Perch of the Thames, which is also noticeable for its fine colouring, probably owes its superior gastronomic attractions to the great purity of the stream above locks, as well as to the wide range in the choice of food, spawning-ground, &c., which it affords; but in whatever waters the fish is bred, it is seldom other than palatable, as well as wholesome, and it is on this account a frequent item in the invalid's dietary. Izaak Walton indeed mentions a German proverb which would give it a very high place as a comestible—"More wholesome than a Pearch of Rhine,"— and quotes a learned authority to the effect that it possesses a small stone in the head thought to be very "medecinable," and which was at one time an ingredient in our Pharmacopœia.

The figures below give a representation of the scales on the lateral line of the Perch and Ruffe.

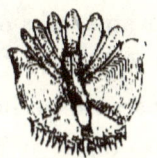
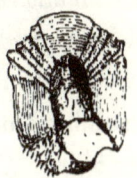

Scale of Perch.   Scale of Ruffe.

The Perch lives long out of water (resembling in that respect the Carp and Tench species), and if carried with care, and occasionally moistened, will in cold weather exist for several hours in this condition,—not unfrequently undergoing a journey of thirty or forty miles without serious injury. Yarrell states that they are constantly exhibited in the markets of Catholic countries, where doubtless they are a popular article of 'fast;' and on these occasions, when not sold, they are taken back to the ponds from which they came, to be re-produced at another opportunity.

The size to which the Perch will attain is somewhat doubtful. The largest specimen that I ever remember to have met with was preserved in a small inn in Perthshire. It was very imperfectly stuffed, and had no doubt shrunk considerably in the operation; but the label stated that it weighed 7 lbs. when caught, and from its appearance it certainly could not have weighed less than six. Perch of 2 and 3 lbs. are by no means uncommon, and specimens of

even 4 lbs. are probably less rare than may be supposed.
Such fish have been taken in the Pen Ponds, Richmond
Park ; and Pennant records the capture of one in the Ser-
pentine which weighed 8 lbs.   Donovan speaks of a Perch
of 5 lbs., caught in Bala Lake.   "Ephemera" (the late
Edward Fitzgibbon) mentions having seen a specimen which
weighed 4 or 5 lbs.   One of 6 lbs. was taken by Mr. Hunt,
of Brades, Staffordshire, from the Birmingham Canal ;
and two fish of 8 lbs. each are stated to have been caught,
the one in the Wiltshire Avon, and the other in Dagenham
Reach, Essex.   One is recorded by Izaak Walton as having
been taken by a friend, which measured two feet in length ;
and in the ' Sure Angler's Guide,' the author says that
he saw the figure of a Perch drawn in pencil on the door of
a house near Oxford, which was twenty-nine inches long,
and he was informed that it was the outline of a living
fish.

It is not probable, however, that either of these sizes
represents the maximum attainable by the Perch under
favourable circumstances, even in British waters ; and they
probably reach a much greater weight in Scandinavia and
other northern countries.   The Danube breeds enormous
Perch ; and Schäffer informs us that in the Church of
Lulea, Lapland, the head of one is preserved which is nearly
a foot long—giving the entire length of the fish at some-
where about $3\frac{1}{2}$ feet.

The annexed table of the comparative weights and measures of Perch, which, with several other similar scales,

has been kindly furnished me by Mr. Charles Wright, of the Strand, may possibly be useful to the angler when unprovided with the means of weighing his fish. It will, Mr. Wright assures me, be found to be generally accurate when the fish are in season.

Length. inches.	Weight. lbs. oz.		Length. inches.	Weight. lbs. oz.
9	0 12		18	3 5½
10	0 13¼		19	3 15¼
11	0 14¾		20	4 9½
12	1 0		21	5 5¼
13	1 4¼		22	6 2½
14	1 9¼		23	7 0½
15	1 14½		24	8 0¼
16	2 5½		25	8 15¾
17	2 13¼			

After the Pike, the Perch is the most fearless of our game fish, often following a bait up to the very surface of the water, or side of the boat, when he presents a really splendid appearance—the jaws open, the spines erect, and the whole fish instinct with energy and fire. On these occasions he frequently remains for several instants bristling like a porcupine, as if threatening reprisals on those who have presumed to balk him of his prey—retiring at length in sullen wrath with his face still turned towards his assailants.

The coarsest bill of fare and the most primitive cookery are usually sufficient to tempt his appetite—a fact from which it results that he not uncommonly has the benefit of the tyro's first angling-experiments. His favourite food

consists of minnows, of which he can devour an extraordinary number; but failing these, any small fry, worms
(especially brandlings), insects, frogs, caterpillars, and grubs
of all sorts are good baits.

Mr. Jesse informs us that if a bottle of live minnows be
sunk at the bottom of a hole or other resort of Perch, it
will in a day or two attract large numbers to the spot,
when they may readily be taken by a similar bait dropped
quietly amongst them. In order to preserve the minnows
alive, the stopper of the bottle should consist of a piece of
perforated zinc, or other substance of a porous nature, so
as to admit free ingress and egress of the water. This
experiment I have never had an opportunity of trying,
nor do I remember any writer who mentions having done
so ; but it is quoted by many.

The extent to which the Perch will gorge himself with
his favourite food may be illustrated by a fact within the
knowledge of most anglers. When the fish has filled his
stomach with minnows so that he can positively swallow
no more, he will still endeavour to bite and, if possible,
masticate others; and it is by no means uncommon under
these circumstances to hook and capture a Perch with the
tails of the minnows which he has already partially swallowed, and been unable to pouch, protruding from his
gullet : when thus gorged, he often ejects a portion of his
prey on being landed. From this it may be inferred that
fish, like many other animals—including man himself, in
the first degree—find a gratification in the exercise of their

predatory instincts, even when the natural appetite has been fully satiated.

A very singular, if not unparalleled, instance of the voracity of the Perch occurred to me when fishing in Windermere. In removing the hook from the jaws of a fish, one eye was accidentally displaced, and remained adhering to it. Knowing the reparative capabilities of piscine organization, I returned the maimed Perch, which was too small for the basket, to the lake, and, being some-what scant of minnows, threw the line in again with the eye attached as a bait—there being no other of any description on the hook. The float disappeared almost instantly; and on landing the new-comer, it turned out to be the fish I had the moment before thrown in, and which had thus been actually caught by *his own eye*. This incident proves, I think, conclusively, that the structure of cold-blooded animals enables them to endure very severe injuries and wounds without experiencing material inconvenience; a fact which may tend to remove any qualms of conscience felt by anglers on the score of the sufferings supposed to be inflicted on their captures.

How far the spines of the Perch protect him from the assaults of other fish—especially of the Pike—is not quite certain. In many fishings both in England and Scotland, small Perch are considered the favourite baits for the Pike, which does not seem to be at all deterred by their spiky appearance. Moreover, as the Pike always swal-lows his prey head-foremost, whilst the spines of the Perch are capable only of projecting backwards—shutting down like the props of an umbrella upon pressure from in front —it would not appear that they could impede the operation of swallowing, but that, on the contrary, they would naturally rather assist it than otherwise—in the same way that the 'beard' of an ear of barley assists it in forcing a way through the sleeve of a coat or other obstructed passage.

The effect of these back-action *chevaux-de-frise* is curiously illustrated by a circumstance of not unfrequent occurrence in Sweden. Large Perch swallow the baited hooks of stationary night-lines, and then enormous Pike gorge the hooked Perch in their turn. In this case, though the Pike is seldom or never actually hooked, yet, on the fisherman's drawing in his line, the Perch sets so fast in his throat that he is unable to get rid of it, and both are taken *. That the spines of the Perch are very formidable weapons, of which they readily make use, is proved by an instance recently witnessed in a stock-pond near Weybridge, where one of these fish, of about half a pound, attacked a Pike of the same weight,—the result being that after a prolonged contest, carried on by both combatants with great fury, the Pike was apparently either killed or stunned, and lay motionless on the bottom, belly uppermost. Mr. Francis informs me, however, that Perch themselves certainly do not object to these spines, so far as

* Gosse's Natural History.

swallowing is concerned, and that in a vivarium he has often observed them take with avidity smaller members both of their own and of the Ruffe species.

In the preliminary chapters on Ichthyology I alluded to instances which had at different times come under my observation of clear sight in fish. I will here mention one to show how very acute is this sense in the Perch, for the opportunity of witnessing which I am indebted to the kindness of Mr. Bartlett, the eminent Superintendent of the Zoological Gardens in the Regent's Park :—In the large Aquarium which will be familiar to many of my readers were placed two plate-glass tanks, one containing a Pike, and the other half a dozen Perch. These fish took no notice of our entrance ; and in order to show how supine they were to everything around, Mr. Bartlett directed the keeper to walk several times past their tanks as if about to feed them. He did so, but failed to evoke the smallest symptom of interest or recognition. Mr. Bartlett then ordered him to walk *away* from them towards the cupboard where the net with which the baits were caught was kept, desiring me to observe the effect. The keeper accordingly crossed the room (about 30 feet wide) in the direction indicated, when instantly the stolid demeanour of the fish—both Pike and Perch—gave way to the most intense excitement. They rushed to and fro across their enclosures, straining their noses against the glass, erecting their fins, and exhibiting every token of agitation ; and when the keeper having taken the net proceeded with it

towards the bait-tank, the whole shoal fastened their eyes
upon him, following every movement, and constantly veer-
ing round, as if under magnetic attraction, towards whieh-
ever párt of the room he turned. I should mention
that this oecurred in the afternoon—the usual time of
feeding being in the morning; but by Mr. Bartlett's di-
reetion the feeding had been on this occasion postponed
until my visit. It is therefore evident that these fish
knew where the net was kept—that the keeper was going
to fetch it—and that his doing so was a necessary preliminary to their being fed. These Perch had been five,
and the Pike ten years in the Zoological Gardens, having
inereased in weight during that time a quarter of a pound,
and a pound and a half, respectively.

As may be gathered from the foregoing ineident, Perch
are by no means difficult to tame : Mr. Jesse sueceeded,
after a few days only, in inducing them to feed from his
hand. Bloch mentions having watched them depositing
their ova in a vessel kept in his own room; and I am informed that the Pereh of the Zoologieal Gardens, already
referred to, increase their numbers by an annual shoal of
young fry, which are hatched and reared under the eyes of
hundreds of visitors.

A comical anecdote, turning upon this faeulty of ready
acclimatization, is related by the author of 'Fishes and
Fishing.' A eountry gentleman was anxious to induce a
London friend to visit him, and knowing the latter to be a
very keen angler, bethought him of adding the temptation

of a "day's fishing in his private water" to the usual
attractions of a suburban villa. The bait took. A day was
fixed; and punctual to his appointment arrived the sportsman, with the usual assortment of rods, reels, lines, &c.
He was all impatient to be at his work; but his host per-
suaded him first to partake of luncheon; after which he introduced him to "his water"—which proved to be an ornamental basin, in width about equal to the length of one of
the rods the visitor had brought with him. The chagrin
and disappointment of the latter may be imagined; but
upon the assurance that there really were fish in the pond,
he put his tackle together and adjusted a bait. It had
hardly touched the water before he hooked and landed a fine
Perch; another and another followed, and by the time his
friend came to summon him to dinner, he had thirty-five
fish in his basket. "Well," said the kind-hearted host,
"I am glad you have had such sport; I caused three dozen
to be put in the day before yesterday." "Indeed," re-
plied the angler, "then I will come back and catch the
thirty-sixth after dinner."

Though attaining their greatest perfection in clear, sharp
streams, Perch thrive well on clayey or sandy bottoms,
preferring generally a water of a moderate depth and current, and frequenting holes, mill-dams, hollow banks, and,
in summer, the under-currents of wears. In winter their
favourite haunts are back-waters and eddies; and at this
time of the year they feed best about the middle of the
day, more particularly if bright and warm. They usually

swim in large shoals. Their spawning-season is at the end of April or the beginning of May; and so prolific are they, that a specimen weighing half a pound has been found to contain 280,000 ova. The eggs are deposited in strings which hang about the weeds and rocks, and when seen through a bright sunlight present a beautiful appearance, almost resembling festoons of pearls.

Of the Perch family only two fresh-water species are known to exist in this country—the common Perch, and the Ruffe or Pope. Deformed Perch are, however, by no means uncommon both in England and on the Continent. Sir John Richardson has given us an interesting account of some of these, which I shall take the liberty of quoting. "A deformed variety of Perch, with the back greatly elevated, the tail distorted, and bearing the local name of *Rudaborre*, was noticed by Linnæus at Fahlun, in Sweden; and similar monstrosities occur at Elgsjön in Ostrogothia, and in other lakes in the North of Europe. Deformed Perch are also found in Llyn Raithlyn, in Merionethshire. Such a fish is figured in the volume of Daniel's ' Rural Sports' devoted to Fishing and Shooting, p. 247. Perch almost entirely white inhabit the waters of particular soils; and I am indebted to the kindness of G. S. Foljambe, Esq., of Osberton, for specimens of a variety of Perch from Ravenfield Park ponds, near Rotherham, in Yorkshire, the seat of Thomas Walker, Esq., which, when received in London, were of a uniform slate-grey colour with a silvery tint; and this peculiarity of colour is retained when the living fish are transferred from the park ponds to other waters."

I have myself taken several specimens of deformed Perch in some ponds near New Brighton, Cheshire; and in other neighbourhoods they do not appear to be very uncommon. Thomas Hurtley, in his account of some natural curiosities in the environs of Malham, near Craven, Yorkshire, speaks of the Perch of Malham Water, which after a certain age become blind. A hard yellow film covers the whole surface of the eye, when the fish gradually acquires a black hue. These Perch frequently attain the weight of 5 lbs., and are only to be taken with a net that sweeps the bottom, where they feed on Loaches, Miller's Thumbs, &c.

The Perch is the *Perke* of the Greeks, the *Perca* of the Romans, the *Pergesa* of the Italians, the *Börs* or *Persch* of Prussia, the *Aborre* or *Tryte* of Scandinavia, the *Perche* of France, and the *Flussbarsch* of Germany.

Characteristics of the common Perch.—Gill-rays 7. Two back-fins, distinct, separated; rays of the first all spinous, those of the second flexible. Length of head as compared to body, 2 to 7. Teeth small, uniform in size, curved backwards; situated on both jaws, vomer, and bones of palate. Fore gill-cover notched below, serrated on posterior edge. Gill-covers bony, ending in a flattened point. Scales rough, hard, and not easily detached. Colours (when in good condition): upper part of body greenish brown, fading into a yellow-white below; sides marked with dark transverse bands; first back-fin brown and spotted; second back-fin, and pectoral fins, pale brown; ventral, anal, and tail fins bright vermilion.

Fin-rays: D. 15−1+13 : P. 14 : V. 1+5 : A. 2+8 : C. 17.

Genus *ACERINA*.*

THE RUFFE or POPE.

(*Acerina vulgaris*.*)

The Ruffe belongs to the Second Division of Perches, which have seven gill-rays but only one back-fin, and is closely allied to the common Perch in appearance and general form, as will be observed on a comparison of the engravings of the two fish, the similarity extending also to the most remarkable of their instincts and habits. Like the latter fish, the Ruffe is predatory and gregarious, being almost always found in company with others of its own or of the Perch species, and feeding voraciously upon minnows, young fry, worms, and aquatic insects ; it selects the same haunts, and spawns at about the same period. Of the distinctions between the two fish the most marked is to be observed in the back-fins, which, although in both instances composed partly of spinous and partly of flexible rays, are

* From the Lat. *acer*, rough, and *vulgaris*, common.

in the case of the Pope united in the centre, thus forming a single long fin slightly indented, whilst in the Perch they form two entirely distinct fins. This peculiarity of the double dorsal fin is confined amongst British fresh-water fish exclusively to the Perch, to the Burbot, and to the Salmon family.

It is singular that the Ruffe, so nearly resembling the Perch in most of its characteristics, should yet differ in one so marked as the nature of the waters which it inhabits; but whilst the Perch lives indifferently in streams and ponds, and apparently thrives equally well in both, the Ruffe is never found, so far as I am aware, in other than running water. Although, however, a purely river-fish, and considered as by no means unpalatable food, it is seldom sufficiently numerous in this country to become an object of exclusive attention to the angler, but is usually taken incidentally whilst in pursuit of other fish, and more particularly when raking for Gudgeon,—the small larvæ and other insects turned up in this operation possessing apparently an equal attraction for both species. The Ruffe also, like the Gudgeon, is very easily tempted by a red worm, which, if offered in judicious proximity to his nose, he will rarely or never refuse.

From its resemblance to the latter species in its colouring, and to the Perch, as already pointed out, in form and habits, the Ruffe has been considered by some authors to be a hybrid between the two,—that is, to be produced from the ova of the one vivified by the milt of the other: for this opinion, however, there does not appear to be any sufficient foundation.

The figure shows the marking of the cheek and gill-covers in the Ruffe.

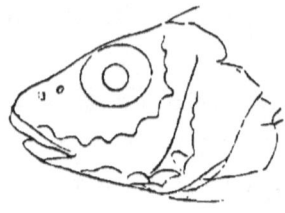

It has been remarked elsewhere that fish are capable, under certain circumstances, of exhibiting considerable attachment for others; and this is often seen in the case of fish kept for some time together in the same receptacle. When thus situated they not unfrequently contract a strong affection for one another, insomuch that, if by any chance they are separated, they mope, or refuse their food, and in some cases actually die of grief. An instance of this attachment in the Ruffe species is mentioned in the 'Philosophical Transactions,' vol. ix. :—

"Two Ruffs were placed by Mr. Anderson in a jar of water about Christmas, and in April he gave one of them away. The fish that remained was so affected that it would eat nothing for three weeks, until, fearing that it might pine to death, he sent it to the gentleman on whom he had bestowed its companion. On rejoining the other it ate immediately, and very soon recovered its former brisk-ness." This, if the fish were of different sexes, may possibly have been the "pining away for love, and wasting lean," alluded to by Burton in his 'Anatomy of Melancholy;' but if of sexes similar, then clearly it was the passion of friendship in its most platonic phase. A good example of the parental instinct in fish is afforded by the proceedings of the male of the Stickleback, alluded to in the next chapter.

The first notice of the Ruffe is attributed by Cuvier to Dr. Caius, a contemporary of Gesner. Dr. Caius found it in the river Yare, near Norwich, and sent a drawing of it to Gesner, by whom it was published in his famous treatise 'De Piscibus.' It was christened by Dr. Caius *Aspredo*, which is a translation of our name Ruffe, or Rough—a derivation easily accounted for by the hard, unpleasant feel of its scales. In most of the rivers of this country, and particularly the Thames and Isis, it is found in greater or less numbers, and, though stated to be unknown in Spain, Italy, and Greece, is an inhabitant of the more northern European latitudes.

In length the Ruffe seldom exceeds 4 or 5 inches, but I once saw a specimen which measured upwards of 7. Its spawning-season is April; and it deposits its ova amongst the rushes and flags at the margin of the water, to which they adhere from their glutinous nature.

Characteristics of the Ruffe or Pope.—Gill-rays 7. One back-fin, but with an indentation at the junction of the spiny and flexible rays, the fore part being spinous, and the hinder part flexible. Teeth very small, numerous, and uniform, situated on jaws and front of vomer. No scales on the head. Fore gill-cover notched gill-cover ending in a point. Colouring of upper part of body and head generally, light olive-brown, merging into a yellowish brown on sides, growing silvery white towards the belly; back, back-fin, and tail spotted with brown; pectoral, ventral, and anal fins pale brown.

Fin-rays: D. 14+12: P. 13: V. 1+5: A. 2+5: C. 17.

The vignette gives a magnified representation of the *Argulus foliaceus* of Jurine, a parasite occasionally found on Trout, Pike, and other fresh-water fish. The figure on the left represents the upper surface in a male, that on the right the under surface in a female, and the small figure in the centre the inseet of the natural size.

ARGULUS FOLIACEUS.

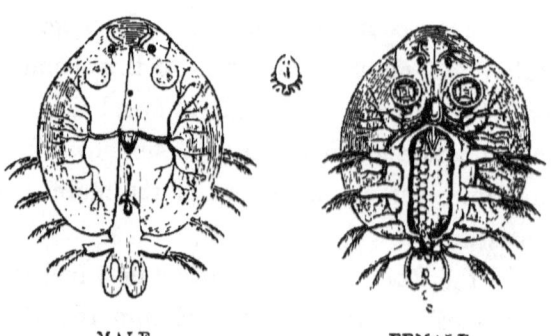

MALE.   FEMALE.

CHAPTER VI.

Series I. *BONY FISHES.*   Family "*WITH HARD CHEEKS.*"
Order I. *ACANTHOPTERYGII**.   Genus *COTTUS*†.

THE RIVER BULLHEAD, or MILLER'S THUMB.

(*Cottus gobio* ‡.)

Characteristics of the Family "with Hard Cheeks."—This family comprehends a number of fish, in all of which the appearance of the head is singular, being variously mailed, or defended by hard spines or scaly plates. They have many characteristics in common with the Perch family. Their principal distinction consists in the suborbital bone being more or less extended over the cheek and jointed on to the gill-cover.

THE genus *Cottus* contains several species belonging to this family, of which, however, we have only one in this country—the River Bullhead, or Miller's Thumb. The distinguishing characteristics of all the species of the genus

---

* Spiny-finned fishes (see p. 36).   † *Cottus*, from *kotte*, the head, Gr.
‡ *Gobio*, a gudgeon, Lat.: may be roughly translated as the 'large-headed Gudgeon.' Sometimes called 'Tommy Logge.'

E

are that they have the head more or less flattened, with teeth in both jaws and in front of the vomer; the gill-covers furnished with spines; the gills with six rays, and large openings; the body slender and without scales; and two back-fins.

The Bullhead is an inhabitant of many of the fresh waters of Europe from Italy to Sweden; and most English streams which in their course run over either sand or gravel produce this fish. It is also common in Scotland, but exceedingly rare in Ireland. Its principal food consists of the larvæ of water-insects, the ova of other fish, and minute fry; and being remarkably voracious it rarely or never refuses to bite at a small worm, or other grub, dropped sufficiently near its immense mouth.

Its favourite haunt is among loose stones, under which, from the peculiarly flattened form of its head, it is enabled

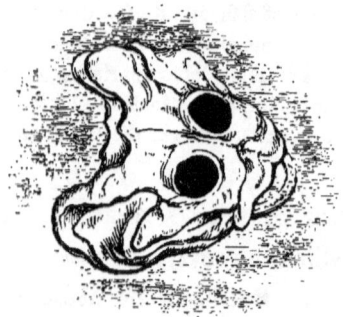

to some extent to thrust itself, thereby obtaining a partial hiding-place. This security, however, like that of the Ostrich, is rather fancied than real; for the eyes being thus blinded, whilst the body remains exposed, it falls an easy prey to the prowess of the village urchins, who, in Switzerland, spear it with a small javelin as it lies *perdu*. When disturbed it darts away in a puff of mud with considerable celerity.

Whether the fish is ever captured in this country for edible purposes, I am not aware : M. Risso says that it is eaten in Italy ; Matthiolus, an eminent physician of the sixteenth century, commends it highly for its " taste and nourishment ;" and Wilson, the naturalist, ascertained that its flesh when boiled becomes red, like that of the salmon. In Russia the Bullhead is used by some as a charm against fever, while others suspend it horizontally, carefully balanced by a single thread ; and thus poised, but permitted at the same time freedom of motion, they believe that it possesses the property of acting as a weathercock, and of indicating, by the direction of the head, the point of the compass from which the wind blows.

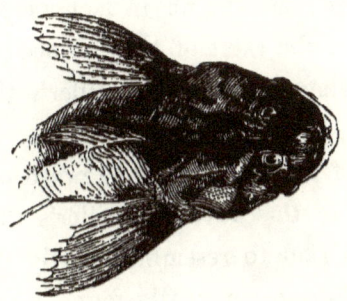

Yarrell gives an ingenious explanation of the term " Miller's Thumb" bestowed upon this fish. He considers that it has reference to the peculiar form of the head, which, as will be seen by the engraving, is smooth, broad, and rounded, like the thumb of a miller. "It is well known," he observes, "that all the science and tact of a miller are directed so to regulate the machinery of his mill, that the meal produced shall be of the most valuable description that the operation of grinding will permit when performed under the most advantageous circumstances. His profit or his loss, even his fortune or his ruin, depend upon the exact adjustment of all the various parts of the machinery in operation. The miller's ear is constantly directed to the note made by the running-stone during its rotation over the bed-stone, the exact parallelism of their two surfaces, indicated by a particular sound, being a matter of the first consequence; and his hand is as constantly placed under the meal-spout, to ascertain by actual contact the character and qualities of the meal produced. The thumb by a peculiar movement spreads the sample over the fingers; the thumb, in fact, employed with tact, is the gauge of the value of the produce; and hence have arisen the sayings of 'Worth a miller's thumb,' and 'An honest miller hath a golden thumb*,' in reference to the amount of profit that is the reward of his skill. By incessant use in this way, the miller's thumb acquires a form which is said to resemble exactly the shape of the head of the fish so constantly found in the mill-stream, and called the Miller's Thumb." This name also occurs

* Ray's Proverbs.

in Beaumont and Fletcher's comedy of 'Wit at several Weapons,' and in Merrett's 'Pinax.' The origin of the name "Bullhead" is sufficiently obvious.

The Bullhead seldom exceeds four or five inches in length; it begins to spawn about April, and continues for several months, during which time the abdomen of the female is frequently so distended with eggs as to present almost the appearance of a cow's udder.

Characteristics of the River Bullhead.—Head large, depressed. Teeth in both jaws and in front of vomer, small, sharp; none on bones of the palate. Fore gill-cover armed with one spine; gill-rays 6. Body naked, without scales. Two back-fins united by a membrane. General colour of body above dark brownish black; sides lighter, with small black spots; under surface of head and belly white. Fins spotted.

Fin-rays: D. 6 to 9+17 or 18: P. 15: V. 3: A. 13: C. 11.

FABRICIUS' SEA-BULLHEAD.

Genus *GASTEROSTEUS* *.

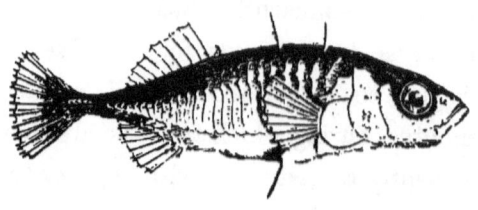

THE ROUGH-TAILED STICKLEBACK.

(*Gasterosteus trachurus* †.)

The characteristics common to the Stickleback genus, of which we have in this country six species, are—the body generally scaleless, and more or less plated or mailed on the sides; one back-fin, with simple or free spines before it; the ventral fins with one strong spine and one ray; the bones of the *pelvis* pointed behind, forming a cuirass; the swimming-bladder simple; and the branchiostegous or gill-rays three.

In order to save space and avoid repetition, I shall here give a short account of the habits and characteristics of the Sticklebacks generally, so far as they are common to the several species, appending, under the head of each individual fish, only such peculiarities as may serve to distinguish it from its congeners.

Though small and apparently insignificant, the *Gas-*

* *Gasterosteus*, the Gr. name for the Stickleback—literally 'bony-bellied'—from *gaster*, the belly, and *osteon*, a bone.

† *trachurus*, 'rough-tailed,' from *trachys*, rough, and *oura*, the tail, Gr.

terostei are amongst the most interesting, at least to the naturalist, of all our pond and river denizens, exhibiting in their diminutive forms a very considerable amount of courage, capacity, and even affection. If the Pike is the tyrant of the water, the Stickleback is certainly its knight-errant: now, with sheathed weapons and glittering in green and purple, he tenderly woos the object of his dcvotion, or armed *cap-à-pie* patrols a watchful sentinel before her nuptial bower; now he fiercely disputes with rival claimants the possession of a favourite nook, or bristling with spines charges through the liquid plains in search of other Sticklebacks as pugnacious and more penetrable than himself.

The movements of Sticklebacks in confinement are described by those who have watched them as being most warlike. When a few are first turned in, they swim about in a shoal, apparently exploring their new habitation. Suddenly one will take possession of a particular corner of the tub, or, as it will sometimes happen, of the bottom, and will instantly commence an attack on his companions ; and if either of them ventures to oppose his sway, a regular and furious battle ensues: the two combatants swim round and round each other with the greatest rapidity, biting and endeavouring to pierce each other with their spines, which on these occasions are projected. Contests of this sort frequently last several minutes before either will give way ; and when one does submit, imagination can hardly conceive the vindictive fury of the conqueror, who,

in the most persevering and unrelenting way, chases his
rival from one part of the tub to another, until fairly exhausted with fatigue. The Stickleback also uses his spines
with such fatal effect, that one has been known during a
battle absolutely to rip his opponent quite open, so that he
sank to the bottom and died. Three or four parts of the
tub are occasionally taken possession of by as many little
tyrants, who guard their territories with strict vigilance;
and the slightest invasion invariably brings on a battle.
During these internecine combats the colours of both belli-
gerents frequently undergo a marked and extraordinary
change, those of the victor becoming a deep crimson on
the belly and green on the back, and the vanquished losing
both his brilliancy and spirit together. These, it should
be observed, are the habits of the male fish alone: the
females are quite pacific—appear fat, as if full of roe—and
never assume the brilliant colours of the male, by whom
they are unmolested.

    An amusing account of the sort of relationship exist-
ing between the Stickleback and Pike families is given by
Dr. Badham *.   " By old Pikes," he says; "Sticklebacks are
held in yet greater abomination than Perch, and not without good reason, seeing the havoc they commit amongst
the young and unwary Pickerels. It is only by personal
suffering that fish, any more than men, ever buy wisdom;
growing Pikes no sooner begin to feel the cravings of
hunger, and to find they have large mouths, well furnished

* Fish Tattle, p. 300.

with teeth on purpose to cater for it, than they proceed to make preliminary essay upon the smallest fish within reach; these are commonly the *Gasterostei*, or Sticklebacks, who, observing the gaping foe advance against them, prepare for the encounter by bristling up their spines in instinctive readiness to stick in his throat, instead, as he supposes, of going smoothly down into his stomach. This induces a dreadful choking disease, which we venture to call ' stickle-backitis,' by means whereof many a promising young Jack is cut off ' *in cunabulis.* '"

I have alluded to the affection exhibited under certain circumstances by this species. The parental instinct in the generality of fish is feeble, perhaps indeed wholly absent; and the exceptions are therefore the more worthy of observation. Amongst the most remarkable of these may be classed the Sticklebacks, which not only display considerable regard and solicitude in the rearing of their progeny, but even build nests for their reception. For the most complete and interesting notice of these we are indebted to the researches of Sir John Richardson; and his account, which will amply repay perusal, will be found in the third edition of Yarrell's British Fishes*. From this I shall take the liberty of introducing a few extracts, in a somewhat condensed form.

The Rough-tailed and Smooth-tailed Sticklebacks, then, according to D'Orbigny, usually construct their nests on the soil at the bottom of the paternal ditch or rivulet,

* Vol. ii. pp. 75 92.

whilst the Ten-spined species, on the contrary, select for
a building-site the broad leaves or fibrous roots of aquatic
plants. The two former build nests in shape somewhat
like mole-hills, while the nest of the latter rather resembles a muff, or the nest of the Wren, or Long-tailed Tit.
On the approach of the spawning-time, which is about
May, or a little later in the summer, the male commences
operations by collecting in a convenient locality a quantity
of grass-stalks, wiry water-mosses, and other fibrous matters, which he cements with the mucus that exudes from
his skin,—creeping for this purpose backwards and forwards
over the materials. In the Smooth-tailed species, the foundation is usually laid of straws, having their ends carefully
tucked into the gravel; other straws are laid across, and
similarly secured by the fish placing his snout on the end
of each straw, and then raising his body vertically so as to
press it down. Confervæ and such like are then woven
into a mass above, through which the water can have free
passage. In the centre of this a dome-like hollow is preserved, and on the top a small round hole, the edges of
which are strengthened with particular care, and rounded off
by tucking in the loose fibres; whilst every now and then
the architect pauses in his task and hovers over the nest,
agitating the water with his fins as if to try the stability of
the structure. In the Rough-tailed species the bottom of
the nest is first finished, then the sides, and lastly the top,
which is covered carefully over, a small hole being left on
one side for an entrance. This labour completed, the

builder seeks out a mate, and conducting her with many
caresses to the nest, introduces her into the nuptial chamber. In a few minutes she has laid two or three eggs, after
which she bores a hole on the opposite side of the nest to
that by which she entered, and makes her escape. The
nest has now two doors, and the eggs are exposed to the
cool stream of water, which entering by one door flows out
at the other. On the following day the male goes again
in quest of a female, and brings back sometimes the same,
sometimes a new mate, and this is repeated until the nest
contains a considerable number of eggs. Next the male
watches a whole month over his treasure, defending it
stoutly against all invaders, and especially against his
wives, who have a feminine curiosity to look at the eggs.
When the young are hatched and able to do for themselves,
the anxieties and active vigilance of the male cease.

Before this time, however, arrives, his duties are of a
most onerous character, as may be gathered from an instance which fell under the notice of Mr. Warington. The
male guardian moved continually across the clear space
in every direction; and his vigilance was greatly taxed,
for other fish in the tank larger than himself used their
utmost endeavours to snap up the young brood. The
little creature, however, drove them all off, seizing their
fins and striking furiously at their heads and eyes. He
also defeated the attempts made by a strange female to
deposit her eggs in the same place. As the young fry
gained size and strength they were inclined to stray, but

the male parent constantly brought the stragglers back within the allotted precincts.

A good account of the nest-building process has been given by the same author. Several beautiful Smooth-tailed Sticklebacks, male and female, the latter full of spawn, were introduced by him into a miniature pond. The male fishes immediately took up certain positions, each defending his own against all intruders with pertinacity. On the following day, one of the males was industriously employed in building a nest behind a piece of rock-work; and it was perceived that he had already constructed a small hole as round as a ring, with a broad margin. This spot he guarded with the utmost jealousy, continually starting from his post, and attacking the other fish with extraordinary ferocity. To quiet the turmoil, Mr. Warington netted the pugnacious fish; but no sooner was it removed from the water than the other Sticklebacks darted to the spot, and pulling out a mass of eggs, devoured them before their defender could be replaced in the vivarium.

During the nesting- and spawning-season the male fish is beautiful beyond description—the eye of a resplendent green with metallic lustre, the lower part of the throat and body bright crimson, and the back ash-green, the colours glowing as if lighted up by an internal heat. The males are generally distinguishable from the females by the pink colour of the belly; in the latter the back is green, and the cheeks, flanks, and belly silvery white; both sexes, however, are more brilliant in the spawning-season.

The Sticklebacks feed usually upon grubs of all sorts, small insects, and minute fry and other animal matters, and are remarkable for their extraordinary voracity, being in fact the only species which, without hook or snare, will suffer themselves to be taken rather than resign their prey. They are believed to be excessively destructive to the ova of other fish; and it has been considered a doubtful race in this particular between the little Eels and the Sticklebacks, as to which devour the greatest quantity. The partiality of the latter for all sorts of ova, and their restless and inconsiderate rapacity sometimes entail a singular death: they dart into the lumps of frog-spawn with which in March and April the ditches abound, and, their spines preventing retreat, are there suffocated. It is by no means uncommon to find two or three Sticklebacks thus choked in a single bed of spawn. This fact has, I believe, hitherto escaped the notice of naturalists. It seems probable that Stickleback-life rarely exceeds two or, at most, three years.

The Rough-tailed Stickleback (a representation of which, of the natural size, is given at page 78) is very generally distributed throughout most parts of England, Ireland, and Scotland, inhabiting indifferently fresh and salt, running and stagnant waters; and, although maturing but few eggs, the numbers of individuals are so great as, according to Pennant, to have enabled a Lincolnshire labourer to earn four shillings a day during a considerable period by catching and selling them at the rate of a halfpenny a bushel—the fish in this case being used as manure. They are also used for the same purpose near the River Welland, in which, about once in eight years, they are caught by the cart-load. Mr. Salter assures us that both Sticklebacks and Sprats make excellent food for poultry, which are very fond of them, and fatten amazingly; and Taylor says that with their prickles cut off they are a good bait for Perch.

Characteristics of the Rough-tailed Stickleback.—Length seldom exceeding 2½ inches. Upper and lower jaws armed with bands of small teeth; none on vomer, bones of palate, or tongue. Spines on back capable of being raised or depressed at pleasure. Sides defended for about three-fourths of their height by twenty-six flat, strap-shaped plates, of which fifteen are before the vent. A series of plates along ridge of back; spines rising from three largest.

Fin-rays: D. III.+9: P. 10: V. 1+1: A. 1+8: C. 12.

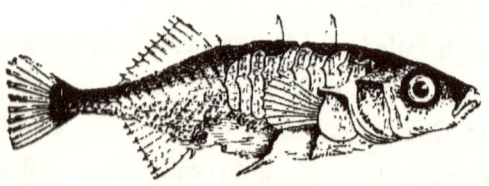

THE HALF-ARMED STICKLEBACK

(*Gasterosteus semi-armatus* *)

is distinguished from the last-named species by the want

* *semi-armatus*, half-armed, Lat.

of defensive plates along the sides of the tail, and by the somewhat larger size of the teeth ; in other respects it differs but little, occurring in similar situations, and frequently in the same shoal. The fin-rays are—

D. III.+10: P. 10: A. 1+9: C. 19.

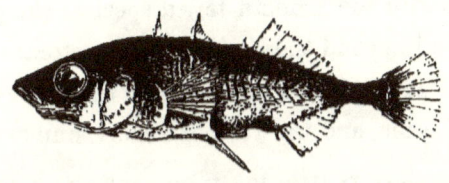

THE SMOOTH-TAILED STICKLEBACK.

(Gasterosteus leiurus *.)

This species is distinguished from those preceding it by the side armour-plates, ten in number, extending no further than the ends of the rays of the pectoral fin,—the whole length of the body behind these being smooth and soft, and without scales.

Fin-rays: D. III.+10: P. 11: A. 1+8: C. 12.

---

* leiurus, smooth-tailed, from leios, smooth, and oura, a tail, Gr.

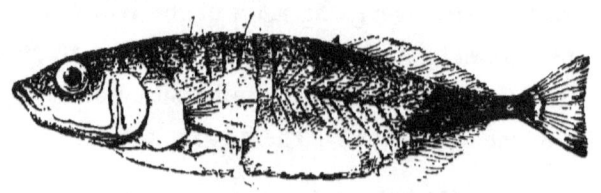

THE SHORT-SPINED STICKLEBACK.

(*Gasterosteus brachycentrus* *.)

In the number of side-plates the Short-spined Stickleback agrees with the Smooth-tailed species; the plates also do not extend beyond the limits of the pectoral fin. It is, however, of much larger size, whilst the spines are considerably shorter, and the vertebræ more numerous.

Fin-rays: D. III.+13 : P. 10 : A. 1+9 : C. 12.

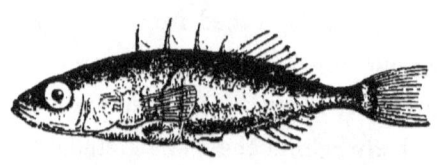

THE FOUR-SPINED STICKLEBACK

(*Gasterosteus spinulosus* †)

is distinguished by having four spines on the back. It is likewise exceedingly small, the figure being double the

---

* *brachycentrus*, literally 'with short prickles,' from *brachys*, short, and *centron*, a prickle, Gr.   † *spinulosus*, spiny, Lat.

natural size. The specimens examined were taken in Scotland; and, so far as I am aware, none are recorded to have been captured south of the Tweed. They have all the varied colours of the other species of the genus, except the bright red and scarlet sometimes found in the males.

The fin-rays are: D. IV.+8: P. 9: V. 1: A. 1+8: C. 12.

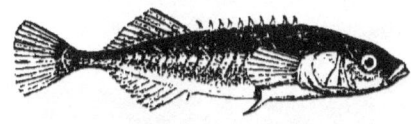

THE TEN-SPINED STICKLEBACK.

(Gasterosteus pungitius *.)

The Ten-spined Stickleback varies in length from 1½ to 2¼ inches, and, though not nearly so numerous as the Three-spined species, is found in most of the creeks near the British coasts, as well as in many of our rivers, up which it is supposed to migrate in shoals in the spring. It is readily distinguished from all other species by the nine or ten spines on the back, and by its sides being perfectly smooth, without any armour-plates. The general colour is yellowish or olive-green on the back; sides and belly

* pungitius, from pungo, I prick, Lat.

silvery white, with minute black specks; fins yellowish white. The fin-rays are—

$$D. IX.+10: P. 11: V. 1+5: A. 1+9: C. 12.$$

The figures below represent two states of the Stone-fly (common Caddis-worm) of anglers.

PHRYGANEA GRANDIS.

CHAPTER VII.

Series I. *BONY FISHES.*
Order II. *MALACOPTERYGII ABDOMINALES* *.

Family *CYPRINIDÆ* †.
Genus *CYPRINUS* ‡.

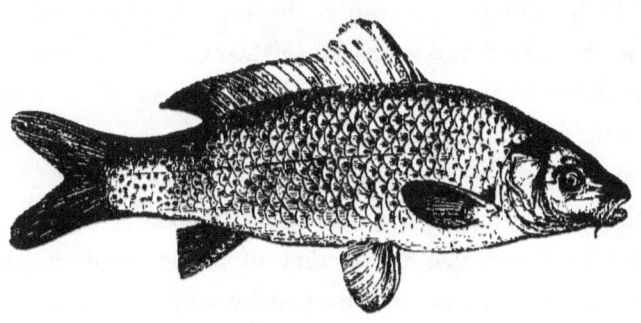

THE COMMON CARP.

(*Cyprinus carpio* §.)

Characteristics common to all the Carp Family.—Fin-rays almost entirely flexible. Ventral fins suspended to the abdomen behind the pectorals, without being attached to the bones of the shoulder. Mouth shallow ; lips commonly fleshy ; jaws feeble, generally without teeth. Powerful teeth in the throat. Only one back-fin. Body scaly. Very few gill-rays.

HAVING concluded the first Order, *Acanthopterygian* fish, or those having numerous spines on the fins, we now come to the *Cyprinidæ,* which form Cuvier's first family of *Malacopterygii,* or fishes which have almost all their fin-rays soft and flexible.

The distinguishing characteristics of *Cyprinus* or true

---

* Abdominal soft-finned fish (see p. 37).
† The Family of the Carps.
‡ *Cyprinus,* a Carp.
§ *carpio,* the Carp, Lat.

Carp (the first genus of this family) are—the body being always covered with large scales; a single long back-fin; the lips fleshy; mouth small; teeth in the throat, but none in the jaws; and three gill-rays.

Of the groups composing the Carp family generally, some are to be found in greater or less abundance throughout almost all the warm and temperate parts of the globe, —India and China producing the greatest variety, and Germany the greatest number of the particular species under notice. Austria and Prussia especially abound with Carp, which form a staple commodity of traffic; and in such request are fresh-water fish as articles of food in parts of these countries, that, according to Yarrell, an acre of water will let for as high a rent as an acre of land. The Carp is an inhabitant also of most of the lakes and rivers of Russia and Eastern Siberia; and Valenciennes states that it thrives and reaches to an extraordinary size in the Caspian.

The common Carp is so well known to most fishermen and others as hardly to require description. It exists, either in ponds or rivers, in tolerably equal distribution throughout the whole of the counties of England, and in some of those of Ireland and Scotland, where, however, the water appears less suited to it.

Although the Carp is not unfrequently found in rivers, yet stagnant water appears to be its natural element, and in ponds it breeds fastest and reaches its greatest size. Large Carp are occasionally taken in the Thames; and in some of its tributaries the fish is also found in tolerable abundance and of heavy weight: of these, the Wey, in Surrey, contains probably the finest specimens, though I believe they are rarely caught.

Of all fish, the Carp family generally are perhaps the least carnivorous; and, indeed, their teeth, which are placed in the throat, are entirely unsuited for purposes of seizing or retaining prey. Their food consists of soft vegetable substances, insects, and occasionally of worms or grubs. Mud is often found in their stomachs, having been swallowed, it may be, on account of the minute worms or other animal matters it contains; and I have met with instances in which small fish have been disgorged by them. This is, however, an occurrence by no means common.

The engraving represents one-half of the teeth in the throat of the Carp, Tench, Roach, and Barbel, with the

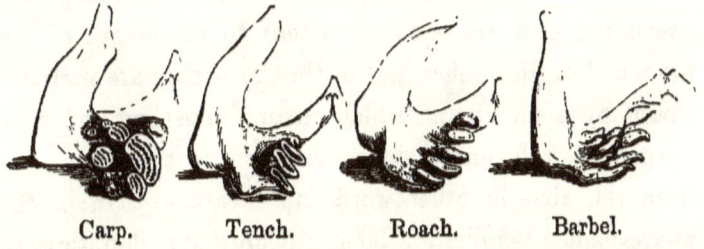

Carp.　　　Tench.　　　Roach.　　　Barbel.

bone on which they are placed, both of the natural size, as exhibited in specimens of about half a pound weight each. It will be seen that the crowns, or upper surfaces, of the teeth of the Carp are furrowed, and altogether present a very similar appearance to those of ruminating animals. These teeth masticate the food by working against a gristly plate in the roof of the throat, in front of which will be found the soft fleshy mass commonly known as "Carp's tongue;" the real tongue, however, is placed as usual between the limbs of the mandible, and is small and inconspicuous.

Although the *Cyprinidæ* are ranged amongst the Soft-finned fishes, many members of the family have one or more of the rays of the dorsal or anal fin strong and pointed, and toothed behind. These rays constitute a connecting link between the Soft- and Spiny-finned Divisions, though from the latter they are distinguishable by having the *joints* of which they were originally formed still obscurely discernible in the adult fish, whilst the spines in the *Acanthopterygii* are constructed of only a single piece. The spines in the latter are, besides, much more numerous.

In the Salmon and Herring families the openings between the gills are equal in extent to the length of the branchial or gill-arches, but in the Carps they are partially closed by a membrane which retains moisture, and thus keeps the gills longer in a condition to absorb oxygen from the air—in other words, to breathe—than in the above-named families; a bountiful provision, doubtless to enable the fish to survive occasional droughts in hot climates. By this means also the fish can live for an unusually lengthened period entirely out of water—for so long, indeed, that I have taken a basket of Carp a considerable journey in a broiling August day, with no more moisture than could be obtained from a damp cloth, and they have been alive and ready to swim about at the end of it. In Holland this peculiarity is well known and acted upon, insomuch that it is by no means an uncommon practice with the Dutch to fatten Carp for the table by hanging them in a cool cellar in a net full of damp moss for three weeks or a month, and feeding them with bread and milk, which is passed into their mouths with a spoon. They refresh the fish now and then by sprinkling the moss with water.

There is a singularity in the structure of the interior supports of the gill-leaves in the Carp, which no doubt has a good deal to do with its power of enduring this sort of amphibious existence : each of these supports is bony ; whilst in the Perch it is formed partly of bone and partly of cartilage, and in the Bream, Barbel, and Pike wholly of cartilage. The number of the gill-leaves varies considerably in different fish. In the Gudgeon, according to Milne-Edwards, there are about 55 in a row, in the Tench 96, in the Barbel 106, and in the Carp 135. The air-bladder in Carps is generally large, and is divided by a short narrow neck or necks into two or more cells or chambers. The woodcut represents a section of this bladder in the

common Carp, with a probe introduced between the two compartments.

Although Carp are the most shy and difficult of capture of any species with which we are acquainted, they are one of the easiest to tame. They feed readily in stews, and will come for their meals, according to some authors, at the ringing of a bell—certainly at the sound of their keeper's voice. Mr. Bradley, who was a great observer of the habits of fish, relates an instance of this :—" At Rotterdam, in a garden belonging to M. Eden, I had the pleasure of seeing some Carps fed, which were kept in a moat of considerable extent. The occasion of my seeing these creatures was chiefly to satisfy me that they were capable of hearing. The gentleman having filled his pocket with spinach-seed, conducted me to the side of the moat. We remained quiet for some time, the better to convince me that the fish would not come till he called them. At length he called in his usual way, and immediately the fish gathered from all parts of the moat in such numbers that there was hardly room for them to lie by one another." The same sort of thing may be witnessed in the waters of some public gardens near Rotterdam. In these ponds the Carp are also in the habit of following visitors about, in expectation of food ; and one immense fellow, with a side as broad as a flitch of bacon, and an appetite that seemed insatiable, actually pursued me for nearly a hundred yards along the side of the bank, until, my stock of bread being exhausted, I was fain to try experiments with some paper pellets, when he sailed off in magnificent disgust. This fish must have weighed, I should think, at least 15 lbs.

Mr. Jesse says of some Carp and Tench which were kept by him, that " they were soon reconciled to their situation, and ate boiled potatoes in considerable quantities; and the former seemed to have lost their original shyness, eating in his presence without any scruple." My experience agrees with Mr. Jesse's. I have now three sturdy little fellows, in a vivarium within a few yards of me, that will readily take anything I throw them, and almost out of my fingers. These fish have been in the house for nearly a year, and are apparently doing well and growing. One of them affords a good instance of the 'hard-dying' qualities of the species. He was 'killed' in the usual manner, and consigned, with others, to the cook, in whose care, however, after some hours, he began to show signs of revival. A kind-hearted damsel compassionately transferred him to the vivarium, where he has since thriven, showing no effects of his narrow escape, save a scar on the back of the head, which he will probably never lose.

There is a pretty instance on record of the taming of the Carp by a little American girl. The child, who was not six years old, lived close to the bank of a pond in the village of Rockynook, near Kingham, Massachusetts. She began by throwing crumbs into the water. " Gradually the fish learned to distinguish her footsteps, and darted to the edge whenever she approached; and at last they would even feed out of her hand, and allow her to stroke their scaly sides. The control of Van Amburgh over his wild beasts was not more complete than that which this child attained

over her finny playmates, who rejected all overtures from
the rest of the neighbours, and would have nothing to do
with any but their tried friend." They would trust no one
else, let him come with food ever so tempting; and when
a few years afterwards the child unfortunately died, during
a visitation of cholera, the fish are said to have shown the
most marked symptoms of distress, swimming disconso-
lately up and down at the spot where their protector was
wont to look for them, and refusing the food offered by the
good-natured townsfolk. "Thus," as the writer adds, "it
will be seen that even fishes are not so cold-blooded but
that they will recognize the *law of kindness*" *.

At Sir J. Bowyer's, near Uxbridge, Mr. Bradley tells us,
there is a pond full of tame Pike which can be called
together at pleasure. Mr. Salter † was acquainted with a
person who for several years kept, in a water-butt, a Perch,
which came to the surface for his food whenever his owner
tapped on the side of the butt. According to Ælian, the
Chad was lured to its destruction by the sound of castanets.
Professor Rennie‡ states that in Germany this fish is still
taken by nets hung with rows of little bells arranged so
as to chime in harmony; and, without going back to the
story of Amphion and the Dolphins, or the old Scottish
Harper who, according to the ballad, "harp'd a fish
out o' the sa't water," we may find hundreds of well-
authenticated anecdotes, leading clearly to the conclusion

* Boston Transcript, United States.
† Preface to Angler's Guide.   ‡ Alphabet of Angling.

that fish have a very considerable perception of external sounds.

A rather annoying proof of the acute hearing at least of the Carp species is nightly furnished me by the three individuals in my vivarium, already referred to. Every evening, when the bell is rung for family prayers, these fish commence springing and splashing about in the water, continuing their efforts for five or ten minutes with a noise and vivacity exceedingly distracting to the attention, and in the highest degree indecorous.

The Carp was a well-known fish in the times of the ancient Greeks and Romans, though apparently held in no very high estimation. It is mentioned by Aristotle and Pliny, the former naming it *Kuprinos*, or *Kuprianos*, from whence probably originated the Latin term *Cyprinus*, and also the modern appellations *Karp* (Swedish), *Karpfe* (German), *Carp*, *Karpe*, and *Carpe* (English, Danish, and French), *Carpa* (Spanish), and *Carpione* (Italian).

When, and whence, the Carp was first brought into this country—if indeed it was really an introduced fish at all—is involved in obscurity. Leonard Mascall, a gentleman of Sussex, claims to have been the importer both of the Carp and of the Pippin; but Mascall's time was 1600, whilst numerous notices of the Carp appear nearly a century before that date. The old couplet quoted by Izaak Walton—

"Hops and turkeys, carps and beer,
Came into England all in a year"—

appears also to have been written under a poetic license;

for Carp are mentioned in the 'Book of St. Albans,' the earliest English work on Angling extant, published in 1481, in which the authoress, Dame Juliana Berners, calls it a "deyntous fish, although scarce,"—whereas turkeys eame from America about 1521, and hops were unknown until 1524. Therefore, notwithstanding the probability of some of the varieties of the Carp having been introduced at one time or another from Germany, or other part of the Continent, there seems to be every reason for believing that the common Carp is an aboriginal of this country.

The difference in the shape of the scales in the Carp and in one of its principal varieties is shown in the engravings.

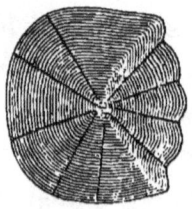
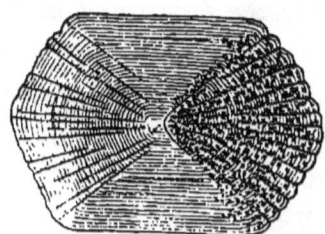

Crucian Carp.   Common Carp.

According to Ephemera*, Carp "in our rivers very rarely reach the weight of 6 lbs., and as seldom 12 lbs. in our ponds." I hold this to be an entirely erroneous view. I am acquainted with many waters, both stagnant and running, in which the usual weights are greatly in excess of those named ; the first instances that occur to my memory

* Notes to Ephemera's edition of Walton, p. 147.

may be mentioned: the River Wey, near Byfleet; and several large ponds at Wimbledon, belonging, a few years ago, to Mrs. Marryatt and to Mr. Beaumont. In all these waters I have frequently seen Carp which averaged nearly double the weights quoted above; and in the lake in Wimbledon Park I took on one occasion, with a landing-net, a specimen weighing upwards of 19 lbs. Much larger fish are, however, by no means unknown; whilst in Holland and other Continental states they sometimes exceed 30 and 40 lbs. in weight *.

Of English Carp, the largest *on record*, so far as I am aware, appear to have been a brace weighing 38 lbs., sent by Mr. Ladbroke, from his park at Gatton, Surrey, to Lord Egremont, as challenge-specimens to compare with the Carp of Sussex †. A Carp is mentioned as having been taken from a piece of water at Stourhead in 1793 which was 30 inches long, upwards of 22 inches in girth, and which weighed 18 lbs. At Weston Hall, Staffordshire, the seat of the Earl of Bradford, is preserved the painting of another which weighed 19½ lbs., and was caught in a lake called the " White Sitch." These are the few large fish that happen to have been chronicled from English waters; but I am convinced that many much larger ones have been taken.

* Valenciennes, Histoire des Poissons.
† Daniel's Rural Sports.

Comparative Lengths and Weights of Carp *.

Length. inches.	Weight. lbs. oz.		Length. inches.	Weight. lbs. oz.	
9	0	7¾	20	5	5¼
10	0	11	21	6	2¾
11	0	14¾	22	7	1½
12	1	2⅓	23	8	1¾
13	1	8¼	24	9	3½
14	1	14½	25	10	6¾
15	2	4	26	11	11
16	2	11½	27	13	2
17	3	4½	28	14	10
18	3	14½	29	15	4
19	4	9	30	16	0

The growth-rate of Carp has been approximately computed at 3 lbs. during the first six years, and 6 lbs. before their tenth year. They grow much faster, however, in warm climates, and also probably in stews, when well fed. The following is recommended as a recipe for fattening them :— " Barley-meal, half a gallon; chalk, in powder, 1½ lb. (very clean); clay, a sufficient quantity to make a stiff paste. Place this in the stew or pond, in a net (of not too small meshes), suspended about a foot from the bottom. When all is sucked away but the clay, place fresh in the net or nets." This recipe is said to have been employed by the old monks; but the chronicler adds, " Now, how the Carp are to suck away the barley-meal and chalk, leaving the clay behind, appears difficult to understand." This seems a pertinent question. Probably wheaten or other flour would be a better ingredient.

* See p. 59.

A hundred—a hundred and fifty—even two hundred
has been stated as the number of years attained by the
Carp under the most favourable circumstances. Supposing, however, that this should be an exaggeration, there
is no doubt that many of the fish which were introduced
into the ponds at Versailles, &c., in the reign of Louis the
Fourteenth (say 1690) are either still living, or were so a
very short time before the Revolution of 1830. Dr. Smith,
in his 'Tour to the Continent,' mentions them, and observes that they had grown white through age. Valenciennes refers to others in the basins at the Tuileries
which would also come when *called by their names*; and
Buffon assures us that he had seen, in the fosses of the
Ponchartrain, Carp which were known to be upwards of a
century and a half old.

It is a curious fact that great age and exclusion from
the light produce apparently the same effects, both on fish
and other animals,—the skin or scales undergoing a sort of
bleaching process, either from a gradual drying up of the
invigorating juices of the body, or from the want of the
sun's rays. In the case of fish and reptiles whitened by
exclusion from the light, it is an almost universal rule that
the eyes are so much undeveloped as to produce total
blindness. The fish taken in the Mammoth-caves of Ken-
tucky are blind, and of a white, colourless hue, as also is
a species of Crawfish found in the same subterranean
waters. The *Proteus anguinus*, inhabiting the caves of
Illyria, exhibits the same peculiarities. This singular

creature, which is apparently a link between the reptile and the fish, presents in every respect the appearance of a blind white eel, with four very thin eft-like legs near the extremities. When swimming, these legs fold back against the sides, and appear to answer no purpose except to balance the animal when at rest on the ground. The specimen which I examined was about a foot long, and was presented to Mr. Buckland by a gentleman who brought it from the cave of Adelsberg, near Trieste. Its lungs or gills were double, one pair being on the inside and one on the outside of the neck; but I could not discover that it ever came to the surface of the water to breathe: it appeared to sleep constantly; and its motion in swimming, when disturbed, was exactly like that of an eel. It was always necessary to keep it covered up, as upon lengthened exposure to the light its life and its colour ebbed away together.

Through the kindness of Sir Emerson Tennent, I had recently the opportunity of examining some newly-discovered Mud-fish found under the surface of the paddy-fields of Ceylon. The medium in which they exist is of about the consistency of pea-soup; and their eyes are so small as to be almost imperceptible. In this case, however, the fish retain the natural colour. We may presume that all these blind creatures obtain their food by scent.

According to Blumenbach, the Carps have the largest brain, in proportion to their size, of any fresh-water fish. They are certainly the most difficult to take by bait, and,

whether accidentally or on purpose, have a singular habit,
on occasion, of cutting through the angler's line with the
sharp spine of their dorsal fin. It also seems to be a well-
established fact that when they perceive a net approaching
they will bury their noses in the mud of the bottom, and
refuse to move, even though the leads of the net sweep
heavily over them. By this means they escape. If, however, they should happen to be dragged up by the net, they
will frequently endeavour, like the Grey Mullet, to spring
over the top: in fact there is no doubt that the Carp quite
merits his *sobriquet* of the "Water-Fox."

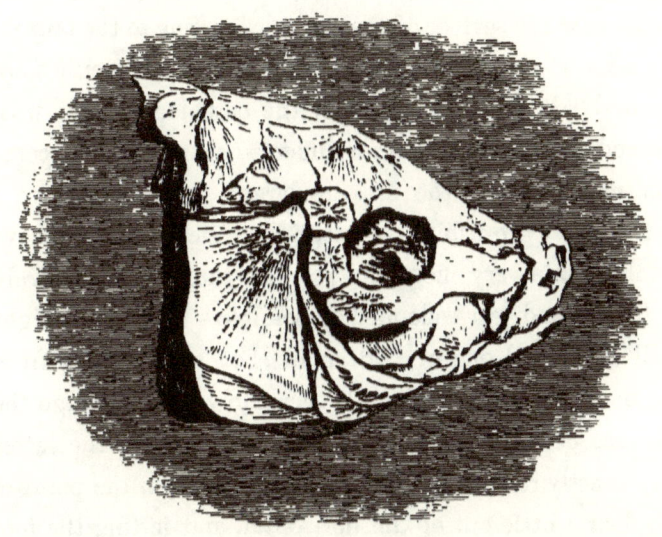

The chamber for lodging the brain is particularly well
closed and compact, as will be seen by a reference to the
engraving.

During the winter months it is probable that Carp retire almost wholly into the mud, or under roots, hollows,
and weeds, and at this time they are hardly ever to be
taken with a bait*. In the summer months they frequently
lie sucking, in the weeds, in a sort of lazy state, each
"suck" making a very distinct and unmistakeable noise.
It very much resembles the sound made by a pig, to which
animal, indeed, a big Carp has always appeared to me to
bear a striking likeness, both in face and character. When
not sucking or basking, the Carp usually swims about in
shoals near the surface of the water, returning to the bottom
to feed.   Early in the morning and late in the evening are
the best times for fishing; but the catching of Carp with
the rod and line is always a difficult and uncertain operation, particularly if the fish are large.   I will here give a
method of Carp-fishing in stagnant waters which I have
usually found very successful †.   Let the line be entirely
of fine, round gut—clouded if possible—with a very light
quill float, and one or two small shot about a foot from
the hook.   Plumb the depth accurately; and arrange the
distance between the float and the shot so that the latter
may exactly rest *on the bottom*, weighing down the point of
the float a little out of the horizontal, and letting the foot
of gut below, and the bait, lie on the ground.   Fix the rod
in the bank, and keep perfectly quiet.   When a bite is per-

* *Vide*, amongst other authorities, White's 'Selborne.'

† Since writing the above, I have ascertained that this plan is also
recommended by Mr. Wright in his clever work on Fishes and Fishing, p. 32.

ceived, do not strike until the float begins to move away. It constantly happens, however, that the Carp will not be taken either by this or any other mode of fishing with which I am acquainted; but if he is to be caught at all, it is thus.

The baits for Carp are, worms, gentles, greaves, grains, and various sorts of pastes, of which, however, I believe the plain white bread-crumb paste is the best, as well as the most easily made. About midsummer a little honey may be added. The above baits—either simply, or mixed with clay, or bran, or both, according to the nature of the pond or current—will form a good ground-bait, which should be thrown in over night on the spot where it is intended to fish. A few gentles, or bits of chewed bread, occasionally added when fishing, are generally advantageous.

It is curious that this ground-baiting should have been practised more than sixteen hundred years ago; it is described by Oppian, who says that the paste was made with scented cheese and flour, which was divided into little pellets and scattered in by the fisherman to attract the fish.

A singular expedient for catching Carp is suggested by Mr. Fitzgibbon in his ' Notes to Walton.' "A correspondent," he says, "not long since wrote to me for advice. He had a pond in which were many large Carp; and although he had angled for them in due season from February to October during seven years, he had not succeeded in capturing them. I advised him to line with hurdles the bank of the pond at the spots where he meant to fish— to ground-bait those spots with red worms, gentles, and especially with sweet paste, for three or four days—to then take his rod, and, supporting it on a bifurcated prop (cut off the branch of a tree) inserted in the bank behind the hurdles, to place on his line a hook broken off at the bend, that is, without barb or sharp point—to bait this harmless hook with sweet paste, and to sink it nearly to the bottom of the already ground-baited water. The Carp will soon take this bait; and finding they can do so with impunity, they will become bolder hourly. Replacing the bait every time it is nibbled off, and continuing to do so for three or four days, commence then angling in earnest: with the same rod and line, but with a barbed hook baited exactly as before, come behind the hurdle, and, with very light float, angle cautiously. My correspondent acted on my advice, and succeeded in catching as many of the large Carp as he wanted."

This is doubtless a very ingenious plan; but, with all due deference to Mr. Fitzgibbon, I think that most fishermen might feel somewhat disinclined to sit for "three or four days" crouched behind a hurdle, without the possibility of catching anything—unless indeed it were a stroke of rheumatism.

I was once witness to a very curious occurrence, where a Carp—usually such a timid and dainty feeder—took in succession two hooks baited with worms, on two different lines, and was itself taken simultaneously by both, one hook being fastened on each side of its mouth: the youths to whom this singular accident happened were brothers. The distance between their two rods and baits at the time the fish took the latter could not have been less than several yards, and the floats disappeared almost at the same moment, both anglers striking together, and the Carp being lifted out between them.

The Carp is extraordinarily prolific—so much so that the roe of a single female, if allowed to arrive at maturity, would be an ample stock for many acres of water. In a fish of 9 lbs. weight Bloch found 600,000 eggs, and Schneider 700,000 in one of 10 lbs. weight. Even these numbers, however, astonishing as they are, sink into insignificance when compared with those of the ova of the Sturgeon. In the Volga, where this fish grows to from 13 to 16 feet long, 200 lbs. of roe have been taken from one specimen, which, at the rate given by Pallas, viz. five eggs to the grain, would make a total of 7,000,000. From one of these Volga Sturgeon, captured in the winter of 1769 and measuring 17 feet, 720 lbs. of roe were taken, containing on the same calculation 25,200,000 eggs. This account, however, applies only to Sturgeon of Northern waters, for M. Petit found less than 1,500,000 ova in a large specimen from the south of Europe. The same gentleman counted 60,000 eggs in a Smelt, 350,000 in a Tench, 50,000 in a Roach, 6000 in a Shrimp, from 12,000 to 21,000 in a Lobster, 4000 in a Crab, 36,000 in a Herring, 9,000,000 in a Cod, 1,500,000 in a Mackerel, 1,000,000 in a Sole, and the same number in a large Flounder. Even the liquor of the Oyster contains incredible multitudes of small embryos covered with little shells, perfectly transparent, and swimming nimbly about. A hundred and twenty of these, side by side in a row, would not, it is asserted, exceed one inch in length. Besides these young Oysters, the liquor contains a great variety of animalcula, five hundred times less in size, which emit a phosphorescent light. The census, however, does not end even here; for there are still to be added to the list of inhabitants three distinct species of worm, called the oyster-worm, which under a powerful microscope shine in the dark like glow-worms.

The Carp spawns towards the end of May or the beginning of June, according to the temperature of the water and the season; and it is supposed to continue spawning occasionally for four or five months, and always for a longer period than most other fish. The ova are deposited upon weeds, amongst which the female is followed by two or three males, thus securing the impregnation of a large proportion of the eggs. The fish is in season for the table from October to April.

M. Valenciennes characterizes the woodcut at the beginning of this chapter as the best engraving of the Carp that he had seen.

Characteristics of the common Carp.—Body covered with large scales, in about twelve rows between ventrals and back-fin; a single very long back-fin. Lips fleshy. Mouth small, and without teeth. Throat-teeth in three rows on each side, the inner row composed of three with broad flat crowns which are furrowed, somewhat resembling those of ruminating animals. Two barbels or beards at each corner of the mouth. First back-fin ray short and bony; the second also bony, notched on the posterior surface, as likewise the first ray of anal fin. Tail deeply forked. Colouring, generally, golden olive-brown, head darkest; belly yellowish white; fins dark brown. Scales covered with a thick mucus or epidermis. Vertebræ 36.

Fin-rays: D. 22: P. 17: V. 9: A. 8: C. 19.

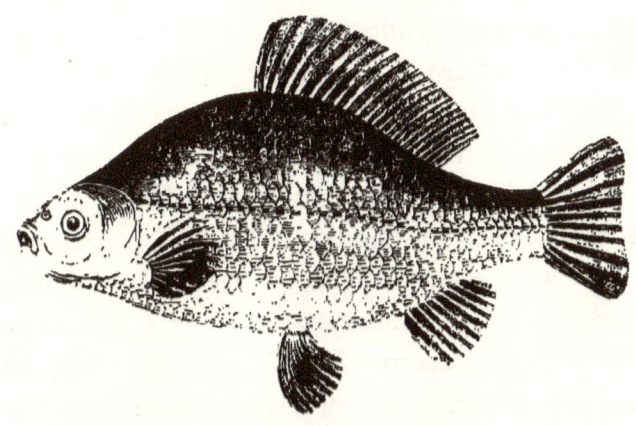

THE CRUCIAN or GERMAN CARP.

(*Cyprinus carassius* *.)

This fish is of an entirely different shape from the common Carp, rather resembling the Bream in depth of body and formation of head; and it also differs materially, though not to such a remarkable degree, from its allied species, the Prussian Carp, as will be seen on a comparison of the engravings. The head of the latter is much rounder and more Chub-like, and its depth of body is considerably

* Probably derived from the Swedish name *Karussa*.

less. Until lately, however, the Prussian and Crucian Carps were included under one and the same name; but Yarrell, having very carefully examined several specimens of both fish, was of opinion that they were distinct, and I have separated them accordingly. Indeed the Prussian Carp bears a very strong resemblance to the Golden Carp, or common Gold-fish, whilst the Crucian Carp, as already observed, has many points in common with the Bream.

The Crucian Carp is a comparatively rare fish, never, Mr. Yarrell states, having been taken, within his knowledge, except in the Thames, between Hammersmith and Windsor. I believe, however, that it exists in some ponds in Surrey, already mentioned, and that it is found in a small piece of water on Putney Heath, locally named 'Elger's Pond.' I cannot state this as a positive fact, having no specimens of the fish preserved, and never having actually compared them with the Prussian Carp; but I have frequently caught Carp in the pond in question which were certainly either Prussian or Crucian, and which, to the best of my memory, closely resembled the figure in the preceding page. These fish never much exceeded a pound in weight. Yarrell, however, refers to one which weighed 2 lbs. 11 oz.

The Crucian Carp is well known in France, where it is called *Carassin*. It is the *Ruda* or *Karussa* of Sweden, and the *Carouche* of Prussia. It is common in all parts of Scandinavia, affecting particularly muddy, grassy lakes; and it is also plentiful in the pools and marshes of Russia and Siberia, forming in those countries an important article of food. In the vicinity of Yakutsk it is taken with nets in the winter, at which time it is quite torpid. The fishermen select the largest, and return the others to the water, where they revive with spring. Even when the lakes are frozen to the bottom the fish survive, and, on the arrival of a thaw, issue from the mud in which they had buried themselves *. Ekström tells us that the Crucian Carp is a very indolent fish, never quitting its native spot unless compelled to do so. It keeps almost constantly near the bottom, approaching the surface only in warm, sunny weather. Its food is the same as that of the common Carp. It spawns about June—earlier or later according to the fineness of the season—and at this time the fish collect in dense shoals and move quickly about. The eggs, which are deposited amongst the weeds, are soon hatched, but the growth of the fry is slow.

The principal characteristics of the Crucian Carp are :—

Scales large. Comparative length of head to depth of body as 1 to 2, and to the whole length of fish, tail included, as 1 to 5. Depth of body compared with total length of fish as 2 to 5. Tail nearly square at the end. Lateral line straight, containing 34 punctured scales, with 7 scales above it to the base of the back-fin, and 6 below it to the base of the ventral fin. Mouth toothless; throat-teeth in a single row (containing 4 teeth) on each side; no barbels. Colour of upper part of body rich golden brown, becoming lighter and more yellow towards the belly; fins dark brown.

Fin-rays: D. 4 | 17: P. 14: V. 9: A. 3 | 6: C. 19.

---

* Pallas's Zoographia.

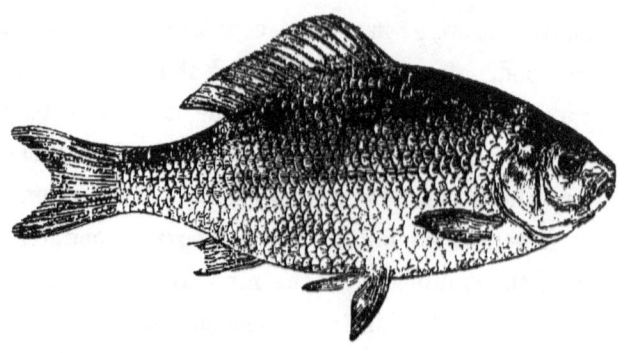

THE PRUSSIAN or GIBEL CARP.

CROUGER, *Warwickshire.*

(*Cyprinus gibelio *.*)

The Prussian Carp is found in several counties of England, and probably exists in many others where it has not hitherto been noticed. It is particularly common in the neighbourhood of the Thames. It spawns about the end of April or beginning of May, and is exceedingly prolific, the roe containing a great quantity of eggs. Though known to be very numerous in some situations, this fish seldom bites freely, and consequently but little success usually attends the angler. The flesh is white and agreeable. In habits and food the Prussian Carp closely resembles the preceding species; and it is so tenacious of life, that it has been known to survive after having been kept out of the water thirty hours.

Principal characteristics of the Prussian Carp.—Comparative length of head to depth of body more than 1 to 2; and to whole length of

---

* *gibelio,* Latinized form of the Prussian name Gibel.

fish, tail included, as 1 to 5; comparative depth of body to the same, 1 to 3. Head obtuse or Chub-like, eyes small, body rather short and thick. Scales large. Number of lines of scales the same as in the Crucian Carp. Mouth small, toothless; throat-teeth as in the last species. Tail forked at the end. Colour: upper part of back and head olive-brown, sides lighter; belly almost white; the whole shining with a brilliant golden metallic lustre. Back-fin and upper part of tail brown, tinged with orange; pectoral, ventral, and anal fins orange-red. Vertebræ 30.

Fin-rays: D. 4 | 16 : P. 14 : V. 9 : A. 3 | 6 : C. 19.

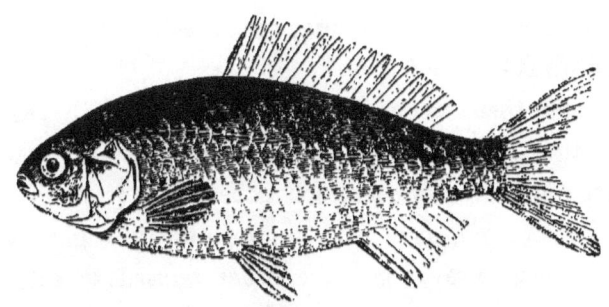

THE GOLD CARP.

COMMON GOLD- AND SILVER-FISH.

(*Cyprinus auratus* *.)

This fish, from its brilliant colouring and ready power of adapting itself to every variety of food and climate, is a favourite ornament of the drawing-room in England and in many other countries, and as such needs but little description.

* *Cyprinus*, a Carp, *auratus*, golden, Lat.

The earliest specimens ever seen in Europe were presented to Madame de Pompadour; but there is no doubt
that they were originally imported from the East, probably
from China, at some time during the sixteenth or seven-
teenth century.   China is still preeminent for its Gold-
fish, of which Pennant informs us that the most beautiful
kinds, both for elegance of shape and richness of tinting,
are taken in a small lake in the Province of Che-kyang.
They are the constant ornaments of all fashionable houses,
and the general pets more especially of the ladies, whose
pleasures in that country must, we can imagine, be somewhat limited.   It is their practice to call their Gold-fish
with a whistle to be fed.

Besides their attractive appearance, Gold-fish recommend themselves by another agreeable quality, that of
entertaining affection for each other.   It is mentioned
that a person who had kept two together in a glass gave
one of them away, when the other refused to eat, and
showed evident symptoms of unhappiness, until his companion was restored to him*.

The Gold-fish will breed very readily in this country in
small ponds or tanks, and especially if the temperature of
the water be high.   In many manufacturing districts where
the supply of cold water for the engines is inadequate, the
heated water is retained in small ponds, to be used over
again when cool.   In these tanks, the usual temperature
of which is about 80°, it is a common practice to keep

* Jesse's Gleanings.

Gold-fish, to consume the refuse grease that would other-wise impede the cooling of the water by collecting on the surface; and under these conditions they multiply with wonderful rapidity. Six fish were put into a dam of this description, and they increased so fast, that at the end of three years, when accidentally poisoned by an escape of ver-digris, their progeny were taken out by wheelbarrowsful.

The Gold-fish is susceptible of almost infinite variations, not only in colour but even in the number and shape of the fins, some having double anal fins, others triple tails; some a very long back-fin, others a very short one; and one specimen is mentioned which had none whatever. M. De Sauvigny * has given representations of eighty-nine varieties of this Carp, embracing almost every shade and combination of silver, orange, and purple. They are, how-ever, useful as well as ornamental in some countries, where they form a not uncommon article of diet. In size they seldom exceed 10 inches, five of which are attained, under favourable circumstances, during the first year. The young fry are dark-coloured, almost approaching to black.

* Histoire Naturelle des Dorades de la Chine.

Genus *BARBUS* *

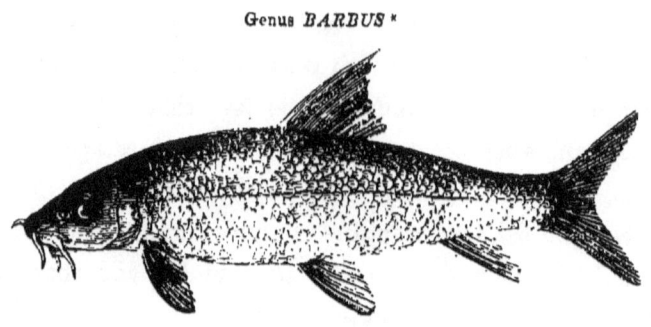

THE BARBEL.

(*Barbus vulgaris* †.)

The Barbel is distinguished from the last genus (*Cyprinus*) in having the back and anal fins short instead of elongated, with a strong bony ray in the dorsal fin,—the mouth also being furnished with four barbels or 'beards.'

Although, in an angling point of view, less wary and difficult of capture than the Carp, the Barbel, both in its natural state and in confinement, is the shyest and most untameable of all our fish, except perhaps the Loach, exhibiting a degree of reserve and intolerance of observation rarely met with. In the spring, however, when the fish seek the gravelly shallows to spawn, they become very lively, and at this season may frequently be seen tumbling and rolling about, with their bodies half out of the water, like a shoal of porpesses. Amongst some specimens kept in a vivarium, it was observed that, when they fancied no one was looking, they would plunge and rub themselves

* 'Bearded,' from *barba*, a beard, Lat.   † *vulgaris*, common, Lat.

against the brickwork, and otherwise show considerable signs of playfulness.

The name 'Barbel,' as already noticed, is derived from the barbs or beards at the corners of the mouth, which are given to the fish to assist it in feeling its way about in deep and, consequently, more or less dark waters, and probably also for the purpose of enabling it to detect the nature of the substances with which it comes in contact. Of the species provided with these barbs, viz. the Carp, Tench, Gudgeon, Loach, and Burbot, all find their food principally, or wholly, on the bottom; and generally the fact of a fish being 'bearded' affords a correct index to its habits.

The food of the Barbel consists principally of slugs, worms, grubs, and occasionally of small fish; and in order to procure these it turns up the gravel and loose stones with its nose, in very much the same manner that a pig furrows a field with its snout. The baits for the fish are lob-worms, greaves, gentles, cheese, caddis-worms, and many others; but of these the first three (here placed in their order of merit) are, in my opinion, much the best. Three styles of fishing also, one of which is peculiar to the Barbel, are commonly employed for its capture. These are—ordinary float-fishing, Nottingham-fishing (a clever variation of float-fishing), and leger-fishing, which is the specialty of the art, and was, until late years, almost wholly confined to the Thames and its *habitués*. A good chapter on the subject will be found in Baily's Angler's Instructor, p. 43.

It is essential in all cases to ground-bait some hours previously the spot at which it is intended to fish for Barbel. For this purpose bran, clay, and boiled greaves, worked up together into balls of about the size of a small cocoa-nut, form a good mixture; gentles or chopped worms may be added with advantage, but clay and any of the before-mentioned materials will answer the purpose. Another excellent ground-bait to which the Thames fishermen are very partial is made by putting handfuls of whole lob-worms into hollow clay balls, some of the heads and tails of the worms being left sticking through the sides. In all ground-baiting, however, the great principle to be observed is, that the ground-bait should be similar in kind, but inferior in quality, to the bait used on the hook,—so that the suspicions of the fish may be lulled by the former, and their appetite excited by the latter. Lob-worms may usually be obtained in great abundance upon damp lawns and gravel-walks by searching for them late in the evening with a lantern. They should be kept in fresh damp moss, changed every three or four days to prevent its getting sour. In choosing baits for the hook, worms without knots in them should be selected. The last two observations hold good with regard to every description of worms and worm-fishing.

The Barbel spawns in May or June, depositing its ova, which in a large fish sometimes number 7000 or 8000, in the gravelly or shingly beds of the stream, where they are immediately covered by the parent fishes. These eggs are vivified, in warm weather, between the ninth and fifteenth day.

The spawners, so soon as they have recovered a little strength, make their way into the swiftest stream they can find, such as weirs, mill-tails, &c., to scour and brace themselves, beginning to get into condition again in a few weeks, and being in the best season for the angler until September and October, when the frosty nights drive them from the streams and shallows into the deeper waters. Here they will be found until the spring; and in these quiet deeps and eddies they are to be caught, if anywhere, during the winter months. At this period, however, especially if the weather is very cold, it is of comparatively little use to fish for them, as they lie in a sort of semitorpid condition, and refuse to move. So inanimate are they, that the fishermen not unfrequently provide themselves with hoop landing-nets, which they place near the Barbel, and with a pole literally push them in. Shoals sometimes collect under the shelter of a sunken punt or other tidal obstruction, lying one over the other as closely as they can pack, and when thus congregated are often taken by being "hooked foul." I have also been assured that boys and others who are good swimmers will dive into the water and take them with the hand from under the banks and holes.

Barbel are numerous in many parts of the world; but their natural habitat appears to be the warmer parts of Europe, and it is stated by Cuvier that in localities favourable to them they will grow to 10 feet long. They are plentiful in the Danube, the Rhine, the Elbe, and the Weser, in almost all the rivers flowing into the Black Sea, and in the Volga, where they attain the weight of 40 and 50 lbs. On the banks of this river the natives make a kind of fish-glue or isinglass of the bladder, boiling the roe and feeding their geese and poultry with it. The fish themselves are sold at Astrakan at about £9 the thousand.

The Barbel is a native of many parts of England, and is exclusively a river-fish. It abounds particularly in the Trent and the Thames, in the latter being so numerous, that in the neighbourhood of Walton and Weybridge as much as 280 lbs. weight are said to have been taken by a single rod in one day. At Temple Weir, near Marlow, I have also known some extraordinary baskets to be made; and at Newlock a gentleman, who is well known as an accomplished angler, once hooked, and was broken by, a fish which he played for *upwards of an hour* without ever succeeding in getting a sight of it. The probable size of this Barbel may therefore be imagined. In this country the usual weight of the fish does not exceed 10 lbs.; but they are occasionally taken as large as 15 lbs., and one is mentioned as having been caught in the River Lea which weighed 19 lbs.

A table of the relative lengths and weights of the fish is annexed.

Length. inches.	Weight. lbs.	oz.	Length. inches.	Weight. lbs.	oz.
12	0	9½	25	5	8
13	0	12¼	26	6	3
14	1	0	27	6	14½
15	1	3	28	7	11¾
16	1	7¼	29	8	9½
17	1	11¾	30	9	8
18	2	0¾	31	10	7½
19	2	6½	32	11	8½
20	2	12¾	33	12	10½
21	3	4	34	13	13½
22	3	12	35	15	1½
23	4	4½	36	16	1½ *
24	4	13¾			

As will be gathered from the anecdote above related, the Barbel is exceedingly strong and makes a powerful fight, showing as much sport as almost any fish of the same size, except perhaps the Salmon-Trout. It is, however, in small esteem for the table, at which it very seldom makes its appearance. A strong jelly may be extracted from the flesh by boiling it down; but whether this is wholesome as an edible I am unable to say.

It has been remarked that many species of the Carp family have the power of emitting a guttural sound under water, although the mechanism by which this is effected is not understood—no air-bubble escaping from the mouth of the fish at the time. Amongst the species producing these sounds the Barbel is particularly noted†.

* See p. 59.

† Valenciennes, Histoire des Poissons, xvi. 14.

Besides those already mentioned, *the principal characteristics of the Barbel are*—Mouth toothless; throat-teeth in three rows on each side, the rows numbering 2, 3, and 5 respectively. Body elongated. Length of head compared with total length of fish as 1 to 5; depth of body less than length of head. Head elongated, wedge-shaped; upper half of jaw much the longer. Upper lip circular and fleshy. One pair of barbels at the front of the nose, and a single one at the end of upper lip on each side. Third ray of back-fin largest and strongest, toothed on its hinder surface. Tail deeply forked at the end. Colour: general hue of upper part of head and body greenish brown, becoming yellowish green on sides; cheeks, gill-covers, and scales tinged with bronze; belly white; back- and tail-fins brown, tinged with red; pectoral, ventral, and anal fins pale red.

Fin-rays: D. 4 | 8: P. 16: V. 9: A. 3 | 5: C. 19$\frac{4}{4}$.

Genus *GOBIO* *.

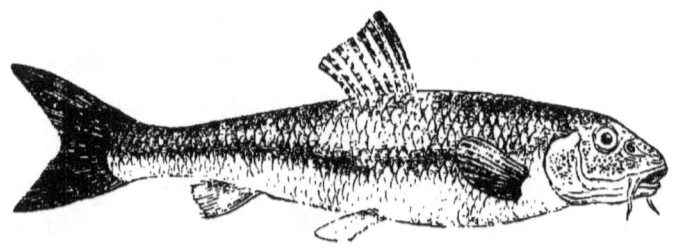

THE GUDGEON.

(*Gobio fluviatilis* *.)

The species of this genus, or more strictly subgenus, have, like those of the last, the back- and anal fins short at

* *Gobio*, the Gudgeon; *fluviatilis*, of the river, Lat.

the base ; their mouths are likewise furnished with beards ; but they have no strong bony ray at the commencement of either dorsal or anal fins.

The Gudgeon, which in this country is represented by a single species, is principally interesting to anglers as a bait for other fish, although, from its instinctive readiness to bite, and general simplicity of behaviour, it has many admirers amongst the fairer sex, who frequently become very skilful in its capture. I once had the pleasure of forfeiting a pair of gloves to a young lady who laid a wager that she would catch ten out of a dozen bites, " nibbles included "—and actually did it.

Notwithstanding, however, this somewhat feminine reputation, there is no doubt that for male minds also Gudgeon-fishing occasionally possesses a peculiar fascination ; and it is mentioned as a fact that the clergyman of a parish near Hampton Court, who was engaged to be married to a bishop's daughter, lingered so long over this sport as to arrive too late for the ceremony ; whereupon the lady, piqued at his neglect, refused to be united to one who preferred his basket to his bride *.

Like the Barbel, the Gudgeon feeds at the bottom, its food consisting of worms, insects, larvæ, spawn of other fish, and such matters ; and, when angling, it is usual to rake the bed of the river in order that the fish may be attracted to the spot by the animalcula, blood-worms, &c. which are disturbed in the operation. These blood-worms, often

* Jesse's Angler's Rambles, p. 4.

found by thousands on the surface of mud, seem to be formed of ten or twelve small connected globes, diminishing in size towards the tail. The mouth is the largest part, and appears to be perpetually wide open, with three little prongs or forks protruding. In colour the whole creature is of a bright crimson; and its structure, which is always sufficiently curious, becomes positively beautiful when placed under a magnifying-glass. Near Whitehall-stairs the surface of the mud has a deep-reddish tint, owing to the innumerable quantity of blood-worms; and it is the vulgar superstition that this appearance was never seen before the decapitation of Charles the First.

Once, when fishing, a singular accident occurred to me in connexion with the Gudgeon. I was spinning for Pike, with one of the former fish for bait, in a deep part of the Thames below Harleyford, when I felt a slight check and increase of weight on the line; supposing it to be a weed, I drew in the tackle, when to my surprise a live Gudgeon was found attached to the dead one, and fast hooked through the lip. Either, therefore, the second fish had attacked the first, from the propensity common to many animals of destroying wounded members of their own species, or because he mistook the hook in the latter's lip for a choice morsel which he wanted to take away from him. This explanation appears to be the most probable, as the mouths of the two fish were actually touching each other, being fixed by one and the same hook.

Gudgeon are never found except in waters having some

degree of movement. They swim in large shoals, appearing to delight in such streams as have a moderate current with sandy or gravelly bars across.

Most English rivers and canals produce these fish, occasionally in such numbers, that I have known as many as twelve dozen to be taken at a single throw of the casting-net; and Thompson mentions they were so numerous in the Newforge mill-stream, on the Lagan, Ireland, that the miller's dog at that place was in the habit of catching them with his mouth, and devouring them in quantities.

Gudgeon rarely exceed 8 inches in length, and are seldom so long: they spawn in May, amongst stones in shallow waters.

Characteristics of the Gudgeon.—Body elongated, in shape very nearly resembling that of the Barbel. Length of head to total length of body as 1 to 5; depth of body less than length of head. Upper jaw the longest. Mouth toothless; throat-teeth in two rows on each side, numbering 3 and 5 respectively, but sometimes fewer on one side; teeth tapering, and curved at tips. Scales of moderate size. One barbel at each side of mouth. Tail-fin deeply forked at the end. Double air-bladder. Colour: upper part of head, back, and sides olive-brown, spotted with black; belly and lower portion of body white; pectoral, ventral, and anal fins nearly white, tinged with brown. Back- and tail-fin mottled brown.

Fin-rays: D. 9: P. 15: V. 8: A. 7: C. $19\frac{5 \text{ or } 6}{5 \text{ or } 6}$.

Genus *TINCA* *.

THE TENCH.

(*Tinca vulgaris* *.)

In addition to the characteristics of the preceding genus (the Gudgeons) it may be mentioned of the Tenches that they have very small scales, and beards of a corresponding size, with a thick coating of slime or mucus over the body.

The common Tench is the most tenacious of life of any fresh-water fish except the Eel. I have known one of them live for a whole day with the gimp of a double jack-hook passed under the skin from gill to tail, the fish being meanwhile cast about from place to place on the water, and suspended in a most unnatural position. In fact, such is the perfection of the organs of the species, that they have been proved by experiment to be able to breathe when the quantity of oxygen is reduced to the 5000th part of the bulk of

---

* *Tinca*, the Tench; *vulgaris*, common, Lat.

the water—river-water ordinarily containing about one part
of oxygen in a hundred.

In this country the Tench is, like the Grayling, a somewhat local fish, preferring ponds to rivers, and of the latter
those which are slow and deep and which cut their channel
through strata of marl or loam ; in these situations, however, it never breeds so fast as in ponds, nor does it usually
attain the same size. Pits from which brick-clay has been
dug often abound with Tench ; and a bucketful have been
known to be taken out of a hole of this sort not wider than
a boy could jump over, and where the weeds were so thick
as to be almost solid. In fact, like the Carp, with which
they have many habits in common, they appear to prefer foul
and weedy to clear waters ; and such as produce the one
species will very constantly be found to produce the other.
In weight the Tench seldom exceeds 5 or 6 lbs., although
heavier specimens are occasionally caught ; the largest on
record weighed somewhat over 11 lbs. and was taken from
just such a pit as that above described, where it had probably battened for half a century. The account of its capture is given by Daniel * :—

" A piece of water which had been ordered to be filled
up, and into which wood and rubbish had been thrown for
years, was directed to be cleared out. Labourers were
accordingly employed ; and, almost choked up by weeds
and mud, so little water remained that no person expected
to see any fish, except a few Eels ; yet nearly two hundred

* Daniel's Rural Sports.

brace of Tench of all sizes, and as many Perch, were found. After the pond was thought to be quite free, under some roots there seemed to be an animal which was conjectured to be an otter: the place was surrounded; and on opening an entrance among the roots a Tench was found of most singular form, having literally assumed the shape of the hole in which he had of course for many years been confined. His length from eye to caudal fork was 33 inches; his circumference, almost to the tail, was 27 inches; his weight 11 lbs. $9\frac{1}{4}$ oz.: the colour was also singular, his belly being that of a Charr, or vermilion. This extraordinary fish, after having been inspected by many gentlemen, was carefully put into a pond, and at the time this account was written, twelve months afterwards, was alive and well."

As to the gastronomic qualities of the Tench, opinions differ. The fish, however, is white and firm, and is considered nutritious,—though, like the Eel, it would appear to be palatable in a precisely inverse ratio to the cleanliness of its abode, improving in gustatory attractions as it approaches more nearly in colour and diet the composition of its habitual mud. Thus, "Tench were taken out of Munden Hall Fleet, Essex, which was so thick with weeds that the flue-nets could hardly be sunk through them, and where the mud was intolerably fetid and had dyed the fish of its own hue, which was that of ink; yet no Tench could be better grown, or of a sweeter flavour." . . . "In a clear pond at Leigh's Priory a quantity of Tench were caught, of about 3 lbs. weight each, of a colour the most golden and beautiful; but when dressed and brought to table they smelt and tasted so rankly that no one would eat them." By washing the slime off the fish with warm water before cooking, the muddy taste is said to be removed.

Tench were certainly amongst the list of monkish delicacies, as may be gathered from the fact that, of our ponds which were formerly stews attached to abbeys and other monastic establishments, a large proportion remain stocked with them. In some extensive tracts of water near Yarmouth these fish are still bred in large quantities as a marketable commodity; they are fattened on a mixture of greaves and meal until fit for the table, and, thus prepared, they, as Walton says, " eat pleasantly," and form a by-no-means contemptible addition to the *cuisine*.

The ordinary food of the Tench consists of various soft-bodied aquatic animals and vegetable matters; and the best bait for them is a well-scoured brandling—the method of angling being similar to that already recommended for the Carp (p. 106). They will bite all through the spring and summer, particularly at the former period, and after or during a mild shower of rain; but in winter they probably lie torpid and bury themselves in mud and weeds.

For the Tench has been always claimed the royal gift of healing by touch; and he has been supposed to possess, in the slime with which he is thickly covered, a natural balsam for the cure of himself and others. Rondeletius says that at Rome he saw a great recovery effected by applying a Tench to the feet of a sick man. But, without trenching

on the domain of the miraculous, there are certainly
many accounts on record of the restoration of sick and
wounded *fish* by contact with the Tench; and it would
be presumptuous indeed in any one to assert that such
a provision for the necessities of this numerous class is
impossible in the beneficent scheme of creation. The following, mentioned by Mr. Wright, is one out of a hundred
of such alleged instances that might be quoted :—

"A gentleman, who was unfortunately unable to leave
the house for some time through an accident, amused
himself by making small artificial flies, which he did very
neatly. He kept some Minnows, and a Tench about 2¼
inches long, in a very large wide-mouthed bottle; all the
Minnows had died except one; my friend was just finish-
ing a fly as I went into his room, and he held it upon the
surface of the water in the bottle as he was often in the
habit of doing; the Minnow darted at it so rapidly, that
he could not withdraw the fly in time to prevent the hook
from pricking the Minnow; the little fish descended three
parts of the way down the bottle, poised himself for a
moment, with his nose pointing downwards, then swiftly
went the remainder of the way, rubbed his nose during a
few seconds against the side of the Tench, and again swam
about as lively as before. We both joined in the opinion
that it is really no fable as to Tench being the Esculapius
of fish; for here was an example before our eyes of a fish
being wounded, and immediately instinct directed him to
seek a remedy."

Camden, in his ' Britannia,' also alludes to this circumstance. "I have seen," he says, "the bellies of Pikes
which have been rent open, have their gaping wounds
presently closed by the touch of the Tench, and by his
glutinous slime perfectly healed up."

Equally numerous, if not perhaps more credible, are the
testimonies to the fact that the Pike, destructive and insatiable towards all else, has yet that "grace of courtesy"
left in him that he spares to molest his physician, even
when most pressed by hunger: amongst other angling authorities, Oppian, Walton, Camden, Hollinshed, Bowlker,
Salter, Williamson, Hofland, and Fitzgibbon, all acknow-
ledge to more or less faith in the truth of the assertion.
Salter says, "I have known several trimmers to be laid at
night, baited with live fish, roach, dace, bleak, and tench,
each about 6 or 7 inches long; and when those trimmers
were examined in the morning, both eels and jack have
been taken by hooks baited with any other fish than Tench,
which I found as lively as when put into the water the preceding night, without ever having been disturbed. This has
invariably been the case during my experience; neither have
I met with one solitary instance to the contrary related
by any of my acquaintance, who have had numerous opportunities of noticing the singular circumstance of the
perfect freedom from death or wounds which the Tench
enjoys over every other inhabitant of the liquid element,
arising from continual conflicts with each other."

To try the experiment, I recently procured some small

Tench, and fished with them as live-baits for a whole day
in some excellent Pike water, but without getting a touch.
In the evening I put on a small Carp, and had a run
almost immediately. I also tried some Pike in a stock-
pond with the same Tench, but they would not take them;
and though left in the pond all night—one on a hook, and
one attached to a fine thread—both baits were alive in the
morning, some Pike teeth-marks, however, being visible
upon the hooked fish.

These are facts, which I mention without expressing any
opinion as to the truth or otherwise of the theories before
alluded to.

The idea of the Pike abstaining from injuring his physician, the Tench, has been thus admirably versified :—

> "The Pike, fell tyrant of the liquid plain,
>   With ravenous waste devours his fellow train :
>   Yet, howsoe'er by raging famine pined,
>   The Tench he spares—a medicinal kind ;
>   For when, by wounds distrest or sore disease,
>   He courts the salutary fish for ease,
>   Close to his scales the kind physician glides,
>   And sweats a healing balsam from his sides."

A less poetical explanation of this abstinence is given
by Bingley, who suggests that, as the Tench is so fond of
mud as to be constantly at the bottom of the water, where
the Pike cannot find him, the self-denial of the latter may
be attributed to more natural causes.

The Tench is common in Holland and in most of the
European lakes, and is said to have been introduced into

England about the year 1514. A few exist in Scotland and Ireland. It is the *Ysgreten* of Wales, the *Sutare* of Sweden, and the *Schleihe* of Germany. The fish spawns, with some variations, about the middle of June, or, according to Willughby, when wheat is in blossom; and M. Petit found nearly 350,000 eggs in one specimen.

Characteristics of the common Tench. — Length of head compared to total length of body, excluding tail, as 2 to 7. Head rather large and blunt. Mouth small, toothless, with a small barbel at each corner. Throat-teeth in a single row on each side, 4 on the right side and 5 on the left. Scales very small. Back- and anal fins destitute of bony rays. Ventral fins in the male very large, and concave on the inside, reaching far enough to cover the vent; in the females smaller and less powerful: the males and females may be distinguished by the size of these fins. Pectoral fins large and rounded. Tail, in young fish, concave, afterwards straight, and in old fish convex. General colour greenish olive and golden; fins darker; lips flesh-colour.

Fin-rays: D. 11: P. 17: V. 10: A. 10: C. 19.

Genus *ABRAMIS* *

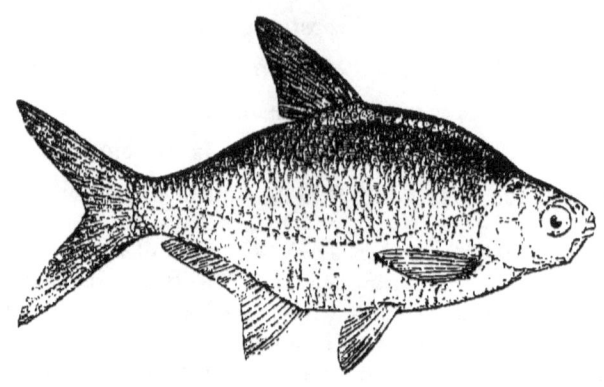

THE BREAM, or CARP-BREAM.

(*Abramis brama* *.)

We now come to the Breams, which are distinguished from the thick-skinned Carps by their bright nacry scales. Unlike the latter fish and the Barbel, they have no strong bony rays in the fins, nor any beards at the corners of the mouth. The body in all the species is deep and thin, or compressed, the outlines above and below being very convex: the base of the back-fin is short, and placed further back than the ventral fin, whilst the base of the anal fin is very long.

If we may credit the French proverb quoted by Izaak Walton, that " He that hath Breams in his pond is able to bid his friend welcome," these fish would seem to be in considerable request on the Continent as an edible. In England they are seldom considered worth cooking. Few

* *Abramis,* a Bream, Gr.; *brama,* the Bream, Lat.

fish, however, afford the angler better sport, as they are exceedingly strong and vigorous, sometimes weighing as much as 7 and 8 lbs.*, and by no means shy biters. They are also useful as stock for ponds, or to feed Pike, being hardy and of quick growth. The ova in one female have been counted, and found to be 130,000.

A comparison of the skull of the Carp-Bream, as shown in the woodcut, with that of the common Carp at p. 105,

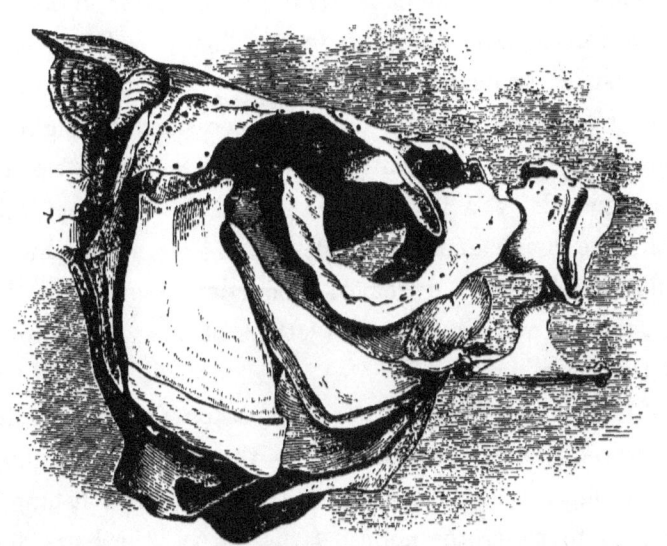

Skull of Carp-Bream.

will exhibit in a marked manner the differences in struc-ture between the two craniums, and the relative superiority of the latter.

---

* Baily, in his Angler's Instructor, records the capture of a Bream in the Trent which weighed 17 lbs.

In its distribution the Carp-Bream is an inhabitant of all the central districts of Europe, as well as those northward to St. Petersburg, Finland, and Scandinavia. Some of the lakes of Ireland also produce it in large quantities. In England it is found in many counties, appearing to thrive best in large open sheets of water, and in slow rivers where the stream occasionally widens out into broads or deeps. Of the rivers near the metropolis which breed this fish, perhaps the Mole and the Medway are the most noted. They are also very numerous in the Thames at Weybridge just below its junction with the Wey, and in the latter river higher up towards Wisley are occasionally caught of very large size. I recently examined a specimen weighing upwards of 5 lbs. taken thence; the scales of this fish were rough and almost file-like, from a small whitish tubercle which is a periodical production common to the species, as well as to several others of the Carp family, at the spawning-time.

Large "takes" of Bream are occasionally made in the Weybridge Deep above referred to, the method of angling found most successful being the "Nottingham fishing" alluded to under the notice of the Barbel, the baits and ground-baits for which are also those most killing in Bream-fishing. The fish are gregarious, and their food consists of worms, slugs, aquatic insects, and vegetable substances: they spawn in May.

Characteristics of the common Bream.—Throat-teeth cylindrical, with smooth crowns adapted for bruising, placed in single rows, five teeth on each side. Mouth small, toothless, without barbels. Scales placed in curves on the fore part of the back, a naked place behind the ventrals. Length of head to body as 1 to 3. Head small, nape of neck depressed. Body deep and flat, very convex above and below, scales comparatively small. Scales of lateral line varying in number from 52 to 58. Tail long, and deeply forked at the end. Colour: generally yellowish white, becoming yellowish brown by age. Cheeks and gill-covers silvery white; fins light-coloured: pectoral and ventral tinged with red—back, anal, and tail-fins with brown.

Fin-rays: D. 11: P. 17: V. 9: A. 29: C. 19.

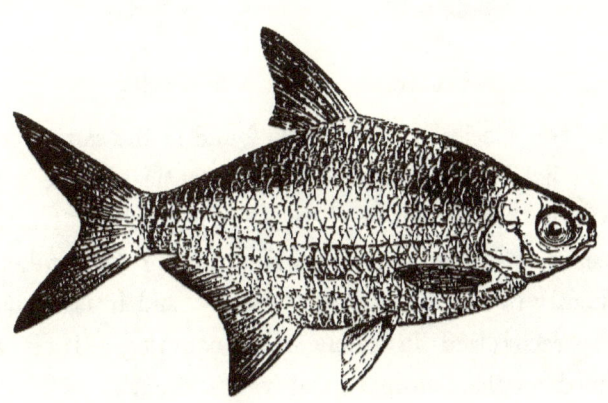

THE WHITE BREAM, or BREAM-FLAT.

(*Abramis blicca.*)

The principal points in which this fish differs from the common or Carp-Bream are—(1) its colour, which is silvery instead of yellow; (2) its size, which rarely exceeds 1 lb., whilst that of the Carp-Bream frequently reaches 7 and 8 lbs.; and (3) its teeth (throat-teeth), which are in

two rows on each side, numbering 2 and 5 respectively,—
those of the Carp-Bream being placed in only one row on
each side, numbering 5. This last point of difference is
so obvious and easily verified that no mistake can possibly
occur. Other minor distinctions will be observed on a
close comparison of the fish. The annexed figures show
the relative size and shape of the scales.

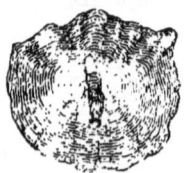

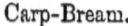

Carp-Bream.   Bream-flat.

The two species are frequently found in the same waters,
and in habits and food are nearly identical. The White
Bream is known to exist in Cambridgeshire, Notting-
hamshire, Norfolk, and Dumfriesshire. I have taken it
frequently in the River Wey in Surrey, and it is probably
locally recognized in many other counties. It is also
common on the Continent and in Scandinavia. It is best
fished for with roach-tackle and a red worm or gentle,
and has this singular habit—by which it may be constantly
recognized, even before it has been seen—of rising instead
of descending with the bait; in consequence of which the
float, in lieu of being drawn under water, is laid flat upon
the surface. The fish takes a bait readily, but often spits
it out again, from being too indolent to swallow it. The
Swedish fishermen call it *Aetare*, or the Glutton.

In the Bavarian dialect the term *blicke* is applied to fishes that have a silvery glitter in the water *, whence the specific name *blicca*, given to it on account of the brightness of its colour as compared with the Carp-Bream.

The principal characteristics of the White Bream are—

Throat-teeth hooked, in two rows as above stated. Length of head compared with that of body alone as 1 to 3. Head larger, and fleshy portion of tail comparatively deeper, than in the Carp-Bream. Scales larger than those of the latter. Lateral line not quite so low down, and with fewer scales, numbering 46 or 50. Relative position of fins very similar; fin-rays different in number. Colour, generally, of the sides bluish white, without any of the golden-yellow lustre observable in the Carp-Bream. Ventral and pectoral fins tinged with red.

Fin-rays: D. 10: P. 14: V. 9: A. 23: C. 19.

THE POMERANIAN BREAM.

(*Abramis Buggenhagii* †.)

Besides the differences which will be immediately observed on a general comparison of this fish with the two

* Heckel and Kner.
† Latinized name of discoverer, Buggenhagen.

preceding species, it may be readily distinguished both
from the White and Carp-Bream by the number of throat-
teeth on each side, which are in two rows numbering 5
and 3 respectively, instead of, as in the former, in two rows
of 5 and 2, and, as in the latter, in a single row of 5. It
is also distinguished by the greater thickness of its body,
which is equal to half its depth, whilst in the other two
the same measurement is only equal to one-third of the
depth. The anal fin is shorter and has a smaller number
of rays than that of the Bream-flat, which, again, presents
a similar proportion as contrasted with the Carp-Bream.
It is a very rare fish, being only known to inhabit a few
waters, amongst which may be mentioned the River Lagan
near Belfast, a pond at Bottisham in Cambridgeshire,
some water near Wolverhampton, and the preserves at
Dagenham Reach, Essex, well known to London anglers.

It was first discovered in Swedish Pomerania by M. Buggenhagen, and has derived its appellations from both these
sources. The Pomeranian fishermen are greatly pleased
when they take this fish in their nets, as they believe
that the other Breams will follow it, even to their own
destruction; the name they have given to it consequently
signifies a guide or conductor. It only attains the length
of 15 or 16 inches. Besides those already mentioned, its
characteristics are—

Length of head compared to total length of body as 1 to 5; depth at
the deepest part as 1 to 3. Head small and pointed. Mouth small,
toothless. Throat-teeth in 2 rows (numbering 5 and 3 respectively)

on each side. Number of scales in lateral line 52. Vertebræ 41. Colour: over upper part of head and back dark blackish blue, becoming lighter on the upper part of sides; lower part of sides and belly silvery white; fins bluish brown, more or less tinged with brown.

Fin-rays: D. 12: P. 17: V. 19: A. 19: C. 19.

Genus *LEUCISCUS* *.

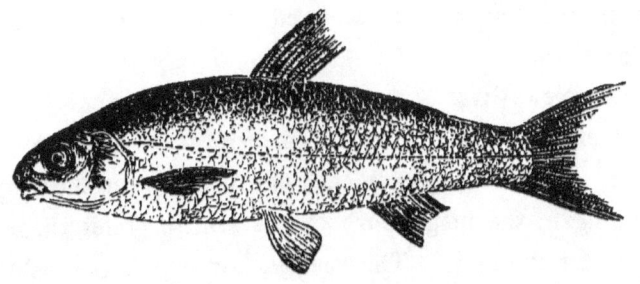

THE DACE, DARE, or DART.

(*Leuciscus vulgaris* †.)

Generic characteristics: the anal fin short at the base, as well as the back-fin, and without strong bony rays at the commencement of either: no beards. The genus may be divided into two sections: the first having the dorsal fin almost exactly over the ventrals, and the second having the dorsal placed considerably further back.

The common Dace, *Leuciscus vulgaris*, is a bright, graceful fish, and makes a gallant fight when hooked, rising

* *Leuciscus*, Gr. for Dace; the diminutive of *leukos*, white.
† *vulgaris*, common, Lat.

freely at the fly, and in many rivers giving the angler
capital sport. The species is very numerous in the Thames,
and particularly in the neighbourhood of Richmond, where
they grow to a large size—6 inches from eye to commencement of tail-fin being the minimum under which, by Act
of Parliament *, it is illegal to take them. The same
statute limits the capture of Roach in the Thames to such
as measure 8 inches; but it is to be feared that where one
fish is basketed above these standards, a hundred are taken
below them.

The New River, near Hornsey, has the reputation of
producing very fine Dace, specimens of three-quarters of a
pound each being by no means uncommon; and the people
residing in the neighbourhood are said to prefer them to
Trout for the table. The species, however, is not held in
much estimation by fish-epicures generally.

   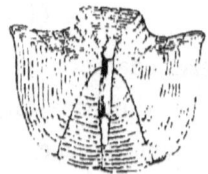

Scale of Dace.   Scale of Graining.

In this country the Dace usually inhabits clear, quiet
streams, where it swims about in shoals or sculls, spawning
in June, and feeding upon grubs, water-insects, and other

* 3rd Geo. II. cap. xxi.

soft substances. A small red worm is perhaps, next to the artificial fly, the best bait for it, though it occasionally takes both paste and gentles. The fish itself forms an excellent live-bait for Pike, particularly in thick water, as its scaling is brilliant so as to be easily seen, and its whole appearance glittering and attractive.

The Dace is exclusively a river-fish.

Principal Characteristics of the Dace.—Length of head compared with length of head and body (without tail-fin) as 2 to 9; depth of body compared with whole length as 1 to 5. Muzzle pointed. Mouth rather large. Eye and scales smaller than in a Roach of similar size. Body elongated; back very little convex. Number of scales in lateral line 52. Dorsal fin commencing rather further back than in the Roach, the first ray being behind the middle of the body. Throat-teeth in two rows (numbering 2 and 5) on each side, conical, curved inwards at the points. Colour: upper part of head and back dusky blue, growing paler on the sides, and white on the belly; cheeks and gill-covers silvery white; back- and tail-fins pale brown; the other fins almost white, with a tinge of pale red.

Fin-rays: D. 9: P. 16: V. 9: A. 10: C. 19.

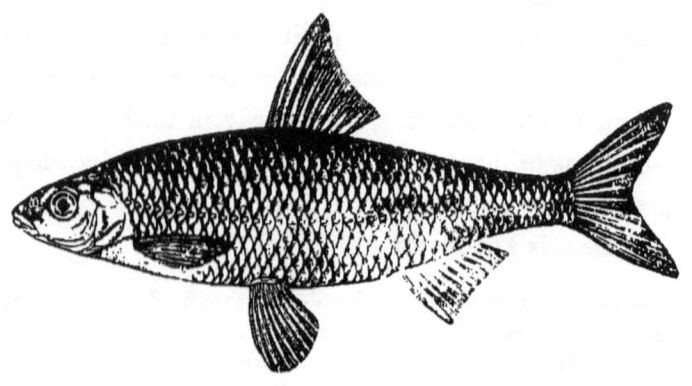

THE ROACH.

(*Leuciscus rutilus *.*)

The Roach—or, as it is technically named, the " Red
Dace," from the scarlet colour of the fins—is a great
favourite with London anglers, who, at any time between
August and May, may be seen perched, regardless of
safety, upon projecting trees, bridge-buttresses, and, indeed, every other accessible ' coigne of vantage ' between
Battersea Fields and Walton on Thames, or clustering
on the hundred-and-one lock-gates with which the pretty
River Lea is intersected almost to its source.   From these
perilous eminences they contemplate—and we may presume are also contemplated by—the intelligent *Leuciscini*, which, notwithstanding, seldom fail to find their way,
in greater or less numbers, into the cockney's basket.   The
Londoners, in fact, bear away the palm from all com-

Leuciscus, a Dace, Gr. ; *rutilus*, red, Lat.

petitors in Roach-fishing—a department of angling, be it said, demanding by no means a small amount of quickness of hand and eye. Mr. Jesse, who has amusingly classified the several orders and *genera* of Thames anglers, gives the Roach and Dace fishers a very high rank for skill and patience, and believes that they very seldom attempt, or understand, any other branch of the gentle craft.

The largest shoals of Roach appear in the Thames about the middle of May or early in June, when they ascend from the lower parts of the river to deposit their spawn in the higher reaches, fighting their way up the strong rapids with persistent energy, until they find a suitable spot. This migration, it has been thought by some authors *, takes place from the sea; but the opinion seems to be erroneous, as all experiments have tended to prove that the Roach will not live in salt water †. A similar annual exodus of this fish has been noticed in Loch Lomond and elsewhere. The Roach deposit their spawn on the surface of weeds in shallow water, and whilst in the act of spawning may sometimes be observed by hundreds together, with their back-fins out of water: a very few days suffice to complete the reproductive process, and the fish then seek swift gravelly shallows on which to scour themselves. These they soon quit, however, for quieter currents, where they remain several months, retiring about October into the deeps and still waters for the winter, and always selecting a gravelly or sandy bottom in preference to a muddy one.

* Donovan's History of British Fishes.   † Montagu, MS.

In the nature of its food, the Roach resembles the Dace, feeding, however, principally at night, and by day swimming about in large shoals near the bottom. The best general bait is the gentle*; but pastes of various kinds, worms, and prepared greaves† are sometimes equally killing,—though the first is better adapted for stagnant than running waters, where it is liable to be frequently washed off the hook. Boiled wheat, brewers' grains, and most of the ground-baits recommended for Carp and Bream will be found successful in Roach-fishing. The tackle ought to be of the finest; and the bait should swim at the bottom in rivers, and at from six inches to two feet from the ground, according to the depth, in ponds.

Roach will not unfrequently take the artificial fly, especially when first scouring themselves after spawning; and during the last few years I have caught some very fine specimens when dapping for Chub with the imitation grasshopper. A ludicrous incident in connexion with the fly-catching propensities of the Roach is mentioned in a recent work on Angling:—A gentleman passing by the Round pond on Clapham Common, observed these fish rising freely at the swarms of hovering *ephemeræ*; and wishing to try whether they would not be equally susceptible to the artificial insect, sent back for a fly-rod, &c., and a small fly. The Roach, however, in this instance refused to be enticed; but a fine Newfoundland dog which was

---

* To keep gentles in the winter months, let them be put in a bottle full of earth, corked up, and placed in a cool situation.　† See p. 154.

swimming about, snapping impotently at the gnats and midges, perceived the apparently drowning insect, and dashed at it,—" taking the death" with a plunge like a heavy Salmon, and being fairly hooked in the jaws. Away went the astonished dog towards the opposite shore—away went the line — and away went the equally astonished angler himself, who, anxious to save his tackle, and being withal of somewhat pursy and plethoric habit, was obliged to make desperate efforts to keep up with his novel *détenu*. Finding himself thus chased by what must have appeared to him to be a man brandishing a huge whip, the dog made for home as fast as his legs could carry him, followed by the shouts of the spectators, and also by his unwilling captor, who, despite his obesity, gallantly maintained the race, springing over " bank, bush, and scaur," and steering his prisoner safely through opposing furze-brakes, until he landed him at his master's domicile.

It once happened to me to hook a wild duck in a somewhat similar manner in Loch Lochy, except that in this instance the cast, which was made with a spinning bait, was intentional. The duck was " hooked-foul" under water in the act of diving, and continued submerged until netted at the side of the boat. The author of the ' Angler's Rambles ' mentions an anecdote of a hare being thus taken with a trout-fly as she was attempting to swim a river. The fly, adroitly cast, stuck into the fur of her back, and, as her captor remarked, landed her " *comfortably.*"

Curious instances are related of birds and other animals

accidentally swallowing fish-hooks. Within my knowledge,
both waterhens and cats have been caught in this manner.
Ducks are the constant victims of their incautious rapacity,
and barn-door fowls have not unfrequently been tempted
to destruction by the allurements of a baited minnow or
seductive " green drake." An instance of the latter is
mentioned by Mr. Wright :—A gentleman fishing with
May-flies in the river Wye, went into an inn on the road-
side, leaving his rod in the portico, where a fine white
cock took a fancy to the fly, and became hooked in the soft
part of the beak. Feeling the hook, the intruder prepared
to beat a hasty retreat, and in so doing pulled down the
rod, with which he was running away in great alarm ; but
the angler, hearing the noise, sallied forth, gave chase,
and regained his departing paraphernalia, when the cock
mounted into the air, and was with some difficulty brought
down and secured.

A correspondent of the 'Field' newspaper, writing
under the signature of a "Coquet-sider," relates another
curious capture, in which a Water-Wagtail was the
victim. "I was fishing," says this gentleman, " in the
Coquet, in 1861, with a Francis-fly, obtained from Mr.
—— (dressed on abominably thick gut—this by the way),
when, in making a longish cast, a Wagtail swooped and
took the Francis. It attempted to soar into the air, but
the weight of the line soon exhausted its strength, and after
playing it a short time, with a sudden jerk I released my interesting visitor. Considering the way in which Mr. Francis

walks into the small birds, it is not to be wondered at that they should have a peck at him when opportunity offers."

The woodcut represents a scale from the back of the Roach and Chub.

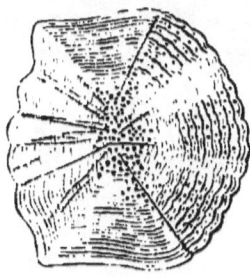 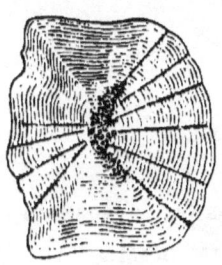

Roach. Chub.

As before indicated, the Roach spawns about the end of May or the beginning of June, when the scales become rough to the touch. The largest specimen that I am aware of having been taken is that mentioned by Pennant, which weighed 5 lbs.

The principal characteristics of the Roach are—

Length of head compared with whole length of fish, tail included, as 1 to 5; depth of body at commencement of back-fin to length of body alone, without head or tail-fin, as 2 to 5. Muzzle rather sharp. Mouth small, toothless. Nape of neck rising suddenly, and profile of back more convex than that of abdomen. Scales somewhat large, marked with concentric and radiating lines; 43 in lateral line. First dorsal ray exactly midway between point of nose and end of fleshy part of tail. Tail deeply forked. Throat-teeth in single rows on each side, 6 on left side, 5 on right. Colour: upper part of head and back dusky green, lighter on sides; silvery white on belly, cheeks, and gill-covers; back- and tail-fins pale reddish brown, pectoral fins orange-red, ventrals and anal fin bright red.

Fin-rays: D. 12: P. 17: V. 9: A. 13: C. 19.

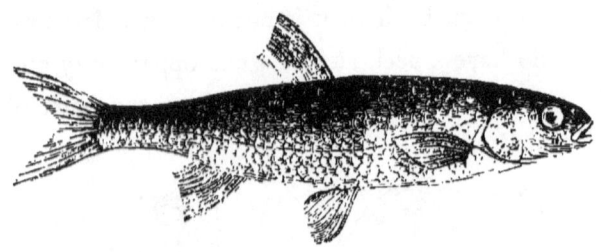

THE DOBULE ROACH.

(Leuciscus dobula*.)

This fish is common in many of the Continental waters, amongst others in the Oder, Elbe, Weser, and Rhine, and the smaller streams that fall into them.   It inhabits also large lakes, seeking to enter rivers from March till May for the purpose of spawning.   In this country it is exceedingly rare, insomuch as to be hardly ever met with: the specimen from which the engraving is taken—a young male fish 6 inches long—was caught by Mr. Yarrell in the mouth of the Thames.

Its principal characteristics were—

Body slender in proportion to its length.   Head compared to length of head and body alone, without tail, as 2 to 9; depth of body equal to length of head.   Nose rather rounded; upper jaw longest.   Mouth toothless; throat-teeth in two rows (numbering 2 and 5) on each side. Pectoral fins rather long and narrow.   Ventral fins rising slightly in advance of the back-fin.   Tail considerably forked.   Scales moderate-sized; 50 in lateral line.   Colour: upper part of body dusky blue; brighter on sides; silvery white on belly, cheeks, and gill-covers; back- and tail-fins dusky brown, the other fins orange-red.

Fin-rays: D. 9: P. 16: V. 9: A. 10: C. 19.

---

* *Leuciscus*, a Dace, Gr.; *dobula*, Continental name.

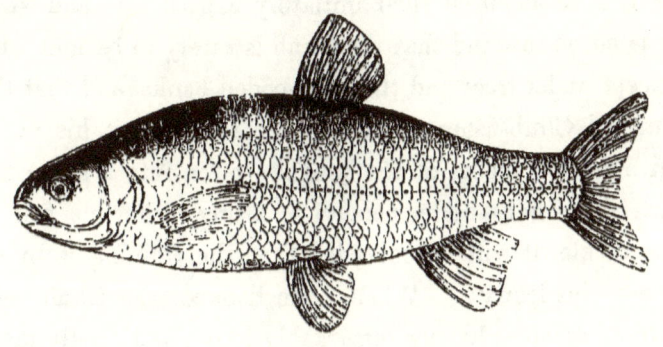

THE CHUB.

(Leuciscus cephalus*.)

The Chub, or "Large-headed Dace," is the *Penci* or *Cochgangen* of Wales, and the *Skelly* of Scotland and of the Cumberland Lakes, though by no means to be confounded with the Ullswater *Schelly* (the Gwyniad), a very different fish, which will be mentioned in the course of the following pages. The *Chevin* is also a local name for this species.

The Chub is very common throughout England, though held in but small estimation, except as affording amusement for the rod and line. In this point of view, however, it deserves honourable mention, as it is a fine, powerful fish, often reaching the weight of 5 and 6 lbs., and, from its readiness to rise at the natural or artificial fly, offering a particularly favourable subject for the young fly-fisher's first essays. In this school not a few of the masters of the

* *Leuciscus,* a Dace, *cephale,* the head, Gr.

craft have acquired their initiatory experience; and when it is borne in mind that the Chub is rarely to be met with except under trees and thickly-wooded banks, and that the finished Chub-fisher must be prepared to cast his fly to within a few inches of the boughs—often into a space the size of his hat—under penalty of losing either his fish or his tackle, it will be conceded that the training is by no means inadequate. When once hooked, the Chub very seldom escapes, having remarkably tough and gristly jaws, or being, as it is termed, 'leather-mouthed.'

The best flies are black and red palmers and Marlow buzzes, varied according to the state of the water, weather, &c.; and both are greatly improved by the addition of a gentle, or a small piece of white leather, on the point of the hook. An artificial caterpillar similarly arranged, and leaded so as to sink slowly, is a very deadly bait, especially in deep waters, as is also a natural caterpillar, cockchafer, or grasshopper, used with a short line by "dibbing" over the bushes. The sinking bait has this great advantage, that it may be thrown as a fly, and does not require frequently renewing. For bottom fishing and ground-baiting, the best baits are those recommended for the Carp, Bream, and Barbel, including greaves*, and with the addition of Minnows in the earlier part of the summer.

---

* *To prepare Greaves or 'Scratching.'*—Break the greaves with a hammer, and boil them (in sufficient water to cover them) for twenty minutes, frequently stirring them to prevent burning. Leave the greaves in the saucepan until cold and stiff, when they are fit for use.

Length. inches.		Weight. lbs. oz.	Length. inches.		Weight. lbs. oz.
9	....	0 12	17		2 13¼
10	....	0 13¾	18	....	3 5½
11	....	0 14¾	19	....	3 15¼
12	....	1 0	20	....	4 9½
13	....	1 4¼	21	....	5 5¼
14	....	1 9¼	22	....	6 2½
15	....	1 14½	23	....	7 0½
16	....	2 5½			

The Chub usually spawns in May or in the latter end of April, selecting for this purpose a shallow gravelly bottom under weeds. After spawning, it rushes into the sharpest and swiftest streams it can find to recover strength, and is supposed to be ready to bite almost immediately †. The taking, however, of this or any other species within at least a month after spawning is an unworthy practice which should be discouraged by all true sportsmen, as the fish are then weak, ravenous, and unfit for food.

In June or July the Chub moves into deeper waters, especially beneath banks overhung with trees or bushes, and will be there found until October or November, when it takes up its winter-quarters, in quiet swims, under willow-beds, amongst roots, by sunken piles, or in any other cover affording a good shelter. It may be at once distinguished, both from the Roach and Dace, by the size of the head, and by the dark chocolate, almost black, tint of its back and tail-fin. This colouring is particularly conspi-

* See p. 59.   † Baily's Angler's Instructor.

cuous in the water, where the fish presents an immediate
and striking contrast to the other species of the same
genus. The lips are also peculiar in colour, being so white
as to be easily observed when opened in taking the fly
or other bait at the surface, even at a distance of 10 or
15 yards. Its food and haunts have been already sufficiently indicated.

Characteristics of the Chub.—Length of head compared with full
length of body, excluding tail-fin, as 1 to 4; depth of body rather
greater than length of head, which is wide and blunt at the muzzle.
Mouth large, toothless; throat-teeth in two rows (numbering 3 and 5)
on each side. Scales very large—from whence is derived the local
name "Skelly"—44 in the lateral line. Back-fin commencing halfway between the point of the nose and end of fleshy portion of tail.
Tail-fin large and somewhat forked. Colour: all the upper part of back
brownish black, the edge of each scale being the darkest part; sides
bluish white, becoming silvery white on belly; back- and tail-fins very
dark brown; pectorals reddish brown; ventrals and anal fin reddish
white; cheeks and gill-covers golden yellow.

Fin-rays: D. 10: P. 16: V. 9: A. 11: C. 9.

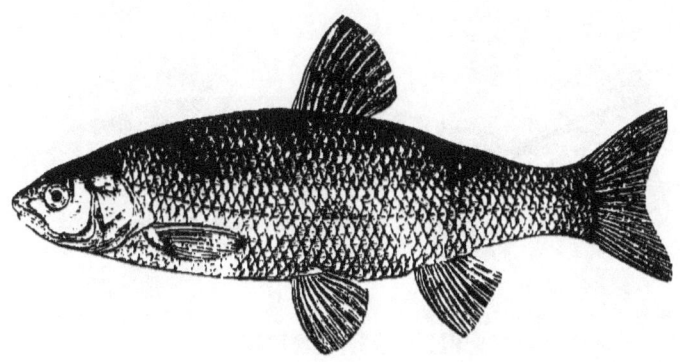

THE IDE.

(*Leuciscus idus* *.)

This fish is very generally diffused over all the middle and northern portions of Europe, as well as the brackish bays of the Baltic, and the large rocky Scandinavian lakes, from which, in the earlier summer months, it finds its way into the rivers to spawn. A specimen of the species is stated to have been taken in the mouth of the Nith by the late Dr. Walker, but it seems to be very doubtful whether the fish in question was not in fact a Chub.

The principal characteristics of the Ide are—

Head large; muzzle blunt. Mouth small, without teeth; upper jaw rather the longest. Outline of back convex, that of belly nearly straight. Scales large. Throat-teeth in two rows (numbering 3 and 5) on each side. Colour: upper part of body very dark bluish black; sides bluish grey; belly white; pectoral fins orange; ventrals and anal fin red and white; back- and tail-fins grey. Vertebræ 41.

Fin-rays: D. 11: P. 17: V. 11: A. 13 or 14: C. 19.

---

* Latinized form of Continental name.

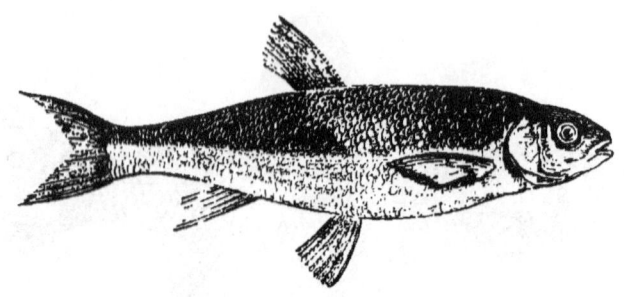

THE GRAINING.

(*Leuciscus Lancastriensis* *.)

The Graining is a very rare and local fish, in habits and food somewhat resembling the Trout, the mode of angling for it being also similar. It affords very good sport, and is said to rise so freely when in the humour, that it is often easy to fill a creel in a day's fishing. Sometimes, though not commonly, the specimens exceed half a pound in weight; and their flavour is considered superior to that of the Dace †, to which fish they bear a considerable resemblance in many points.

The Graining is never found in ponds: the rivers in which it is known to exist are, the Mersey, near Warrington; the Alt, Lancashire; the Leam, at Leamington; two or three streams in the townships of Burton Wood and Sankey, and several others near Knowsley Park, forming the source of the River Alt. It is also found in the Lakes of Neuchatel and Thun.

<hr>

* *Leuciscus*, the Dace, Gr.; *Lancastriensis*, of Lancaster, Lat.
† Bainbridge's Fly-fisher's Guide.

Principal Characteristics of the Graining.—Length of head compared to total length of body and tail-fin as 1 to 6; depth of body to the same as 1 to 5. Nose more rounded than in the Dace, the upper line of head being straighter; lower edge of fore gill-cover less angular; dorsal profile less convex. Back-fin commencing exactly half-way between point of nose and end of fleshy portion of tail, whilst in the Dace it commences further back; all the fins somewhat longer in proportion; scales rather larger; number in lateral line 48. Fleshy part of tail long and slender. Throat-teeth in two rows (numbering 2 and 5) on each side. Colour: upper part of head and body pale drab, tinged with red, and separated from lighter parts of body below by a well-defined line. Cheeks and gill-covers silvery yellowish white; all the fins pale yellowish white.

Fin-rays: D. 9: P. 17· V. 10: A. 11: C. 19.

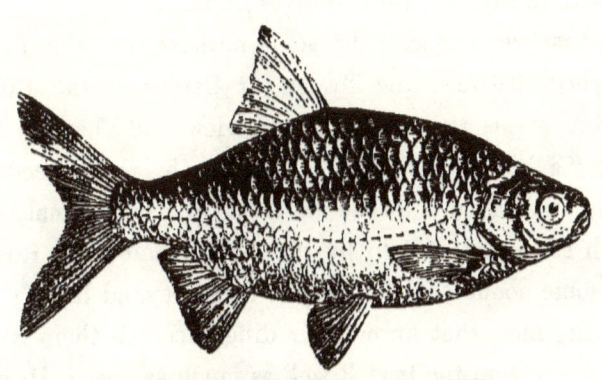

THE RUDD, or RED-EYE.

(*Leuciscus erythrophthalmus* *.)

With the Rudd we begin the second series of the *Leuciscini*, or Dace genus, viz. those in which the back-

* From *erythros*, red, and *ophthalmos*, the eye, Gr.

fin commences considerably behind the line of the ventral fins; and to this section belong three other British species, the Azurine, the Bleak, and the Minnow.

The Rudd is an exceedingly handsome fish, surpassing in beauty of colouring all its congeners. The general hue of the body is a reddish gold, varying according to the light in which it is seen; the eyes and fins are tinted different shades of crimson and scarlet; the cheeks and gill-covers rich yellow, as also the sides and belly, though less vivid; and the upper parts of the back and head greenish blue. From these peculiarities of colouring, it is needless to say, the Rudd derives its name.

It has been supposed by some authors that this fish is a hybrid between the Bream or Carp and the Roach. Walton seems to have held this view. " There is," he says, " a kind of bastard small Roach, that breeds in ponds, with a very forked tail, and of a very small size, which some say is bred by the Bream and right Roach; and some ponds are stored with these beyond belief; and knowing men that know their difference call them Ruds: they differ from the true Roach as much as does a Herring from a Pilchard. And these bastard Roach are now scattered in many rivers, but, I think, not in the Thames." Elsewhere he adds, " Some say that Breams and Roaches will mix their eggs and milt together; and so there is in many places a bastard breed of Breams, that never come to be very large or good, but are very numerous." The species here referred to were no doubt the true Rudd

and the Breamflat, and it is much to be regretted that
we have not greater means of testing the accuracy of
these opinions. Certainly neither of the fish grow to any
large size, 1½ or 2 lbs. being the extreme limit: and as
to their numbers, I am acquainted with many waters that
literally swarm with the former; whilst of the latter
eighteen hundredweight are stated to have been taken in
the Trent at a single sweep of the net.

The notion of hybrids amongst fish is not confined to
the Rudd and Breamflat; as already mentioned, it has
been supposed that the Ruffe is a cross between the Perch
and the Gudgeon, an opinion which has arisen from its
resemblance to the one in its colouring, and to the other
in shape and habits. Mr. Wright, alluding to the subject, says, "This view may appear at first very extraordinary, seeing that the Perch are constantly preying upon
Gudgeons, and cannot therefore be supposed to form any
friendly connexion; but it may be easily accounted for
thus :—the Gudgeon, with ova at maturity, in endeavouring to escape from the Perch, might, and most likely would,
deposit some of their eggs, whilst the Perch would as probably deposit a portion of vivifying milt upon them; and
this would so continually occur, as to give reason for the
great number of hybrids in rivers where the two fish
abound, even if the hybrids themselves have no power of
reproduction.... This year, 1855, nearly the middle of
May, I have a Ruffe or Pope full of ova: there is, in my
opinion, every reason to think that this fish is a hybrid;

and here is ample proof that it is capable of producing its own species, which, from the quantity of ova in the specimen now before me, must be very numerous."

Many naturalists have disputed entirely the existence of hybrids among fish. This, however, is certainly a mistake, as such hybrids have been actually produced by placing fish of different species in sufficient numbers in the same vivarium. The experiment was tried with perfect success by Mr. Bartlett with the common Carp and Goldfish, the result being that the ova and milt became intermixed, and many nondescript varieties were produced; but whether these fish possessed the power of renewing their species, and what would have been the nature of such progeny if bred, is a different question, for the solution of which the experiment was unfortunately not carried far enough to furnish any data. It is indisputable, however, that hybrids exist amongst birds, and even plants, which are capable of reproduction. At Syfran, on the River Krymsa, they breed the Astraean Swan-Goose; this breed intermixes with the common Goose, and its progeny will couple with each other *.

A similar cross has for some years been bred at the Zoological Gardens, between the Tufted Duck (*Fuligula cristata*) and the Castaneous Duck (*Nyroca leucophthalma*), the new species exhibiting very marked and well-defined characteristics. The male Nyrocas have a singular habit, when courting, of suddenly jerking back the head and

* Pallas's Travels in Siberia.

neck to the utmost possible stretch, uttering at the same time a note which sounds like "look! look!" This, Mr. Bartlett informs me, is their mode of showing off in the eyes of their innamoratas; but the effect when witnessed in a number of individuals at the same time is most ridiculous.

To return. The Rudd is a very bold biter, breeding indifferently in all sorts of waters, and on this account, as well as from its being remarkably prolific, forms a useful stock-fish for the feeding of Pike and other predaceous species. As a bait for the former, it is particularly worthy of the troller's notice, the scarlet colour of its fins giving it a bright and attractive appearance in the water, and its un-

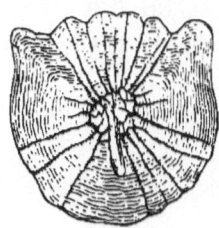
Scale of Rudd.

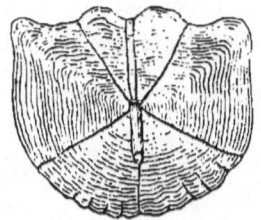
Scale of Azurine.

usual tenacity of life enabling it to survive a long course of piscatory calisthenics. In habits and food the Rudd resembles its allied species the Roach,—the baits, &c., used for the two fish being also similar.

The Rudd is found in all parts of the Continent and Great Britain. It is the *Shallow* of Cambridgeshire, the *Roud* of Norfolk, and the "Roach" (or fish commonly so called) of Ireland. From the true Roach, however, it may be at once distinguished upon the most superficial comparison.

The Rudd spawns in April or early in May.

Principal Characteristics.—Length of head compared with length of head and body only, as 2 to 7; depth of body to the same as 1 to 3. Head small; nose rather blunt. Nape of neck rising abruptly; profile of back and belly very convex; fleshy part of tail narrow. Dorsal fin commencing further back than the ventrals, its base standing over the space between ventral and anal fins. From point of nose to commencement of pectoral fins, thence to origin of ventral fin, and again to commencement of anal fin are three very nearly equal distances. Mouth toothless; throat-teeth in two rows (numbering 2 and 5 respectively) on each side. Scales large; number in lateral line about 40; in oblique line ascending to back-fin, 7; in descending line to ventral fin, 4. Colour (see remarks at p. 160).

Fin-rays: D. 10: P. 15: V. 9: A. 13: C. 9.
(Irish Rudd from Lough Neagh have one ray more in the dorsal and anal fins.)

THE AZURINE.

(*Leuciscus cœruleus* *.)

The Azurine, which was first added to the British list by Yarrell, is, in England, found only in a few localities in the neighbourhood of Knowsley, the seat of Lord Derby, by whom the specimens from which the engraving is taken were supplied.

It is very hardy and tenacious of life, and its flesh is said to be firm and of good flavour. In its food, and in the baits used for its capture, it resembles the Carp; and the largest specimen known to have been taken was not supposed to have exceeded 1 lb. in weight. The local name for the Azurine is the Blue Roach. It spawns in May.

Its principal characteristics are—

Depth of body compared with length of head and body only, as 2 to 7. Distinguished from the Rudd by the slate-blue colour of the back, the silvery whiteness of the abdomen, and by its white fins. Nose blunt; head small and depressed; back and belly rather convex. Mouth small, toothless; throat-teeth in two rows (numbering 2 and

---

* *Leuciscus*, a Dace, Gr.; *cœruleus*, blue, Lat.

5 respectively) on each side.   Scales large, and differing from those of the Rudd (*vide* woodcut); scales in lateral line about 42.   Lateral line concave.   Dorsal fin commencing halfway between eye and end of fleshy portion of tail; pectoral fins rather long, reaching nearly to the origin of the ventrals, which arise considerably in advance of the dorsal fin, thus bringing that fin over the space between the ventral and anal fins.   Fleshy part of tail narrow; tail-fin deeply forked.

Fin-rays: D. 10: P. 15: V. 9: A. 12: C. 19.

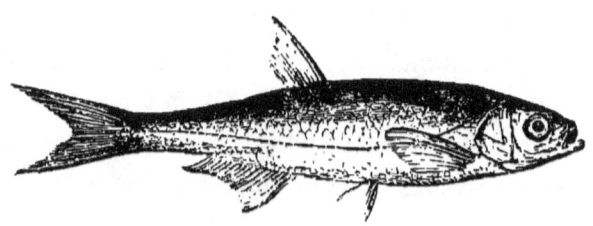

THE BLEAK.

(*Leuciscus alburnus *.*)

This fish much resembles a Sprat in form and general appearance, and makes a good spinning-bait for Pike or Thames Trout.   It is, however, a "surface-swimmer," and, as such, much too delicate, and easily killed on being taken from the water, to be used in "live-baiting."   The Bleak abounds in the Thames, and in most other rivers producing Roach and Dace.   It is a very playful and sportive fish, and on a summer's evening may be seen perpetually darting about and leaping at the midges which would fain flit

* *Leuciscus*, a Dace, Gr.; *albus*, white, Lat.

out their three hours' existence over their native stream.
Whipping for Bleak used to be a favourite amusement
with our ancestors, and even with the classical anglers of
ancient times :—

> " Quis non et virides vulgi solatia Tincas
> Norit, et Alburnos prædam puerilibus hamis?"

By the young Waltonians of the present day, however,
Bleak-catching is voted *infra dig.*, and the little fish is
seldom molested unless for the purpose of bait.

Another prolific cause of the destruction of Bleak has
much diminished of late years, viz. the manufacture of
"patent pearls," as they were called, in which the Bleak's
scales played a prominent part. On the inner surface of
these is found a silvery pigment, to which they owe their
brilliant metallic lustre; and this colouring-matter was
universally used in the bead-trade for imparting a pearly
tint to their wares. So great was at one time the de-
mand, when the fashion of wearing imitation pearls was at
its height, that the price of a quart-measure of scales varied
from one guinea to five. At one factory alone, in Paris,
10,000 pearls were issued per week; and when it is considered that each pound of scales cost the lives of 4000
fish, and that this pound only produced four ounces of pigment, some estimate of the destruction effected amongst the
Bleak may be formed. The Thames fishermen gave themselves no trouble beyond stripping off these valuable appendages, throwing away the fish when scaled. Roach
and Dace, and some other species, also furnished a colour-

ing-substance, though of inferior quality, the best of all
being procured from the Whitebait; and it was the custom
amongst hawkers regularly, before selling any "White-fish"
as they were termed, to supply the bead-makers with their
scales.

The method of obtaining and using the pigment was,
by first washing, and then soaking the scales until the
colouring-matter descended to the bottom of the vessel
in the form of a pearly precipitate, whence it was removed by small tubes and injected into thin hollow glass
beads of various sizes. These were then spread on sieves,
and dried in a current of air. If greater solidity appeared
to be necessary, a further injection of melted wax was
resorted to.

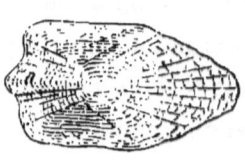
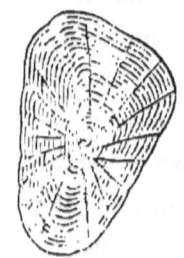

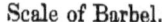

Scale of Barbel.   Scale of Bleak.

At present the material for making artificial pearls is
supplied by the swimming-bladder of the Argentine, or
Tiber Pearl-fish. The bladders are placed in spirits of
wine, and when required for use are taken out and steeped
in a solution of isinglass until all the pearly particles have
been detached, the method of injection being as before.

It occasionally happens to the angler to catch pearls ready-made. These are found in the large river-mussel, which, as is well known, will not unfrequently swallow a worm or other ground-bait, taking so fast a hold with its shell-lips as to be fairly hoisted out of the river's bed and basketed. An instance recently occurred near Tweed Mill, Coldstream, where a boy, who was worm-fishing for Trout in the Chapel brook, caught a mussel 4 inches long and 2 broad containing no less than forty fine pearls of different sizes, some of which were thought to be worth ten shillings each.

It has several times happened to me to take mussels whilst fishing; but, either owing to my want of luck, or lack of inquisitiveness, I have hitherto discovered nothing in them more valuable than mud. There is another species of mussel, never, I believe, found on these shores, called the "Nacre," from which mother-of-pearl is procured; this shell-fish grows to the length of 2 feet, and, according to Oppian, enters into copartnership with a small species of crab, which permanently resides within its shell, and in return for this lodging-accommodation caters for the 'board' of both parties.

Most fishermen will have, on occasions, remarked Bleak swimming round and round in circles with their heads above the surface of the water, as if suffering from vertigo. These gyrations are caused by thin white tapeworms, sometimes as much as 9 or 10 inches long and three-tenths of an inch wide, which get into the intestines of the fish,

I

and occasion great pain or irritation. Fish thus affected are called by the fishermen mad Bleak; and as they are observed to be found only where rivers are turbid, it would appear probable that the worms are generated through the foul state of the water. In an article in the 'Mirror'* on medical quackery, it is asserted that these tapeworms are used by quack doctors to exhibit in their windows.

The most certain method of taking Bleak is with a single gentle at the end of a very fine casting-line, used without shot, and with a piece of cork the size of a pea 3 or 4 feet above the bait, to serve as a sort of float—*a few gentles also being from time to time scattered into the river to attract the fish.* The hook should be small enough to be entirely concealed in the gentle. For this fishing a light fly-rod is the most agreeable as well as most effective weapon.

The Bleak swims usually in large sculls, spawning in May; its length seldom exceeds 6 or 7 inches. The term Bleak, which has reference to its shining white appearance, is derived from a Northern word signifying to bleach or whiten,— *Blik* (Danish), *Blick* (Swedish and German), 'glance,' 'glimmer.'

A few dozen Bleak marinated form an excellent breakfast dish.

Characteristics of the Bleak.—Length of head compared with total length, tail included, (about) as 2 to 9. Depth of body equal to length

---

* Vol. i. 1826.

of head. General shape of body Dace-like, but easily distinguished by the relatively backward position of the dorsal fin, and by the body being much more compressed, or flatter. Nose pointed; under-jaw longest. Scales moderate-sized; number in lateral line about 47. Mouth small, toothless. Throat-teeth in two rows (numbering 2 and 5 respectively) on each side. Colour: back bluish green; sides, belly, cheeks, and gill-covers silvery white; all the fins nearly white. Vertebræ 43.

Fin-rays: D. 10: P. 17: V. 9: A. 18: C. 19.

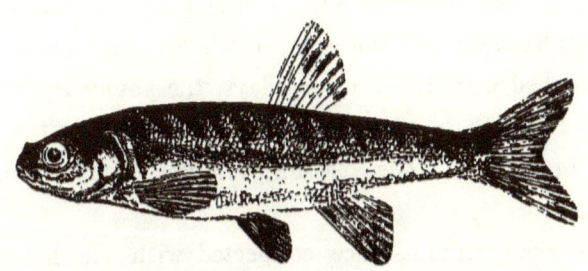

THE MINNOW, or PINK.

(*Leuciscus phoxinus* *.)

As its names† express, the Minnow is a small, dainty, tapering fish; it is, indeed, the smallest of all our Carp family. It very rarely exceeds 3 inches in length; but its numbers in many of the brooks and canals of Great Britain, over which it is generally distributed, are almost incredible.

* *Leuciscus*, a Dace, and *phoxinos*, name of a fish (from *phoxos*, conical or tapering), Gr.

† The term 'Minnow' is said to be derived from the Lat. *minimus*; and 'Pink' from the bright-red colour of the belly in summer.

I 2

Like the last-noticed species, the Minnow is exclusively
a river-fish, and swims in large shoals, inhabiting usually
such streams as also contain Trout, and preferring gravelly
or sandy bottoms. Its food consists of water-weeds, worms,
and small portions of animal matter; and, from its active
and amusing habits, it is a favourite denizen of the vivarium, where, however, it has never been known to live
beyond three years. The Minnow forms an excellent bait
for Pike, Perch, Trout, and Chub. It spawns in June,
at which time the head will be found to be covered with
small tubercles; and the eggs, which are very numerous,
are hatched within five or six days, the young fry reaching the length of three-quarters of an inch by the first
week in August. The spawning-process occupies only a
few days.

A curious circumstance connected with the habits of
this species is related in Loudon's Magazine of Natural
History. "On crossing a brook," says the writer, "I
saw from the foot-bridge something at the bottom of the
water which had the appearance of a flower. Observing it
attentively, I found that it consisted of a circular assem-
blage of Minnows. Their heads all met in a centre; and
their tails diverging at equal distances and being elevated
above their heads, gave them the appearance of a flower
half-blown. One was larger than the rest; and as often
as a straggler came in sight, he quitted his place to pursue
him, and, having driven him away, returned to it again
—no other Minnow offering to take it in his absence.

This I saw him do several times. The object that had been attracting them all was a dead Minnow, which they seemed to be devouring."

The young Minnows when first hatched are quite transparent, except the eyes, which are large and dark. In this state, the larvæ of the May-fly, and other ephemera, are their greatest enemies, and the diminutive fry seem to be perfectly aware that they owe their safety to concealment, when exposed immediately burying themselves again in the gravel.

Principal Characteristics of the Minnow.—Length of head compared to length of head and body (excluding tail-fin) as 1 to 4; depth of body not quite equal to length of head. Scales very small. Tail-fin rather large and forked; back-fin short at the base, and placed behind the ventrals. Mouth small, toothless. Throat-teeth in two rows (numbering generally 2 and 4) on each side. Colour: top of head and back dusky olive, mottled; sides pale satin-colour; belly white, pink in summer; back- and tail-fins brown; the other fins lighter.

Fin-rays: D. 9: P. 16: V. 8: A. 9: C. 19.

Genus *COBITIS* *.

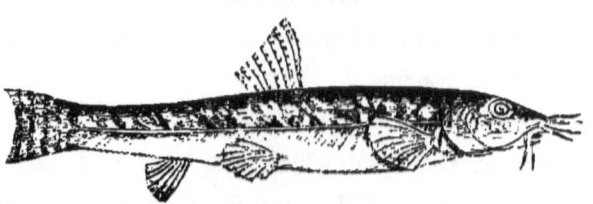

THE LOACH.

(*Cobitis barbatula* †.)

The Loaches form the last genus of our *Cyprinidæ*, or
Carp family, and are somewhat allied to the Gudgeon in
appearance, as well as in many of their habits.   The most
remarkable characteristics of the genus are the number of
'barbels' about the mouth, which vary from six to ten,
and the air- or swim-bladder being enclosed in a bony
cell behind the head, as shown in the magnified representation annexed.

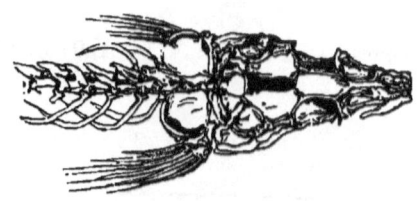

Bony Capsules of the Air-bladder.

This air-bladder is considered by Professor Owen to exist
principally in subserviency to the organ of hearing.   The
other features are, the dorsal and opposite ventral fins

* The Loach genus, from the diminutive of *Kobios*, a Gudgeon or
small fish, Gr.   † *barbatula*, with a little beard, Lat.

short, and placed far back; the mouth toothless; throat-teeth numerous, pointed, and situated in a single row only on each side; the body covered with very small scales, none on the head; three gill-rays.

The common Loach, Beardie, or Stone-Loach, by all of which names the fish is known, is found in most parts of the three kingdoms, affecting particularly clear gravelly brooks, where it is by no means uncommon, although, from its habit of lurking under stones, in search probably of larvæ and other insects, it frequently escapes notice; it is not, however, a purely river-fish, as I have often taken very fine specimens in a small stagnant pool near Roehampton. When disturbed by the moving of its stony shelter, it darts away with great rapidity.

It has been remarked elsewhere, that 'bearded' fish, like the Loach, are known to feed at or near the bottom of the water, for which purpose their beards or barbels are of valuable assistance, and that such fish have usually a low standard of respiration and a high degree of muscular irri-tability. In animals possessing this constitution we have reason to believe that there exists also great susceptibility to any electrical changes affecting the element in which they reside; and hence the restless movements of Eels and other ground-swimmers so commonly observed during thunder-storms.

The Chinese, who breed and rear great quantities of Gold-fish, find that thunder injures, and sometimes kills them. Lobsters are known to exhibit terror at the sound of thunder, and are even said to be apt to cast their claws upon an unusually loud clap,—an effect which may be attributed to spasmodic action of the muscles under electrical influence. If fishes of opposite habits, such as surface-swimmers* and ground-swimmers, are put together into the same vessel of water and a slight galvanic discharge is passed through the fluid, the ground-swimmers, with the lowest degree of respiration, will be the most agitated.

The Loach seldom exceeds 4 or 5 inches in length, and feeds upon worms and water-insects. Its flesh is considered excellent; and in some parts of Europe it is held in such high estimation for delicacy and flavour as to be frequently transferred, at the cost of considerable trouble and expense, from the rivers it naturally inhabits to others in the neighbourhood of noblemen's estates. It is said that Frederick the First of Sweden went to the length of having it imported into that country from Germany for his own particular eating †.

This little fish appears to be entirely incapable of swimming about like the majority of its class. When in confinement it remains during the greater part of the day motionless at the bottom of the vivarium, but towards evening, and also in showery weather, often comes to the top by a violent wriggling movement of its eel-like body: having reached the surface, it is totally unable to remain there, either by continuing its efforts, or by that easy float-

* See p. 10.   † Linnæus, Fauna Suecica.

ing motion which most fish practise so gracefully, and which would seem to be rather the result of volition than of muscular action. The moment its exertions cease, the Loach falls heavily and languidly to the bottom, dropping from rock to rock, or from leaf to leaf, until it finds a resting-place, on which, be it stone or plant, it will remain for hours without stirring.

"I have seen it," says Mr. Newman, "apparently balanced crosswise on the edge of a vertically-placed stone: aquatic progress seems to be the result of powerful exertion of the vertebræ. It is excessively voracious, and will consume an incredible number of small worms; as soon as it seizes one it stirs up the sediment in the vivarium, making the water so cloudy that the fish becomes invisible. The lid of the nostril stands up like a little horn on each side of the face. It is unconquerably shy."

The Loach spawns in March or April.

Principal Characteristics of the Loach.—To those already given in the beginning of the notice may be added the following:—Length of head compared with length of body alone (excluding head and tail) as 1 to 4. Depth compared with head and body alone as 2 to 11. Nose rounded, pointing downward; top of head flat. Mouth small, placed underneath like that of a Barbel; upper jaw longest; 4 beards on upper lip, and 1 at each side of the mouth. Vertebræ 36. Colour: head, body, and sides clouded and spotted with brown on a yellowish-white ground; belly and under surface white or yellowish white; all the fins spotted with dark brown, back-fin and tail the most so; irides blue.

Fin-rays: D. 9: P. 12: V. 7: A. 6: C. 19.

THE SPINED LOACH.

(Cobitis tænia*.)

The Spined or Ribbon-shaped Loach is a much rarer
fish than the last-named species, and, from its smaller size
and similar constant propensity for lurking under stones,
its habits are either but little known, or they have not
been distinguished from those of the common Loach. The
Spined Loach, sometimes also named Groundling, has been
found in the Trent, near Nottingham †, in the Wiltshire
streams ‡, in Warwickshire, and in the Lodes, or Leads,
as they are termed, which run into the Cam. It is very
possible, however, that it also exists in many other waters
where it has hitherto escaped notice. It has not been
found in Ireland.

This fish seldom exceeds 3 inches in length, and is
usually much smaller, the engraving representing a specimen of the natural size. When touched it emits a
peculiar guttural sound, resembling that already referred
to in the Barbel and one or two others of the Carp
species.

The Spined Loach may at once be distinguished from

---

* *Cobitis*, a Loach, Gr.; *tænia*, a ribbon, Lat.

† Berkenhout's Synopsis of the Natural History of Great Britain,
&c.   ‡ Turton's British Fauna.

the common Loach by its head being armed with forked moveable spines, situated behind the nostril, below each eye; the form of the body is also still more slender and ribbon-shaped, the mouth and eyes are relatively smaller, and the pectoral fins longer and narrower. The general colouring is very similar in both fish, but in the Spined species the side is traversed by a conspicuous row of dark-brown spots. The air-bladder is enclosed as in the common Loach.

Fin-rays: D. 8: P. 9: V. 7: A. 6: C. 15.

DUM CAPIMUS CAPIMUR.

CHAPTER VIII.

Series I. *BONY FISHES.*   Family *ESOCIDÆ* †.
Order II. *MALACOPTERYGII ABDOMINALES* *.   Genus *ESOX* ‡.

THE PIKE.

(*Esox lucius* ‡.)

Characteristics of the Pike Family.—Head depressed, large, oblong, blunt. Body elongated, rounded on the back; sides compressed, covered with scales. Dorsal fin placed very far back, over anal fin. Jaws, palatine bones, and vomer furnished with teeth of various sizes.

Contains only one genus, *Esox*, the characteristics of which are consequently similar to those above named.

THE Pike, from its high rank as a game fish, as well as from its edible qualities, deserves to command next to the Salmon and Trout the attention of anglers; but whilst the habits and history of the latter have been made, over and over again, the subject of elaborate treatises and minute exhaustive investigations, those of the former—if not as important, at least equally interesting—have been passed over for the most part with merely superficial notice.

---

* " Abdominal soft-finned fishes " (p. 37).   † The Family of the Pikes.
‡ *Esox*, a Pike ; *lucius, the* Pike, Latin names.

There has always appeared to me something peculiarly attractive in the Pike—its size, its reckless courage, and the dash and *élan* with which it " takes the death." Its very ferocity has an interest; and I confess to a feeling almost of affection for the gallant and fearless antagonist with whom I have had so many encounters.

The Pike, of which we have only one recognized species in this country and on the Continent, is common to most of the rivers and lakes of Europe and North America* and the more northern parts of Asia, and, according to the

* Although there is but one species of the Pike (i. e. *Esox lucius*) found in the waters of Great Britain and recognized in those of Europe, the rivers and lakes of North America produce a great many varieties, all possessing more or less distinct characteristics. Into the details of these it is not necessary to enter; but the following is a list of the principal species which appear to have been clearly demonstrated to be distinct :—The Mascalonge (*Esox estor*) and the Northern Pickerel (*Esox lucioides*), both inhabitants of the great lakes; the common Pickerel (*Esox reticulatus*), indigenous to all the ponds and streams of the Northern and Midland States; the Long-Island Pickerel (*Esox fasciatus*), probably confined to that locality; the White Pickerel (*Esox vittatus*), the Black Pickerel (*Esox niger*), and *Esox phaleratus*, all three inhabiting the Pennsylvanian and Western waters.

Of the species above enumerated the first two are the types, all the others following, more or less closely, the same formation as to comparative length of snout, formation of the lower jaw, dental system, gill-covers, &c.

As regards the European Pike, it seems probable that there may be varieties yet to be discovered, as Dr. Genzik informs me that he has found some specimens which had teeth like the fangs of a viper—capable of being erected or depressed at pleasure,—a circumstance the more remarkable as the jaws also of the fish are furnished with extra bones to increase the size of its gape, very similar to the corresponding bones in the Viper-conformation.

author of ' British Fishes,' and most other writers, was probably an *introduced* species into English waters.   From
this view, however, with due deference to the authority of
so eminent an ichthyologist, I must dissent, on the following grounds.   Yarrell bases his opinion upon the great
rarity of Pike in former times in England, which he proves
thus :—

   " That Pike were rare formerly may be inferred from
the fact that, in the latter part of the thirteenth century,
Edward I., who condescended to regulate the prices of the
different sorts of fish then brought to market, . . . fixed the
value of Pike higher than that of fresh Salmon, and more
than ten times greater than that of the best Turbot or Cod.
In proof of the estimation in which Pike were held in the
reign of Edward III., I may refer to the lines of Chaucer—

> ' Full many a fair partrich hadde he in mewe,
> And many a breme, and many a *Luce* in stewe.'

   " Pike are mentioned in an Act of the 6th year of the
reign of Richard II. (1382), which relates to the forestalling
of fish.   Pike were dressed in the year 1461 at the great
feast given by Geo. Nevil, Archbishop of York. . . . Pike
were so rare in the reign of Henry VIII., that a large one
sold for double the price of a house-lamb in February ; and
a Pickerel, or small Pike, for more than a fat capon."

   But to what does this amount ?   Simply that at some
periods of our history Pike were scarcer, or more esteemed,
and as a consequence more valuable, than at others.   Nor
is this apparent scarcity, as I think I shall be able to show,

at all difficult of explanation without any reference whatever to the cause which would appear to be assigned—namely the recent introduction of the fish. Even on this supposition, however, the argument fails, as it will be observed that Pike were actually cheaper in the thirteenth than in the fifteenth century, being valued in the former (the reign of Edward I.) at "little more than the Salmon"—then a very common fish,—whilst in the latter (the reign of Henry VIII.) they sold "for double the price of a house-lamb."

But, as before observed, the comparative scarcity of Pike is readily explicable on other grounds. It is well known that, as late as the close of the fifteenth century, it was the custom for most great houses, abbeys, and monastic establishments to have attached to them preserves or stew-ponds, containing supplies of fresh-water fish. In this way the productive ponds of the country must, in great measure, have been monopolized, and their owners, being generally wealthy people, would, we can imagine, but rarely allow their produce to find its way into the open market. Thus purely fresh-water fish became a delicacy only within the reach of the rich, and hence the high price of *every description* of such fish, as shown by existing records. The Salmon, on the contrary, being procurable in great abundance from the sea—and lacking therefore this artificial stimulus—would naturally realize only a fair market value in proportion to other descriptions of food.

The numerous and widely-differing dates which have

been assigned by authors for the introduction of the Pike furnish another argument in favour of the view advocated; and as we find mention of the taking of the fish in England as early as the reign of Edgar *, and considering also that it is diffused throughout the length and breadth of the British Islands, and is apparently indigenous in all climates which are not tropical, there appears to be every reason for concluding that it was an aboriginal, and not an introduced, inhabitant of our waters.

It would seem, indeed, that a chilly or even frigid latitude is essential to the well-being of the Pike. Thus in Norway and Sweden, Siberia, and the lakes of Canada and Lapland it reaches its full development, breeding in vast numbers, and commonly attaining the length of 4 or 5 feet, whilst it rapidly degenerates on approaching warmer latitudes—diminishing in geographical distribution with the spruce fir, and ceasing entirely in the neighbourhood of the Equator.

For the numerous names by which the Pike is known, various derivations have at different times been suggested, having all more or less aptness. Of these, however, the common term ' Pike,' or ' Pickerel,' is probably the only one derived from our own language; and this would appear to have originated in the Saxon word *piik*, signifying ' sharp-pointed,' in reference doubtless to the peculiar form

* Leland states that a Pike of great size was taken in Ramesmere, Huntingdonshire, in this reign.

of the Pike's head—thus, by the way, furnishing an incidental concurrent testimony in favour of the indigenous character of the fish.

In Sweden it is named *Gädda*, and in Denmark *Giedde*, *Gedde*, *Gede*, or *Gei*, of which the second term is identical with the Lowland Scotch, *Gedd*. M. Valenciennes has printed a long list of the names which the fish bears amongst the Sclavonic and Tartar races, none of which seem to have any relation to those by which it is known on the western coasts of Europe. The Scandinavian name had its origin, probably, in the sharpness of the teeth of the Pike, and the consequent danger of injury to those who attempted to handle it; for we find a similar word, *Gede* or *Geede*, used to designate a 'goat' in Danish, and *Gedehams* to signify a 'hornet.'

The derivations for the French names of *Brochet* or *Brocheton*, *Lance* or *Lanceron*, and *Becquet*, seem to be obvious; the first evidently owes its origin to the spit-like shape of the body, the second to the speed with which the fish darts in pursuit of its prey, and the last *sobriquet* to the flattened or duckbill-like form of the muzzle.

The ancient classical name of the Pike was *Lucius*, under which it is mentioned by several old writers; and from this root have doubtless sprung the terms *Luce* or *Lucie* (the 'White Lucie' of Shakespeare and of heraldry*), as well as the *Luccio* or *Luzzo* of the Italians and the *Lucie* of the French.

* Moule's Heraldry of Fish, p. 50.

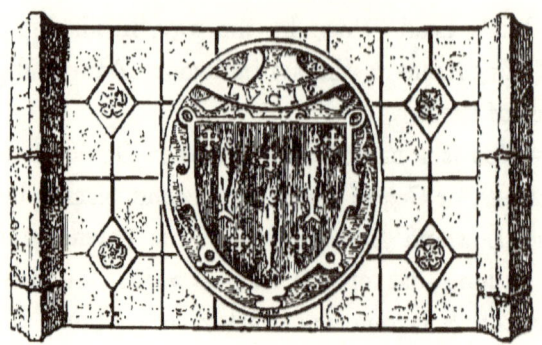

ARMORIAL BEARINGS OF THE LUCIES.

Nobbes suggests that the name *Lucius* is derived " either *a lucendo*, from ' shining in the waters,' or else (which is more probable) from *Lukos*, the Greek word for *lupus* : for as," says he, " the wolf is the most ravenous and cruel amongst beasts, so the Pike is the most greedy and devouring among fishes.   So that *Lupus Piscis*, tho' it be proper for the Sea-wolf, yet it is often used for the Pike itself, the Fresh-water Wolf."

To the ancient Greeks, so far as we are aware, the Pike was a stranger; or if known, has escaped notice in the writings of Aristotle.   In the works of several Latin authors it is mentioned, and is stated to have been taken of very great size in the Tiber; but it has been doubted by naturalists whether this fish—the *Esox* of Pliny—is synonymous with the *Esox*, or Pike, of modern ichthyology. One of the earliest writers by whom the Pike is distinctly chronicled is Ausonius, living about the middle of the fourth century, and who thus asperses its character :—

> "Lucius obscurus ulva lacunas
>   Obsidet. Hic, nullos mensarum lectus ad usus,
>   Fumat fumosis olido nidore popinis."

> "The wary Luce, midst wrack and rushes hid,
>   The scourge and terror of the scaly brood,
>   Unknown at friendship's hospitable board,
>   Smokes midst the smoky tavern's coarsest food."

The age to which the Pike will attain has been always
a debated point. Pennant mentions one ninety years old.
Pliny considered it as the longest-lived, and likely to reach
the greatest age, of any fresh-water fish ; while Sir Francis
Bacon, agreeing in this view, yet limited its probable maximum to forty years.

There is no doubt that, in Persia, Pike are occasionally taken of very great size, arguing a corresponding lon-
gevity ; and a Russian naturalist, with the euphonious name
of RzACZNSKI, alludes to one which was proved to have
survived to little short of centenarian honours.

The famous story of the Pike with the brass ring round
its neck that was put into the Kaiserwag Lake by one of
the German Emperors, and there lived to the age of 267
years, is probably familiar to all, as it has been a staple
commodity with the book-writers and book-makers of
every generation since the sixteenth century. This is, I
think, about the place at which the great "Ring Story"
might be expected to make its appearance—which, however, it would certainly not have done, were it not that I
am enabled to present my readers with what I hope may
be considered as a not uninteresting addition to the goodly

fabric which fact and fiction have so long united to raise.
This is a facsimile of the actual ring itself, as it was clasped

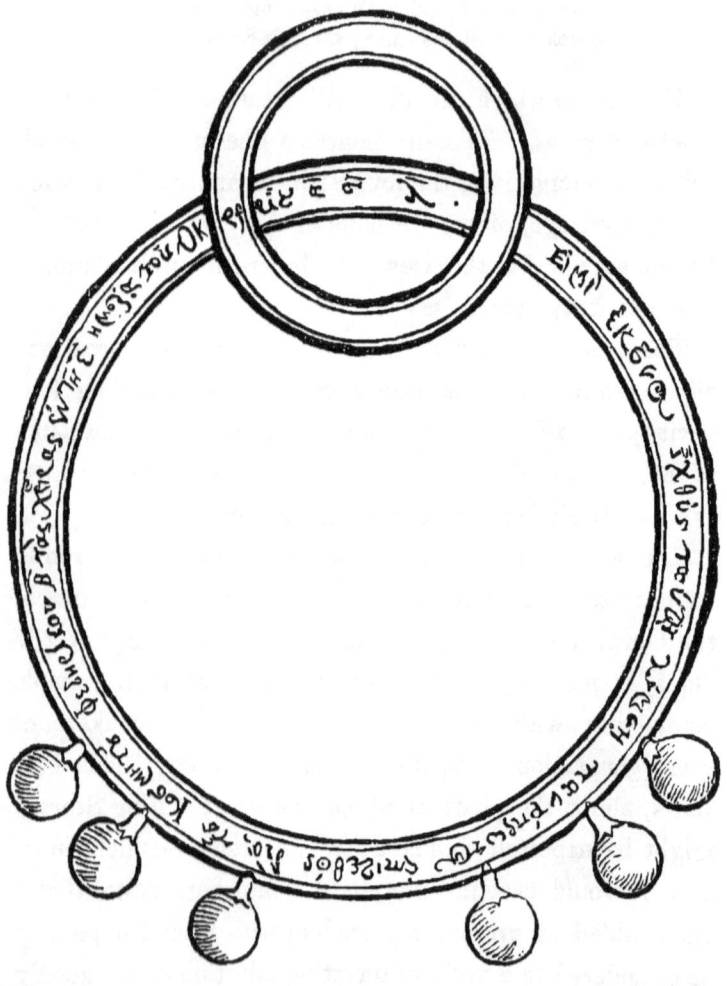

into the gills of the fish by Frederick II. six hundred years
ago; and on it may be deciphered in full the often-quoted

Greek inscription, " I am the fish which was first of all put into this lake by the hands of the Governor of the Universe, Frederick the Second, the 5th of Oct. 1230."

For this interesting relic, of which the figure is an exact transcript, I am indebted to the research of Mr. Francis Buckland, by whom it was discovered in an old black-letter copy of Gesner's famous work, published in Heidelberg, A.D. 1606*.

It is singular that this engraving should have escaped the notice of the numerous commentators by whom the story has been invested with its present almost historical celebrity; but, so far as I am aware, it has never been produced, nor its existence referred to, by any English writer. Leham, indeed, mentions having seen a drawing of both Pike and ring, in a tower on the road between Heilbronn and Spires; but it does not seem to have occurred to him to have it copied. He informs us, however, that, as late as the year 1612, the water from which the fish was taken was still named *Kaiserwag,* or the ' Emperor's Lake.' The ring and the skeleton of the Pike are stated to have been long preserved in the cathedral at Mannheim, the skeleton measuring 19 feet; but, upon subsequent ex-

* " Icones Animalium Quadrupedum Viviparorum et Oviparorum quæ in Historia Animalium Conradi Gesneri, Lib. I. et II., describuntur. Heidelberga: Anno MDCVI."

There is an old, English translation of this work: " C. Gesner's History of Four-footed Beasts and Serpents, by Edward Topsel; whereunto is added the Treatise of Insects or lesser living creatures, as Bees, Flies, &c., by T. Muffet; the whole revised by J. Nowland." 1658.

amination by a clever anatomist, it was discovered that the bones had been lengthened to fit the story—in other words, that several vertebræ had been added.

A critical comparison of the various accounts upon which the general authenticity of the legend rests would be beyond the limits of the present work, although such an examination, did space permit, might possibly not be without interest. Taking, however, all the circumstances of the case into consideration, as well as the amount of concurrent testimony produced, there appears to be no reason to doubt that a Pike of extraordinary size and age was actually taken at the place and time stated. It is to be observed, in estimating the probabilities of the narrative, that it was certainly the custom in earlier times to put metal rings into the gill-covers of fish; and as late as 1610 a Pike was taken in the Meuse bearing a copper ring, on which was engraved the name of the city of Stavern and the date of 1448. Even now the practice is not entirely extinct. Sacred fish are still to be found in different parts of the world. Sir J. Chardin saw, in his travels in the East, fish confined in the court of a mosque, with rings of gold and silver through their muzzles—not for ornament, but, as he was informed, in token of their being consecrated to some Oriental deity, whose votaries, not content to leave transgressors to his resentment, took upon themselves the task of retribution, and killed upon the spot an Armenian Christian who had ventured to violate the sanctity of the place. This Eastern custom is also alluded to by Moore in his "Fire-worshippers " :—"The Empress of Jehan-Quire used to divert herself with feeding tame fish in her canals, some of which were, many years afterwards, known by the fillets of gold which she had caused to be put around them."

*   *   *   *

> " Her birds' new plumage to behold,
>> And the gay gleaming fishes count
> She left all filleted with gold,
>> Shooting around their jasper fount."
>
> *Hinda.*

In natural connexion with this part of the subject—the limit of age in the Pike—occurs that of its probable growth and size when suffered to attain to full development. It has been the custom amongst modern writers to affect a civil disbelief in the accounts of very large Pike handed down to us by numerous credible witnesses; and the prevailing impression appears to be that a weight of 30 or 40 lbs. is about the real maximum attained. I could easily refer, however, to many attested examples of Pike having been taken in the British Islands up to the weight of 70, 80, and even 90 lbs.; but a single instance, too well authenticated to admit of doubt, will suffice. I refer to the case of the Kenmure Pike—mentioned also by Daniel in his 'Rural Sports,' and by Dr. Grierson and other authors —the weight of which was 72 lbs. It was taken in Loch Ken, Galloway, a sheet of water belonging to the Castle of Kenmure, *where the head of the fish is still preserved,* and may be seen by any one sufficiently curious or sceptical to desire ocular demonstration.

To the Hon. Mrs. Bellamy Gordon, of Kenmure Castle, my best acknowledgements are due for an interesting account, written on the spot, of this gigantic Pike* and its captor, as well as for a photograph of the head of the fish as it now appears, with its proportions. These latter would be searcely intelligible without the assistance of the photograph; but, to give a general idea of the size of the fish, I may quote one measurement—that across the baek of the head, the width of which was *nine inches.*

I have lately received from Dr. Genzik, of Lintz, who has kindly furnished me with much valuable information concerning the Continental Pike, some facts in regard to the size attained by these fish in Bavaria, the Tyrol, &e., whieh may probably be new to many of my readers. He assures me that, in the fish-markets of Vienna, Lintz, and Munieh, Pike are not unfrequently exposed for sale of 80 and 90 lbs. weight and upwards,—that the fishermen on the Danube, near Strudel and Wirbel, have legends of Pike 15 and 20 feet long, which break through all their nets,—and that at Traunkirehen, on the Gmünden Water, there are still living some fishermen who declare that about twenty years ago, when dragging the lake, they enclosed a Pike longer than either of their boats, and that they began, as they expressed it, "to say their prayers, thinking the

* This account was written by the Rev. George Murray of Balmaclellan. In the Ashmolean Museum, Oxford, the head of a Pike is stated to have been preserved, the owner of which weighed 70 lbs.; but the Curator of the Museum informs me that this head is not now in the collection.

enemy was on their nets; the Pike, however, with one spring, jumped over the nearest boat and escaped."!

At Oberneukirchen Dr. Genzik himself saw a Pike, taken out of a large tank or preserve, which, after being cleaned, weighed 97 lbs. and some ounces; and an officer of Tyrolese Rifles informed him that whilst at Bregentz during the past autumn (1862), he was present when a Pike was caught weighing upwards of 145 lbs.

These accounts, received direct from such an unquestionable source, go some little way towards acquitting the original historians of the "Emperor's Pike" of the charge of hyperbole, and confirm the probability of the statement of Bloch, that he once examined a portion of the skeleton of a specimen which measured 8 feet.

The accompanying table shows the comparative lengths and weights of the Pike. (See p. 59.)

Length. inches.	Weight. lbs. oz.		Length. inches.	Weight. lbs. oz.
15	1 0		29	7 9
16	1 4		30	8 6
17	1 8		31	9 3
18	1 13		32	10 2
19	2 2		33	11 2
20	2 7		34	12 2
21	2 12		35	13 4
22	3 2		36	14 7
23	3 8		37	15 11
24	4 0		38	17 0
25	4 8		39	18 6
26	5 5		40	20 0
27	6 1		45	32 8
28	6 13		Girth 21 inches.	

There has always been a moot point connected with the weight of this fish, viz. at what size it ceases to be a "Jack" and becomes a "Pike." Walton says, at 2 feet; Sir J. Hawkins, at 3 lbs.; Mr. Wood, at 2 lbs.; Salter, at 3 lbs.; Hofland, at 3 lbs., or when it exceeds 24 inches in length; "Piscator" (Practical Angler) says 4 lbs.; "Glenfin," 3 lbs.; Mr. Blaine, 4 or 5 lbs.; Carpenter, 3 lbs.; "Ephemera," 4 lbs. in his Notes to Walton, and 3 or 4 lbs. in his 'Handbook of Angling'; whilst Captain Williamson recognizes no distinction, but calls them indiscriminately Pike and Jack. Under these circumstances, and considering that the distinction—unlike that between the Salmon and Grilse—is purely arbitrary, it would appear to be desirable that for the future an 'act of uniformity' be passed; and as the majority of writers seem to favour the 3 lbs. qualification, that standard might perhaps be adopted by general consent as the point at which the young Pickerels 'cast off the Jack' and assume the full dignities of Pike-hood.

The rate of growth of the Pike has been by different authors variously estimated at from 1 to 5 lbs. a year; but these estimates do not, generally, appear to be based on any very reliable grounds, still less upon actual experiment, and therefore go but a little way towards advancing our knowledge of the subject. My own experience leads me to believe that the growth-rate is susceptible of very great variation, depending upon the nature of the water, and the amount of food supplied to the fish, but that in the *open waters*—at least in England—it seldom averages more than 1 lb. a year during the first two years, and from $1\frac{1}{2}$ to 2 lbs. a year afterwards, decreasing again after eight or nine years to about the original ratio. This average is not very different from that given by Bloch as the result of his observation. It cannot, of course, be taken as any index of what may be done by keeping Pike in rich preserves, or fattening them in stews, as the capacity of the Pike for food is well nigh inexhaustible, and is in analogy with its powers of digestion, the marvellous rapidity of which has been aptly described as resembling the action of fire.

To procure positive data, however, upon this point must clearly be a matter of great difficulty. From frequent opportunities of witnessing the feeding and management of Pike in stews, I should say that a fish of 5 or 6 lbs. would eat, if permitted, at least twice its own weight of fish every week*; whilst, on the other hand, it can be almost starved for a very considerable period without suffering perceptibly; and in one instance already alluded to, namely that of the Pike in the Zoological Gardens, the

---

* As an instance of this, it is mentioned that eight Pike, of about 5 lbs. each, consumed nearly 800 Gudgeons in three weeks, and that the appetite of one of them was almost insatiable. There is no doubt, however, that this dietary is far below the limit which might be reached. Mr. Stoddart, in his 'Angler's Companion' (p. 298), makes a curious calculation of the ravages committed by Pike in the Teviot, and also states that in some lochs in Scotland the fish has been known to eat its own weight of baits every day.

increase of weight has only been 1½ lb. in ten years. This capacity of existing under such opposite extremes of diet throws an additional difficulty in the way of drawing, from the growth-rate in stews (where only it can be conveniently tested), a correct deduction as regards that in ordinary waters, as we are deprived of the means of gauging the amount of food really required.

Of one point, however, I have fully convinced myself, viz. that during the first year the maximum growth, in open waters, does not much exceed half a pound. The grounds of this conclusion are briefly as follow :—Pike spawn in March or April : in June, when Pike-fishing properly commences, I have not unfrequently taken, and seen taken, with the net, small Jack of about *an ounce*, or a little more, in weight; in September, again, I have constantly taken them, with a minnow, of *three or four ounces*; and in January and February specimens of from *five to seven ounces*; whilst I have never within my memory caught the smaller-sized fish at the later periods, or *vice versâ*,—thus pointing clearly to the inference that at these seasons there were young Jack of those respective sizes, *and none others*—in other words, that the different sizes represented the different stages of growth. These I believe to be the fish of about ¾ lb. of the following season.

A remarkable instance of the Pike's rapidity of digestion was communicated to me by Mr. H. R. Francis * as having occurred some years ago, whilst he was fishing in the

* Author of the 'Fly-fisher and his Library,' &c.

neighbourhood of Great Marlow. He observed a Pike lying in the weeds in an apparently semitorpid condition, and succeeded, with the aid of a landing-net, in securing it, when a large eel was found to be sticking in its throat, the head portion of which was actually swallowed and partially digested, whilst the tail, still alive and twisting, protruded from the jaws. The same gentleman caught in the Thames a Pike weighing 9 lbs. with a moorhen in its gullet, by which it was being suffocated; and on another occasion a fish of five pounds that had one of three pounds half swallowed, but made, notwithstanding, an effort to take his spinning-bait, and was hooked foul in the attempt.

Since the above was put into type, I have been favoured by Captain S. H. Salvin with a curious *pendant* to one of these anecdotes. Captain Salvin had until recently in his possession a tame Cormorant, which had been for many years trained to catch fish for his master by diving,— amongst other odd captures made by it being that of a *Water-hen*, which it secured and brought to the bank after an exciting chase. Within the last few months, however, the career of the feathered angler has been tragically cut short: whilst diving one day as usual, he was seized and crushed to death by a Jack, which was itself choked in its endeavours to swallow him.

The weight of this Jack was only 2½ lbs.

The Pike is a true cosmopolitan in his feeding. Fish, flesh, and fowl are alike acceptable to him : animal, mineral, and vegetable—his charity embraces them all. Nothing, in short, that he can by any means get into his stomach comes amiss to him; and imperial man himself has on more than one occasion narrowly escaped being laid under contribution to his larder.   His own species enjoy no immunity from this universal rapacity; on the contrary, it is believed, and with good reason, that more young Jack are destroyed by their parents than by any, or perhaps all other enemies put together.

A proof of this omnivorous instinct in the fish may be found in the fact that watches, spoons, rings, and other articles have been frequently taken from the Pike's maw; and several authors have asserted that it also feeds upon the pickerel-weed, a common species of water-plant.   I have often known Pike to run at and seize the lead of a spinning-trace; and on one occasion, at Newlock on Thames, Mr. Francis caught a fish which had thus attempted to swallow his lead, and which was entangled and held fast by the gimp lapping round behind the gills.

Without recapitulating the numerous instances of voracity cited by other authors, I may mention a few which have come within my own knowledge.

One of the most remarkable of these occurred during the last few years to Mr. L—, of Chippenham, Wiltshire. This gentleman had set a trimmer in the River Avon over night, and on proceeding the next morning to take it up, he found a heavy Pike apparently fast upon his hooks. In order to extract these, he was obliged to open the fish, and in doing so perceived another Pike of considerable size inside the first, from the mouth of which the line proceeded. This fish it was also found necessary to open, when, extraordinary to state, a *third* Pike, of about $\frac{3}{4}$ lb. weight, and already partly digested, was discovered in the stomach of the second. This last fish was, of course, the original taker of the bait, having been itself subsequently pouched by a later comer, to be, in its turn also, afterwards seized and gorged.

Occurrences of a somewhat similar nature are by no means rare ; one striking example has been already mentioned, and on several occasions I have myself taken Pike with others in their stomach, but I never remember to have met with a well-authenticated instance in which the cannibal propensities of the fish were so strongly and singularly displayed as in that above referred to.

Of the indiscriminating character of the Pike's appetite a more amusing illustration could not perhaps be given than the following, communicated to me by Mr. Clifton, who was an eye-witness of the occurrence : — Upon a piece of water belonging to Wandle House, Wandsworth, some toy vessels were being sailed, at the stern of one of which was attached a small boat fancifully decorated with green and gilding. As the little craft swept briskly across the pool, with her boat in tow, a Pike suddenly darted from the water and grasped the latter in his jaws, retreating as instantaneously towards the bottom, and well nigh capsizing the whole flotilla in his efforts to drag his capture along with him. To this task, however, his strength was apparently unequal, and a fresh breeze springing up, the submerged nautilus reappeared on the surface and continued her voyage, but had hardly got fairly under way when the Pike again dashed forward to the attack, seizing her as before, and continuing every half-dozen yards the process of alternately swallowing and ejecting, until she grounded on the opposite bank.

The best-authenticated instance of attempted *man-slaughter* on the part of a Pike is one which occurred, within a comparatively recent date, in Surrey. The particulars are given by Mr. Wright:—

"In the Reading Mercury a statement appeared 'that a lad aged fifteen, named Longhurst, had gone into Inglemere Pond, near Ascot Heath, to bathe, and that, when he had walked in to the depth of about 4 feet, a huge fish, supposed to be a Pike, suddenly rose to the surface and seized his arm. Finding himself resisted, however, he abandoned it, but still followed, and caught hold of the other hand, which he bit very severely. The lad, clenching the hand which had been first bitten, struck his assailant a heavy blow on the head, when the fish swam away. W. Barr Brown, Esq., surgeon, dressed seven wounds, two of which were very deep, and which bled profusely.'

"I wrote to this gentleman, who very politely obtained, and sent this day, Sept. 18, 1857, the whole account, in writing, from the young man's father (Mr. George Longhurst, of Suuning Hill), which I give as I received it:—

"'*Particulars of an Encounter with a Fish in the month*

of June 1856.—One of my sons, aged fifteen, went with three other boys to bathe in Inglemere Pond, near Ascot Race-Course; he walked gently into the water to about the depth of 4 feet, when he spread out his hands to attempt to swim; instantly a large fish came up and took his hand into his mouth as far up as the wrist, but, finding he could not swallow it, relinquished his hold, and the boy, turning round, prepared for a hasty retreat out of the pond; his companions, who saw it, also scrambled out of the pond as fast as possible. My son had scarcely turned himself round when the fish came up behind him and immediately seized his other hand, crosswise, inflicting some very deep wounds on the back of it; the boy raised his first-bitten, and still bleeding, arm, and struck the monster a hard blow on the head, when the fish disappeared. The other boys assisted him to dress, bound up his hand with their handkerchiefs, and brought him home. We took him down to Mr. Brown, surgeon, who dressed seven wounds in one hand; and so great was the pain the next day, that the lad fainted twice: the little finger was bitten through the nail, and it was more than six weeks before it was well. The nail came off, and the scar remains to this day.

" ' A few days after this occurrence, one of the woodmen was walking by the side of the pond, when he saw something white floating. A man, who was passing on horseback, rode in, and found it to be a large Pike in a dying state; he twisted his whip round it and brought it to

shore.   Myself and my son were immediately sent for to
look at it, when the boy at once recognized his antagonist.
The fish appeared to have been a long time in the agonies
of death; and the body was very lean, and curved like a
bow.   It measured 41 inches, and died the next day, and,
I believe, was taken to the Castle at Windsor.'

" There can be no doubt," Mr. Wright adds, " that this
fish was in a state of complete starvation . . . .   If well-fed,
it is probable it might have weighed from 30 to 40 lbs."

The same gentleman also mentions that he was himself
on one occasion a witness, with Lord Milsington and
many other persons, to a somewhat similar occurrence,
where, during the netting of the Bourne Brook, Chertsey,
one of the waders was bitten in the leg by a Pike which he
had attempted to kick to shore.   This fish, which was afterwards killed, weighed 17 lbs.

I am indebted for the following to Dr. Genzik :—" In
1829 I was bathing in the Swimming-School at Vienna
with some fellow-students, when one of them—afterwards
Dr. Gouge, who died a celebrated physician some years
ago—suddenly screamed out and sank.   We all plunged
in immediately to his rescue, and succeeded in bringing
him to the surface, and finally in getting him up on to the
hoarding of the bath, when a Pike was found sticking fast
to his right heel, which would not loose its hold, but was
killed, and eaten by us all in company the same evening.
It weighed 32 lbs.   Gouge suffered for months from the
bite."

This recalls the story of the Pike which was said to have attacked the foot of a Polish damsel—a performance the more ungallant as the ladies of Poland are celebrated for their pretty ankles.

'Bentley's Miscellany' for July 1851 gives an account of the assaults of Pike upon the legs of men wading; and the author has himself had the privilege of being severely bitten above the knee by a fine Thames fish, which sprang off the ground after it was supposed to be dead, and seized him by the thigh—where it hung, sinking its teeth deeply into a stick which was used to force open its jaws.

More examples might easily be adduced; but the above are sufficient to prove that in rare instances, and when under the influence of either extreme anger or hunger, a large Pike will not hesitate to attack the lords (and ladies) of creation.

Such being the case, it is hardly necessary to say that it is by no means uncommon for animals, often of large size, to be similarly assaulted, and, in the case of the smaller species, devoured, by this fish. Accounts are on record of otters, dogs, mules, oxen, and even horses being attacked. Poultry are constantly destroyed by the Pike,—"the dwellers in the 'Eely Place,'" as Hood punningly says, "having come to Picc-a-dilly:" sometimes the heads of swans diving for food encounter instead the ever-open jaws of this fish, and both are killed; whilst among the frogs he is the very "King Stork" of the Fable, his reign beginning and ending with devouring them. He will even seize that most unsavoury of all morsels, the toad, although in this ease the inherent nauseousness of the animal saves it from being actually swallowed,—its skin, like that of the lizard, containing a white, highly acid secretion, which is exuded from small glands dispersed over the body.

There are also two little knobs, in shape like split beans, behind the head, from which, upon pressure, the acid escapes.

To test this, I have sometimes, whilst feeding Pike, thrown to them a toad instead of a frog, when it has been immediately snapped up, and as instantaneously spat out again; and the same toad has thus passed through the jaws of nearly every fish in the pond, and escaped with but little injury after all. The effect of this secretion may also be observed in the case of a toad being accidentally seized by a dog, which invariably ejects it at once with unequivocal signs of disgust.

Pike will attack both the land- and water-rat; occasionally pouching them, but more frequently treating them as in the case of the toad,—a fact confirmed by Captain Williamson, who adds: " But whether owing to the resistance that animal (the rat) makes, which I have witnessed to be very fierce—and that under water too—or whether owing to the hair or scent displeasing them, I know not; but they do not appear to be very partial to the quadruped. I have repeatedly seen rats pass such Jacks as were obviously on

the alert without being attacked, though the former seemed
to have all their eyes about them and to keep close in
shore."

Rats which have once been gripped by a Pike rarely
appear to recover. They may not unfrequently be found
dead in the weeds, bearing evident marks of the fish's
teeth; and one very large brown rat which I thus found
had the head and fore part of the body crushed almost flat
by the pressure to which it had been subjected. The
marvel, however, is, not that these animals should often
die of their injuries, but that they should ever succeed in
escaping from the triple *chevaux de frise* with which the
jaws of the Pike are armed. An anecdote, taken from
Mr. Buckland's charming collection of 'Curiosities of
Natural History,' illustrates the formidable nature of these
teeth, even when at rest.

"When at Oxford," he says, "I had in my rooms the
dried head of a very large Pike, captured in Holland. It
was kept underneath a book-case. One evening, whilst
reading, I was much surprised, and rather alarmed, to see
this monstrous head roll out spontaneously from below
its resting-place and tumble along the floor; at the same
time piteous cries of distress issuing from it. The head
must be bewitched, thought I; but I must find out the
cause. Accordingly I took it up, when, lo and behold!
inside was a poor little tame guinea-pig, which was a pet
and allowed to run, with two companions, about the room.
With unsuspecting curiosity master guinea-pig had crept

into the dried expanded jaws of the monster, intending, no doubt, to take up his abode there for the night. In endeavouring to get out again he found himself literally hooked. Being a classical guinea-pig, he might have construed '*facilis descensus Averni*,' it is an easy thing to get down a Jack's mouth; '*sed revocare gradum*,' &c., but it is a precious hard job to get out again."

The scratched prisoner was only at last rescued from his Regulus-like incarceration by Mr. Buckland cutting a passage for him through the fish's gills, and thus enabling him to make his exit *à tergo*.

To the sharpness of the teeth in the mouth of this particular Pike I can bear witness, having received unpleasant proof of the fact when carelessly withdrawing my hand from an examination of its contents.

The engraving represents one side of the lower jaw-bones of the Pike, and the position of the large canine teeth.

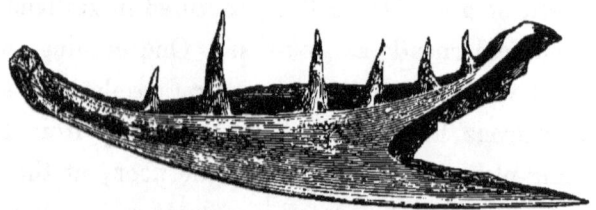

In consequence of the inconvenience experienced in extracting hooks from the mouths of these fish with the ordinary short disgorger, I recently caused a ' disgorger-blade,' if I may so term it—made, of course, without edges of any sort—to be inserted in my fishing-knife, by which the length of the disgorger was doubled, and its power and readiness for use very greatly increased. The advantage of this arrangement of the disgorger, both in trolling and other fishing, suggested the advisability of extending the principle so as to embody in the same knife the rest of the Angler's *desiderata*, and thus spare him the necessity of collecting and stowing each individual article before starting for the river. I am aware that knives intended to fulfil the object have been already produced; but they have generally been excessively clumsy and expensive, and have either not embraced the really essential implements, or have sacrificed their efficiency to a number of others which are practically useless.

The engraving on the next page represents the form and arrangement of a fishing-knife which will, I believe, be found to contain all that is *really* required, viz.—a powerful blade suited for crimping or other general purposes (marked 3), a ' disgorger-blade ' (4), a minnow-needle (6), an ordinary baiting-needle (7) (the last two slipping into a box (1) in the handle of the knife), a sharp-pointed pricker (5) (an exceedingly useful instrument for unpicking knots, loosening drop flies, separating feathers, &c.), and last, not least, a strong corkscrew.

I have furnished Messrs. Weiss, of No. 62, Strand, London, with the pattern for this knife, which they inform me they can supply, of the best materials and workmanship, for 12*s*. 6*d*. (or about their price for an ordinary double-bladed pocket-knife).

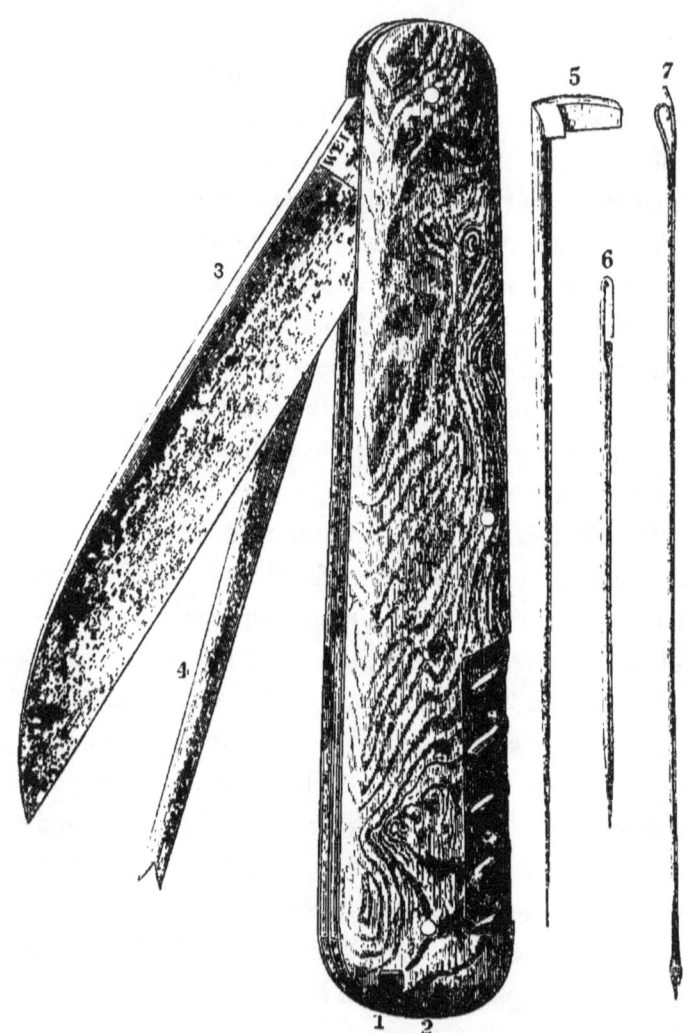

FISHING-KNIFE.

To return. Sometimes the Pike lies in ambush, protruding only its eyes and grim muzzle through the weeds, when the movement of seizing a prey is little beyond a quick turn of the body and an opening and shutting of the jaws; but generally he takes it with a rush and a flash, emerging so suddenly and with such startling energy, that I have, in more than one instance, known an angler literally drop his rod from the effects of sheer terror.

In this boldness and absence of all artifice the Pike offers a strong contrast to the equally voracious but cunning and secretive Fishing-Frog, or 'Angler'*, as it is named, from its habit of angling for its prey. This fish is furnished with two slender tapering rays on the top of the head, like fishing-rods, one of which is flattened out at the end into a form resembling a bait, its attractions being heightened by a shining silvery appearance. The Angler, lying on the bottom, stirs up the mud with its fins, and, thus concealed, elevates its bait-like appendages, moving them temptingly to and fro, until a sufficient number of curious spectators or intended diners have collected, when it opens its immense mouth and at once swallows them all.

Dr. Houston, in a lecture before the Royal Society of Dublin, exhibited the skeleton of an Angler 2½ feet in length, in the stomach of which was a cod 2 feet long; inside the cod were two whitings of the natural size, con-

* *Lophius piscatorius.*

taining in their turn scores of half-digested fish too small
and numerous to be counted. 'Angling' would therefore
appear to be a successful method of procuring food.

Another fish, the Star-gazer (*Uranoscopus scaber*), has
recourse to a similar device,—waving about in the mud
the beards with which his lips are furnished, and which are
mistaken for worms—a stratagem also adopted by the great
Silurus glanis, or 'Sly,' the largest of the European fresh-
water species. This fish, according to Agassiz, exhibits
a notable instance of parental affection. "The male
Glanis," he says, "is conspicuous amongst river-fishes for
the great care it takes of its young: for the female, having

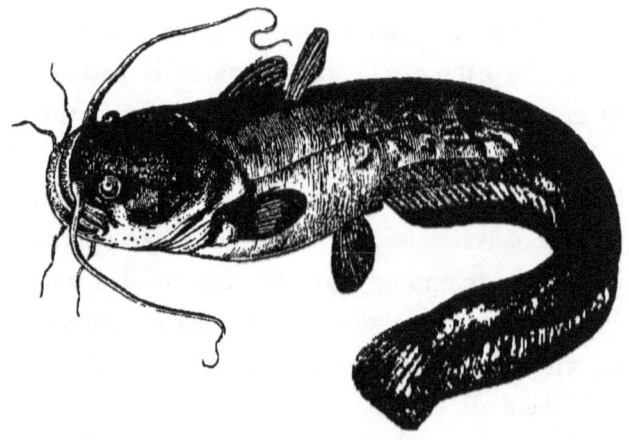

SLY SILURUS.

brought forth, departs; but the male remains watching by
the eggs for forty or fifty days to keep off the attacks of
other fishes, which he does by rushing movements, and

making a noise and moaning, whereby he is discovered to the fishermen, who entice him into shallow places by moving thither the spawn, as he will not even then desert it."*

A somewhat similar instinct is exhibited (though in a less degree) by the unprepossessing-looking River Bullhead and by the Lump-Sucker. The Stickleback also builds a nest for its eggs, as already mentioned, and likewise the Black Goby and the Hassar: the latter of fibrous plants; and the former of clay—burrowing galleries like rats' holes, in the soil, where it spends the greater part of the year. The affection of the Hassar for its egg is shamefully misused by man for its destruction: a small basket is held before the door of the nest, and the structure slightly shaken, when, furious, with extended fins, its enraged guardian darts into the fatal basket†.

Of all the methods of procuring food practised by fish, perhaps the most singular is that of the Chætodon of India and its allied species. This fish literally *shoots* its prey. When it perceives a fly or other insect settle upon an overhanging bush or leaf, it approaches as cautiously as possible, gradually bringing its head and nose close to the surface of the stream, and remaining for an instant motionless whilst taking aim, with its eyes fixed upon the insect: suddenly it darts at it a drop of water from its

* Agassiz, Proc. Amer. Acad. of Arts and Sciences, November 12, 1856.

† Hartwig, The Sea and its Wonders.

snout with such strength and precision as rarely fail to bring down its object—often from a distance of 5 or 6 feet. This illustrates, by the way, the acute nature of the sight of fish.

Whilst alluding incidentally to these 'hunting' species, as they may be termed, I should not omit to mention the Remora or Sucking-fish, also called *Echeneis*, from two Greek words, signifying that the fish holds or stays ships in their course—a fabulous power attributed to it by ancient authors. The Remora is furnished with an appa-

THE REMORA.

ratus on the back of the head and shoulders which enables it to adhere with great force to other fish, or to the bottoms of vessels; and this peculiarity is, or was formerly, made use of by the West Indians, who let it go with a cord fastened to the tail, when the Remora attached itself to other fish, or to turtles, and both were drawn out together. By this means a weight of several hundred pounds has been sometimes raised from the bottom. Columbus mentions the Remora, and says that it will allow itself to be cut to pieces rather than relinquish its hold.

The Pike and many other predaceous species exhibit a similar reluctance to quit their grasp of a prey once seized;

I have witnessed this tenacity occasionally in the case of both Eels and Perch; and the Stickleback, as is well known, will let itself be pulled out of the water by its hold of a worm.

On one occasion, for the sake of experiment, I fastened a large cork to a string, and drew it across a Pike-pond, giving it at the same time an irregular, life-like motion. It was quickly seized by a fish of about 2 lbs., which made a most determined resistance, running out the twine as if really hooked, and only relinquishing its grasp of the cork when within arm's length. The experiment was repeated several times with a similar result.

This illustrates a fact of great importance to Pike-fishers, and one which is of especial significance in the case of Spinners : namely, that Pike will constantly make a considerable fight, and even allow themselves to be dragged *many yards*, by the obstinacy of their hold, *without ever having been pricked by a hook*—shaking the bait out of their mouths when almost in the net. It is highly desirable therefore to take care always to strike very sharply when thus fishing, and to repeat the stroke until a violent tearing struggle is felt; such a struggle almost invariably beginning the moment a fish really feels the hooks, and being easily distinguished from that sluggish resistance, sometimes absolute inaction, exhibited when it is only holding on.

When fishing with a gorge-bait, if a large number of small bubbles rise from the spot where it is evident, from the direction of the line, that a Pike which has taken the bait is lying, it is, according to a clever writer on this subject *, a certain sign that he has not yet pouched. As a rule, however, it is a mistake to suppose that bubbles are occasioned by fish; and when they are so caused, Captain Williamson considers they may be regarded as a symptom that the fish will not bite, being already satiated, and the bubbles arising from the digestive process. " The bubblers," he says, " will always refuse the bait. Wounded fishes, especially Jacks, evince their pain in this manner, as they do also their disquietude when unable to swallow their prey." I confess it appears to me more probable that the bubbles in this case arise rather from the uneasiness of the fish at being unable to get *rid* of the bait already pouched—and the hooks of which have begun perhaps to be felt—or from the tickling of the line in the throat and jaws.

A ludicrous circumstance once happened in the feeding of two Pike kept in a glass vivarium. A bait was thrown in about midway between the fish, when each simultaneously darted forward to secure it, the result being that the smaller fish fairly rushed into the open jaws of the larger, where it remained fixed, and only extricated itself with difficulty and after a lapse of some seconds.

As instances of the attacks of Pike upon the larger animals, Dr. Genzik informs me that he once saw a fox caught by an immense pike, in the Great Rosenberg Tank,

* Captain Williamson, The Complete Angler's Vade-Mecum, p. 194.

Bohemia—then nearly dry. The fox was shot in the water; and as the pike would not loose its hold of his throat, both were pulled out together. The fox had evidently come to poach upon the ducks in the tank, and must have been not a little astonished at finding himself the subject of such a singular detainer.

For another incident of a somewhat similar nature I am also indebted to the researches of the same naturalist, who found the account printed at the foot of an old engraving by Ridinger, now in a collection at Munich. Of this curious picture Dr. Genzik has kindly procured me a photograph, as well as a copy of the story underwritten, of which I append a translation :—

" In the county of Wolffstein, at Pyrbaum, some forty years ago, the following true event occurred :—

" Whilst fishing in the great pond, a large pike of about 18 or 19 lbs. weight was caught; this was to be brought at night to the Castle at Pyrbaum; but it escaped (sprung out), as the vessel in which it was placed was not properly watched, and the persons who carried it came home empty; so they were sent back, with others, provided with torches, to seek for the pike. When they arrived at the place where the pike was lost, they observed a fox in the wheat, who, even on their approaching him, remained standing still; whereupon they hurried nearer, and perceived that the pike had hold of the fox by the snout, and had so bitten into it that they could not release it. So the fox was killed, and the living pike was brought to the Castle.

" Graciously communicated on the 19th May, 1763, by His Serene Highness Carl August von Hohenlohe and Gleichen.

" Johann El. Ridinger ; Aug. Wind ;

Martin El. Ridinger."

This may be cited as an instance of the ' ruling passion strong in death.' The picture gives a very vivid idea of the whole scene by torchlight, with the fox and pike in the foreground, the latter holding the former by the snout.

Occasionally, however, the Pike is himself a victim. The Otter is his worst enemy, and generally comes off victor in those desperate combats with which the watery realms must be too frequently convulsed, could we but see what goes on under their placid surface. A more exciting spectacle, in its way, than such a struggle between these two hereditary antagonists it would be difficult to conceive. On the one hand, the Otter, dark, noiseless, and treacherous, writhing with eel-like suppleness to secure a position from which to fix the fatal grip ; on the other, the Pike, an impersonation of concentrated ferocity, flashing across the arena, with eyes glaring and jaws distended—or even in death striving to fasten his teeth into the throat of his foe *.

The otter is not, however, the only antagonist to the attacks of which the adult Pike is exposed : according to

---

* It is a fact that when angry the Pike erects his fins, much in the same way that a cat bristles up his fur, or a porcupine his quills; and this has been noticed by several of his biographers.

Mr. Lloyd, the author of 'Scandinavian Adventures,' it appears that it is a circumstance by no means uncommon in the North of Europe for this fish to become the prey of a feathered enemy, the eagle, which pounces upon him when basking at the surface of the lakes. In this case, where very large, the fish has been known to carry the bird under water, when the latter, being unable to disengage his talons, is generally drowned. Dr. Mellerborg informed Mr. Lloyd that he had seen an enormous Pike with an eagle thus riveted to his back—both lying dead, in a field previously flooded but from which the water had receded; and on another occasion the actual contest with all its vicissitudes was plainly witnessed. The Pike, when first seized, was lifted by the eagle some height into the air; but his weight, combined with his struggles, soon carried both down again to the water, under which they sank. Presently the eagle reappeared on the surface, uttering piercing cries, and apparently making great efforts to extricate his talons. All, however, was in vain; for, after a prolonged resistance, he finally disappeared in the depths of the lake. An incident very similar is also related by the author of the 'Angler in Ireland' as having occurred on one of the wild loughs of Connemara.

Amongst his own class the Pike reigns supreme, although it has been asserted that, from its superior momentum, a trout or salmon of equal weight would have the advantage in a pitched battle. I doubt it much. What chance these fish have against the Pike is shown

L

by the effect of introducing the latter into trouting and
salmon waters, where the new-comer speedily dispossesses
the rightful tenants.   Witness, for instance, the ravages
committed in the Canterbury River, in the Wandle*, in
the Colne near Draycot and Cowley †, in the Teviot ‡, and
in Lochs Katrine, Lomond, Awe, and Jurit § in Scotland; and the same thing is known to have taken place
in many of the best Irish waters, where the Pike is still
continuing to spread and multiply, displacing by degrees
the Trout and other indigenous races.   Salter says, "I
have known instances of Pike entirely destroying every
fish in a pond, and then making a prey of each other
till there has been but one left."   If, therefore, as it has
been asserted, the fish was really imported into this
country, it is evident that it has borne the expatriation
without much detriment to its constitutional vigour or
productiveness.

Indeed, *how* Pike spread is a problem which it has
perplexed naturalists to explain.   A stream, or pond, or
loch, reserved perhaps for centuries to the docile phleg-
matic Carp, or 'star-stoled Trout,' suddenly begins to show
symptoms of a falling off; the next year matters are
worse; the water is dragged, and the first fish to come
up in the net is probably a Pike.   How the Pike came
there, or who put it there, remains unexplained; but the

---

* Practical Angler, p. 242.   † Wright's Fishes and Fishing.
‡ Stoddart's Angler's Companion.
§ Stoddart's Scottish Angler, p. 57.

cause of the depletion of the water is no longer a mystery. Some authors have accounted for these singular immigrations by supposing that the Pike, like the Eel *, actually travels overland in wet weather from one pond to another † ; and several curious circumstances, which have recently come to my knowledge, would appear to lend some colour to the supposition.

A gentleman who has had considerable experience in the management of fish was witness to one of these apparent migrations. " My brother and myself," he writes to me, " were starting on a fishing-expedition at about 3 o'clock in the morning, when, happening to pass my breeding-ponds—distant some half a dozen yards from the main stream—we found a Pike jumping and working about in the wet grass, and evidently making for the river, towards which it had already proceeded two-thirds of the way when our arrival cut short its journey. The dewy state of the grass, at the time standing for hay, would have enabled me to detect any appearance of footsteps had such been near the ponds, and negatived the idea of the stews having been visited by poachers, either biped or quadruped. This circumstance, I think, may possibly explain what has often puzzled me—namely, how it is that so many large Pike are put into the ponds, and that so few are ever forthcoming when required."

* See instances alluded to in the Chapter on Eels.

† See, amongst other works, The Complete Angler's Vade-Mecum, p. 137.

It is to be regretted, in the interest of science, that the traveller was not allowed to continue his progress, so that we might have had a fact instead of an hypothesis to add to our knowledge of the subject. There seems to be no doubt, however, that if a Pike is placed near the bank of a river or lake where it has no means of seeing the water, it will, by instinct, immediately begin to jump in the proper direction.

A somewhat analogous case to the above was communicated to me by a gentleman who happened to be present on the occasion. Mr. Newenham, an English resident at Antwerp, in order to test the migratory theory, caused two contiguous ponds to be excavated, and stocked one with Pike, and the other with small Roach, Dace, &c. At the end of the second day he caused both ponds to be emptied, when it was found that several of the Pike from pond No. 1 had made their way by some means into pond No. 2, and had destroyed a great part of the fry.

A singular fact, pointing indirectly to the same conclusion, once came under my own observation. A pool 5 or 6 yards square, for the reception of small fish, had been constructed close to a stew-pond containing Pike; the work had been finished in the afternoon, and the pond left to fill. On visiting it the next morning, I was surprised to find it already occupied by a Jack of about $\frac{3}{4}$ lb. weight, which had contrived thus early to take possession.

Perhaps, however, the most remarkable occurrence of this description is one which recently happened in the

Zoological Gardens. In the Aquarium at this institution was a glass tank containing the Pike to which I have elsewhere alluded. During the night the tank broke, and the Pike, being thus left dry, was discovered the next morning by the keeper and his assistant making its way steadily towards a small piece of water at some distance. I measured the space between the tank and the spot reached by the fish, and found it to be a little more than 24 yards. The keeper informed me that when picked up the Pike had still plenty of strength remaining and was quite lively, and he had no doubt that, if left to itself, it would have succeeded in reaching its destination,—a feat, however, which it would probably have had reason to regret, as the water in question was nothing less than the *Otters'* pond.

Walton was too close an observer of the habits of fish not to notice the mysterious appearance of Pike in unstocked waters; but he was driven to account for it by adopting one of the many fallacies held by Gesner and his contemporaries. " It has been observed," he says, " that where none (Pike) have been put into ponds, yet they have there found many .... 'tis not to be doubted but that they are bred some by generation, and some not, as namely of a weed called pickerel-weed,—unless learned Gesner be much mistaken; for he says this weed and other glutinous matter, with the help of the sun's heat, in some particular months and some ponds apted for it by nature, do become Pikes. But doubtless divers Pikes are bred after this

manner, or are brought into some ponds some such other
ways as is past man's finding out, of which we have daily
witnesses."

The absurdity of Gesner's theory is sufficiently obvious:
it probably arose from the fact that Pike are fond of lying
in beds of pickerel-weed, and not unfrequently deposit
their spawn amongst it.

The notion, which is on a par with the popular belief in
chopped horsehair thrown into ponds becoming Eels, and
other similar superstitions, is alluded to in the 'Piscatory
Eclogues' :—

> " Say, canst thou tell how worms of moisture breed,
>   Or Pike are gender'd of the Pickrel-weed ?
>   How Carp without the parent seed renew,
>   Or slimy Eels are form'd of genial dew ?"

The most obvious explanation of the ' spontaneous breeding' of Pike would appear to be, that the impregnated
spawn is conveyed from one place to another by aquatic
birds, frogs, and other amphibia, either sticking to their
bodies, or swallowed, but undigested; but this would not
explain the discovery of full-grown fish under the circumstances before alluded to.

The sudden appearance of Pike at certain times is not
less remarkable than their unaccountable *dis*appearance
at others. There is no doubt that in seasons of great
heat or unusual drought, when ponds or reservoirs have
become rapidly dried up, the Pike that were in them
have vanished in a very extraordinary manner, and that

upon the return of the water they have been immediately found in apparently undiminished numbers. The phenomenon is not, however, confined to the *Esocidæ*; the same thing has been observed with regard to Carp and Tench; and it is a curious circumstance, of the truth of which I have been frequently assured by those who have witnessed it, that in New South Wales, where great droughts are common, the large frogs of the country will mysteriously disappear in the manner described, and cannot be found even by digging deep into the mud. Their croaking also, one of the most constant and striking sounds in Australian bush-life, ceases altogether. Yet on the first fresh of rain they at once reappear in their pools as numerous and noisy as before.

Sir Emerson Tennent, in his admirable 'History of Ceylon,' gives a highly interesting account of the fish inhabiting the tanks and reservoirs of that island. Many of these pools, he says, are twice in each year liable to be evaporated to dryness, till the mud of the bottom is converted into dust, and the clay cleft by the heat into gaping apertures. Yet within a very few days after the change of the monsoon the natives are busily engaged in *fishing* in these very spots. This operation may be seen in the lowlands which are traversed by the high road leading from Colombo to Kands, the hollows on either side of which, before the period referred to, are covered with dust; but when flooded by the rains they are immediately resorted to by the peasants with baskets, in which the fish are encircled and taken out by the hand. These fish are mature and full-grown; and the spots where they are thus found are in the interior, and too far from either seas or rivers to permit of their appearance being explained by the questionable theory of " fish-showers,"—even putting aside the conclusive fact that the adult fish, measuring from 9 to 12 inches, have been, over and over again, actually dug up at a depth of several feet from the surface. Mr. Whitting, Chief Civil Officer of the Eastern Province, was a witness on several occasions to these disinterments,—the buried fish being a species of *Anabas* closely resembling the *Perca scandens* of Daldorff. Yarrell's theory, therefore, that the reappearance of the fish is caused by the impregnated ova of one rainy season being left unhatched until the next*, cannot be admitted as accurate. The correct solution is doubtless that given by Sir Emerson Tennent. He considers that, as the water decreases, the fish seek relief from the heat by burying first their heads, and finally their whole bodies in the ground, gradually working their way deeper down as the moisture is dried up from the surface—in fact, that they ' æstivate ' in dry earth, as eels and other fish are known to hibernate in mud.

These burying-fish are by no means confined to Ceylon. They exist in the Gambia†, in the Mareb of Abyssinia‡, in

---

* British Fishes, Introd. vol. i. p. xxvi.

† *Lepidosiren annectans*, Linn. Trans. 1839.

‡ Quatremère's Mémoires sur l'Egypte, tom. i. p. 17.

Guiana*, Surinam†, and many other places; and Dr. Hancock, in a paper on the fish of Demerara, mentions a species of the Pike family, the Yarrow, which is remarkable for the same singular habit.

There does not appear, however, to be anything peculiar in the structure of the gills or fins of the English Pike to enable it either to exist for any considerable period in mud, or to travel overland from one pool to another. Such travelling-fish are found both in Ceylon and elsewhere; but in every instance it would appear that nature has given them peculiar organs or conformation to fit them for the performance of these journeys, which are usually undertaken in search of water or more plentiful food on the drying up or exhaustion of their pools. The travelling-fish of China, for instance, are in the habit of crossing the paddy-fields from creek to creek, sometimes many hundred yards apart; and this they effect, according to the Chinese, by means "of a kind of leg" ‡.

The American Flat-headed Hassar, again, a description of which is given by Dr. Hancock in the 'Zoological Journal,' makes, during seasons of drought, considerable journeys overland, marching in large droves at night, and moving (about as fast as a child would walk) by means of a strong bony ray in the pectoral fin. This ray it uses as an arm, or crutch, propelling itself, by the tail, with a

* *Callichthys littoralis*, Zoological Journal, vol. iv. p. 243.
† *Loricaria*, Sir J. E. Tennent's History of Ceylon.
‡ Kirby's Bridgewater Treatise.

series of small jerks,—its motion when advancing resembling it is said that of a two-footed lizard. The body of this fish is enveloped in strong plates, which, like those underneath the serpent, probably facilitate its progress; and the Indians affirm that it is furnished with an internal reservoir of water sufficient for its journeys, so that the body, even if wiped dry with a cloth, immediately becomes moist again. This assertion there seems to be no reason to doubt, as analogous provisions are observed in several other migratory species: one of the Flying-fish, and a species called 'Swampines,' belonging to the genus *Hydrargyra* (discovered by Bosc in the fresh waters of Carolina), are furnished with a membrane which enables them when travelling to close the mouth and gills, thus retaining moisture sufficient for short *trajets*. These journeys the 'Swampines' perform by leaps, frequently in droves of thousands together, directing their course with unerring instinct towards the nearest water, and furnishing, during their migrations, food for a vast number of birds and reptiles. Their organ of motion is a long rough-edged spine, situated as in the Flat-headed Hassar. The 'Dorcas' of Guiana*, and several species belonging to Siam†, also progress by much the same means.

Of the travelling-fish of Ceylon the most common is a sort of Perch, called by the natives *Kavaya*, which grows to the length of about 6 inches, having its head round and

* Sir R. Schomburgk's Fishes of Guiana.
† Sir J. Bowring's Siam, vol. i. p. 10.

covered with scales, and being furnished with strong teeth
or spines under the gill-cover. Aided by this apparatus,
says Sir Emerson Tennent, "this little creature issues
boldly from its native pools and addresses itself to its
toilsome march, generally at night, or in the early morning
whilst the grass is still wet with dew; but in its distress
it is sometimes compelled to travel by day, and Mr. E. L.
Layard on one occasion encountered a number of them
travelling along a hot and dusty road under the mid-day
sun."

Mr. Morris, the Government Agent of Trincomalee,
writing of these fish, says:—"I was lately on duty in-
specting the bund of a large tank at Nade-cadua, which,
being out of repair, the remaining water was confined in
a small hollow in the otherwise dry bed. Whilst there,
heavy rain came on, and, as we stood on the high ground,
we observed a pelican on the margin of the shallow pool
gorging himself; our people went towards him and raised
a cry of 'fish! fish!' We hurried over, and found numbers
of fish struggling upwards through the grass, in the rills
formed by the trickling of the rain. There was scarcely
water enough to cover them; nevertheless they made
rapid progress up the bank, on which our followers collected about two bushels of them, at a distance of 40 yards
from the pool. They were forcing their way up the knoll,
and, had they not been intercepted, first by the pelican,
and afterwards by ourselves, they would in a few minutes
have gained the highest point, and descended on the other

side into a pool which formed another portion of the tank."

Equally singular are the habits of some of the fishes of the *Lophius* or "Fishing-frog" family, already alluded to, which have the fins convertible into feet or paddles:

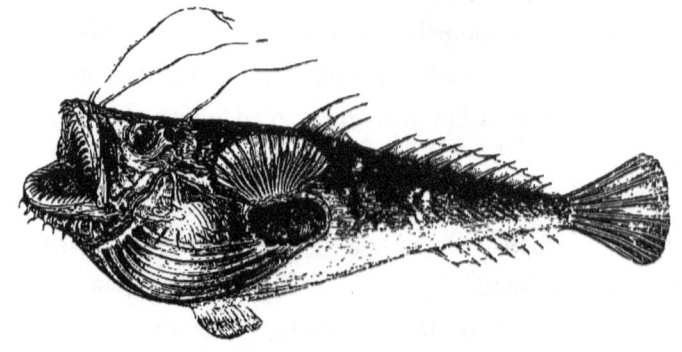

LOPHIUS PISCATORIUS.

by these they are enabled to crawl or flop about over sand and mud; whilst one species, the *Lophius histrio*, has been known to live for two or even three days out of water, and can progress upon dry land *. The Sargo, also, a native of India, which will exist for four or five days in a dry jar— and is in this manner brought alive to the Calcutta market —will travel considerable distances in damp weather, and is so frequently found leaping about in wet grass after rain as to have given rise to the notion of fish-showers.

Another curious mode of progression is that of a little

* Communication from Dr. Buckland to the Ashmolean Society at Oxford, June 1843.

fish (*Salarias alticus*), also a native of Ceylon, which has the faculty of partially ascending beaches and other steep places. This species darts along the surface of the water, and by a sort of wriggling motion of the body, with the assistance of the pectoral fins and gill-covers, scuttles up the wet stones with the utmost ease and rapidity, climbing the smooth surfaces of the rocks in search of flies, and adhering so closely as not to be detached by repeated shocks of the waves. It even ascends the roots of the mangroves with which the littoral of most parts of Ceylon is lined, and exhibits such nimbleness that it is almost impossible to lay hold of it,—scrambling to the edge and plunging into the sea upon the slightest attempt at molestation.

The most extraordinary of all these performances is that of the *Perca scandens*, or Climbing Perch, a native of some parts of the East, which not only travels overland, but actually ascends trees, in pursuit of the crustaceans upon which it feeds, having been taken at an altitude of many feet from the ground. The structure of this fish peculiarly fits it for the exercise of this remarkable instinct. Its gill-covers are armed with a number of spines, by which, used as hands, it appears to suspend itself. Making its tail a lever, and standing as it were on the little spines of its anal fin, it endeavours to push itself upward through the interstices of the bark by the expansion of its body, closing at the same time its gill-covers that they may not impede its progress; then, reaching a higher point, it opens them again. Thus, and by bending the spiny rays of its dorsal fins to right and left and fixing them in the bark, it continues its journey upwards.

As before observed, however, all these travelling-fish are more or less expressly equipped by nature for the purpose; and though I have alluded to them as examples, interesting in themselves, of the migratory instinct, more complete and corroborative testimony must be produced before we accept as proved the theory that any British fishes, other than Eels, are capable of similar, or even less lengthened efforts. But to return :—

Although, from its vigorous and unsparing destructiveness, the Pike has many detractors and few apologists, it must not be supposed that it is altogether without any of the softer instincts. On the contrary, it has been known to exhibit, under particular circumstances, a very decided amount of friendship, and even affection, especially in the conjugal form. An instance of this is on record, where a female Pike was taken during the spawning-season, and nothing could drive the male away from the spot at which its mate had disappeared; and the author of the 'Practical Angler' refers to a similar occurrence which happened under his own observation. The Pike has also occasionally exhibited considerable signs of grief at the departure of other fish from a vivarium in which they had been for some time fellow-prisoners.

I cannot here resist quoting an amusing account, given by Dr. Badham, of the uxoriousness of another predatory species, the Cossyphus—often mentioned by ancient writers on Halieutics :—

"The Cossyphus, according to Aristotle, makes the best of mates, 'una contentus conjuge,' as good Roman husbands in the olden time were fond of recording on their tombstones; but if so, Oppian has taken great poetical liberties with his reputation, describing him as the 'Great Mogul' of the deep. According to this author, he possesses an immense gynæcium, sufficient to keep him perpetually in hot, albeit in cold, water. Having found suitable *gîtes* for his numerous females, he ascends the waters, and from a transparent watch-tower looks down into their bowers, an open-eyed sentinel, whose jealousy day and night never remits, not so much as to permit him to taste food. As the time for expecting a new posterity approaches, his anxiety, we are told by his biographer, knows no bounds : he goes from one to the other, and back again to the first, making inquiries of all; but as the pains and perils of Lucina proceed, the liveliest emotions of fear and anxiety are awakened in his breast. As some distracted matron wanders in her agitation backwards and forwards, and suffers, by sympathy, all the daughter's pains in her own person, so the agitated Cossyphus roams incessantly about, disturbing the waters as he moves from place to place.

"The fisherman, tracking these movements, drops a live bait, properly leaded, right on the top of one of the ladies in roe; the Cossyphus, supposing this an invasion of his seraglio, flies at the intruder open-mouthed and is immediately hooked,—his dying moments being further embittered by cruel taunts from the trawler, who, after the insulting manner of Homer's heroes, reviles him by all his mistresses, and bids him mark the seething caldron on the lighted shore, prepared expressly for his reception. His favourites, on losing their protector, leave their hiding-places, and getting, like other 'unprotected females,' into difficulties, are speedily taken." *

The 'one virtue' to which, amongst a thousand crimes, the name of the Pike has been linked is gratitude: it has been asserted that he never attacks his physician, the Tench. To this subject I have already referred in the notice of the latter fish.

Superstition, which has touched almost everything sublunary, has not spared the Pike. Some of the qualities and influences attributed to it are not a little singular. Nobbes tells us that " his head is very lean and bony, which bones in his head, shaped like a cross, some have resembled to things of mysterious consequence. . . . If these comparisons smell anything of superstition, yet as to physical use those bones may be profitable: For the jaw-bone beaten to powder may be helpful for *pleurises* and other complaints; some do approve of it as a remedy for the pain in the heart and lungs; others affirm that the small bones pulverized may be fitly used to dry up sores; and many the like Medicinal qualities are attributed to the Pike's head. An ancient Author writing of his Nature of things,

* Fish Tattle, p. 27.

does discover a stone in the Brain of the Pike, much like unto a chrystal. Gesner himself, the great Naturalist, testifies that he found in the head of a little Pike two white stones. . . . Gesner likewise observes that his heart and galls is very medicinable to cure agues, abate feavers, &c., and that his biting is venomous and hard to be cured." (The latter assertion is undoubtedly true, as pointed out in its effects upon rats; but it is to be attributed to the punctured shape of the wounds inflicted, rather than to any poisonous qualities in the Pike's tooth.) Writing in the reign of Charles II., Siebald says that the heart of a Pike is a remedy against febrile paroxysms, that the gall is of much use in affections of the eyes, and that the ashes of the fish are used to dress old wounds. These, and the rest of his statements on medical subjects, have the formal approbation of the President and Censor of the Royal College of Physicians of Edinburgh *. Mr. Blakey mentions that the little bone in the form of a cross, already referred to, has been worn by the credulous as a talisman against witchcraft and enchantment, and that in some of the districts of Hungary and Bohemia it is still considered an unlucky omen to witness before mid-day the plunge of a Pike in stagnant waters †.

The roe of this fish provokes violent vomiting and other disagreeable symptoms ‡, and used to be included,

---

* Encyclopædia Britannica, vol. xii. p. 253.

† ' How to Angle and where to go.'

‡ Natural History of Fishes, by S. J., p. 67 (publ. 1795).

with that of the Barbel, in ancient Pharmacopœias. It was prescribed as an emetic, but its effects are stated to have been most deleterious; and an enthusiastic physician, Antonio Gazius, who tried conclusions on his own person with two small boluses, was nearly killed by the dose, and has recorded his sensations as a *caveat* to all future experimentalists.

The haunts of Pike vary considerably at different times of the year, and also vary with the nature of particular waters; but it usually prefers a still, unfrequented spot plentifully supplied with weeds and flags, selecting if possible a gravelly or sandy bottom. The neighbourhoods of reeds, docks, bulrushes, and the broad-leaved waterlily are its favourite resorts; and of these, a flooring of lilies, with from four to six feet of quiet current over it, and a wall of reeds at the side, springing from the bottom, is the best—

> " A league of grass washed by a slow broad stream
>   That, stirr'd with languid pulses of the oar,
>   Waves all its lazy lilies and creeps on. . . ."

Indeed, it may be said that the reed and the lily are to the Pike what the hollybush is to the woodcock. In lochs and meres, it commonly frequents the most shoal and weedy parts, small inlets and little bays, or the mouths of streams where minnows or other fry congregate; and in rivers, back-waters and dam-heads, eddies between two streams, or in fact any water that is weedy,

of moderate depth, and not too much acted upon by the
current. As a general rule, Pike will be found during the
summer in or close upon the streams, and in winter, after
the first heavy flood, in the large eddies and deeps. At
the latter season the fish feed best about mid-day, with a
breeze and a warm sun; and in the summer months, at
morning and evening, with a cloudy sky and plenty of wind.
A hot, sultry day is always inimical to success in Pike-
fishing; as also a muddy or flooded state of the water: a
full water, however, if not discoloured, is very favourable.

As regards both game and edible qualities the pond
Pike bears no comparison to its river congener, standing in
about the same relationship that the Pike of Holland does
to that of England. This distinction was once amusingly
illustrated by a fishmonger: "You see, sir," said he, " we
reckon it's pretty much about the same as the difference
between an Englishman and a Dutchman."

The British fish, however, differ materially in point of
excellence according to the quality of the water and the
nature of the food. Those produced by the Thames are
firm and of good flavour. " Horsea Pike, none like," has
been a well-known proverb for upwards of a century; and
the fish of the Medway, which, near the mouth of the
river, feed upon Smelts, are supposed to possess a particularly fine taste in consequence. Probably the worst Pike
are those bred in the Scotch lochs.

When in high season, the general colour of the fish is
green, spotted with bright yellow, whilst the gills are of a

vivid red; when out of season, the green changes to a greyer tint, and the yellow spots become pale.

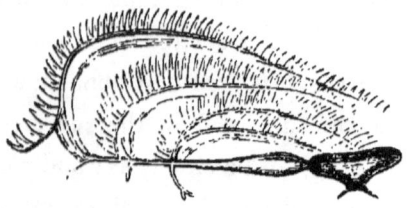

Section of the gills of the Pike.

The Pike spawns about March or April, according to the climate, forwardness of the spring, and other local circumstances,—the young females of three or four years old taking the lead, and the dowagers following. For this purpose they quit the open waters in pairs, and retire into the fens, ditches, or shallows, where they deposit their spawn amongst the leaves of aquatic plants; and during this period the male may often be observed following the female about from place to place, and attending upon her with much apparent solicitude. As many as 80,000 eggs have been counted in one fish. When the spawning-process is complete, the fish return again into the rivers, and are then for some weeks in a state of partial stupefaction, and unfit for food. In rivers they begin to be in condition again about June, and are in their best season in November; but in still waters the recuperative process is much slower. On the Thames, within the City jurisdiction, which extends up to Staines, Pike-fishing is illegal between the 1st of March and the 31st of May.

Principal characteristics of the common Pike.—Body elongated, nearly uniform in depth from head to commencement of back-fin, then becoming narrower; body covered with small scales; lateral line indistinct. Length of head compared to total length of head, body, and tail as 1 to 4. Back- and anal fins placed very far back, nearly opposite each other. From point of nose to origin of pectoral fin, thence to origin of ventral fin, and thence to commencement of anal fin are three nearly equal distances. Pectoral and ventral fins small; rays of anal fin elongated. Tail somewhat forked. Shape of head long, flattened, and wide; gape extensive. Lower jaw longest, with numerous small teeth round the front. The sides with 5 or 6 very large and sharp teeth on each side (see engraving at p. 206). Upper jaw somewhat duck-billed. Teeth on vomer small; on the palatine bones larger and longer, particularly on the inner edges: none on superior maxillary bones. Head covered with mucous orifices placed in pairs. Cheeks and upper parts of gill-covers covered with scales. Colour of head and upper part of back dusky olive-brown, growing lighter and mottled with green and yellow on sides, passing into silvery white on belly; pectoral and ventral fins pale brown; back-, anal, and tail-fins darker brown, mottled with white, yellow, and dark green.

Fin-rays: D. 19 : P. 14 : V. 10 : A. 17 : C. 19.

OMNIA VINCIT AMOR.

CHAPTER IX.

Series I. *BONY FISHES.*   Family *SALMONIDÆ* †.
Order II. *MALACOPTERYGII ABDOMINALES* *.   Genus *SALMO* †.

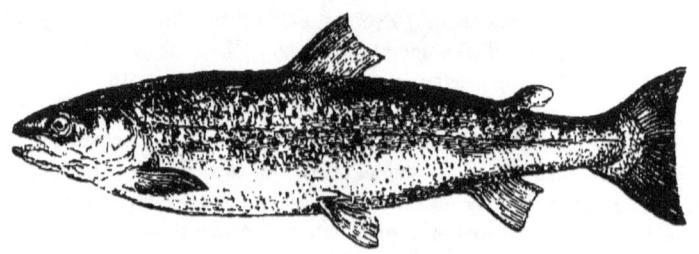

PARR, 1st state.   SMOLT, 2nd state.   GRILSE, 3rd state.

SALMON, all other states.

(*Salmo salar* †.)

Characteristics common to all the Salmon and Trout Family.—Bodies scaly; two back-fins, all the rays of the first fin soft; the second fin adipose or fatty, without rays; numerous gill-rays. Air-bladder large and simple. Form and arrangement of the jaws and teeth varying considerably.

WE have in Great Britain several genera of this family, of which the first genus (*Salmo*) embraces all fish following the common Salmon and Trout as their types. The characteristics distinguishing these species are,—the head smooth; teeth on the vomer ‡, the tongue, both bones of the palate, and on all the jaw-bones above and below;

---

* "Abdominal Soft-finned Fish" (see p. 37).

† *Salmo*, Lat. for a salmon; *salar*, having reference to the Latin *salarius*, of salt.   ‡ See p. 35.

gill-rays varying in number, generally from 10 to 12, but sometimes unequal upon opposite sides; a great part of the margin of the upper jaw formed of the maxillary * bones.

Until within the last thirty years very little was known of the natural history of the Salmon, the united lore of those most interested in the fisheries amounting to little beyond the fact that the fish ascended the rivers to spawn during the spring and summer—spawned—and descended again to the sea within the following two or three months.

Since the period referred to, however, and especially during the last few years, the researches of ichthyologists and the experiments which have been conducted on a large scale by enterprising and scientific men have thrown a flood of light upon the subject, converting doubts into certainties, theories into practice, and generally advancing our knowledge of the subject to a point which promises to be productive of most important reforms in the management of our exhausted Salmon-fisheries, and in the establishment of new ones.

Amongst those who have been most active in prosecuting these experiments, and in bringing their results prominently before the public, might be mentioned Mr. Hogg, Mr. Shaw, of Drumlanrig, Mr. Young, Mr. Ashworth (proprietor of the Galway fisheries), Mr. Yarrell, Sir William Jardine, Mr. Buist (who superintended the Stormontfield experiments on the Tay), Sir John Richardson, Mr. C. F.

* See p. 28.

Walsh, Mr. Buckland, Mr. William Brown, Mr. Ffennell (Commissioner for the Irish fisheries), Mr. Francis Francis, Colonel White, and many others, whose names will always be associated with the successful introduction of fish-culture into this country.

From the writings and experiments of these gentlemen, as well as from those reported from time to time in the 'Field' newspaper and other public journals, I have not hesitated to make use of such facts and illustrations as appeared necessary to place the subject clearly, and I trust comprehensively, before the reader. This object will perhaps be best effected by prefixing to any general observations a summary of the most important of what may be designated 'proved facts' in the natural history of the Salmon,—that is, facts no longer open to discussion, but admitted to have been actually demonstrated. They may be enumerated as follows:—

Proved Facts in the History of the Salmon.

1. Salmon and Grilse invariably spawn in fresh water if possible,—both the eggs, and the young fry whilst in the Parr state, being destroyed by contact with salt water.

2. The eggs are usually deposited on gravelly shallows, where they hatch in from 80 to 140 days, according to the temperature of the water. Eggs remaining unhatched beyond the latter period will seldom hatch at all, possibly from having been destroyed by the low temperature.

3. The eggs deposited by the female will not hatch under any circumstances unless vivified, after exclusion, by the milt of the male; and—at least up to the period of migration—there is no difference whatever in fry bred between Salmon only, between Grilse only, between Salmon and Grilse, between Salmon and Parr, or between Grilse and Parr.

[*Note*.—The female Parr cannot spawn; but the male Parr possesses, and constantly exercises, the power of vivifying Salmon and Grilse eggs.]

4. The fry remain one, two, and, in some cases, three years in the rivers as Parr before going down to the sea, —about half taking their departure at one year, nearly all the others at two years, and the remainder (which are exceptional) at three years old.

5. All young Salmon-fry are marked with bluish bars on their sides until shortly before their migration, up to which period they are Parrs; they then invariably assume a more or less complete coating of silvery scales and become Smolts,—the bars, or Parr-marks, however, being still clearly discernible on rubbing off the new scales.

6. The young of all the species here included in the genus *Salmo* have at some period of their existence these bluish bars; and consequently such marks are not by themselves proofs that fry bearing them are the young of the true Salmon (*Salmo salar*).

7. Unless the young fish put on their Smolt dress in

M

May or early in June and thereupon go down to the sea, they remain as Parrs another year; and without Smolt scales they will not migrate, and cannot exist in salt water.

8. The length of the Parr at six weeks old is about an inch and a half or two inches; and the weight of the Smolt before reaching the tidal wave from one to two ounces.

9. In at least many cases, Smolts thus migrating to the sea in May and June return as Grilse, sometimes within five, generally within ten weeks, the increase in weight during that period varying from 2 to 10 lbs., the average being from 4 to 6 lbs.; and these Grilse spawn about November or December—go back to the sea—and (in many cases) re-ascend the rivers the next spring as Salmon, with a further increase of from 4 to 12 lbs. Thus, a fish hatched in April 1854, and marked when migrating in May 1855, was caught as a Salmon of 22 lbs. weight in March 1856.

10. It appears certain, however, that Smolts do not always return during the same year as Grilse, but frequently remain nine or ten months in the sea, returning in the following spring as small-sized Salmon.

[*Note.*—It will thus be seen that the fry of the Salmon are called *Parrs* until they put on their migratory dress, when they become *Smolts* and go down to the salt water; *Grilse* if they return from the sea during the first year of their migration; and at all other periods *Salmon.*]

11. It has also been clearly proved that, in general,

Salmon and Grilse find their way back to spawn to the rivers in which they were bred—sometimes to the identical spots,—spawn about November or December,—and go down again to the sea as "spent fish," or "Kelts," in February or March,—returning, in at least many cases, during the following four or five months as "clean fish," and with an increase in weight of from 7 to 10 lbs.

[*Note.*—Shortly before spawning, and whilst returning to the sea as Kelts, or spent fish, Salmon are unfit for food, and their capture is then illegal. "Foul fish" *before* spawning are, if males, termed Red fish, from the orange-coloured stripes with which their cheeks are marked and the golden-orange tint of the body; the females are darker in colour, and are called Black fish. *After* spawning the males are called Kippers, and the females Shedders or Baggits.]

This, in a condensed form, is the present state of our positive knowledge as regards the leading facts in the history of the Salmon. They will be referred to more fully in the course of the following pages.

DISTINCTIVE MARKS OF SALMON AND TROUT.

The first points upon which the Angler will look for information are the number and names of the several British species of the genus *Salmo* (Salmon and Trout properly so called), and the distinctions by which each may be most easily recognized.

These I shall divide into three groups * :—

* This grouping commends itself not only by its simplicity and convenience of classification, but also by such broadly marked distinc-

1. The Silver, or Migratory species (*i. e.* those migrating to and from the sea) ;

2. The Yellow, or Non-migratory species ; and,

3. The Charrs, or Orange- and Red-coloured species.

Between these three groups no difficulty can well arise, the general colour of the first being always more or less greyish-silver, that of the second golden or yellow, and that of the third, especially on the under part of the body, crimson and orange of various degrees of brilliancy. Dismissing here, therefore, the last two groups, to be again referred to in their proper order, I shall restrict myself at present to the first group only—viz. the Silver, or Migratory species.

These are three in number; and they include, according to the opinions of the most eminent ichthyologists, the whole of our migratory *Salmonidæ*, under whatever local names they may occur.

They are :—

    The true Salmon (Parr, Smolt, Grilse)—*Salmo salar* ;

    The Bull-Trout (also called Grey Trout, Sewin, and
        Roundtail)—*Salmo eriox* ; and

    The Sea-Trout or Salmon-Trout—*Salmo trutta.*

We now come to the specific distinctions between these three fish, which, as their general colour and appearance are very similar, will be illustrated by reference (1) to the form of the gill-covers, (2) to the number and situation of

---

tions in regard to habit, structure, &c., as must override distinctions founded upon any mere technical differences.

the teeth, and (3) to the size and shape of the tail-fin,—in other words, by the principal organs of respiration, mastication, and motion, which are admitted to be amongst the most important and unvarying in piscine structure.

First, *differences in the form of the gill-covers* *.—These differences afford by far the readiest and most certain test for distinguishing between the species above named. They are so obvious, that, upon comparing the gill-covers of either of the fish with the figures here given, its identi-

Salmon.   Bull-Trout.   Sea-Trout.

fication must be a matter of ease. It may be remarked, however, that the hinder margin of the whole gill-cover in the true Salmon forms nearly a *semicircle*, whilst that of the Bull-Trout approaches more closely to a *right angle*, and both differ completely from the same parts in the gill-cover of the Sea-Trout. The position and shape of the several parts of which the gill-covers are composed also vary considerably, as already pointed out at page 52.

* The position of these is shown at page 30. They are often erroneously called "gills,"—the real gills, however, being the red spongy substance which they cover.

Secondly, *differences in the arrangement of the teeth.*— These will be useful to the angler principally as furnishing a ready means of distinguishing the Sea-Trout from the true Salmon and the Bull-Trout—the difference between the teeth in the two latter species being little beyond a question of size.

The distinguishing characteristic in the dental arrangement of the Sea-Trout is, that the teeth on the vomer, or central bone in the roof of the mouth (marked 1 in 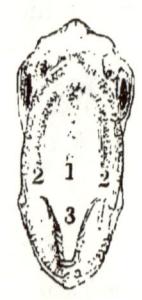 the engraving*), are more numerous than in either of the other species, and often remain, as here drawn, extending a considerable distance along the bone, whilst in the true Salmon and Bull-Trout they are almost all lost upon the first migration to the sea, only two or three being left on the most forward end of the bone; and these, in old fish, are frequently represented by a single tooth, or entirely disappear. Even in the Sea-Trout, however, the teeth on the vomer diminish in numbers as the fish gets older, and will often be found in a cluster only at the end of the bone; but they are always retained in greater numbers than in the true Salmon and Bull-Trout. The teeth generally, also, of the Sea-Trout are finer and more numerous than in the other

---

* The number of rows and general arrangement are very similar in the several species of the genus *Salmo*. For names of teeth, bones, &c., see p. 35.

two species, the Bull-Trout possessing the longest and strongest amongst the three fish, and the Salmon those of medium size—short, stout, and pointed.

Thirdly, *shape and size of the tail-fins.*—These are a less certain test than the teeth and gill-covers, as they vary much in different stages of growth; and, with the diagrams of the former already given, an appeal to them will be found superfluous. They are usually, however, as follows:—

SALMON.	BULL-TROUT.	SEA-TROUT.
Tail-fin deeply forked when young, less so at 3rd year; at 5th year nearly or quite square. ·	Becomes square at an earlier period than in Salmon, and afterwards gradually convex.	Less forked than in Salmon of same age; becomes ultimately square. Tail shorter and smaller than in Salmon.

The shape and position of the other fins also vary, though in a less degree; and as they may be sometimes found useful in deciding upon exceptional or doubtful specimens, they are given under the "Characteristics" at the end of the notice.

By a little attention to the foregoing points, and by comparing the gill-covers as shown in the engraving with those of the specimens in his basket, the young Salmon-fisher will speedily acquire a knowledge of the proper names of the several species, and be able to distinguish them at a glance*.

* It is suggested to the inexperienced angler, before starting on his

To induce the Angler to do this, by the avoidance of technicalities and by placing the subject plainly before him, is the aim of the present work; and if it should be successful only in a very small degree, it will have amply repaid whatever labour has been expended upon it.

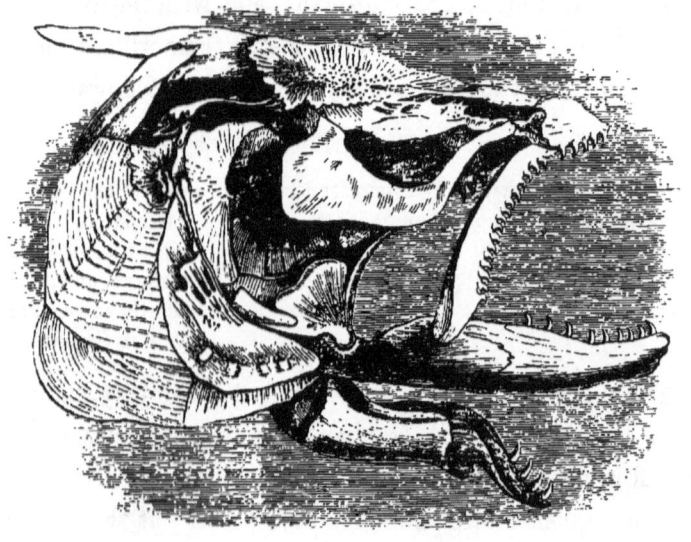

BONES OF THE HEAD OF THE SALMON.

first campaign, to visit a fishmonger's shop and there examine carefully the different fish, comparing their gill-covers, teeth, &c., with the illustrative diagrams herein given. This will probably be sufficient to enable him at least to recognize the three species when he sees them on the bank of the river.

CHAPTER X.

In offering a few further observations on the general history of the true Salmon (*Salmo salar*), I have adopted the sequence suggested by its natural habits, as likely to be that most easily followed and most convenient for reference. Thus, commencing with the ascent of the fish in the early spring and summer, its course will be briefly sketched from the tidal wave up the river to the spawning-ground, and back again to the sea,—the gradual changes of colour and condition being at the same time pointed out. Returning then to the spawning-beds, where the ova should be approaching the time of hatching, the growth and habits of the young fry will be traced from the egg until their migration to the salt water as Smolts, their subsequent return as Grilse, and, finally, as Salmon.

Ascent of Salmon from the Sea : Fresh-run Fish.

Sooner or later during the spring and summer months a proportion at least of the Salmon in the bays and estuaries of the coast make their way up the rivers for the purpose of spawning—their general colouring at this period being a brilliant silvery white, merging into a bluish black with a few dark spots on the upper part of the body and head. When first ascending from the sea, Salmon are termed "fresh-run " fish, and are then in the most perfect condition both for the rod and the table.

The marks by which a fresh-run fish may be known are, the bright, silvery hue of the belly and sides, and the comparatively loose adherence of the scales—more particularly in the Grilse. In the case also of Salmon just fresh from the sea, a species of parasite, or sea-louse, may be frequently found attached to the fish. These, however, are killed by a few hours' contact with fresh water.

In some rivers the ascent and spawning-time of the Salmon are much earlier than in others. This is often the case in rivers issuing from large lakes, in which the water has previously undergone a sort of filtering process and has become warmer, owing to the greater mass and higher temperature of its source; whilst, on the other hand, streams which are liable to be swollen by the melting of snows, or cold rains, or which are otherwise bleak and exposed, are later in season, and yield their principal supply when the great lake rivers are beginning to fail. Two of the Sutherland streams offer good examples of these operating causes. One, the Oikel, springs from a small exposed alpine pool some half mile in breadth; the other, the Shin (a branch of the Oikel), takes its rise in the deep sweeping waters of Loch Shin and its tributary lakes. The Shin joins the Oikel about five miles from the sea. Early in the spring, all the Salmon entering this common mouth diverge at the junction, pass up the Shin, and thus return, it would appear, to their own warmer stream, whilst very few keep the main course of the Oikel until a much later period.

A somewhat analogous effect, indirectly traceable to the same cause, has been pointed out by Dr. Heysham * as observable in several of the Cumberland † rivers. The Salmon, during winter and spring, evidently prefer the Eden to either the Esk, Caldew, or Peteril, although the Eden and the Esk pour their waters into the same estuary, and, in fact, are only separated at their mouths by a small promontory. There is hardly an instance, he states, of a Salmon entering the latter until the middle of April or beginning of May—a circumstance referred by the fishermen to the difference in temperature between the two streams,—the waters of the Eden, they allege, being considerably warmer than those of the Esk, which, from the shallow and rocky character of the bed of the Esk, appears not improbable. Be this as it may, it is an indubitable fact that snow-water prevents fish from running up even the milder stream of the Eden. The Caldew and the Peteril, again, pour their waters into the Eden, the one at, and the other a little above Carlisle; yet up neither of

* Catalogue of Cumberland Animals.

† In Cumberland, *Mort* and *Spod* are names applied indiscriminately to the Salmon and Salmon-Trout, the former term being used for fish weighing between 2 and 5 lbs., and the latter for smaller fish. (Dr. Davy, Angler in Lake District.) The fishermen of the Ribble in Lancashire call Salmon of one year old, *Smelts*; next year they are *Sprods*, in the third *Morts*, in the fourth *Fork-tails*, in the fifth *Half-fish*, and in the sixth and thereafter, *Salmon.* (Willughby.)

these rivers do Salmon ever run, unless at the spawning-season, and then but in small numbers.

The rule, however, which would appear to be inferred from the instances quoted is far from being invariable; and as it has been found that the time of Salmon ascending and spawning frequently differs in neighbouring rivers of the same district—in some cases even where their sources and channels are of a precisely similar nature—it is very possible that we have yet to learn the true cause of the variation.

The order in which fish ascend rivers is—allowing for the variations already pointed out—generally somewhat as follows :—

First come the strong, early runners. These are succeeded by the Grilse, and by the small "Spring Salmon" which have probably never ascended at all as Grilse, but have remained in the sea since the Smolt state—a period of from eight to ten months, as noticed in "Proved Facts," No. 10. The scales of these spring Salmon are not easily rubbed off like those of the Grilse, and their tails are not so forked. A few of them generally appear with the early-running fish. As the season advances, the larger fish and those heavy with spawn begin to work their way upwards from the mouths of the rivers and estuaries towards the higher reaches; and such fish continue ascending from the sea until the close of the autumn, or, if the river be an early one, of the summer.

Even as late as November and December, and the January and February following, a few fish continue to run which have been usually considered as " barren "—without capability of spawning ; but this notion has been proved by Mr. Ffennell * to be erroneous, as upon dissection he found that the females had ova in them perfectly developed, although not larger than mustard-seed, whilst in the males a thin thread of milt was always discernible. These fish, of which many ascend the Tay in November and the three following months, remain nearly a year in the fresh waters before spawning, and although their colours gradually become darker in consequence, they are to all intents and purposes " clean fish " †, and are exceedingly good eating.

The appearance of these so-called barren Salmon at a time when most fish are spawning, or are just recovering from the process, illustrates what I believe to be the most important fact connected with the history of the Salmon, and one which does not appear to have been hitherto understood, although following as a natural corollary to the propositions of Mr. Ffennell, and hinted at by Mr. Brown in his account of the Stormontfield experiments, viz. that the principle of a *divided migration* is not confined to the Parrs on going to the sea, or to the Smolts

* See Appendix to Report of Commission of House of Lords on the Salmon Fisheries.

† "Clean fish" is used as the antithesis to "foul fish"—a term applied to all Salmon which have either not recovered from the effects of spawning, or in which the roe or milt has arrived at a considerable degree of maturity.

on their return from it, some as Grilse and some as spring Salmon, *but that it also extends to the old and adult fish after spawning*—one portion of these latter coming back into the rivers during the following summer, and the rest not until the spring succeeding it; in other words (and this is the gist of the whole), that at least a proportion of Salmon *spawn only every alternate year* *.

The design of this law or instinct—which, when once apprehended, will be found to explain many of the perplexities in the history of the Salmon—is intelligible enough, viz. to ensure a supply of clean fish throughout as large a portion of the year as possible, and to enable each river to support the greatest stock,—a result which could only be obtained by such a provision as the above. It is also doubtless intended to ensure an equal distribution of the fish throughout the whole length of the river. These Salmon, by ascending thus early, before their spawn is at all matured, are vigorous, and able to overcome the obstacles in their upward course to the extreme sources of the river—to which those fish which remain in the sea

---

* An analogous fact was observed by Dr. Davy with regard to the spawning of the common Trout. Dr. Davy was in the habit of opening the fish he caught, and by this means he discovered that, as the spawning-season approached, only about one half of the females had visible eggs, whilst in the other half there were *no signs of the development of the ova.* Charr, also, are frequently taken in Windermere in high condition in October and November, which is their regular spawning-season,—a fact which would seem to point to the possibility of the rule of alternate spawning-years holding good in the case of all the fish here included under the genus *Salmo.*

until heavy with spawn could never penetrate. But to return.

During the early part of the season, the Salmon in the rivers, which do not at once ascend, remain in or near the mouths, most commonly advancing with the flood, and retiring with the ebb of the tide—unless captured by any of the contrivances hereafter mentioned; but as the season progresses they get gradually further into the fresh water beyond the influence of the sea, and at about this time will be found to be becoming full of roe, and more or less out of condition and unfit for food, according to their forward state as breeding-fish. In fact, the edible qualities of the Salmon when ascending rivers depend entirely upon the state of the development of the milt or roe. Even in the salt water this loss of condition follows upon the maturing of the spawn; and when fish are precluded from entering rivers by want of a rise in the tide, or other cause, the development takes place as in the stream, and the Salmon assume the reddish-coloured tints distinctive of spawning-fish.

With the approach of the spawning-time, the anxiety of the Salmon to ascend increases, and they shoot up rapids with the velocity of arrows, and make wonderful efforts to surmount cascades and other impediments, frequently clearing a height of two or three yards at a bound. It has been calculated that, when swimming, or rather darting at full speed, the Salmon will glide through the water at the rate of about 1500 feet per minute, or 2,160,000 feet (up-

wards of 400 miles) per day—a pace which, if it could be
maintained, would speedily carry the fish round the world.
Marvellous stories are related of Salmon-jumps, some altogether incredible, others, to say the least of it, highly
improbable.   No doubt the depth of the water from which
they take their spring materially influences its height;
but, as a general rule, the limit of the perpendicular leap
certainly does not exceed 12 or 14 feet; or, if they rise
higher than that, the effort is aimless, and they are dashed
down again by the current before they have recovered their
energy.   Frequently they are killed by the exhaustive
violence of their exertions, and sometimes they alight upon
the rocks and are captured.   This is the case at the falls
of Kilmorac, on the Beauly in Inverness-shire (forming
the head of one of the finest Salmon-runs in the North),
where the peasantry are accustomed to lay branches of
trees on the edge of the rocks, and thus intercept the
return of such fish as miss their leap ; and the same thing
is mentioned as taking place at the Cataract of the Lilley
in Ireland *.   The extraordinary exertions of the Salmon
to surmount the falls at the former spot have been graphi-
cally described by Mr. Mudie in the ' British Naturalist.'

This writer mentions that "amongst the wonders which
the Frasers of Lovat used to show their guests" was a
voluntarily-cooked Salmon.   For this purpose a kettle of
boiling water was placed upon the flat rock on the south
side of the fall, close by the edge of the water, and the

* Hartwig, The Sea and its Living Wonders.

company waited until a Salmon fell into the kettle and was thus boiled in their presence.

A curious leap was recently made by a Salmon in Dumfriesshire. Two young ladies residing in the neighbourhood of Thornhill were walking by the bank of the River Nith, when they saw a large Salmon almost stranded in a shallow creek. They walked into the water and succeeded in driving the fish up a sort of *cul-de-sac* from which there was no escape, and were stooping to secure it *when it sprang completely over their heads,* and falling on the dry land was captured and carried home in triumph. The achievement was, I believe, chronicled at the time in some of the local papers; but I can vouch for its authenticity, having received the account direct from the two principal performers.

The invention of ladders or stairs by which the Salmon are enabled to surmount high weirs and other obstructions is one which, if judiciously applied, is likely to prove of infinite value to the fisheries, and will, it is to be hoped, come into yet more general use. These ladders may be constructed so as not in any way to diminish the waterpower of mill-streams or lessen their supply — matters which have hitherto given rise to much dispute and embroilment between the rival owners of mills and of Salmon rivers. One form of the stair is shown in the engraving. A portion of the side of the dam or fall—properly that highest up the stream, as the point towards which Salmon naturally make their ascent—is partitioned off and inter-

sected at considerable distances by transverse steps of wood
or stone, each intersection crossing about two-thirds of the

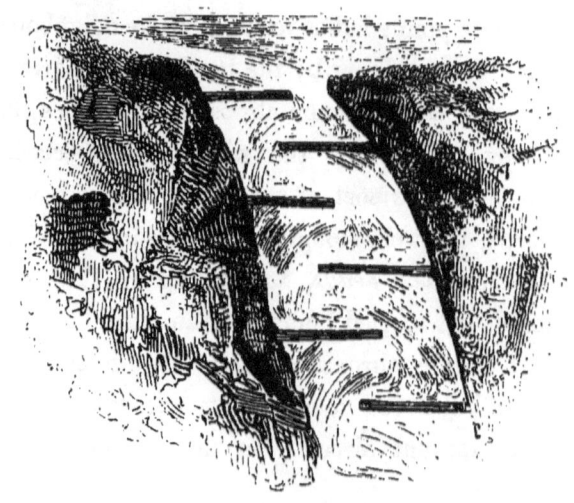

whole width, and the fish are thus, step by step, taken up to
a height of 30 or 35 feet, or higher if necessary.

One of the most singular of the habits of the Salmon in
rivers is that of affecting from generation to generation
particular spots, and even individual stones. Almost all
Salmon streams contain several such *gîtes*, known perhaps
only to the poachers of the neighbourhood, or local fishermen; and such is the partiality of the fish for them, that
if one tenant is caught, another almost immediately takes
its place, sometimes within half an hour afterwards.
When fish were running freely, I have known as many as
three to be taken in the same day from behind a single

stone. This is one amongst other reasons why no angler should ever, if he can avoid it, fish a strange river without a competent guide or keeper to point out the best pools and most likely casts; and when such a pool is reached, every yard of it should be carefully and closely fished over, if necessary with a change of flies, before it is quitted for less certain finds. In some waters, such as the Tweed, the minnow is occasionally more killing than the fly *, and in periods of summer droughts the worm is not unfrequently a deadly bait.

With the advance of the season the fish begin to gain the upper and shallower reaches, or spawning-grounds; and at this time all the Salmon and Trout species resident in fresh water, both migratory and non-migratory, acquire, in lieu of their brilliant spring tints, a dusky-yellowish exterior, accompanied by a considerable increase of mucus or slime,—the fins also becoming more muscular. As the important operation approaches, these colours undergo a still further deterioration, the general hue of the body in the

---

* BOB-FLIES or DROPPERS.—I may perhaps here mention incidentally a method of fastening drop-flies on Salmon casting-lines which I have found very successful, and which, I believe, is not generally known. The object sought to be attained is, of course, that the fly should remain for the longest possible time standing clear from—in fact, almost at right angles to—the line, with the least amount of knotting or thickening, and the greatest facility for changing. To secure the first, it is absolutely necessary that the casting-line should be *stiffened* at the point of intersection. This is effected by joining there two lengths of gut in a *single fisherman's-knot*, leaving about half an inch over at each end. The knot having been drawn straight and close, these two ends should be lapped down to the line with a few

males assuming a browner or more golden tinge, and the cheeks being marked with orange-coloured stripes; the lower jaw elongates, and a gristly projection or horn turns

---

turns of light-coloured silk, as shown in fig. I of the accompanying engraving; and the effect of this arrangement will be found to be that the casting-line at that point is trebly stiffened, with scarcely a perceptible increase of thickness or clumsiness. Over the central knot the loop of the drop-fly should be passed in the usual manner and drawn close (fig. 3 ⊛).

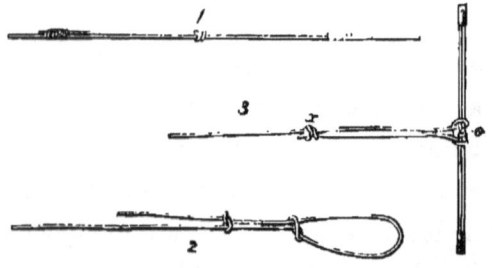

For the tying of these loops, and all others used in fishing, I have, I believe, succeeded in hitting upon a new and considerably improved form of knot,—the ordinary loop being both clumsy and crooked (a serious drawback to the perfect set of the fly), and, in thick gut, very difficult to manipulate. My knot (fig. 2, and *x* in fig. 3) is simply a new application of the principle of the ordinary single fisherman's-knot, thus: a half-knot is made, about an inch and a half or two inches from the end of the gut of the fly, *but not drawn quite tight*; the end of the gut is doubled over and passed back again through the opening on the same side from which the end issues; and then again, with this end, a further half-knot (embracing the main link) is made below the first. Both half-knots are then pulled tight, and drawn together. This produces the smallest possible knot, and one which will never draw and is perfectly straight.

Of course the foregoing knots, so far as regards flies, are only applicable to those used in Salmon or Sea-Trout fishing, or where very fine tackle is not essential.

upwards from the points, which is used by the Salmon as an organ of offence in its contests with other fish. In this state the males are called " Red fish," or are said to be "on the reds." The females are somewhat darker in colour, and are known by the name of " Black fish."

The Spawning-beds.

The usual time of spawning is from November until the latter end of January or the beginning of February; but there are exceptional rivers both earlier and later, as already pointed out; and it is probable that many of the so-called " barren fish," entering the fresh water in November and December, spawn in the succeeding October.

The process of spawning is as follows:—A pair of fish, male and female, select a gravelly shallow suitable for the purpose, which is generally occupied also by other spawners, both Salmon and Trout, as well as by a considerable number of male Parrs. These latter, as stated in " Proved Facts," No. 3, are perfectly qualified to continue their species, and they perform a most important part in the reproductive process; for the attentions of the male Salmon being constantly distracted by the necessity of protecting the spawning-bed from the intrusion of other fish, the ova of the female are during these absences vivified by the milt of the Parrs *. The female deposits her eggs in shallow furrows in the gravel, to which they adhere

---

* According to the experiments of Mr. John Shaw (subsequently confirmed by those at Stormontfield), male Parrs attain to the breeding-

by a thin coating of glutinous matter, the male at the same time shedding his milt over them. Whether these furrows are made conjointly by both spawners, or by the female fish only, and whether the snout or the tail is the organ used in the delving process, have been disputed points amongst naturalists. From the concurrent testimony, however, of those who have had the best opportunities of observation, it now appears certain that the trenches are made by the tail of the female fish only, and that the male takes no share whatever in the more laborious portions of the parental duties.

The only extra-matrimonial function that he performs consists in exerting an unwearied vigilance to protect his seraglio from the invasions of rival males, all of whom he assiduously endeavours to expel,—living, in fact, in a perpetual state of active hostilities. The female, regardless of the frequent absences of her lord during these contests, and probably satisfied with the presence of the male Parrs, proceeds with her operations by throwing herself, at intervals of a few minutes, upon her side, and whilst in that position, by a rapid action of the tail, she digs a receptacle for her eggs, a portion of which she on each occasion deposits, and, again turning on her side, covers it up by a renewed action of the tail; thus alternately

state in about eighteen months from the time of hatching. The females, it would appear, never become prolific whilst in the Parr state unless they are amongst the exceptional fish, alluded to in "Proved Facts," No. 4, which remain over the third year in the rivers before migrating.

digging, depositing, and covering ova until the whole are laid,—a process usually occupying a period estimated by different authorities at from 3 or 4 * to from 10 to 12 days †.

Although, as I have stated, the male takes no share in the drudgery of the *ménage*, his duties are of by no means a light nature; the conflicts with other males, if brief, are incessant; and it sometimes happens, when a rival is either very fond or very fierce, that the domestic supremacy is only to be maintained at the cost of a prolonged and desperate fight. A good instance of this is described by Mr. Shaw :—

"On the 10th of January, 1836, I observed a female Salmon of considerable size (about 16 lbs.), and two males, of at least 25 lbs., engaged in depositing their spawn. The spot which they had selected for that purpose was a little apart from some other Salmon which were occupied in the same manner, and rather nearer the side, although still in pretty deep water. The two males kept up a perpetual contest during the whole of the day for possession of the lists, and in the course of their struggles frequently drove each other almost ashore, and were repeatedly on the surface, displaying their back fins, and lashing the water with their tails."

Perhaps, however, the most graphic account of a com-

* Paper by Mr. John Shaw in the Transactions of the Royal Society of Edinburgh.

† Ellis, On the Natural History of the Salmon.

bat of this sort is the following, which I extract from
Mr. Newman's 'Zoologist'*:—"We have this week to
narrate a more remarkable occurrence, in the character of
the Salmon, than any we have yet had the opportunity of
recording. The facts are these :—While several cuttermen
of the Preventive Service were on their rounds the other
day, and patrolling along the Findhorn, between Glen-
ferness and Dulcie Bridge, they observed an unusual
commotion among the spawning-beds of the ford. On
approaching the spot, two large male Salmon were
seen engaged in mortal combat for a female. Never did
chivalric knights do battle for the hand of lady fair
more fiercely than those buirdly lords of the flood. The
tranquil bosom of the stream was lashed into foam by
the struggles of the finny antagonists,—the object of the
fray in the mean time beating silently about, ' spectatress
of the fight.' From the appearance of the stream—dyed
with blood, and gradually assuming its former smooth surface—it was evident that the contest was over. One of
the Salmon, at last, flounders on the surface—dead ; and
the victor, it may be conjectured, exhaustedly bore off his
prize.

"The men, who had the curiosity to watch the fight, as
a proof of their story conveyed the dead Salmon to the
nearest dwelling, that of Mr. George Mackintosh, March
Strype, near the entrance of the secluded valley called The
Streens. The victorious Salmon had torn off the flesh, or

* For the year 1847, p. 1650.

rather fish, along the back from head to tail, to the very bone. In the movement of Salmon-spawning, the males have often been seen chasing one another; but such a fray as this has not been witnessed by the oldest fisher or poacher on the Findhorn."

The weapon of attack in all these battles appears to be the cartilaginous horn or excrescence on the point of the lower jaw, which is used as a sort of battering-ram, the fish, as described by Mr. Walsh, rushing on open-mouthed, and turning on his side in striking. In the ease of the male fish being captured or killed, the female retires to the nearest large pool in search of a fresh mate, with whom she returns and completes the process of depositing her eggs*. This she will repeat several times if her partner be removed; and it is mentioned as a fact by Mr. Young* that nine male Salmon in succession have been thus killed from the side of a single female, who then brought back with her, as companion, a large yellow *Trout*. In consequence, we may suppose, of the arduous nature of his military duties and reddish colour at this period, the term 'old soldier' is frequently used to designate the male Salmon after spawning; and I recently examined an old soldier in which the whole of the back and head was one mass of scars and wounds. It is probably owing to these exhaustive contests that the finding of the male Salmon dead on the fords in December and January is a matter

* See Evidence before Committee of the House of Commons, 1824, 1825.

of frequent occurrence, whilst such a thing as a dead female is hardly ever seen.

The female, however, does not enjoy a total immunity from danger; she is especially liable to the assaults of that most terrible of all piscine foes, the Otter—an enemy who is particularly active at the spawning-season, when the fish are heavy and unwieldy with roe. An account of an attack by one of these animals upon two Salmon in the spawning-beds is mentioned in the 'Field' of November 15, 1862 :—

" Last week, close to the weir of Foxford, on the Ballina River, an Otter got into collision with two Salmon. The first he seized hold of; but after a severe struggle, lasting several minutes, it got away : he went in pursuit of the fish again, and met a second Salmon, which, after some hard work in a rapid stream, he succeeded in mastering, and carried to the weirs, where he left it on a wall. He then immediately returned to the spot where he had lost the first Salmon, and was not long before he found it ; and as it was not able this time to make any fight, owing to its previous injuries, he carried it off to where he had left the other on the weirs. Then dropping it, he commenced to eat the one he had first brought there, for no other reason, that I can see, than that it was the largest : just, however, as he was enjoying himself, a keeper arrived, and shot him. One Salmon was 15 lbs., and the other 9 lbs. in weight, male and female—both heavy in spawn."

RETURN OF SALMON TO THE SEA AS "SPENT FISH"
AFTER SPAWNING.

After spawning, the adult fish are for some time in a
very weak and exhausted state, and have not energy sufficient immediately to return to the sea.   They usually
drop down from the spawning-grounds, or 'redds,' to the
first quiet deep, where they remain until their strength
is somewhat recruited.   They then continue falling back
with the winter and spring floods, descending from pool to
pool, and avoiding as much as possible weirs and rapid
currents, until they reach the sea, where they quickly
recover their condition, to ascend again (at least in many
cases) in the autumn or succeeding spring for the same
purpose as before,—always remaining, however, for a considerable period in the brackish water or tideway before
making either decided change.

After the conclusion of the spawning-process, Salmon
are called 'spent' or unclean fish, or 'Kelts'; and at
this time they are quite unfit for food—indeed almost poisonous—and their capture is prohibited by law.   Spawned
male fish are also termed Kippers, and females Shedders
or Baggits—names by which they are frequently mentioned in Acts of Parliament relating to the Salmon-
fisheries.   Lately-spawned Kelts may be recognized by
their dark unhealthy colour, lanky flaccid appearance, and
by the enlargement of the vent.   Their gills also are almost
invariably found to be infested by a species of white worm*

* This insect, the *Lernæa Salmonis* of Linnæus, is improperly called

N 2

or maggot, which adheres firmly to the inside of the gill-covers, and from which they are released by contact with the salt water,—a similar release from other parasites being obtained on passing to the fresh water from the sea.

Within a period of five or six months after their return to the salt water, it has been proved that at least a proportion of Kelts find their way back to the upper reaches of the river as clean fish, having gained in weight during that time from 7 to 10 lbs. The Duke of Atholl has for some years caused all Kelts taken with the rod in his waters to be marked with a numbered copper or gutta-percha ticket fastened to the tail, stating the time when caught and the then weight,—the increase of weight attained being also noted upon the fish being subsequently recaptured. The annexed table exhibits the increase of weight in three instances.

CAUGHT AS KELTS OR SPAWNED FISH RETURNING TO THE SEA.		RETAKEN ASCENDING THE RIVER AS CLEAN FISH.	
1859.	Weight. lbs.	1859.	Weight. lbs.
No. 21—Feb. 14	10	No. 21—Aug. 18........	17
No. 76—March 2	11½	No. 76—Aug. 18........	17
No. 95—March 29	12½	No. 95—Aug. 12........	19

These figures speak for themselves, and show the folly of destroying, in a comparatively worthless condition, fish

---

a maggot, as, according to Dr. Fleming, it never changes its state, or becomes a fly. The most singular species of parasite to which Salmon are subject is the Lamprey or Stone-sucker, which in several instances, recently reported, has been found attached to them, having bored a deep hole through the skin.

which in so short a time would return to the same spot almost doubled in size and trebled in value.

Whilst descending to the sea in the spriug months Kelts are a great annoyance to anglers, as at this time they are ravenous for food, rising greedily at any sort of fly, and, though not so strong and obstinate as clean fish, often taking up more time in landing than can conveniently be spared. No one should, however, be permitted on any pretence to kill or keep such fish; and anglers using the gaff in their capture should be proceeded against with the utmost rigour *.

* The following question and answer on this subject recently appeared in the 'Field':—

"*Killing unclean Salmon.*—In the full season, with fair rod and line, a person hooks a salmon—his attendant gaffs it—and, on being landed, it proves to be a kelt, or old fish. Is the person, under such circumstances, liable to a penalty for killing an unseasonable fish? If he is liable, it must be always necessary to land your salmon with a large unwieldy net, and the handy little gaff can be of very little use; for it is to be presumed that very few people can distinguish between a kelt and a fresh-run salmon until they have landed him. The gaff, of course, always kills the fish.—CONSTANT READER. [The angler is unquestionably liable.—ED.]"

A further communication subsequently appeared in the same paper. The facts referred to are well worthy of the attention of salmon-fishers.

"*The Use of the Gaff.*—I would beg to call the attention of all true salmon-anglers to the necessity which exists for some legal provision against the use of the gaff in the early part of the season: there is such, I believe, in the Tweed Act. To prove this, I would mention that I have been out three times with the rod this season on two small rivers hereabouts, and landed nine large salmon, every one of them spent fish. Using a large landing-net, these fish were returned to the river unhurt; but had they been gaffed, nine fine fish would have been lost to all intents and purposes. I have heard since of some

That spawned fish improve greatly in condition before they leave the fresh water there is no room to doubt, although they are never really fit for the table until their return from their sea-trip. Mr. Brown, in his excellent little book, 'The Stormontfield Experiment on the Salmon,' from which I have taken the liberty of extracting the above table and much valuable information, instances a case in point:—

"On the 4th of May, 1861, we hooked a fish on the Stanley water, and, as the fishermen assured us the kelts had all left the river, we were flattering ourselves with the prospect of landing a fresh-run salmon. He fought well for liberty, and twice did he make his appearance, and was pronounced clean by the fisherman who had the gaff extended, when his eye caught the glittering copper medal attached to the tail. We ordered the gaff to be laid aside, but had to give the fish another run before it could be lifted out without injury. It turned out to be a male fish, and had a copper medal fastened round his tail, on which was stamped 'Atholl, No. 78.' He weighed 16 lbs.; and, but from being a little lank at the tail, might have passed muster for a clean fish (there were no maggots on his gills), as the fisherman thought he was until we showed him the

mere pot fisher having killed eleven fish in one of these small rivers, every one of them, I will venture to say, spent fish.—GEORGE MO-RANT, Jun. (Shirley House, Carrickmacross.)"

It occasionally happens that the gills of the Salmon are wounded by the hook, in which case the injury invariably proves fatal. This also holds good in regard to other species of fish.

vent, which was too much enlarged for a fish that had not lately spawned. After having carefully returned him to the river, we noted the number, and apprised the Duke of the circumstance, when his Grace was so obliging as to send us the following account of the fish :—

> "'Dunkeld, May 9, 1861.
>
> "'The Duke of Atholl presents his compliments to Mr. Brown, and is very much obliged for his civility in forwarding particulars of the capture of a marked fish. The Duke thinks it may interest Mr. Brown to learn that the Kipper No. 78 was caught on the 1st of April by Mr. Evans, above Logierait. It then weighed 13¼ lbs.'"

This fish had consequently recovered lost weight in the fresh water, since spawning, to the extent of 2½ lbs. in five weeks.

It is evident, therefore, that Salmon do, under certain circumstances, improve rapidly in condition before returning to the sea; and hence the expression, " A well-mended Kelt," which is common amongst fishermen. Kelts in this state are almost as bright and silvery-looking as the really clean fish, and are not unfrequently sold as such in towns; but the head is disproportionately large, owing to the body not being properly filled up; and upon opening the gill-covers, the white worm, before mentioned, will almost invariably be found adhering to them. When cooked, the fish emits a disagreeable odour, and as an article of food is unwholesome.

HATCHING OF THE EGGS AND GROWTH OF THE YOUNG FRY.

Leaving now the exhausted and more or less ill-con-

ditioned Kelts to recruit themselves in their salt-water
bath, we return to the spawning-bed where the eggs are
approaching the time of hatching.

Into this bed, during the preceding three months, a
dozen females have each poured the germs of, say, from
seventeen to twenty thousand Salmon *, which, if they
all arrived at maturity, would represent in approximate
figures some three million five hundred thousand pounds'
weight of wholesome food, or a money-value of about
£160,000. Unfortunately, however, the fry in fact added
to the stock of the river are a mere fraction, and those
that survive to return as Grilse a very trifling fraction
of these numbers. The latter have been calculated by
Mr. Brown at about one in every 1000, and by Messrs.
Ffennell and Ashworth at one in every *six thousand*, of
the original deposit of ova.

The causes of this destruction are numerous. From the
first laying of the egg until the plunge of the young Smolt
into the tidal wave, and even afterwards in the broader
waters of the estuary or open sea, a hundred wholesale
depredators lie in wait for it. First there are the shoals
of hungry fish of all kinds which prowl about the fords,
pressing close behind the spawner, and ready to fight for
the possession of her eggs almost before they are laid;
then come the voracious larvæ of the May-fly and Stone-

* Appendix to Report of Committee of House of Commons, 1824–5.
A thousand eggs, however, to every pound weight of Salmon is about
the usual allowance.

fly, the Water-shrimp, and a host of kindred insects, which work their way in amongst the gravel and destroy, perhaps less ostentatiously, but not less certainly.

If the egg escapes these perils, and having performed its protective mission releases its charge in due course, fresh dangers await the delicate and immature nursling: again, the trout and the wild-duck, and even the parent salmon themselves, hunt it out in its sheltering creeks and crevices; and hundreds of fry are daily sacrificed on a single spawning-bed by this means*: last of all comes man, who wantonly, either for amusement or for the sake of a single dish, fills his basket with produce which, if allowed to pass to the sea, would have returned in a few weeks worth a pocketful of gold. With these various enemies besetting every period of their existence, it ceases to be a matter of surprise that the percentage of fry attaining the Grilse stage should be as trifling as it is; the only wonder is that it is not still smaller.

Many causes of destruction, however, menace the ova of the Salmon besides those enumerated: a winter flood perhaps sweeps down the river, and buries a whole brood under a foot of sand-drift; not only the duck and the grebe, but all sorts of water-fowl and amphibia perform their share of the work of depredation; and though we know but little of the habits of the Smolts when once in

---

* A yellow Trout is now preserved in the Museum of the Literary and Antiquarian Society weighing 1½ lb., from the stomach of which ten full-grown Parrs and Smolts were taken.

the salt water, it may be conjectured that their adversaries here are not less active and numerous than those of the river. I have not included the Water-ouzel in the list of the undoubted riflers of spawning-beds. Formerly, from having been in the habit of watching them working about over the gravel of such spots, I was of opinion that their object was certainly to get at the eggs there deposited; but the recent examinations which Mr. Buckland has made of the crops of some of these birds—shot, as I should have said a few months ago, *in flagrante delicto*—without in any case discovering a trace of ova, lead me to doubt the truth of the allegations hitherto made against them.

The contents of the crop were, in every instance, found to consist almost wholly of beetles and other aquatic insects, which it seems probable were engaged in destroying ova at the time of being themselves seized by the Water-ouzel; but whether, in delving amongst the gravel for these insects, the bird does not at the same time expose the ova below to other enemies, appears to be a somewhat pertinent question. There is no doubt that the proprietors of the Spey salmon-fishings formerly rewarded the destroyer of a Water-ouzel with permission to fish during "close-time."

A remarkable instance of the havoc committed amongst unhatched eggs by the Trout was lately communicated to me by the Keeper of the Thames Angling Preservation Society at Hampton. When employed during the past season in procuring Trout-ova in a stream at High Wycombe, he observed a pair of Trout spawning on a shallow ford, and another just below them devouring the ova as fast as they were deposited by the spawner. The Keeper netted all three fish; and in the stomach of the third, which was in very good condition, were found upwards of two ounces of solid ova, or about 300 eggs. Some of these were placed in the breeding-apparatus, and have since hatched.

In striking contrast to this wholesale system of destruction must appear the exceedingly small percentage of loss attending the artificial impregnating and hatching of the ova as now practised on a large scale in many places in the United Kingdom and on the Continent. This percentage would seem to have reached its minimum in the present year's hatching at the Thames Society's Establishment at Hampton, where, as I am informed by Mr. Ponder, the able Superintendent, it has amounted to only three per cent. on the whole number of eggs introduced into the breeding-boxes. The young fry are carefully reared until they arrive at an age when they can shift for themselves, and are then turned into the river, thus escaping the thousand-and-one enemies to which they would be otherwise exposed. The consequence has been a very decided improvement in the Thames * Trout-fisheries.

* The Thames fishing can never do justice to the labour and expense bestowed upon it, so long as the present number of swans are maintained. The destruction effected amongst the spawn and fry by one of these mischievous birds would be hardly credited by those who have not had ocular proof of the fact from watching them at work on the spawning-beds. All anglers should unite to rid the river of these ornamental pests.

The other species of fish are also multiplying under the judicious management of the Society, to which the thanks and cooperation of all anglers are due.

At Stormontfield also, near Perth, the experiment of hatching and rearing the Salmon has proved eminently successful; for whilst between 1828 and 1852 the rental of the Tay Fisheries gradually declined from £14,574 in the former, to £7953 5s. in the latter year, since the commencement of the artificial breeding in 1853 it has been steadily increasing up to the present time, when it surpasses that of 1828—almost all the other Scotch fishings having fallen off rather than improved during the same period. The total cost of this breeding-establishment is, Mr. Brown states, about £50 a year. The above figures speak more eloquently than words as to the value of artificial fish-culture—an art which has been known and practised by the Chinese for centuries, amongst whom " fish-seed," as they term it, is a regular article of merchandise.

To revert to the spawning-beds.

In from 40 to 60 days after being first deposited in the spawning-bed, the egg begins to show faint signs of animation, and the eye of the embryo fish appears, a scarcely perceptible black speck, gradually increasing in size until the time of hatching—an event which usually occurs in from 90 to 140 days, according to the temperature of the water and forwardness of the spring *.

* This period is liable to great variations. The usual time in Scot-

The actual bursting of the young Salmon from the egg
is most interesting. The operation, which I have frequently watched, takes place thus:—The fish lies in the
shell coiled round in the form of a hoop (as shown in fig. 1

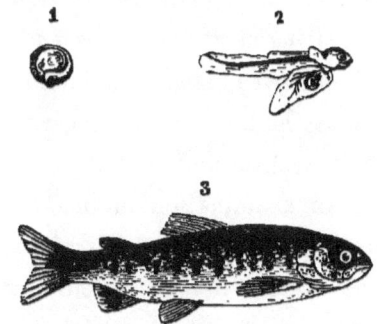

of the woodcut); and the greatest strain being at the back,
this is, of course, the first part to be freed. At this point
the shell splits across, and, after a few struggles, is completely thrown off with a jerk—leaving the red yolk of the
egg, by which the fish is nourished during the first five or
six weeks of its existence, suspended in a conical bag under

---

land is from 100 or 110 to 140 days. South of the Tweed it is often
considerably less. In water of the constant temperature of 44°, eggs
have been hatched in 60 days; whilst in some experiments made at
the Crystal Palace in 1859, several were actually matured in as little
as 30 days (see Report of Proceedings of Zoological Society for 1859,
p. 125). The effect of differences of temperature upon ova cannot be
more curiously illustrated than by a fact mentioned by Sir John
Richardson, viz. that if entangled in the hair of an otter, or in the
feathers of an aquatic bird, an egg may be carried from one pool to
another without detriment, whereas the heat of the stomach of a warm-
blooded animal would arrest its circulation and destroy it.

the stomach (fig. 2).   At this " bag-stage " of its development, the half-formed fry is exceedingly delicate, the dis-
placement of a stone, or the slightest bruise or injury,
proving instantly fatal. Its appearance is also very curious.
The future monarch of the stream is represented by a
mere ragged line, fringed at the edges and almost transparent, the head and eyes being prominent and altogether
out of proportion to the body, which measures only about
⅝ths of an inch in length, and is of a pale peach-blossom
or azure tint.   An examination of one of these newly-
hatched creatures through a powerful microscope exhibits
in perfection the system of the double circulation *, or
passage and repassage of the blood-globules through the
veins and arteries—a fearful and wonderful sight, which
seems to bring the beholder face to face with the great
mystery of life, in at least its visible aspect.

In thirty-five or forty days from the time of hatching, the yolk-bag disappears, and the fry becomes a perfect
little fish of about an inch long (fig. 3), with the fins separated and properly developed, and the tail deeply forked at
the end.   The general colour now also changes to a light

---

* The gills of fish represent the lungs of warm-blooded animals.
The blood, however, after being forced to the gills by the heart, does
not, as in the latter class, flow back again to the heart, to be thence
propelled throughout the body, but proceeds direct to the arteries lying
under the spine, and continues its course to the tail, gradually filtering
its way back to the heart, and thence to the gills, and so on in a continuous circle.   By this arrangement the fish is enabled to exist upon
the comparatively small amount of oxygen contained in the water—in
other words, becomes " cold-blooded."

brown; and the sides are indistinctly crossed by nine or
ten transverse dusky bars, or Parr-marks, characteristic
of all the species of the genus *Salmo* when in an immature
state, and which in the true Salmon remain more or less
visible even in a Smolt or Parr 6 inches long. If the scales
are removed, the marks are much more obvious. It has
been observed that this similarity of marking, or family
likeness, in the young of various species of the same genus,
however different may be the colours of the parents, is not
confined to Salmon and Trout, or to fish as a class, but
is equally noticeable amongst other classes of the Animal
Kingdom. The young of the lion and the puma are as
much marked for a time as those of the tiger or leopard,
or indeed any of the other felines, whether striped or
spotted; and the young of all deer are said, and many are
known, to be spotted, though it is also known that the
greater number of the adult animals are perfectly plain.
The differences in appearance, in fact, between the fry of
the Salmon, Bull-Trout, and Sea-Trout, and probably also
between the fry of the other species of the same genus,
are so trifling as to be scarcely perceptible unless upon very
close examination, and are, moreover, liable to constant
variations with local circumstances. According, however,
to Sir William Jardine, the fry of the common Trout (*Salmo
fario*) may always be distinguished from that of either of
the three migratory species by its having the extremity of
the second dorsal or adipose fin fringed with orange—a
mark easily identified.

Representations of the young of the Salmon, Sea-Trout, and Common Trout, as given by Mr. Shaw (the first demonstrator of the identity of the Salmon and Parr), are annexed.

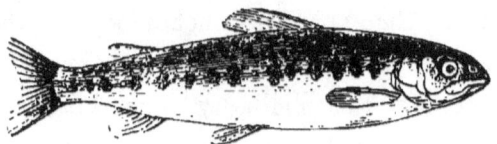

YOUNG SALMON.

YOUNG SEA-TROUT.

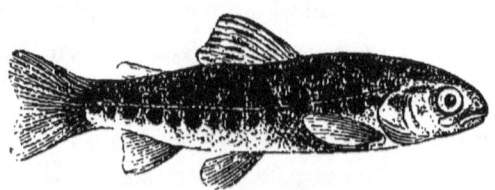

YOUNG RIVER- OR COMMON TROUT.

Up to the period of their first assuming the Parr-marks the Salmon-fry are unable to move about much, owing to the presence of the vitelline, or yolk-bag, which impedes their motions in swimming, and obliges them when at rest to lie perpetually on their backs, unless artificially supported. This support they seek to obtain by placing themselves amongst gravel or in crevices between stones, exhibiting generally a great desire to escape observation—an instinct given to them no doubt for their preservation during so feeble and helpless a condition. On the disappearance, however, of the yolk-bag they come from their hiding-places, and are to be found, on careful search, in the streams in or near which the old Salmon had deposited their spawn during the preceding winter. "Early in April," says Mr. Shaw, "I discovered them in one of these streams, but so young and weak, owing to their very recent emergence from the spawning-bed, as to be unable to struggle with the current where it flowed with any strength or rapidity. They therefore betook themselves to the gentler eddies, and frequently into the small hollows produced in the shingle by the hoofs of horses which had passed the ford. In these comparatively quiet places, and covered by a slight current of a few inches in depth, they continued, with their little tails in constant motion, until my near approach was perceived, when they immediately darted beneath the stones. They remain, with these habits and in the situations just mentioned, during the months of April, May, and even June; but as they increase in size and strength they scatter themselves all over the shallower parts of the river, especially wherever the bottom is composed of fine gravel. They continue, in truth, comparatively unobserved throughout the first summer, being seldom taken by the angler during that season."

At two months old the Parr begins to acquire a more
symmetrical form, and the disproportion in the size of the
head ceases to be observable; at four months the characteristic Parr-marks are clearly defined; and at six months
the fry has reached the length of from 3 to 4 inches, and is
the small-sized Parr so constantly found in salmon-rivers.
Extraordinary variations, however, are discovered in the
growth-rate of fish of similar ages and even belonging to
the same brood—a fact which, I believe, has not been
hitherto satisfactorily explained; and, within certain limits,
the fish of different rivers also vary in this manner not
only in size, but often in shape and colour, as much as do
the qualities of the streams themselves.   Examples of such
differences in form and growth are shown in the engravings
below.

In Scotland the general temperature of the rivers is so
low during the winter, and the consequent deficiency of

insect-food so great, that the whole of the *Salmonidæ* inhabiting fresh waters are well known to lose rather than
gain in weight during that season.

CHANGE OF PARR INTO SMOLTS, AND FIRST MIGRATION
TO THE SEA.

In somewhat more than twelve months from the time of
hatching—that is, between the middle of April and the
early part of June—about half of the last year's Parr
begin to assume the silver coating of scales preparatory to
making their first trip to the sea as *Smolts*. These silvery
scales, which form the distinctive mark of the Smolt
as distinguished from the Parr, are never put on except
when the fish is about to migrate; and without them it
will not migrate at all, and cannot exist in salt water, as
has been proved by experiment. The change commences
by the tail, pectoral, and back-fins acquiring a dusky margin, the whole body of the fish at the same time exhibiting
symptoms of a silvery exterior, with increased elegance
of form. When confined in ponds, the habits also of
the transforming fish undergo a marked alteration. As
Parr they show no disposition to congregate, each occupying its own place, and any intruder upon a post already
tenanted being instantly and forcibly expelled; but as soon
as the whole brood have completed their travelling costume
—an operation usually lasting two or three weeks—they
collect in a shoal, and show their desire to escape by
scouring over the ponds, leaping and sporting, and gene-

rally displaying a greatly increased amount of energy and activity. When their passage to the sea has been barred too long, Parrs in this state have been known to leap some distance on to the shore or barrier, and thus kill themselves.

It has been clearly demonstrated by the proceedings at Stormontfield that about one half the young fry migrate when about a year old—almost all the other half at their second year—and the few remaining at their third year; but the period of the descent is very generally the same in either case, and in all rivers whether early or late, beginning in March and continuing through April, May, and the early part of June—only a few fish continuing to migrate during the subsequent months. The length of the Smolt when migrating varies from $3\frac{1}{2}$ to 7 or 8 inches, according to age and other circumstances. Its full colours are, dark blue or bluish green on the upper half of the body and head with black or carmine-coloured spots, gill-covers and lower half of body silvery, and all the fins much darker than those of the Parr. The silver scales come off upon slight pressure, and the Parr-marks are visible below. (See also p. 241.)

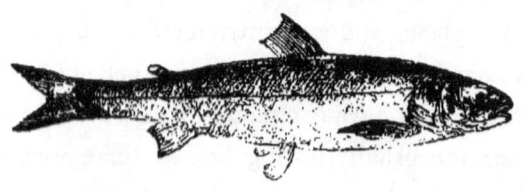

The engraving represents a Smolt from the river Thames,

where the fish was formerly called a Skegger or Scegger, and sometimes Salmon Pink or Brandling. "Lastspring" is also a local name for the Smolt.

When ready to make their trial trip, the Smolts assemble in sculls of from forty to seventy together, passing down the river at the rate of about two miles an hour,—according to some authors, in family groups. "The caution," says a gentleman who was a witness of one of these migrations, "which they exercised in descending the several rapids they met with in the course of their journey was very amusing. They no sooner came within the influence of any rapid current than they in an instant turned their heads up the stream, and would again and again permit themselves to be carried to the very brink, and as often retreat upwards, till at length one or two, bolder than the others, permitted themselves to be taken over, when the entire flock, one by one, disappeared; and then, so soon as they had reached comparatively still water, they again turned their heads towards the sea and resumed their journey." Thus resting in the slack waters, and at intervals braving the rapids and strong currents, they drop gradually down the river, unless on the occurrence of a heavy flood, which sweeps them at once into the sea. On meeting with the tide they remain for two or three days in the brackish water, to fit them for their change of habits, and then go off to the sea altogether.

What becomes of the young fish after reaching the ocean is at present a matter of conjecture. What we do know positively is, that in from six to eight weeks a number return to the same river with an increase in weight of from 2 to 5 lbs.*, and that many of the fry marked when migrating as Smolts in May and June, are sold in the London markets as Grilse in July, August, and September. It is a fair point for conjecture, and would be an interesting subject for future experiment, whether the Grilse returning the same season may not consist principally of the *two-year-old* Smolts, and so on; or whether, should this prove not to be the case, these older Smolts may not represent the larger-sized Grilse, and the younger fish the smaller ones.

Very small Grilse are sometimes caught; and the engraving represents a fish of the extraordinary low weight of 15 ounces. These Grilse, when weighing less than 2 lbs., pass amongst the London fishmongers and in some fishing counties by the name of " Salmon Peel."

* The following fish, marked as Smolts at Stormontfield, on their way to the sea in May 1855, were captured on their return as Grilse during the same year, at the times and of the weights stated :—

July	1	....	3	lbs.	....	July 30	....	7¼ lbs.
July	20	....	5⅓	„		July 31	....	9¼ „
July	21	....	5	„		Aug. 4	....	7½ „
						Aug. 4	....	8 „

Of the habits and food of the Salmon in its various stages whilst in the sea we know little. In his evidence before the Select Committee of the House of Lords in 1860, Professor Quekett stated it as his opinion that Salmon travel some distance along the coasts, and probably into deep water, in search of the ova of the Echinus or Sea Urchin—a species commonly inhabiting a depth of not less than from 6 to 20 fathoms. Professor Huxley disagreed with this view as regards the nature of the food, and believed that it consisted chiefly of a numerous class of small creatures * found in semisolid masses upon the surface frequently of deep water—in fact, that the Salmon swims in a species of animal-soup, in which it has merely to open its mouth and swallow what enters it. Dr. Knox was of opinion that the food consisted of the ova of various kinds of *Echinodermata* (Star-fish, Sea Urchins, Encrinites, &c.) and some of the *Crustacea* (Crab and Lobster family). Faber, in his ' Natural History of the Fish of Ireland,' says, " The common Salmon feeds on small fishes and various small marine animals." Dr. Fleming and several other naturalists have observed upon their partiality for the Sand-eel or Sand-launce—a fact which is confirmed by Sir John Richardson, who states that he has himself taken this fish from their stomach. Sir William Jardine also says that in the north of Sutherland a mode of salmon-fishing is successfully practised in the firths with Sand-eels attached to a buoy or bladder and allowed to float with

* Entomostracous Crustacea.

the tide up the narrow estuaries. The worm, the minnow, and Parr-tail are all, under certain circumstances, known to be deadly baits for the Salmon; and in an essay published in the Transactions of the Highland Society, vol. ii. p. 392, Mr. Alex. Morrison says, "I have taken Salmon within flood-mark, some of which had two, and others three full-sized herrings in their stomachs."

Judging from the perfect arrangement of its teeth and the known habits of its allied species, there can be no doubt that the Salmon is a very voracious feeder,—although the very small amount of food usually found in the stomach has been hitherto a source of difficulty in ascertaining its exact nature. The singularity of this latter circumstance was recently the subject of an interesting correspondence in the 'Field,' in which it was suggested, amongst other less probable explanations, that the gastric juice of the fish was so powerful as to dissolve almost instantaneously whatever was subjected to its action,—another hypothesis being that the fish ejects its food on finding itself hooked or netted. Alluding to these points, Mr. Buckland says,—

"'Waltonian's' observation is very important. It goes to prove that the gastric juice of the Salmon is so highly solvent of animal matter, that digestion goes on very rapidly, and that hence actual food is rarely found in their stomachs. Reasoning from analogy, one would think this likely : the digestion of many kinds of swift-flying birds is very rapid, the reason possibly being that a full stomach would add weight to the body and prevent rapid flight. Why may not this law apply also to fish? Again, many birds, especially carnivorous, have the power of emptying their stomachs by vomiting when danger is near and their activity is to be called into play. Is it not possible that Salmon too may have the power of ejecting their food when they find themselves in trouble either by hook or net?"

A writer in No. 87 of 'Once a Week' says:—"My friend, Mr. Walter Campbell, informed me that he once had a wonderful haul of Salmon at Islay, in an estuary of the sea. He landed 716, and many of them escaped. As the net approached the shore *he saw the fish discharging the contents of their stomachs*, which consisted of small eels."

Be this as it may, one point is certain, viz. that such a marvellously rapid growth as that shown to take place in the Salmon can only be produced by a corresponding supply of nutritious food; and as regards the travelling or otherwise of the fish in the sea, the thousands of Salmon constantly taken in nets along all parts of our coasts are a clear proof that they do rove, at least to considerable distances, from their native rivers and estuaries. From the observations of Sir William Jardine and Dr. Heysham it would appear probable that, when the fish happen to have thus wandered beyond their usual limits, they will at the proper season run up the first stream they meet with, the temperature and condition of which are congenial.

A remarkable instance of the return of Salmon to their own rivers or localities was witnessed in the case of some streams of Sutherland.   The circumstances were as follows :—

" Loch Shin, a piece of water about 20 miles by 14, situate in the heart of the Sutherlandshire mountains, is the immediate feeder of the river Shin, noted for the abundance of its Salmon.   The loch itself has four feeders, middling-sized rivers—viz. the Ferry, Fiack, Garvy, and Curvy—in which, previously to the year 1836, not a Salmon was ever seen, though many were in the habit of entering the loch or lake.   In the year mentioned, at the request of the Duke of Sutherland and Mr. Loch, M.P., Salmon were caught in the river Shin, shortly before the spawning season, and conveyed to the four rivers above named, amongst which they were distributed in due proportion. Mr. Andrew Young, the Duke's Salmon-factor, and our best natural historian of Salmon, was the managing director on the occasion.   In the winter season all the fish spawned, each in the river into which it was put.   Now mark one of the consequences : Salmon at present, and ever since, come regularly to spawn in all those heretofore salmonless rivers, traversing the lake, &c. to do so.   Nay, more ; the fish hatched in the Ferry—at least those that survive long enough—return to the Ferry ; and the fry of the other three rivers return from the sea to them, each Grilse or Salmon entering never-failingly the actual stream that gave it birth.   What wonderful and unerring instinct !

One might think that they would remain in the river Shin, and spawn where their first ancestors had spawned ; but no, they leave their own natal shallows, pass down the lake, through the river Shin, along the Kyle of Sutherland, to the sea, and there having become adolescent, in three months or so they retrace their route, and, after necessary rests on their long voyage, revisit for the first time, but not for the last, if they survive, the scenes of their birth and infancy." *

During their sojourn in the sea after the first spawning, the growth of the Grilse is exceedingly rapid, a considerable proportion at least of such fish returning to the river in the summer and autumn with an increase in weight of from 5 to 9 lbs.   In twelve Grilse of 4 lbs. each which were carefully marked by Mr. Young when descending to the salt water, this was found to be the average increase on their return during the same season.

Whether the growth-rate is as rapid in the after-stages of their existence we have no accurate means at present of judging ; but reasoning from analogy it would appear probable that it decreases somewhat with the advancing age of the fish, and in very old specimens is perhaps comparatively trifling.   Of such Salmon, the largest recorded to have been captured in British waters was a female fish of the weight of 83 lbs., which was exposed for sale in the shop of a London tradesman in the year 1821.   Another of 74 lbs. is alluded to by Pennant ; and Mr. T. Grove,

* Ephemera, 'The Book of the Salmon.'

the well-known fishmonger, of Parliament Street, informs me that he has had Salmon in his possession weighing upwards of 60 lbs. Salter, in one of his works on Angling, refers to the capture of a Salmon of 70 lbs. in the Thames near Laleham in the year 1789, which was subsequently sold to Mr. Howel, a fishmonger in the Minories, for a shilling a pound. The fact of the taking of this fish is confirmed by Mr. Wright, who says that he went off in a boat to see it, and found it "enveloped in nets between two punts which were kept apart by short spars lashed head and stern."

Some very large Salmon have been occasionally caught with the rod. One is noticed by Mr. Lascelles, as taken in Scotland, which weighed 54½ lbs.* The late Sir Hyde Parker captured one in Sweden weighing 60 lbs. A Salmon was caught by Sir H. Davy above Yairbridge in the Tweed, of the weight of 42 lbs.† ; and a former Earl of Home took another from the same waters of the unequalled weight of 70 lbs. within a few ounces.

Not a little singular are the chances by which Salmon and other fish are occasionally killed. A few years ago an 8-lb. Salmon was caught on a light trouting-rod through the casting-line having formed a running noose round its tail; and the same thing has also occurred in several instances with Trout and Chub. I once knew a Pike of 9 lbs. weight taken by the gimp of a spinning-trace twist-

---

* Letters on Sporting, Part i. p. 21.
† Stoddart's Art of Angling in Scotland.

ing fast round the neck behind the gill-covers; and in the Orchy, above Dalmally, an angler caught on one occasion a large Trout, owing to its having swallowed, and apparently been unable to disgorge, a Parr which had taken the fly and was being landed.

But perhaps a still more curious circumstance is the following capture of a Salmon, witnessed during the past season (1862) in the Galway River by Mr. Andrew, of Weybridge, who has kindly furnished me with the particulars:—"When fishing in Ireland during the present year, I was witness to an extraordinary occurrence, viz. a Salmon which had been hooked and played for a considerable time, taking a *second* fly. A Mr. Knowles was wading on one side of the Galway River, and Captain Laurie was fishing from the opposite bank; the former hooked a Salmon and had played it some minutes, at least 40 yards of line being run out, when it suddenly made a dart across the river and took Captain Laurie's fly. Supposing that he had hooked the fish foul, Captain Laurie gave line, and the Salmon was eventually gaffed on Mr. Knowles's side of the river, when it was found that both flies were hooked well in the inside of the mouth in the same corner,—the fly first taken being nearest the lip, and the second a little further down in the mouth. The fish weighed between 10 and 11 lbs."

In a subsequent note Mr. Andrew says, "I have since heard of an occurrence still more singular than that before mentioned—a Salmon taking two shrimp-baits, the second when actually beaten *and just coming under the gaff.*"

Sir William Jardine also gives an instance of rapacity in the Salmon, which confirms the view before expressed as to the voracious feeding-habits of the fish:—

"The fisherman who rents this part of the Tweed, fishing with worms one day last week, had his hooks and tackle taken away by a fish. He put on a new set, and again hooked and killed a Salmon with the former hooks and bait in its jaws. This will prove either extreme voracity in the fish, or little sensibility in the parts of the mouth. I have often before heard fishermen mention analogous facts, but never before knew an instance on which I could depend." *

Both Salmon and Sea-Trout will frequently take the fly or bait not only in brackish water, but in the open sea.

Much controversy and many experiments have been devoted to the question, "Will Salmon live and thrive entirely in fresh water—that is, in lakes or ponds which have no communication with the sea?" The answer appears to be in the negative, so far as all practical purposes are concerned. It has been proved that the fish will so far increase under these conditions as to attain a maximum weight of a few pounds; but the flesh of such fish is comparatively white and insipid, and as an article of food altogether different from that of the sea-bred Salmon.

* Letter to Dr. Richardson, dated St. Boswells, April 15, 1835.

SALMON-TRAPS, NETS, ETC.

The woodcut gives a sectional view of the form of that most deadly of all salmon-traps, the Stake-Net,—the hoop-

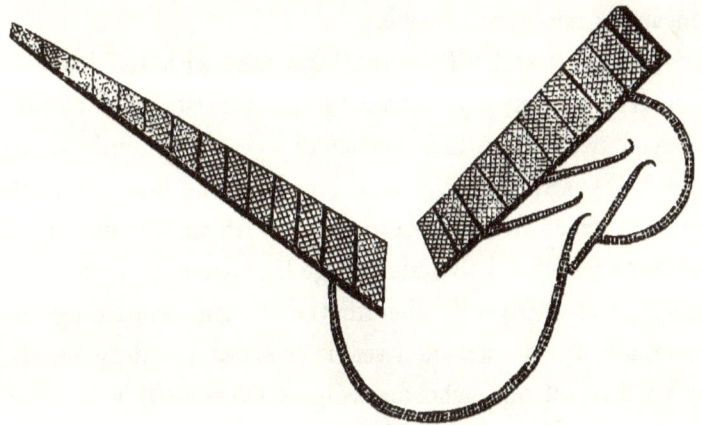

like curve underneath (here represented by a black line) being a sort of network *cul-de-sac* into which the Salmon are guided by the two wings. This 'fixed engine,' which is now fortunately illegal over most parts of Great Britain, is constructed on the shores of estuaries and tidal waters between high- and low-water marks, the concavity of the net being exposed to the flood or ebb tide as the case may be. Frequently double sets of these nets are erected, so as to catch the Salmon both in their ascent and descent.

The "Cruive," another destructive poaching contrivance, is a partially enclosed space built in the wall of a dam or weir, and through which the water passes; the fish as they push up the stream enter this aperture, and, having entered, are prevented by a peculiar contrivance from getting back again.   Escaping these dangers, the Salmon are very likely to be caught in the seins, or drag-nets, with which the open reaches of the river are incessantly swept by means of boats called cobles.

"Halves" and "Bag-nets" are used with the hand in estuaries or tideways.   The former consists of a funnel-shaped net ending in a pocket or bag—the mouth of the net being stretched upon an oblong frame about 3 yards wide attached to a pole or handle. With the flowing of the tide, a number of halve-men range themselves in a close line across the sands with the mouths of their nets facing the current: as the stream rises, it becomes too deep for the man furthest out, who accordingly takes up his net and places himself at the inside extremity of the line—and so on in rotation. On the halve-net being entered by a Salmon, the mouth is immediately raised above water so as to prevent the fish's retreat.   Bag-nets are worked in a somewhat similar manner, by being dropped from stages or platforms projected into the tideway : in this case the fishermen are generally concealed by hurdles.   In Wales a species of net is commonly used termed a "Trammel" or "Horn-net," which is drawn down stream between two Coracles—a small description of boat formed of basket-work and covered with painted canvas or other waterproof material, and light enough to be readily carried on the shoulders.

The assistance of dogs is sometimes found very useful in

netting for Salmon. In the neighbourhood of Hawick, a gang of salmon-poachers, afraid of taking the water on frosty nights, have taught a dog to swim across the river

THE CORACLE.

with a cord in his mouth, which he delivers to a man stationed on the opposite side; the net is then dragged over, the end of the cord again given to the dog, who re-crosses the river with it, and, both ends of the line being thus in the hands of the netters, a clean sweep is made.

In the Correspondence of the Rev. William Hamilton *

* Letters concerning the Natural History of Basalts on the Coast of Antrim.

an interesting account is given of the sagacity of a dog whilst aiding netters in shallow water. The dog takes his post on a ford, or scour, where the current is not very deep, at some distance below the fishermen : if a Salmon escape the net, it makes a shoot down the river in the direction of the sea; and the dog, who has perceived its approach by the ripple on the water, endeavours by every means in his power either to turn it back again or to catch it. Failing in these attempts he at once quits the water, in which the pace of the fish is too much for him, and runs at full speed along the bank to intercept it at the next shallow ford, where another opportunity and a second persevering attempt occur.

In some parts of Wales dogs are occasionally put in requisition by the Salmon-fishermen, appearing to take the greatest pleasure in the pursuit, and exhibiting by turns the most patient watchfulness, energy, or sagacity, as either quality may best advance their masters' interests. "Where the rivers are narrow," says Sir John Richardson, " and the Salmon are caught in a net drawn by men on either bank, dogs are trained to swim over from side to side with the head- and ground-lines of the net, as required. From a correspondent in Devonshire I learn that a clever poacher at Totness, on the Dart, admitted that he had killed many Salmon in the night by setting a trammel, or three-wall net, at the lower end of the deep pools in the river Dart and sending in a dog at the upper end, which dog he had trained to dive like an otter. The Salmon, as soon as the dog dived, immediately dashed into the stream, and were taken in the trammel-net at the lower end of the pool."

Poaching-dogs 'on their own account' are not very uncommon. I have elsewhere alluded to one which regularly depopulated the Lagan mill-stream of its Gudgeon; and the following instance of a notorious Salmon-poacher is mentioned by Lord Home:—

"My uncle who took the 70-lb. Salmon had a Newfoundland dog which was celebrated for catching these fish. He knew the Monday mornings as well as the fishermen themselves, and used to go to the cauld or mill-dam at Fireburn Hill on those days. He took his station on the 'cauld slap,' or opening in the dam by which the Salmon passed up, and has been known to kill from twelve to twenty Salmon in a morning. The fish he carried to the side."

The best part of the story remains to be told. The then Lord Tankerville instituted a Process against the dog, and the case was brought before the Court of Cession,—the indictment being entitled "The Earl of Tankerville versus a Dog, the property of the Earl of Home." Judgment was given in favour of the dog.

This take of "twenty fish in a morning" must certainly have been in the palmy days of the Salmon. By continuing, however, the course of sound legislation lately commenced for their protection and fostering, and especially by the rigorous abolition of all stake-nets, cruives, and other fixed engines, there is no reason why the royal fish * should not again become as cheap in our markets as any other description of food. The Acts of the last three years have come just in time to prevent the final destruction of the fisheries, and to arrest a deterioration which otherwise bade fair to reduce the Sovereign of the British Islands to the necessity of imitating the Scythian queen who prohibited her subjects from eating a particular fish " because there would not be enough left to regale their monarch."

SHOOTING A SEIN NET.

In addition to the family and generic distinctions given at page 238, the Principal Characteristics of the True Salmon are :—

Length of head compared to whole length of fish as 1 to 5. Body elongated ; dorsal and abdominal line about equally convex; lateral line near middle of body, dividing it about equally. Fleshy portion of tail slender. Scales moderate-sized, oval, and thin, easily removed when young, adherent when old. Teeth stout, pointed, and curved, one line on each side of upper jaw, one line on each bone of palate, one line on vomer or central bone in roof of mouth when quite young (loses a large portion on first visit to salt water, and gradually all, or all but one or two on most forward point of bone), one line on each side

* The Salmon-fisheries of the United Kingdom vest in the Crown as a royal prerogative.

of lower jaw, one line ou each side of tongue (occasionally two lines on each side of tongue). See also p. 246 for differences between teeth in Salmon, Sea-Trout, and Bull-Trout. For distinctive shape of gill-covers in the three species, see p. 245; and for shape of tail-fins at various ages in the same, p. 247. Relative position of other fins :—

SALMON.	BULL-TROUT.	SEA-TROUT.
Dorsal fin : — Hiuder origin about half-way between point of uose and end of tail-fin. Third ray longest.	Commences about half-way between point of nose and origin of upper tail-fin rays. Base of dorsal longer than longest ray.	Hinder origin exactly half-way between point of nose and end of tail-fin. Second ray longest, same length as base of fin.
Adipose fin :—Hinder origin half-way between origin of last back-fin ray and end of tail-fin.	Nearer to end of tail-fin than to origin of last dorsal fin ray.	Half-way between origin of last ray of back-fin and end of tail-fin.

To the above it may be added, that in the Salmon the pectoral fin equals two-thirds of length of head, whilst in the Bull-Trout it equals little more than half,—the anal fin also in the former commencing about halfway between origin of ventral fins and origin of lower tail-fin rays, and in the latter nearer to the tail. Colours of Salmon : as Parr, see p. 279; as Smolts, p. 283–4; as Grilse and Salmon when in condition, p. 249; when out of condition, (*before* spawning) p. 260, (*after* spawning) p. 267; as 'well-mended Kelts,' p. 271.

Fin-rays: D. 13 : P. 12 : V. 9 : A. 9 : C. 19. Vertebræ, 60.

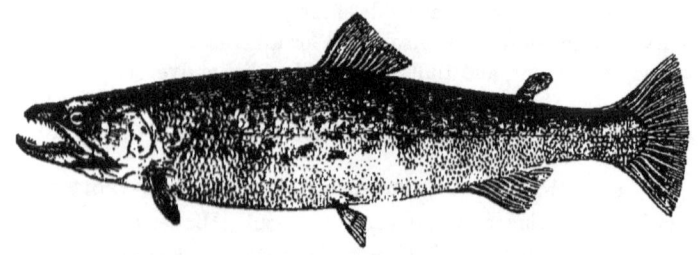

THE BULL-TROUT.

(Grey-Trout, Sewin, or Roundtail.)

(*Salmo eriox* *.)

The Bull-Trout is an inferior fish to the Salmon and
Sea-Trout, both as regards its sporting and edible qualities;
and it is clearly and easily distinguished from them by the
several specific peculiarities already alluded to †.   Valenciennes even goes so far as to class it in a different genus
from the latter.   His distinction, however, appears to be
rather fanciful than real, and I have not adopted it; indeed the general habits, structure, and appearance of the
two fish are so much alike, and in both cases so nearly
resemble those of the Salmon, as to have led many into the
fallacy of supposing that they were actually the young of
that fish, bred between specimens in different stages of
growth.

Some of the distinctions in the habits of the Bull-Trout
are pointed out by Lord Home :—

---

* *Salmo*, a Salmon or Trout, Lat.; *eriox*, specific name.

† For these distinctions see, as regards form of gill-covers, p. 245;
teeth, p. 246; shape of tail-fin and other fins, p. 247 and p. 301.

" The Bull-Trout has increased in numbers in the Tweed prodigiously within these last forty years, and to that increase I attribute the decrease of Salmon-Trout or Whitling,—for the Whitling in the Tweed was the Salmon-Trout, not the young Bull-Trout, which now go by the name of Trouts simply. The Bull-Trout take the river at two seasons. The first shoal come up about the end of April and May. They are then small, weighing from 2 to 4 or 5 lbs. The second, and by far the more numerous shoal, come late in November. They then come up in thousands, and are not only in fine condition, but of a much larger size, weighing from 6 to 20 lbs. The Bull-Trout is an inferior fish, and is exactly what is called, at Dalkeith and Edinburgh, Musselburg Trout. ... A clean Bull-Trout, in good condition, is scarcely ever known to take fly or bait of any description. It is the same in the Esk at Dalkeith. I believe I have killed as many—indeed, I may venture to say, I have killed more Salmon with the rod than any one man ever did, and yet, put them all together, I am sure I have not killed twenty clean Bull-Trout. Of Bull-Trout Kelts thousands may be killed.

" The great shoal of Bull-Trout not taking the river till after the commencement of close-time, are in a great measure lost both to the proprietor and the public."

The more common weight of the Bull-Trout is under 15 lbs., but it is sometimes taken weighing as much as 20 lbs. When a clean fish of this size happens to be hooked it makes a splendid fight, dashing itself repeatedly into the air, and yielding to its fate only after an exhaustive conflict, in which it is aided by the size and great muscular development of the fins, which are larger than those of the Salmon. Like the Salmon, the Bull-Trout ascends rivers to spawn, but somewhat sooner in the season,—the fry, as it is supposed, returning to the sea correspondingly early.

The cut at the head of this notice was engraved from a full-grown male fish of 32 inches in length, from which also the descriptive characteristics at pages 301 and 305–6 were taken. The figure below gives a representation of a younger fish, in which it will be observed that the tail-fin is hardly square at the end, whilst in the adult specimen it is convex.

The Bull-Trout is far from being as common in this country as the Salmon or Sea-Trout. Probably it is better known in the Tweed than in any other river, being there as abundant as either of the other two species; but the Tweed is in this respect exceptional.

Amongst other localities, the Bull-Trout is known to exist in the streams of Devonshire and Cornwall, in the Severn, in several of the rivers of South Wales (where it is called the Sewin), and, according to Dr. Heysham, in some of the Cumberland waters debouching into the Solway Frith. In Ireland it occurs very generally on either side of the northern portion of the island; and Killala Bay, Donaghadee, Florence Court, Belcek, Crawfordsburn, Nanny Water, Ballyhalbert, and Dundrum are all referred to by Thompson as places whence he had obtained specimens.

Sir William Jardine mentions the Bull-Trout as being found in the Annan, Dumfriesshire; and by Mr. Low it is stated to be an inhabitant of the Loch of Stenness, Orkney. The Liddel, which runs through Roxburghshire, appears to have been once renowned for this fish. Sir Walter Scott, in his Notes to the 'Lay of the Last Minstrel,' says there is an old rhyme which thus celebrates the places in Liddesdale remarkable for game:—

> Billhope braes for bucks and raes,
> And Carit haugh for swine,
> And Tarras for the good Bull-Trout,
> If he be ta'en in time.

" The bucks and roes as well as the old swine are now extinct, but the good Bull-Trout is still famous."

The young of the Bull-Trout is the Warkworth Trout and Coquet Trout of Northumberland and Durham.

All laws relating to Salmon apply equally to the Bull-Trout and its young, under whatever local names they may be known.

Principal Characteristics of the Bull-Trout.—Length of head compared to body only, as 1 to 4; general form of body similar to that of the Salmon, but nape of neck and shoulders thicker, and fleshy portion of tail and base of each of the fins more muscular. Teeth of female smaller than those of male (for other particulars respecting teeth see p. 246). Distinctive shape of gill-covers, see p. 245. Shape of tail-fin, see p. 247; relative position of the other fins, see p. 301. Elongation of lower jaw confined to the males only, but not so conspicuous as in the Salmon. Scales rather smaller and more numerous than those of a Salmon of equal size. Colour: when in good condition like that of the Salmon-Trout, p. 312: at spawning-time, (in the *males*) head olive-brown, body reddish- or orange-brown; (in the *females*) blackish grey; in both fish the back-fins reddish brown, spotted with darker brown, tail-fins dark brown, the other fins dusky brown. Vertebræ commonly 59, occasionally 60.

Fin-rays: D. 11: P. 14: V. 9: A. 11: C. 19.

THE SEA-TROUT or SALMON-TROUT.

(*Salmo trutta* *.)

The last of our migratory species is the Sea- or Salmon-Trout, a much commoner fish than the preceding, and as an article of food more valuable and delicate, ranking with, but after, the Salmon. The marks, as regards the gill-covers, teeth, and shape of tail-fins, &c., by which it is to

* *Trutta*, trout, Lat.

be distinguished from this fish and the Bull-Trout have
been already given in full *, and need not here be reca-
pitulated; but it may be observed generally that in appearance it is somewhat rounder or more tapering than
either of its congeners, the form of the gill-lids and proportions of the tail being intermediate between the two.
The scales are also relatively smaller.

It is not only in its edible characters that the Sea-Trout
deserves the good word of anglers. Indigenous in almost
all Salmon or Bull-Trout rivers, and frequently abounding
in streams which produce neither the one nor the other,
there is no fish that swims which will rise so boldly at the
fly, or which, when hooked, shows for its size such in-
domitable—English pluck I was about to say—but at any
rate such gallant and determined courage. In fact, the
bright graceful *Salmo trutta* is the most game and mettlesome, if not, on the whole, the most beautiful fish known
to Europe, or probably to the world.

The Sea-Trout is the *Salar* of the Moselle, so named by
Ausonius in the fourth century—

"Purpureisque *Salar* stellatus tergore guttis."

In habits it closely resembles the *Salar*, or true Salmon,
of modern ichthyologists, and is included in all statutory
restrictions affecting this fish or the Bull-Trout. Writing
of the Sea-Trout, Sir William Jardine says:—"In approaching the entrance of rivers, or in seeking out, as it

* Gill-covers, p. 245. Teeth, p. 246. Tail-fin, p. 247; other fins,
p. 301.

were, some one they preferred, shoals of this fish may be seen coasting the bays and headlands, leaping and sporting in great numbers, from 1 lb. to 3 or 4 lbs. in weight; and in some of the smaller bays the shoal could be traced several times circling it, and apparently feeding. In these bays they are occasionally taken with a common hang-net stretched across; and when angled for in the estuaries with the ordinary flies which are used in the rivers of the South for Grilse, rose and took so eagerly, that thirty-four were the produce of one rod, engaged for about an hour and a half. They enter every river and rivulet in immense numbers *. The food of those taken in the estuaries appeared very indiscriminate: occasionally the remains of some small fish which were too much digested to be distinguished; sometimes flies, beetles, or other insects which the wind or tide had carried out; but the most general food seemed to be the *Talitrus locusta*, or common Sand-hopper, with which some of their stomachs were completely crammed."

The Sea-Trout is the only one of the three White or Migratory species which is at all likely under any circumstances to be confounded with the Yellow Division of Trout, as the difference in the shape of the gill-covers of the common Trout and Sea-Trout is not so marked as to be by itself a sufficient guide for the sportsman. The difference in colour between the two fish—the one being silver and the other golden—is *usually* too obvious to admit of doubt:

* The females are said to enter rivers before the males.

but it occasionally happens, especially when confined for a long time in a loch, that the Sea-Trout acquires a colour not altogether unlike that of the Yellow Trout; and when this is the case, a reference to the *teeth on the vomer or central bone on the roof of the mouth* will always settle the point.

These teeth in the common Trout (and also in the Great Lake Trout) run in *two* distinct rows, whilst in the Sea-Trout they run only in a *single* row. It is to be observed, however, that the arrangements of the teeth require to be rather closely examined, as in the case of the Sea-Trout the points bend alternately to either side, so as to present rather the appearance of a thinly planted double row; whilst in the common Trout the two lines of teeth are placed so that a *space* in one row has a *tooth* opposite it in the other, making the difference appear at first sight to be little more than one of comparative closeness in the setting of the teeth. In regard to the position of these vomerine teeth, the engraving of the mouth of the common Trout at p. 35 is somewhat inaccurate, resembling in fact more nearly the appearance of the single row seen in the mouth of the Sea-Trout.

Great quantities of the Sea-Trout are yearly sent from Scotland to supply the London markets, where they obtain a high price. Those from Perth, Dundee, Montrose, and Aberdeen are considered to be the best fed, as well as of the finest flavour and colour,—the Tweed producing comparatively few. In regard to the latter river, Lord

Home has the following note:—"Of this excellent species I can only repeat that in the Tweed they have almost entirely disappeared. They afford good sport to the angler; but I never saw one above 7 lbs. weight. Of the Phinoek of the Spey, the Hirling of the Nith and Annan*, the Whitling or Whiting of the Esk, all one and the same fish, I can say nothing. There is a little fish, however, which makes its appearance about November and December, but in very small numbers, few only being caught, and those of course with the hook. They are called here Silver-whites, and also Black-tails, from a dusky-blue spot in the centre of the tail-fin. They are a beautiful little fish, resembling much small Sea-Trout; and if not young Sea-Trout, I know not what they are. When caught, the scales, which are of a beautiful silvery whiteness, separate so easily from the fish that on taking it up they stick to the hand, leaving almost the impression behind. The flesh is pink-coloured, and the flavour very good."

The Don, the Spey, the Tay, the Annan, and the Nith, all produce the Sea-Trout in great abundance, as also some of the rivers of Devonshire, where it is called a Truff. It is found in the Severn, and in the Cumberland and Cornwall streams. On the banks of the rivers falling into the Solway Frith, it is termed in its grilse stage a Hirling; and

* Yarrell observes with respect to this fish:—"The specimens of the Phinock or Hirling (the *Salmo albus* of Dr. Fleming) which I have received so exactly resemble the young of the Salmon-Trout on its first return from salt water, that I am unable to point out any sufficiently distinguishing character."

in Wales and Ireland, where it is very numerous, it commonly goes by the name of White-Trout. This fish is the "Fordwich Trout" of Izaak Walton, so named from a village on the Stour near Canterbury, where it still maintains its reputation for being "rare good meat"—according, at least, to the reports of those who have tasted it from the Ramsgate market. Specimens are occasionally taken in the Thames above Putney Bridge by Shad-fishermen in June and July; and Mr. M'Culloch mentions that it is found in a fresh-water lake in Lismore, one of the Hebrides, where it has existed for many years, precluded from ever visiting the sea, but apparently quite reconciled to its prison, and breeding freely *.

From 1 to 5 lbs. is the usual weight of the Sea-Trout, the Irish specimens generally averaging a somewhat larger size than those of England or Scotland. The annexed engraving represents a Sea-Trout in its fourth year, and the figure at the head of this article one of three years old.

The following large specimens are mentioned by Sir John Richardson :—

* Journal of the Royal Institution, No. 34. p. 211.

In July 1840 a male Sea-Trout was taken at Sandstill fishery in the mouth of the Tweed, which was 37 inches in length, 22 in girth, and which weighed 24½ lbs.; and in November 1846 one of 40 inches in length, and weighing 21 lbs., was caught in the Tame near Drayton Manor, and presented by Sir Robert Peel to Professor Owen.

Principal Characteristics of the Sea-Trout.—Length of head compared to body only, as 1 to 4; depth of body compared to whole length of fish also as 1 to 4. Teeth small and numerous, in five rows on upper surface of mouth (see also pp. 246 & 309), those on the vomer, or central bone in roof of mouth, generally extending some distance along it, the points turning outwards alternately to either side; one row on each side of under jaw, and 3 or 4 strong, sharp, and curved teeth on each side of tongue. Distinctive form of gill-cover, see p. 245. Shape of tail-fin, see p. 247. Relative position of fins, see p. 301. Lateral line very nearly straight. Scales adhering closely, in form rather a longer oval than those of the Salmon. Colour when in season : upper part of head and body bluish black, lighter on sides, which are marked (principally above the lateral line) with numerous spots somewhat resembling in form the letter X. Lower part of sides and belly, cheeks, and gill-covers silvery white; back-fins and tail nearly same colour as back; pectoral fins small, and bluish white; anal fin and ventral fins white. Vertebræ 58.

Fin-rays : D. 12 : P. 13 : V. 9 : A. 10 : C. 19.

THE COMMON TROUT.

(Salmo fario *.)

With the Sea-Trout we conclude the list of the Silver or migratory species of the genus *Salmo* †, and come to the second division of that genus, viz. the *Yellow or Golden, non-migratory* ‡ *Trout.*

DISTINGUISHING CHARACTERISTICS OF THE YELLOW DIVISION OF TROUT.

This group is at once distinguished from the last-named by the difference in colour, a mark which, with the one occasional exception in the case of the Sea-Trout, provided for at p. 308–9, will generally prevent the possibility of any confusion. It is also easily distinguished from the Charrs, or Third Division, by the red and orange colours of the latter, and by the additional characteristic of having two complete rows of teeth on the vomer, whilst in the Charrs the vomer has only a few teeth, and those on the most forward part.

* *Salmo*, a Salmon or Trout; *fario, the* Trout, Lat.
† Salmon and Trouts properly so called — ‡ which never go down to the sea.

P

Of the Yellow Trout there are only three generally recognized species in this country—though probably there
exist others yet to be verified.

The admitted species are—

The Common Trout (*Salmo fario*);

The Great Lake Trout (*Salmo ferox*); and

The Lochleven Trout (*Salmo Levenensis*).

In regard to each of these, the specific characteristics
are given in detail at the end of the several notices; but a
few general observations here will enable the reader to
distinguish them without the necessity of resorting to a
minute comparison.

We have not in the present case the same prominent
differences in the shape of the gill-covers and position of
the teeth by which the migratory Trout and Salmon are so
clearly defined, and for ready points of distinction we must
rely upon colour, general appearance, and localities; these,
however, will be found amply sufficient for the purpose.

1. As regards *localities*. — The Common Yellow Trout
breeds indifferently in brooks, rivers, and lakes, whilst
the Great Lake Trout is never found except in or close
to lakes (generally large and deep); and the Lochleven
Trout is confined, so far as we are aware, to Loch
Leven itself and one or two other lochs and lakes in
the county of Sutherland.

2. *Colour.*—The Lochleven Trout has never any crimson
spots on the body, whilst the Common Trout is never,
or hardly ever, without them; and in the Great Lake

Trout the spots are in each case surrounded by a paler ring, sometimes of a reddish hue.

The flesh of the Lochleven Trout is deep red in colour, that of the Great Lake Trout generally orange-yellow, and the flesh of the common Trout pink or white, according to the nature of the water and the condition of the fish.

3. *Length of head.*—The disproportionate size of the head in the Great Lake Trout is very remarkable, it being little less than one-fourth of the total length of the fish, tail-fin included, whilst in the other two species it is not much more than one-fifth. The length of head in the Great Lake Trout is also *greater* than the depth of the body at the deepest part, whilst in the common Trout it is *less*, and in the Lochleven Trout about *equal.*

4. *Tail-fin.*—The tail-fin in the Great Lake Trout (as shown in the engraving, p. 334) is nearly square at the end, and is considerably wider than the widest part of the body, whilst in the other two species it is very obviously narrower than the same measurement.

By bearing these characteristics in mind, the Angler will be at once able to distinguish the species to which his fish belongs. Upon any other mere external peculiarities of colour or shape very little dependence should be placed, as these are liable to constant variation with differences of water, food, or season.

To return to the Common Trout :—This species is so
well known, and is so widely distributed over the whole
of the British Islands and the Continent, as to make any
description of its appearance or habitats superfluous. Indeed, to give a complete account of the former would
occupy a dozen folios, as its colours and shape—except in
the points already referred to—are susceptible of infinite
difference, and vary as much as the qualities of waters
(whether in sources or feeders), geological strata of the
beds, and nature and quantity of food supplied by the
brooks, streams, rivers, ponds, lynns, and lakes in which it
is bred. This diversity of colouring is, in fact, a defence
furnished by nature for the preservation of the fish, which
would otherwise be so plainly visible upon the slightest
change of water or soil as to fall an easy prey to its enemies, whether biped or quadruped; and experiments have
shown that the change is a question of minutes rather than
of days or weeks. Upon its transfer from a light- to a
dark-coloured vessel, or *vice versâ*, the hue undergoes an
instant alteration, and in a very short time assimilates itself
more or less perfectly to that of its new domicile. This is
also the case, though perhaps in a less remarkable degree,
with the Salmon and all other species of river and sea fish.
Thus, for instance, the Trout of Lynn Ogwin, almost the
whole bottom of which is formed of grass, have when first
caught a brilliant emerald gloss over their golden and
yellow tints; and although the waters are of the utmost
clearness and the lake swarming with fish, I was never able

in any one instance to distinguish these from their surrounding green. Again, in the Spean Water, Inverness,
there are several small tarns in which I have frequently
taken fish of almost the colour of ink; yet these tarns
actually join the Spean, where many of the Trout are of a
fine rich yellow,—the cause of the difference being that the
river has at this point a bed of gravel, whilst the tarns are
floored with a deep deposit of black mud. A similar peculiarity has been noticed as regards the black-moss Trout
of Loch Knitching; and Loch Katrine produces a small
description of very dark Trout, which probably owe their
discoloration, as in many other lochs, to the drainage of
bog-moors.

A remarkable example of this variation is given by the
author of 'Wild Sports of the West.' "I never observed,"
he says, "the effect of bottom-soil upon the quality of fish
so strongly marked as in the Trout taken in a small lake
in the county of Monaghan. The water is a long irregular
sheet of no great depth, one shore bounded by a bog, the
other by a dry gravelly surface. On the bog side the Trout
are of the dark and shapeless species peculiar to moorish
loughs, whilst the other affords the beautiful and sprightly
variety generally inhabiting rapid and sandy streams.
Narrow as the lake is, the fish appear to confine themselves
to their respective limits,—the *red* Trout being never found
upon the bog moiety of the lake, nor the *black* where the
under-surface is hard gravel."

Although, however, in all these cases the variations in

colour, shape, &c., are readily intelligible, the circumstance
of two or more distinct qualities of Trout existing in the
same locality in a river or lake, and apparently under precisely similar conditions, is less easily explained. Amongst
the instances of this which I have met with, one of the
most remarkable occurs in the River Laggan, near Moy,
Inverness.

For about a mile after quitting the lake of the same
name, and until it approaches Moy, the Laggan is a deep
sluggish river, winding its way through a channel of clayey
gravel, but on arriving at this point it widens out for
some 600 or 700 yards into a swift, broad stream, resuming
its lagoon-like appearance below the village. The ordinary fish of both these reaches bear very much the general
aspect of the Trout of other Scotch waters, seldom averaging more than $\frac{3}{4}$ lb. in weight, and in colour and taste when
cooked rather pale and insipid than otherwise.

During several successive seasons I had been in the
habit of fishing the Laggan for a week or so at a time,
filling my creel with these Trout, and never observing any
varieties amongst them sufficiently remarkable to call for
notice : when last there, however, in 1862, I had occasion
to catch some spinning-baits, and for that purpose repaired
late in the evening to the swift part of the stream with a
cast of very small flies,—the ordinary Laggan flies being
large yellow or green lake-flies. No fry appeared to be
on the feed ; but after a few casts I hooked, and ultimately
landed, a Trout of somewhat more than 2 lbs. weight, and

totally different from any that I had ever before seen in the
river, or, indeed, in that part of Inverness. This fish was
brilliantly coloured, the pervading tint being a rich yellow
gold spotted with vermilion, and becoming a deep orange
on the belly. The shape of the body and of the small
compact head was also graceful and symmetrical in the
extreme, resembling rather that of the White than of the
Yellow species; and looking back at the many hundreds
of Trout it has been my fortune to take both north and
south of the Tweed, I should say that this fish was the most
beautiful I ever met with.

During the succeeding half-hour I took four more fish,
all upwards of a pound in weight, from the same pool, and
was twice broken by others; and although none of those
afterwards caught quite equalled the first in beauty or size,
they still bore so close a resemblance to it and to each
other, and were so entirely dissimilar to the ordinary run
of Laggan fish, that no doubt could exist as to the identity
of the breed. With the second breakage the last of my
small flies was unfortunately lost; and though I tried
conclusions with several larger varieties, and again the next
evening and on subsequent occasions with the original
pattern, I could not succeed in catching another of these
fish. The villagers said they had never seen such Trout
from the Laggan before. The flesh when boiled was a fine
salmon-colour, and the flavour excellent.

In all cases of this kind a close comparison of the
several characteristics of the fish with those given at the

end of this article (p. 333) should be resorted to, and a careful description drawn up according to the directions at p. 49 to p. 51, with a view to determining whether the fish is entitled to rank as a distinct species, or is only a variety of the common Trout. That such species exist, though as yet undiscovered, I firmly believe, and such is also the opinion of those best qualified to form a judgment; but the want of any knowledge whatever of the natural history of fish on the part of the great majority of sportsmen has hitherto been a principal cause of our lack of reliable information on the subject.

The annexed woodcut, taken from a male Thames Trout

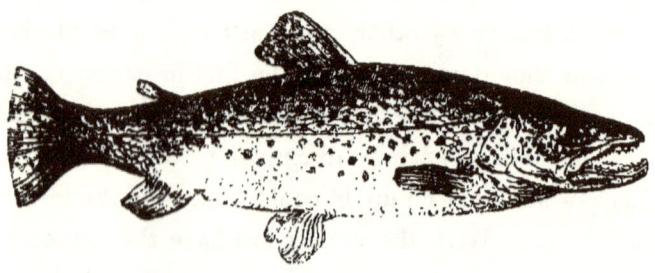

of 11 lbs. weight, and measuring 28 inches, exhibits a remarkable instance of the variations to which Trout are subject. In this fish it will be at once observed that the end of the tail-fin has grown convex through great age, the natural shape being concave, or, when old, square. The length of the head also is somewhat too large for perfect symmetry, as it is longer than the width of the body at its widest part, and closely approaches the proportions of the

head of the Great Lake Trout described at p. 315. The fish
was taken, however, early in the season, so that it was probably not in full condition; and the circumstance of its
being a male would account in some measure for the unusual size of the head—as the gills or respiratory organs in
the male are always longer than in the female fish. From
3 to 10 lbs. is the usual weight of Thames Trout, which tax
to the uttermost the skill and patience of the angler, not
only in the hooking, but also in the subsequent induction to
the landing-net. Indeed, so proverbial are the experience
and sagacity of these highly-educated fish, that it is a joke
amongst the Thames watermen to say that the Trout know
the names of the makers of every bit of tackle used for
their ensnarement. They are considered as excellent eating, and realize a large price, the highest rate ever paid
for one in the London market being *twelve shillings* the
pound.

By the 1st Elizabeth, cap. xvii., no Trout may be taken
in the Thames measuring less than 8 inches from eye to
fork. The legal Thames close-time for this fish is from
the 10th of September to the 25th of January; but the
Thames Angling Association have wisely extended it to the
31st of March—a very proper regulation, which is seldom
infringed by respectable anglers.

Amongst the best localities for Thames Trout may be
mentioned Weybridge, Sunbury, Penton Hook, the Old
Windsor Water, Marlow Weir, and some deep pools above
Oxford. In the Weybridge waters during the past season

(1862) an unusual number of fish were taken, the four
largest being of the respective weights of 11 lbs., 12 lbs.,
8½ lbs., and 8 lbs.,—of which the two first were taken by the
punts of George Keene and Thomas Purdy, and the two last
in that of John Harris, Jun. I can strongly recommend
this fisherman—one of the very best on the Thames—to
any one desiring a good instructor in this somewhat peculiar
branch of angling. A Thames Trout of 15 lbs. weight was
caught in 1835; but the largest of which I can find any
record is one of 16½ lbs., taken by John Harris, Sen., land-
lord of the Lincoln Arms, Weybridge, at Laleham, in 1822.

Many other waters in England produce very large Trout.
At Herdcot House, near Salisbury, there is preserved the
skin of a Trout which was taken from a tributary of the
Avon running through that town. Its weight was 25 lbs.,
and its length 4 feet 2½ inches; in girth it measured 2 feet
1 inch. This is probably the fish alluded to in the ' Transactions of the Linnean Society' as being caught on the 11th
of January, 1822, in a brook some 10 feet wide at the back
of Castle Street, Salisbury. Mr. Powell, at the bottom of
whose garden it was discovered, placed it in a pond, where
it was fed for four months, until it died, when it was found
that it had decreased in weight to 21¼ lbs.

A male fresh-water non-migratory Trout of 30 lbs. weight,
from Lough Neagh, Ireland, was cooked at Brookes's Club
in October 1832. It was beautifully spotted, and its flesh
of good colour and flavour. The length of this fish was
40 inches, and its girth 24 inches.

In the neighbourhood of Downton a Trout was caught with the fly by a Mr. Bailey which weighed 14 lbs.; and in a small tributary of the Trent at Drayton Manor a fish was taken exceeding in weight 21 lbs.* A portrait of this fish is still in the possession of the family of the late Sir Robert Peel.

These weights, however, large as they are, are dwarfed by comparison with those of specimens of the Great Lake Trout of Cumberland and Scotland, and of some of the Trout of the Continental and North American waters. Lakes Michigan and Superior abound with monster Trout of such a size as to set at defiance all attempts to capture them with rod and line †. One of the smaller-sized of these fish (weighing however 72 lbs.) was actually caught by a fisherman in Lake Huron; but it was altogether inferior, both in appearance and flavour, to the beautiful species found in our own streams. Some curious facts respecting the habits of the Huron Trout are mentioned by Feather-stonhaugh in his 'Canoe-Voyage up the Minnay Sotor.' "Upon one occasion," he says, "Mr. Biddle caught one of the Great Trout of the Lake, which, when it was drawn up, had a large White-fish (*Coregonus albus*) in its throat, with the tail sticking out of its mouth, whilst inside the Trout's stomach were two more White-fish, each weighing about 10 lbs. Both these fishes were lying with their heads downwards, and in this manner he had invariably found

---

* Zoologist, 1848, p. 2324.
† Fly-fishing in Salt and Fresh Water, p. 72.

them when inside Trout.   The voracity of this animal
must be great, if, not satisfied with three large fishes, he
must dash also at the bait of the angler.   An Indian who
was a very experienced fisherman explained to my informant
the probable reason why the White-fish are found with
their heads downwards.   He said he had frequently seen
from his canoe, when in still water, the Trout chase the
White-fish; and that whenever the latter perceived the
former near them, they invariably turned round as if to
look their danger in the face, and, making no resistance,
were taken head foremost into the jaws of the enemy,—a
curious provision of Nature, unnerving the weak to feed
the strong.   In the winter-season the Indians cut holes in
the ice where it is transparent, and contrive to drag their
nets beneath it.   They also *spear* the Trout, using upon
such occasions a painted fish as a decoy, which attracts
the minnows : the voracious Trout, perceiving that something is going on, now gets in motion, and the minnows,
aware of his approach by the movement of the water, escape
in a contrary direction, when the Indian, thus apprised
of the quarter whence the Trout is making his advent,
adjusts his spear and transfixes him as he comes up."

There is a species or variety of Trout called the Botling,
mentioned by Dr. Davy * as inhabiting Wastwater, Cumberland, which attains a weight of 10 or 12 lbs.; but I have
hitherto not been fortunate enough to obtain a specimen.
The Botling ascends the lake-streams in the autumn, and

* The Angler in the Lake District, p. 98.

is described as a fierce, powerful fish, frequently attacking the other *Salmonidæ* whilst spawning. In form it is short and deep, with the lower jaw much hooked, or curved upwards; and when full-grown, its girth considerably exceeds its length. In the arrangement of its teeth and spots it resembles closely the ordinary Trout.

The largest of the Irish lakes, Lough Neagh, as well as L. Bofin, L. Corrib, L. Mask, and others, produce a Trout which has been by some naturalists too hastily considered as a distinct species—the Gillaroo. The inner coats of the

THE GILLAROO TROUT*.

stomach in this fish are considerably thickened, so as to afford increased muscular power, and the teeth are remarkably small; but beyond these, and the mere divergences in external form, so little difference appears to exist between it and the common English Trout as to lead to the

* The specimen (a remarkably fine one from Lough Neagh) from which the engraving was taken measured 22 inches in length. In this fish the number of rays of the back-fin was less by two than that of the same fin in the Common Trout. The numbers of the other fin-rays and of the vertebræ were identical.

conclusion that the Gillaroo is only a variety of that species.

Another singular variety—though perhaps it ought more correctly to be called deformity—is seen amongst the Trout of Lochdow, near Pitmain, Inverness-shire, to which it has been hitherto supposed to be confined.   In 1862, however, the author caught such a Trout with the fly in a mountain-tarn of the same county, called Roy, or Roi, from which the picturesque little salmon-river so named takes its source.   The elevation of the loch above the sea-level is considerable, and its appearance striking, as it is situated directly below an almost perpendicular cliff, at the base of which it forms a sort of lynn or caldron.   In some parts it is very shallow, but in others the water is black, and apparently of immense depth; whilst what seems to be the edge of the declivity between the two is bordered, far out in the pool, by a semicircular sweep of bulrushes cut as sharply as if with a knife.

DEFORMED-HEADED TROUT OF LOCH ROI.

This fish, of which the engraving accurately represents the form of the head, is now in the British Museum.   It weighed about 5 ounces, and took the fly during a violent snow-storm in July, when it was so bitterly cold that the rings were frozen to the rod.

Other deformities are not very uncommon amongst Trout. The Hog-backed Trout of Plinlimmon, which is occasionally taken in Bagail Lynn, Shepherd's-pool, is not altogether unlike the Perch in form; and in the river Towey, Carmarthenshire, a fine fish of the Salmon or Trout species was caught, with the net, which had two heads and two tails—the heads being joined on to one neck, and the tails meeting about the centre. The fish was preserved for some time in a small pool at Llangattock, for the inspection of visitors.

The usual spawning-time of Trout is in the latter end of October or November, and thence up to the beginning of February (the operation, however, in each particular fish continuing only about eight days); and at this period the under jaw in the old males exhibits in a modified degree the elongation and upward curving characteristic of the male Salmon at the same time. An example of this is shown in the figure of the Thames Trout at p. 320, in which, from the very considerable age of the fish, the curvature would probably be to a certain extent permanent, but increasing at the spawning-season. In a less aged specimen the curvature would not be so marked.

From the experiments of Dr. Davy, elsewhere commented upon, it appears probable that at least a proportion of Trout, like some Salmon, spawn only in alternate years. The situation chosen for, and the mode of conducting the spawning-process are very similar to those noticed in the Salmon (p. 261),—the eye, however, of the young fish becoming visible in about three weeks, and the egg being usually hatched in from forty to fifty days. The number of eggs, in proportion to the weight of the fish, is about the same as in the case of the Salmon. The yolk-bag is absorbed in from three to five weeks; and in six weeks or two months the young fry are about an inch long and able to shift for themselves. From this time their growth is rapid or slow according to the nature and quantity of their food and other local circumstances.

In order to ascertain the relative nourishment of the different descriptions of food, some interesting experiments were made not many years ago. Trout were placed in three separate tanks, one of which was supplied daily with worms, another with live minnows, and the third with flies. The result was, that the fish fed with worms grew slowly and had a lean appearance,—those dieted on minnows became much larger,—whilst such as were fattened upon flies only, attained in a short space of time extraordinary dimensions, weighing *twice as much as both the others put together*—the quantity of food eaten by them being actually less *.

On another occasion Trout were kept for many years in a store stream, and tested with various kinds of diet, when it was ascertained that in some instances the increase in

* Stoddart, Art of Angling in Scotland.

weight was as much as 9 lbs. in four years (or from 1 to 10 lbs.*).

From the experiments on the different modes of fattening Trout above referred to, it is evident that fish and grubs bear no comparison with insect-food in point of nourishment, doubtless in consequence of the amount of phosphate of lime contained in the latter. Of the insects specially contributing to the food of fish, probably the most nutritious of all are the May-flies, upon which, when arrived at maturity, the adult Trout wreak a signal vengeance for the destruction effected by the larvæ of the one amongst the eggs of the other †—a retributive law of nature, of which many curious examples occur in the animal kingdom.

The May-fly, or, as it is sometimes called, Day-fly (*Ephemera vulgaris*), is well known to fishermen from the immense numbers in which it suddenly appears upon the rivers in spring, swarming over the water and waking into voracious activity every living creature—feathered and scaled—which preys above or below its surface. In such

---

* One of the Trout (a female), which had been regularly fed and weighed during six years, being observed to be falling off in colour and condition, was killed, and found to weigh 7 lbs. Its progressive increase and its decrease are shown in the table :—

Date of weighing.	1835.	1836.	1837.	1838.	1839.	1840.
	lbs. oz.	lbs. oz.	lbs. oz.	lbs. oz.	lbs. oz.	lbs. oz.
April 1	0 12	1 12	3 4	5 4	7 0	7 4
October 1 ..	1 4	2 0	5 0	5 12	7 8	7 0

New Sporting Magazine for Nov. 1840, p. 975.

† See p. 272.

flights do these insects appear, that the Trout may frequently be seen lying with their noses just under water,
sucking them in by the dozen with hardly an effort or
movement; and on one occasion I found in the stomach of
a good-sized fish a mass of Ephemeræ which must certainly
have numbered many hundreds.

The name 'Day-fly' owes its origin to the shortness of
the life of this species. Some live several days; others
take wing with the setting sun and are dead before
morning; and a large proportion, again, measure their
span by minutes, and expire within the hour that gives
them birth. It has been noticed that the May-flies of the
Rhine are always seen in the air shortly before the rising
of the evening star, making their appearance in such clouds
as almost to darken the sky; and, generally, the season
or hour when the chrysalides of the different Ephemeræ
assume their winged condition maintains a kind of regu-
larity in accordance with the temperature of the air or the
rise and fall of the water.

The May-fly remains in the larval, and subsequently in
the chrysalis state for one, two, or three years, and up to
the time of its flight is a purely aquatic insect: the difference between the two stages is shown in the engraving opposite, the figure in the centre representing the form of the
chrysalis, which differs from that of the larva in possessing
rudimentary wings contained in a case on its back. The
sides of both insects, it will be observed, are furnished with
small fringes of hair, which when put into motion serve

as fins or legs for oaring their passage through the water.

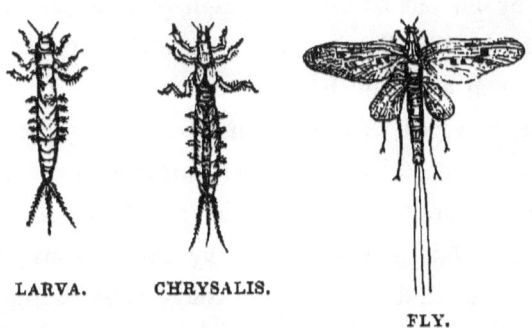

LARVA. CHRYSALIS.

FLY.

When the time arrives for the transformation of the loathsome grub into the brilliant and delicate May-fly, the insect crawls up from the mud in which its hole is bored by the stem of the nearest rush or water-weed, on which it rapidly casts the disfiguring slough, dropping its eggs into the water as it rises from the surface for its first flight. The eggs, from their specific gravity, sink to the bottom, to furnish in another year a new swarm of destroyers for the Trout eggs, and again, when their turn comes, a fresh supply of food for the survivors of their depredations.

The voracity of the Trout when in pursuit of its favourite food sometimes leads to curious results. Dr. Gillespie once saw a Swallow from above and a Trout from below dart upon the same May-fly: down came the Swallow, and up came the open mouth of the Trout, into which, in pursuit of its prey, the Swallow pitched its head. The struggle to get separated was short, but severe; and the Swallow was twice immersed, wings and all, before it disentangled itself from the sharp teeth of the Trout *.

It is by no means an unexampled occurrence for this fish to take a Swallow in grim earnest. One instance at least of such a circumstance is on record. The bird, in this case, however, was not flying, but floating before the wind on the surface of the water, into which it had been shot, when a Trout made a rush at it and carried it out of sight. The fact was witnessed by two persons; and as there were no Pike in the river, there could be no doubt as to the species of the fish by which the Swallow was taken.

Insects of all kinds appear in greater numbers and are observed to exhibit increased activity towards sunset; and this is consequently the best time in the day for taking Trout with the artificial fly, and especially the heavy fish, which until then lie concealed amongst roots, under deep holes, and in other similar shelters. The next best time is during the first freshness of the morning, before the sun gets much power. The Fly-fisher, in fact, cannot be too early or too late at the water; and I have often killed the best fish of the day when it was so dark that I could hardly see my rod and had entirely lost sight of my flies. At both these times larger-sized flies may be used than at others. Small flies are preferable on hot, windless days, or when the water is bright and low. When water is much discoloured with rain so as to become opaque, fly-

* Scrope's Tweed.

fishing is useless ; but such a water when it is clearing, or a full water that is not discoloured, is highly favourable.

The two golden maxims for fly-fishing are, first, to keep as far from the bank and as much out of sight as possible ; and secondly, always to use finer tackle than any one else on the river,—and (your skill being equal) you will always catch the most fish. As it has been cleverly parodied, " Tell me what your tackle is, and I will tell you what your basket is."

Principal Characteristics of the Common Trout (Salmo fario). (Taken from a Hampshire fish, 12 inches in length.)—Length of head compared to length of head and body, without tail-fin, as 1 to 4: depth of body rather greater than length of head. Profile of back and belly about equally convex. Head blunt ; lower jaw longest when the mouth is open, but shutting within the upper jaw on its being closed. Back-fin commencing halfway between point of nose and commencement of upper rays of tail-fin ; third ray of back-fin longest, and longer than base of fin. Small back-fin commencing halfway between origin of large back-fin and upper extremity of tail-fin ; pectoral fin two-thirds of length of head ; ventral fins under middle of first back-fin, and halfway between origin of pectoral fin and end of base of anal fin ; anal fin beginning halfway between origin of ventral fin and commencement of lower rays of tail-fin. Tail slightly forked, very gradually becoming square, or slightly convex in very old fish (as shown in figure, p. 320). Form of gill-cover, see figure at p. 30. Pyloric cæca * seldom exceeding 46 in number. Teeth numerous, strong, and curving inwards, in six rows on upper surface of mouth and jaw, and four on lower. (See also p. 35 ; and for distinguishing features between teeth of Common Trout and Sea-Trout, p. 309.) Teeth (as throughout the Salmon and Trout family) larger in males than in females.

---

* The pyloric cæca are narrow pouches or *culs-de-sac*, more or less numerous, attached to the pylorus or mouth of the intestines.

Number of scales above and below lateral line about 25. Vertebræ 56. Usual colours: back and upper part of sides mottled with numerous dark reddish-brown spots on a yellow ground; eleven or twelve bright red spots along lateral line, with a few more above and below, but liable to constant variation in number, size, and colour; lower part of sides golden yellow; belly and under surface silvery white (often yellowish white); back- and tail-fin light brown, with numerous darker brown spots; small back-fin brown, often with one or two darker spots, and edged with red; pectoral, ventral, and anal fins uniform pale orange-brown. For distinctive colours of young of Trout, see p. 279.

Fin-rays: D. 14: P. 14: V. 9: A. 11: C. 19.

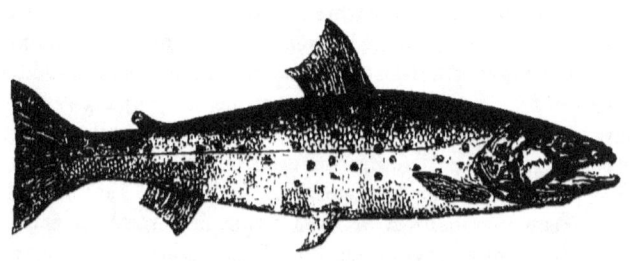

THE GREAT LAKE TROUT.

(*Salmo ferox* *.)

The points in which this fish differs from the Common Trout and Lochleven Trout, and also the distinctions by which it may be most easily recognized, are given at pp. 313–15.

* *Salmo*, a Salmon or Trout; *ferox*, fierce, Lat.

The Great Lake Trout, which is perhaps best known to anglers as the species for which Loch Awe has always been famous, is probably distributed throughout almost all the larger and deeper lochs of Scotland. It occurs to my knowledge in Lochs Ericht, Lochy, Garry, and Laggan, and it has also been recognized in Loch Shin, in Lochs Loyal and Assynt, and amongst some of the Orkney and Shetland Islands. In Ireland it appears to be an inhabitant of all the best-known and most extensive lakes, having been found in Loughs Mask, Melvin, Erne, Corrib, and Neagh, where it is locally named *Buddagh*, the younger and smaller-sized fish being termed *Dolachans*. It is the *Ullswater Trout* and Grey Trout of the English Lake-districts, referred to by Dr. Heysham, and was erroneously considered to be identical with the Great Trout of the Lake of Geneva—a theory contradicted by Agassiz, who pronounced it to be distinct from any of the large Continental species.

The specific name *ferox* has been given to this fish from its extraordinary fierceness and voracity, which are such that, having once seized a bait, it will allow itself to be dragged by its hold for 40 or 50 yards, and when accidentally freed will immediately seize it again. The stomachs of the specimens that I have caught have been constantly found gorged with food. The only way of taking the larger fish is by spinning with a small Parr or other glittering bait towed behind a boat, for which purpose very powerful tackle is required, as the fish is of immense strength, and its teeth as sharp as those of a Pike. As a rule, however, not much success attends the troller for the Great Lake Trout—a circumstance which may possibly be in some measure attributable to the general ignorance of all its habits and of the manner in which it is to be fished for.

The secret of success lies in four points—time, depth, speed, and place : *e. g.*—

Time.—As a rule, *begin* fishing at the time when other people are *leaving off*—that is, about six o'clock P.M. : up to this hour the fish are rarely in a position from which they can by any accident see your bait. From six o'clock until midnight Lake Trout may be caught *.

Depth.—Instead of weighting your tackle to spin at from 3 to 4 feet from the *surface*, lead it so as to sink to within about the same distance from the *bottom*, be the depth what it may.

Speed.—Let your boat be rowed *slowly*, rather than at a brisk, lively pace—as a large Lake Trout will seldom trouble himself to follow a bait that is moving fast away from him ; consequently your bait must possess the speciality of spinning at all events moderately well, or it will not spin at all.

Place.—The place to spin over is where the bank shelves rapidly into deep water—say at a depth of from 15 to 30 or

---

* These fish are essentially night feeders. During the day they lie hid under rocks and in holes, in the deepest parts of the extensive lakes which they generally inhabit, and only venture into fishable water at the approach of evening.

40 feet, according to the nature of the basin: a much greater or much less depth is useless. This is a rather important point, as thereupon it depends whether your bait is ever seen by the fish you wish to catch *.

The annexed figure represents a small example of this species taken from one of the Irish loughs, in which the spots will be observed to be more numerous than in the adult fish.

YOUNG OF GREAT LAKE TROUT.

The Great Lake Trout is almost wholly confined to lochs and deep extensive tracts of water, where it reigns in solitary grandeur, seldom venturing far up or down the streams, and never descending to the sea. It spawns in September.

Principal Characteristics of the Great Lake Trout.—Length of head compared to total length of head, body, and tail-fin about as 1 to 4½ ; depth of body less than length of head. (See also p. 314-15 for comparison with the Common and Lochleven Trout.) Teeth large, strong, and numerous, arranged in six rows above and four below—two of the

---

* The food of the Lake Trout consists of small fish. These are not to be found in any great depths of water, but on the contrary on the sloping shores of the lake, up which, therefore, the Trout comes in search of them, stopping short of the shallows.

upper rows extending along the vomer. Origin of back-fin halfway between point of nose and commencement of upper tail-fin rays; third ray of back-fin longest, and equal to length of base of fin; small back-fin halfway between last ray of large back-fin and end of tail-fin, and directly over origin of last ray of anal fin. Fins generally rather small and muscular. Colours when in season: upper parts and back-fin deep purplish brown, changing into reddish grey, and thence into fine orange on breast and belly; whole body when fresh out of water as if glazed over with a tint of rich lake-colour. Gill-covers and back-fin marked with large dark spots, and whole body covered with markings of different sizes and varying in number in different individuals, being sometimes scattered and of large size, and at others thickly set and of small dimensions. Each spot surrounded by a paler ring occasionally of a reddish hue. Spots becoming more scattered below lateral line; none on belly. (See also p. 314 for comparison of spots in this fish and in the Common and Lochleven Trout.) Pectoral, ventral, and anal fins yellowish green, darker towards the extremities. Tail of great breadth and power—broader than greatest depth of body (see also p. 315), slightly forked when young, becoming square with age; in very old fish slightly convex. Pyloric cæca from 34 to 49 in number. Scales thin and flexible, different in form from those of the Trout, and more circular than those of any of the migratory species.

Fin-rays in specimen from Loch Awe: } D. 13: P. 14: V. 9: A. 11: C. 19.

In specimens from Lough Neagh, one ray less in D., P., & A. fins, and one ray more in C. fin.

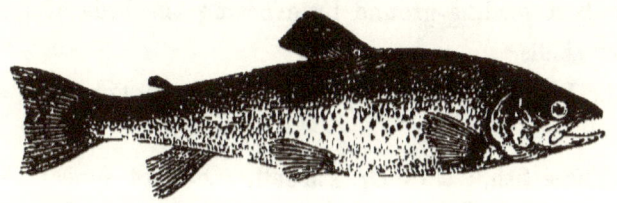

THE LOCHLEVEN TROUT.

(Salmo Levenensis *.)

The Lochleven Trout derives its name from the barren lake, and now dismantled castle celebrated as the prison of the unfortunate Mary Queen of Scots, and perhaps equally well known from having been the scene in which our great novelist has laid the plot of one of his most delightful romances.

The points in which the Lochleven Trout is distinct from the Common Trout and Great Lake Trout have already been referred to at p. 314, and need not be here repeated. It is only necessary to remark that, in the opinion of modern ichthyologists, they are such as clearly entitle the fish to be considered a distinct species, and not merely a variety of the *Salmo fario.* Several such varieties exist in the same waters; but their flesh is white or pinkish, and in flavour they are quite inferior to the real Trout of Lochleven. Of late years, however, these fish have considerably fallen off in colour and condition, owing, it is said, to the partial draining of the loch having destroyed

---

* *Salmo,* a Salmon or Trout; *Levenensis,* of Leven, Lat.

their best feeding-ground by exposing the beds of fresh-water shells *.

The Lochleven Trout spawn in January, February, and March.

"These fish," says Dr. Parnell, "do not appear to be peculiar to Lochleven, as I have seen specimens that were taken in some of the lakes in the county of Sutherland, with several other Trout which were too hastily considered as mere varieties of *Salmo fario*. It is more than pro-bable that the Scottish lakes produce several species of Trout known at present by the name of *Salmo fario*, and which remain to be further investigated."

I have had opportunities of examining many speci-mens of the Lochleven Trout, and their characters agreed closely with those given by Dr. Parnell from a specimen one foot in length. Of these the principal were :—

Head a little more than one-fifth of the whole length, tail-fin in-cluded. Depth of body at the deepest part about equal to length of head. Gill-cover produced behind ; lower margin of operculum ob-lique ; præoperculum rounded ; end of the superior maxillary bone extending as far back as the hinder margin of the orbit. Commence-ment of back-fin halfway between point of upper jaw and a point a little beyond the fleshy portion of the tail. End of back-fin even, sometimes concave. Pectoral fins pointed when expanded ; in Com-mon Trout rounded. Tail-fin long, rather narrow, and concave at the end. Tail-fin rays much longer than in the Common Trout, and pointed at the upper and lower extremities, whilst in the latter they are rounded. Teeth stout, sharp, and curved slightly inwards, situated as in the Common Trout. In the specimen described by Dr. Parnell there

---

* Paper by Dr. Parnell in vol. vii. of the Memoirs of the Wernerian Natural History Society of Edinburgh.

were 32 in the upper jaw, 18 on the lower, 12 on each palatine bone, 13 on the vomer, or central bone in roof of mouth, and 8 on the tongue. Scales small, thick, and adherent, when dry exhibiting a small ridge in the centre of each, not perceived in the Common Trout; 24 in an oblique row between middle back-fin ray and lateral line. Pyloric cæca from 60 to 80. Colours: back deep olive-green; sides lighter; belly inclining to yellow; pectoral fins orange, tipped with grey; back- and tail-fins dusky; ventral and anal fins lighter. Gill-cover (in the specimen described by Dr. Parnell) with 9 round dark spots; body above lateral line with 70 spots, below it 10; back-fin thickly marked with similar spots. Forward extremities of anal and back-fins without the oblique dark bands so constant and conspicuous in many of the Common Trout. Flesh deep red. The Lochleven Trout has never any red spots, and the Common Trout is scarcely ever without them (see also p. 314). It is probable that the Lochleven Trout is identical with the *Fario Lemanus* of the Lake of Geneva.

Fin-rays: D. 12: P. 12: V. 9: A. 10: C. 19.

THE CHARRS.

THE WELSH CHARR.

(*Salmo Cambricus.*)

The Charrs, or, as I have denominated them for the sake

of clearness, the Red and Orange-coloured division of the genus *Salmo* (Salmon and Trouts proper), are exclusively a lake species, never migrating to the sea, and seldom ascending streams unless for the purpose of spawning. They are rarely known to take the fly or other bait; and the interest which they possess, as amongst the least-known and most beautiful of our fishes, is consequently rather for the naturalist than the angler. As a Division or Group they may at once be distinguished from the two other sections of the same genus by the brilliant tints of the belly, which increase in vividness as the spawning-season approaches, and by the comparatively very minute size of their scales.

Our knowledge of the different species of the British Charrs has been until lately in a very unsatisfactory state, principally owing to the constant attempts on the part of naturalists to identify our species with those of the Continent, and more particularly with the *"Ombre Chevalier,"* the Charr of the Lake of Geneva. The consequence has been a vast amount of misapprehension and a general confusion of names and synonyms, which, added to the great difficulty of procuring specimens for examination, has hitherto prevented anything like a reliable classification being arrived at.

Thanks, however, to the researches of Dr. Albert Günther, Custodian of the fish at the British Museum, we are now, we may hope, at the commencement of a new era in this respect. Dr. Günther has enjoyed unequalled advantages in the number of specimens at his command, and has consequently deduced his arguments and conclusions from a direct examination of the fish themselves, without being compelled, as most previous ichthyologists have been, to depend in a great measure upon the confused and often incorrect descriptions of other writers. He has, moreover, taken the trouble to collect and sift the opinions and statements of all previous authorities entitled to be considered as such, and has pointed out where their arguments or conclusions are defective.

The substance of his examinations has been embodied in a comprehensive treatise, from which I shall here present my readers merely with the results.

Three distinct species of Charrs, then, have been distinguished by Dr. Günther as inhabiting different localities in the British Islands [*]. These are—

1. The Welsh Charr, or Torgoch of Llanberris (*Salmo Cambricus* [†]).

2. The Windermere Charr (*Salmo Willughbii* [‡]).

3. The Grey Charr, or Fresh-water Herring of Lough Melvin, Ireland (*Salmo Grayi* [§]).

[*] Since the above was put into type I have been favoured by Dr. Günther with a further paper on the British Charr, in which he adds two more species to the list, viz. *Salmo alpinus* (the Northern Charr), found in Lake Helier, Hoy, Orkneys, and probably in other Scotch waters; and *Salmo Colii*, found in Loughs Esk and Dan, Ireland.

[†] *Salmo*, a Salmon or Trout; *Cambricus*, of Wales, Lat.

[‡] *Willughbii*, of Willughby, Lat.

[§] *Grayi*, Lat., named after Dr. Gray.

It must not be considered that these represent all the species contained in British waters; Dr. Günther's opinion, in which I entirely concur, is that there are probably several others; but they are the only three which the materials at his disposal have at present enabled him clearly to identify. None of these are identical with either of the generally known Continental species.

A brief description of each of the three British Charrs in question may assist the Angler in recognizing them if he should happen to meet with them.

THE WELSH CHARR.

This fish, which is sometimes called in Wales the *Redbelly*, is the *Torgoch* of the lakes of Llanberris and Cawellyn, two deep sheets of water situated on the east and west sides of Snowdon, and is also found in Llyn Coss-y-gedawl —'the lake of the fruitful marsh'—a locality near Barmouth, Merionethshire, from which the specimen represented at the head of this article was taken*. Lake Cawellyn, which is of great extent and profound depth, is faced on one side by a sharp mountainous cliff rising abruptly out of the water, in the deep recesses at the

---

* This was a young specimen only 5 or 6 inches long, the usual length being 9 inches, and the greatest commonly attained 12 inches. These small Charrs are marked with eight or nine cross bars, or Parr-marks, on the sides (as shown in the engraving), which disappear in the adult fish. The size of the head is also proportionally smaller and more depressed over the eyes in the adult fish than in the woodcut.

base of which the Torgoch is supposed to pass the milder seasons of the year in perfect security, only approaching the shallower parts in small shoals about the middle of December.

The general characteristics of the Welsh Charr given by Dr. Günther are—

Body slightly compressed and elongate, its greatest depth being equal to one-fifth or two-ninths of the distance between the snout and root of tail-fin; length of head equal to considerably more than one-half of the distance between the snout and origin of back-fin. Head rather depressed; *space between the orbits of the eyes flat*, its width being less than twice the diameter of the eye. Males with the lower jaw largest; teeth of moderate strength, 6 in each intermaxillary bone *, 20 in each maxillary *. Length of pectoral fin less than that of head, but much more in length than half the distance between its root and the root of the ventral fin. 170 transverse series of scales above the lateral line. Colour: sides with numerous red dots; belly red; pectoral, ventral, and anal fins with white margins.

D. 13 or 14: A. 12 or 11: P. 12 or 13: V. 9.

The following additional particulars are taken from a male fish 9 inches long, of which Dr. Günther gives a detailed description.

Nostrils situated midway between eyeball and end of snout; the anterior nostril round, open, surrounded by a membrane, which is developed behind into a small flap almost entirely covering the smaller, oblong, hinder nostril. (By this character alone, Dr. Günther says, the Torgoch may be distinguished from the Windermere Charr and Fresh-water Herring.) The maxillary bone * extends slightly beyond the hinder margin of the eye, and is armed with from 19 to 21 teeth of moderate size; 6 or 7 teeth in each intermaxillary *; 17 in each mandible; 7 teeth on vomer, forming two sides of a triangle, the point furthest back. Scales very small and thin, and deeply imbedded in

---

* See pp. 28 & 35.

the skin. Gill-covers with numerous black dots, extending backwards above root of pectoral fin and being in immediate contact with it. Vertebræ 61.

The Welsh Charr or Torgoch spawns in November and December, and is in season towards the end of the year *.

The Windermere Charr,

on which Dr. Günther has founded his second species, is an inhabitant of Windermere—or Winandermere as it used to be called—and probably also of several others of the English, Irish, and Scotch waters. Except at the spawning-season they seldom quit the deep bed † of the lake for any of the rivers by which it is either supplied or drained ; and then their partiality for a clear stream and a stony bottom is very conspicuous. Windermere has two principal feeders, the Rothay and the Brathay, the former having a bed of sand, but the channel of the latter being rocky and abrupt : these streams unite at the northern extremity of the lake, and after a short course enter it together. At about the end of October the Charr make their way in shoals up both rivers ; but invariably, before spawning, those

---

* As these fish inhabit situations in which they are almost inaccessible during by far the greater part of the year, it would appear that they ought to be considered as in season during the few weeks in which they can be caught.

† The deepest parts of the lake, with a varying depth of from 50 to 80 yards, are their favourite habitats when not spawning; when spawning, they prefer from 2 to 2½ feet of water both in the river and the lake.

fish which have ascended the sandy bed of the Rothay return and pass up the rocky channel of the sister stream—a preference which appears to be exactly reversed in the case of the Trout. The whole length of the channel over which the Charr spawn is not more than half or three-quarters of a mile—from the mouth of the Rothay up to Skelwith Pool, a reach including several small rock-lakes or tarns. A certain number of fish also spawn in the lake; but it has been observed that they always affect the stony parts, and of these only such as are in the immediate vicinity of very deep water. The process does not commence until a month or three weeks later than in the river; and it is a fact worthy of note that at this period Charr are not unfrequently taken in the highest condition, and without any roe in them. Does not this point to the probability of at least a portion of these fish spawning only every *alternate* year, as already alluded to in the case of the Salmon and Trout?

Like other species of the same genus, the Charrs exhibit a considerable difference in their colouring; and possibly, in some cases, the colours in the males and females also permanently differ. Such a variation is stated to have been observed in the Charr of Ennerdale Lake, Cumberland, the males being more brilliant than the females *; but it has been suggested that the amount of colour may depend not so much upon the question of sex as upon

* Mr. Mascall, communication to the Magazine of Natural History, April 1835.

the constitutional vigour of the individual fish, as witnessed in the periodical assumption of peculiar tints in other animals. Case Charr, Red Charr, Gilt Charr, and Silver Charr are all names which have at different times been applied to the Charr of the British lakes in consequence of the varying intensity of their colouring. Dr. Davy says that the "Silver Charr" of Windermere spawns chiefly in November and avoids the deep portions of the lake, whilst the "Gilt Charr" inhabits only the deepest waters and does not spawn till the beginning of February. It seems a fair presumption, therefore, that some of these variations in colour indicate specific differences, whilst in other cases they are merely local, or dependent on sex or condition.

From 9 to 12 inches is the usual length of the Charr of the Cumberland and Westmorland lakes; but specimens have been occasionally taken as long as from 18 to 24 inches.

Dr. Günther gives the following as the general characteristics of the Windermere Charr:—

Body compressed, slightly elevated, its greatest depth being equal to one-fourth of the distance between the snout and the end of the middle tail-fin rays; length of head equal to a little more than one-half of distance between snout and origin of back-fin. Head compressed; *interorbital space concave*, in width being less than twice diameter of eye. Jaws of male of equal length in front. Teeth of moderate strength, 4 in each intermaxillary, 20 in each maxillary bone. Length of pectoral fin less than that of head, but much more in length than half the distance between its root and the root of the ventral fin. Back-fin rays 12. 165 transverse series of scales above lateral line. Colour: sides with red dots; belly red; pectoral, ventral, and anal fins with white margins.

In a male fish of 11 inches in length, described in detail by Dr. Günther, the number of fin-rays were—
D. 12: A. 12: P. 13 (or 14): V. 9 (or 10) *.
The nostrils were situated immediately before the eye, the hinder nostril widest; and the cutaneous bridge between both not developed into a flap. Maxillary bone extending slightly beyond margin of orbit, armed with from 20 to 21 teeth of moderate size; 4 teeth in each intermaxillary, 17 in each mandible, 2 pairs (4) on vomer, 15 on each bone of palate, and 4 pairs (8) on tongue. Scales very small and thin, those on the back minute and hidden in skin. Gill-covers silvery, lower parts minutely dotted with black; edges not overlapping root of pectoral fin, which is entirely free. Vertebræ 59.

THE GREY CHARR, OR FRESH-WATER HERRING OF LOUGH MELVIN, IRELAND.

This Charr appears to be confined to Lough Melvin; and the account we have of it is still incomplete, and can be considered only as a first step towards a satisfactory history of the species. The flesh is said to be white and soft, and different from that of the Charr of any other lough; but this peculiarity may possibly depend upon the state of the fish at the time of its being caught, as a recent writer on the subject mentions that he has found specimens not inferior in point of firmness, flavour, and the pink colour of the flesh to any Charr in the kingdom.

Dr. Günther gives the following as its general characteristics :—

---

* The figures in brackets show the variations in different specimens.

Body compressed, slightly elevated, its greatest depth being equal to one-fourth of the distance between the snout and the end of the middle tail-fin rays; length of head scarcely equal to more than one-half of the distance between the snout and the origin of the back-fin. Head compressed; interorbital space convex, its width being less than twice the diameter of the eye. Jaws of the male of equal length in front; *teeth very small* (by which character alone, according to Dr. Günther, these fish may be distinguished from all the other allied British or Continental species), 4 in each intermaxillary, 16 in each maxillary. Length of the pectoral fin equal to, or rather more than that of the head, terminating at no great distance from the ventral fin. Back-fin rays 13 or 14. 125 transverse series of scales above the lateral line. Colour: sides with scattered orange-coloured dots; *belly silvery whitish, or with a light shade of red; fins blackish* (thus differing entirely from both the other species).

In a male specimen 10½ inches long the ray-formulary was—
D. 13 (or 14) : A. 12 : P. 13 (or 14) * : V. 9.
Nostrils situated midway between the end of the snout and the forward margin of the eyeball; the hinder nostril wide and round, the forward one being a very narrow vertical slit; both separated by a narrow cutaneous bridge. Maxillary bone extending as far back as the hinder margin of the eye, armed with 16 very small teeth, the hinder ones being quite rudimentary. All the other teeth small, 4 in each intermaxillary bone, 12 in each mandible, 2 to 4 on the vomer, 15 on each bone of palate, and 4 pairs (8) on tongue. Scales very conspicuous, and comparatively much larger than in the other British species; *those on the back very distinct.* Gill-covers silvery, not overlapping root of pectoral fin, which is entirely free. Vertebræ 60.

A tolerably close examination of the characteristics of these three species will probably enable the Naturalist to identify either of them he may meet with; but, as before stated, they are rarely caught with the fly or any other sort of bait. Except at the time of spawning, they inhabit the

---

* The figures in brackets show the variations in different specimens.

deepest and most inaccessible parts of the lakes, and the only chance for taking them (beyond an occasional specimen when fly-fishing for Trout) is to trail a spinning-minnow with a very long line, leaded so as to sink nearly to the bottom.

The following are amongst the lakes known to contain Charr :—

1. A Charr is found in Loch Grannoch, Kirkcudbright-shire, which makes its appearance only during ten days, and never before about the 13th of October. The sexes are stated to be distinct from each other in colour and in the size of the head and of the fins; also in the number of the vertebræ, the male having 60, the female 62–63 ?. Number of eggs found in a specimen 482. Charr are also found in Loch Ennick, Rothicmurchusforrest, and in Lochs Clare, and, I believe, in the sister loch, Coulin.

2. Of other localities in Scotland, Loch Inch and Loch Corr are mentioned. They appear to be inhabited by a species identical with, or similar to, the Charr of Winder-mere—at all events by one different from the "Haddy" of Loch Killin, in Inverness-shire. The latter is very interesting, inasmuch as it seems to be closely allied to the Fresh-water Herring of Lough Melvin. It is only caught when spawning, about the 26th of September.

3. Lough Melvin, producing the Fresh-water Herring, which appears to be confined to that locality.

4. Lough Dan, co. Wicklow, Ireland, inhabited by a Charr exhibiting some of the characters both of the

Northern and Welsh Charr. Specimens have been caught with the fly in summer.

5. Other localities in Ireland are—L. Kindun, L. Gartan, L. Derg, Lake of Luggela, Loughnabrak, and L. Corrib (the Charrs from these localities have a deep-red belly, and apparently approach the Welsh or Windermere Charr in character) ; L. Dan (co. Wicklow) ; L. Esk (co. Donegal) ; Cummeloughs, in the mountains of Cummeragh ; Lake of Inchigeelagh (co. Cork), and one or two other small lakes in this neighbourhood ; L. Neagh ; a lake near Dunfanaghy (co. Donegal) ; L. Eaghish (co. Monaghan). As recently-discovered localities are mentioned Lake Helier, in Hoy, Orkneys ; Loch Druiach, Scotland ; Keswick, Crummock Water, Coniston Water, and Ennerdale Lake, Cumberland ; to which may be added Loch Roy, Inverness-shire (described at p. 326), where, during a violent snow-storm in July 1862, the author took with the fly a small specimen of a very beautiful species of Charr, in shape closely resembling the engraving below, and which will probably prove to be the young of the Northern Charr.

Genus *THYMALLUS.*

THE GRAYLING.

(*Thymallus vulgaris**.)

Generic Characteristics.—Two back-fins; the base of the first very long, with numerous rays; the second small and adipose, without rays. Mouth small, with a squarish orifice; teeth very small and conical; air-bladder large; body elongated, and sides marked with longitudinal bands or lines. Gill-rays 7 or 8.

Whilst yielding to its sister species the Trout in the qualities of dash and obstinate courage, the Grayling is yet a sturdy and mettlesome fish—"a foeman worthy of our steel;" and if the former is the handsomer, the latter must, I think, be admitted to be the prettier species of the two. The Trout has, so to speak, a Herculean cast of beauty; the Grayling rather that of an Apollo—light, delicate, and gracefully symmetrical.

Though abounding to excess in some streams, the Gray-

* *Thymallus,* 'thymy'—from *thymum,* thyme, and *vulgaris,* common, Lat.

ling is a remarkably local and even comparatively rare fish, thriving best in rivers the bottoms of which are composed principally of sandy gravel or loam—a soil highly favourable to the production of the insect-food on which it in a great measure subsists. Rocky or stony bottoms are very inimical to its breeding; and this is probably the reason why, though flourishing in many Continental waters, none exist in those of Ireland or Scotland. Indeed, even in England, a dozen names or so include all our streams which have any right really to be considered as properly Grayling-waters; and these, with hardly an exception, belong to the southern and western portions of the island. The fact is no doubt accurately stated by Mr. Blaine when he says, "Grayling require other peculiarities of location besides those of temperature, such as, for instance, the general character of the water they inhabit, and certain circumstances in the nature of its composition derived from its sources. It is probably owing to the abstraction of some of these requisites that the breeding of the fish in several rivers in which they have been attempted to be naturalized has not been attended with success. In some they soon disappeared; in others they remained, but never thrived; while in some waters though they lived and at first increased, yet they were afterwards observed to shift their quarters to different grounds, in most of which cases it proved, as in the Test of Hampshire, that they migrated from above downwards, probably in search of deeper and more tranquil waters: for the angler cannot fail to observe that Grayling do not, like Trout, affect very rapid shallows and the coldest torrents; on the contrary, they seem to thrive best where milder currents alternate with deep and extensive pools." On these rapids, however—or "stickles," as they are termed—small Grayling may frequently be found, but the large fish rarely except in the spawning-season. The haunts of large Grayling are the deepish and slowly-running tails of streams or pools, a few yards before the formation of fresh shallows; and here they will be found *at all times*, except when spawning.

Notwithstanding the fastidiousness of Grayling in the choice of situation and the quality of water, it has been clearly proved by experiment that they will live in ponds newly cut in hard soil, or in such as have been recently and carefully cleaned out; but in these situations the fish do not breed, and in old muddy ponds rapidly die off.

Some years ago the attempt to introduce Grayling into the upper part of the Thames was made by Mr. Warburton, who turned in a considerable number of store-fish; but they never became acclimatized, and have long since entirely disappeared. A similar effort on a larger scale is now being conducted by the Thames Angling Association, which it is devoutly to be wished may prove successful, though I cannot say that my own anticipations as to the probability of such a result are very sanguine. The small number, however, that have hitherto been caught may perhaps be owing to their never being fished for. It remains to be seen what might be done with the gentle and artificial grass-hopper in the deep, quiet swims towards October and November.

It has been asserted that the Grayling is not, like the Trout, indigenous to this country, but was introduced by the monks on account of its edible qualities—a supposition to which the peculiarity of the local distribution doubtless gave rise; and it is certainly clear that its gastronomic attractions were fully appreciated by the luxurious cleri-cals. Father Sanctus calls it a "Queen of delight"; and Walton tells us that "St. Ambrose, Bishop of Milan, who lived when the Church kept fasting-days, names him as the 'flower-fish' or 'flower of fishes,' and that he was so far in love with him that he would not let him pass with-out the honour of a long discourse." Two circumstances, however, appear to militate against the conclusion that the Grayling was introduced by the monks :—first, that it would be exceedingly difficult to bring the fish over alive from the Continent; and secondly, that it is not found in the streams of Kent, Dorsetshire, Devonshire, or Cornwall, where monastic establishments were formerly most numerous.

In Hampshire and Wiltshire the Grayling is found in the Test, the Wharf, and in both the Avons; in Hereford-shire, in the Dove, the Lug, the Wye, and the Irvon; in Shropshire, in the Teme and Clun; in Staffordshire, in the Hodder, the Trent, the Dove, and the Wye; in Derby-shire, in the Dove; in Merionethshire, in the Dee, between

Curlen and Bala; in Lancashire, in the Ribble; in Yorkshire, in the Derwent, the Ure, the Wharfe, and the Whiske,
near Northallerton; and in Cumberland*, in the Esk and
the Eden. Of these, by far the finest streams are the Dove,
the Lug, the Test, and the Teme. The last-named river
contains, in addition to some remarkably beautiful scenery,
probably the best Grayling-water in the world. It was
in the neighbourhood of the Teme, at Downton Castle,
that Sir H. Davy wrote his ' Salmonia, or Days of Salmon
Fishing'; and within the last few months, through the
kindness of the present owner, Mr. Boughton-Knight, the
author has enjoyed some excellent sport on its banks.

The Teme Grayling has the reputation of being the
finest in England, and when in the height of condition
—that is, in October or November—and just taken from
the water, is certainly one of the most beautiful fish that
can be imagined. At this time the back is of a deep
purple colour, with small dark irregular spots on the sides;
the stomach is brilliantly white, with a fringe or lacing of
gold, and the tail-, pectoral, and ventral fins are of a rich
purplish tint. The dorsal fin is very large—almost disproportionately so—and is covered with scarlet spots and
wavy lines upon a dark ground of reddish brown. The
little velvet back-fin near the tail is also dark brown or
purple, and the whole body is shot with violet, copper, and
blue reflexions when seen in different lights. Properly to
appreciate this colouring, the fish should be laid horizon-

* Heysham's Catalogue of Cumberland Animals.

tally upon the hand to be looked at, in which position its varied tinting is seen to the greatest advantage.

In addition to its delicate colouring the Grayling has been always supposed to possess a peculiar smell, which in my opinion rather resembles the odour of cucumber than that of the thyme from which it takes its designation—*Thymallus*, or 'thymy.' This peculiar odour is also exhaled in a still more remarkable degree by the Smelt.

The name Grayling is probably a modification of 'Graylines,' in reference to the longitudinal dusky-blue bars with which its body is marked.

The size of Grayling varies much in different localities; but they rarely exceed 3 lbs. in weight, and by far the greater number of those taken are under 1 lb. Occasionally, however, they are met with of even a larger size than that above named: T. Lister Parker, Esq., took three fish in the Avon, near Ringwood, which together weighed 12 lbs.: a Grayling of $4\frac{1}{2}$ lbs. weight was killed in the Test, and one of 5 lbs. is recorded to have been taken in the neighbourhood of Shrewsbury.

The food of the Grayling, besides flies, worms, caterpillars, and the like, consists of the larvæ of dragon-flies, May-flies, and other ephemera, remains of the cases of the former and the skins of all of them being frequently found in their stomachs.

Unlike the Salmon species generally, the Grayling never jumps out of water, and is apparently unable to surmount either natural or artificial obstructions or to stem very rapid torrents, being much more prone to going down than up stream. It has the power, however, of raising itself rapidly to the surface, and of descending again with stone-like velocity—a faculty which has been ascribed to the action of the large dorsal fin striking either upwards or downwards against the current, but which is more probably attributable to the unusual size of the swimming- or air-bladder.

The ova of the Grayling are numerous, but considerably smaller than those of the Trout, being about the size of partridge-shot, and when viewed in the rays of the sun have very much the colour of the opal. The body of the embryo fish becomes distinctly visible in about nine days, and the egg itself hatches in fourteen or fifteen days from the date of deposit,—results obtained in the case of the eggs of the Trout in about thirty-five and fifty days respectively.

Their spawning-time is in April or the beginning of May, the fish getting into condition in July, and reaching its prime in October and November, when most of the other *Salmonidæ* are going off. The Grayling has, moreover, the advantage of rarely being so much out of season as to be unfit for food, or unwilling to take a bait if judiciously offered. Sir Humphry Davy, who has given us a very fair history of the fish, considered that it might be fished for at all times of the year, and that when there were flies in the water it would generally take them.

In the winter months the Grayling will commonly rise

at the fly from about twelve o'clock until two, if there is any sun; but at this time of the year the artificial grass-hopper with gentles is by far the most deadly bait.

For instructions in regard to the making and using of these and all other Grayling baits, flies, &c., I would recommend Mr. H. Wheatley's treatise of the 'Rod and Line,' in which will be found not only much valuable, but also a good deal of *original* information *,—adding only a hint which I believe that gentleman does not give—*that when the fish refuse the fly at the surface, they will frequently take it if allowed to sink towards the bottom.*

Principal Characteristics of the Grayling (as found in a specimen 10 inches long).—Head small and pointed, flattened at the top; in length compared to length of body alone, excluding tail-fin, as 1 to 4; body deepest at commencement of back-fin; depth rather more than equal to length of head. Distance between point of nose and commencement of first back-fin equal to one-third entire length, tail-fin rays excluded. Back-fin very long at the base, nearly equal to twice the length of its longest ray; pectoral fins small, narrow, and pointed; ventral fins commencing directly under centre of back-fin; anal fin commencing halfway between origin of ventral fins and end of fleshy part of tail. Opening of mouth when viewed in front squarish; teeth small, numerous, and curved; none on tongue, and only a few on end of vomer, or central bone in roof of mouth, and on the adjoining ends of the bones of the palate, situated in single rows on the jaws. Profile of back slightly convex, that of belly nearly straight. Scales large, 7 in an oblique row above the lateral line. Colour: sides

---

* The 'Rod and Line' (Longman and Co., Paternoster Row, 1849), by H. Wheatley. Mr. Wheatley deserves well of the angling world if only as the first who duly appreciated the importance of *flying triangles* in minnow spinning-tackle. One of his maxims also is invaluable: "*Never throw a fly, or put a bait into the water, without expecting a fish.*"

marked with about 15 dusky longitudinal bands or bars; the general hue becomes darker with age, and about the spawning-season the pectoral fins are reddish with small black spots: for further remarks on colouring see p. 357.   Vertebræ 58.

Fin-rays: D. 20: P. 15: V. 10: A. 13: C. 20.

Genus *COREGONUS*.

THE GWYNIAD.

(*Coregonus Pennanti* *.)

All the species of this genus (the last of the *Salmonidæ*) are more or less like the Herring in their general appearance, from which, however, they are broadly distinguished by the characteristic of two back-fins—the first being greater in height than in length, and commencing before the ventrals, the second adipose or fleshy; the scales large; teeth small, or wholly absent; pre-maxillary bones lying across the front of the mouth, which is small; maxillary bones on sides of mouth, generally oval.

* *Coregonus*, Gr. name for the species; *Pennanti*, of Pennant, Lat.

R

The species of the genus *Coregonus* are numerous in Europe ; and several of them are so similar to each other, that, without further information than we at present possess, and in the absence of any means of making actual comparison between British and foreign specimens, it has been found impossible to pronounce with certainty in regard to their identity *.

Ullswater and several others amongst the Cumberland lakes contain great numbers of the Gwyniad, which in this vicinity goes by the name of *Schelly,* on account of its large scales. It occurs also abundantly in the neighbouring lake of Haweswater, and is in all probability the Coregonus which is known to inhabit the Red Tarn, a small sheet of water near the summit of Helvellyn, elevated more than 2600 feet above the sea-level. Llyn Tegid, near Bala, was also at one time plentifully stocked with Gwyniad; but the introduction of Pike into the lake has, it is supposed, materially reduced their numbers of late years.

The Gwyniad are gregarious, and in spring and summer approach the shore in immense shoals, when many hun-

* Some authors have even asserted the Vendace of Lochmaben to be identical with the Powan of Perthshire, the Schelly of Ullswater, the Gwyniad of Wales, and the Pollan of Ireland ; but, upon a comparison of the specific characteristics, the incorrectness of this opinion is at once apparent. The Irish Pollan is certainly distinct from the two species of *Coregoni* found in the sister island. Pennant considered the Gwyniad as identical with the *Coregonus fera* of the Lake of Geneva, an opinion held also by Willughby, but which has been clearly shown by Valenciennes to be erroneous. Neither is the Gwyniad the Lavaret of Switzerland.

dreds are sometimes taken at a single draught of the net *. They die rapidly on being taken from the water, and are prone to quick decomposition.

The most common length of the full-grown fish is from 10 to 12 inches; and their spawning-time is towards the latter end of the year.

The Pollan or Coregonus of Lough Neagh, Ireland, differs from the Welsh Gwyniad in the following particulars: —in the snout not being produced; in the back-fin being nearer the head; in the smaller number of rays in the anal fin, and in the position of the fin being rather more distant from the tail; also in the back-, anal, and tail-fins being smaller; and in the third ray of the breast-fins being the longest—the first ray being of the greatest length in the Gwyniad †.

Characteristics of the Gwyniad.—Length of head compared with total length of body as 1 to 5. Depth of body at commencement of back-fin rather exceeding length of head. Back-fin commencing about halfway between point of nose and end of fleshy portion of tail: longest ray one-third longer than the base. Adipose fin rather nearer to the end of the tail than to the hinder edge of the back-fin. Breast-fins narrow, pointed, and somewhat shorter than the head, inserted low down on the body. Ventral fins attached under middle of back-fin. Tail forked. Head triangular; jaws nearly equal, the lower just shutting within the upper. A very few minute teeth in tongue and jaws. Eyes large. Lateral line very near middle of side. Scales

---

* Amongst the poorer classes the fish goes by the name of the "Fresh-water Herring," and is salted and cured in a similar manner to its salt-water prototype. The Welsh name "Gwyniad" has reference to its silvery-white colour.

† Proceedings of the Zoological Society of London for 1835. p. 77.

large. Form of body very like that of a Herring. Colour: upper part
of head and back dusky blue, becoming lighter down the sides, with a
tinge of yellow. Cheeks, gill-covers, lower part of sides and belly
silvery white; fins all more or less tinged with dusky blue, especially
towards the edges. Vertebræ 58.   .

Fin-rays: D. 13: P. 17: V. 11: A. 16: C. 19.

BONES OF THE HEAD IN THE COREGONI.

THE POWAN.

(Coregonus Cepedei*.)

Although there are certain points of resemblance between this fish and the Pollan of Ireland, it may be readily
distinguished from it by the peculiar form of its mouth, a
representation of which in two points of view, and contrasted with the same parts in the Pollan (both of the
natural size), is annexed. In the Powan the greater depth
of the upper lip and the large size of the superior maxillary bones will be at once remarked.

In Loch Lomond these fish exist in great numbers, and
are called by the natives *Powans* or *Fresh-water Herrings*.
They are taken with drag-nets from March until September,
and in rare instances have been killed with a small artificial fly : a minnow or natural bait they have never been
known to touch. Early in the morning and late in the
evening large shoals of them are observed approaching the
shores in search of food, and rippling the surface of the
water with their fins as they proceed, resembling in this
respect the Vendace of Lochmaben and the salt-water

* *Cepedei*, of Lacépède, Lat.

Herring. They are never seen under any circumstances in the middle of the day. Their spawning-season is from October to December, and they are in their best condition in August and September.

The Powan rarely grows beyond the length of 15 inches. Its food appears to consist principally of water-insects, larvæ, and small red-worms.

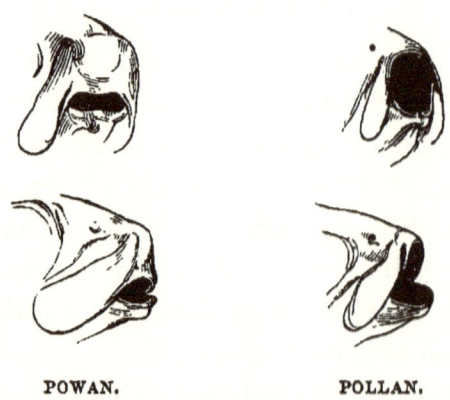

POWAN. POLLAN.

Characteristics of the Powan (Coregonus Cepedei).—Head long and narrow; length about one-fifth of whole body, tail-fin included, and greater than depth of body at commencement of back-fin. First ray of back-fin commencing halfway between point of snout and origin of tail-fin. Adipose fin large and thin. Anal fin commencing halfway between origin of ventral fins and base of middle tail-fin ray. Ventral fins commencing under middle of back-fin. Breast-fins long and pointed, one-sixth the length of the whole fish, tail-fin included. Tail deeply forked; long rays of upper portion curving slightly downwards, giving a peculiar shape to the fin. Gill-cover produced behind; lower margin of gill-cover proper * slanting upwards and backwards. Snout

* See p. 30.

prominent, extending beyond upper lip. Lower jaw shortest. Teeth (about 6) in upper jaw, long and slender; those on tongue shorter and more numerous. Scales large; 8 between lateral line and back-fin, and 8 between lateral line and base of ventral fins. Colour of back and sides dusky blue; belly dirty white; lower portion of back, breast, ventral and anal fins dark bluish grey.

Fin-rays (including two short rays at commencement of back- and anal fins): D. 14: P. 16: V. 12: A. 13: C. 20 *.

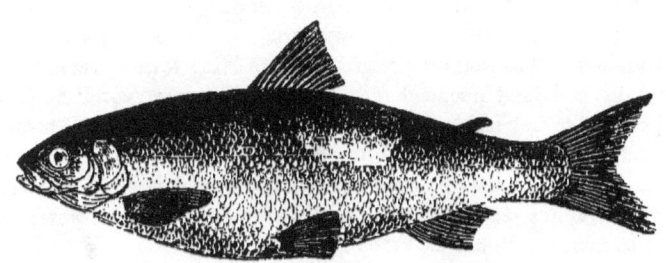

THE POLLAN (OF IRELAND).

(*Coregonus pollan.*)

In habits these fish do not differ in any marked respect from the Vendace of Scotland, or from the Welsh Gwyniad. They abound in some parts of Lough Neagh, and are met with in Loughs Corrib, Derg, and Erne, and probably also in others of the Irish lakes. The specimens from these different loughs vary slightly in external appearance, but will all be found to bear a close resemblance to that re-presented in the engraving, which was taken from Lough

* From Dr. Parnell's description of a Loch Lomond Powan.

Erne. The food of the Irish Pollan is very similar to that of the Powan, described in the last notice.

The female fish attains to a larger growth than the male, the latter rarely measuring beyond 11½ inches in length, whilst the former frequently exceeds 13 inches.

The Pollan spawns in November and December.

Its principal characteristics are :—

Relative length of head to that of body about as 1 to 3½. Depth of body equal to length of head. Jaws equal in length; both occasionally furnished with a few delicate teeth. Teeth numerous on tongue. Lateral line sloping downwards for a short way from gill-cover, and thence passing straight to tail. Nine rows of scales from back-fin to lateral line, and same number thence to ventral fin (row of scales on back and lateral line not included). Third ray of breast-fin longest. Colour to lateral line dark blue, thence to belly silvery; back-, anal, and tail-fins tinged with black towards extremities; breast and ventral fins very transparent except at their extremities, which are dotted faintly with black. Vertebræ 59.

Fin-rays: D. 14: P. 16: V. 12: A. 13: C. 19.

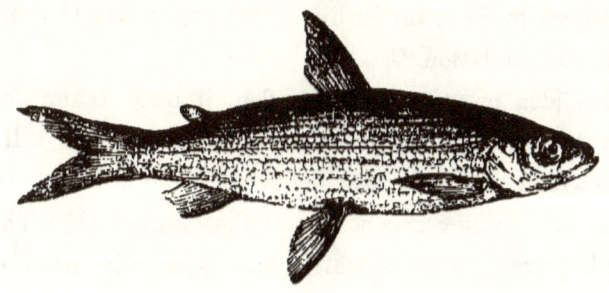

THE VENDACE or VENDIS.

(*Coregonus Willughbii* *.)

Owing to the difficulty of determining synonyms, but little is known of this interesting fish beyond what has been published in the Edinburgh Journal of Natural and Geographical Science, for which we are indebted to Sir William Jardine—and in the Transactions of the Royal Society of Edinburgh, from the pen of Dr. Knox.

In Scotland the Vendace is found only in the lakes in the vicinity of Lochmaben, Dumfriesshire, where some singular opinions and traditions exist regarding it. Sir W. Jardine says, "The Vendace is well known to almost every person in the neighbourhood; and if among the lower classes fish should at any time form the subject of conversation, the Vendace is immediately mentioned, and the loch regarded with pride, as possessing something of great curiosity to visitors, and which is thought not to exist elsewhere. The story that it was introduced into these lochs by the unfortunate Mary Queen of Scots, as

* *Coregonus*, Gr. name of the species; *Willughbii*, of Willughby, Lat.

mentioned by Pennant in his description of the Gwyniad, is still in circulation."*

"An idea prevails that this fish, if once taken from the water, will die, and that its immediate return will be of no avail; and it is also believed that it will not exist in any other water except that of the Castle-loch. These are of course opinions which have gradually, from different circumstances, gained weight, and have at last been received as facts. The fish is of extreme delicacy—a circumstance which may have given rise to the first notion—and the introduction of it must have taken place by means of the spawn : the fish themselves, I am confident, could not be transported alive even a few miles. As to the second opinion, they are not confined to the Castle-loch, but are found in several other neighbouring ones, some of which have no communication with that where they are thought to be peculiar."

"In general habits the Vendace nearly resemble the Gwyniad, and indeed most of the allied species of the genus. They swim in large shoals; and during warm and clear weather retire to the depths of the lakes, apparently sensible of the increased temperature. They are taken with nets only—a proper bait not being yet discovered; and the fact that but little is found in their stomachs has

* According to Dr. Davy, the same species exists in Derwentwater and Bassenthwaite Lakes, Cumberland—a fact which disposes at once of the above ideas. The Vendace occasionally descends the Annan to the Solway Frith, and has been taken in the stake-nets placed in that estuary.

given rise to another tradition, that they are able to subsist without food. They are most successfully taken during a dull day and in a sharp breeze, as they then approach near to the edges of the loch, and swim in a direction contrary to the wind. They spawn about the commencement of November, and at this time congregate in large shoals, frequently rising to the surface of the water, in the manner of the common Herring, and making a similar noise by their rise and fall to and from the surface. The sound may be distinctly heard, and the direction of the shoal perceived, during a calm and clear evening. They are very productive. The Lochmaben lochs abound with Pike, of which they are a favourite food; but their quantity seems in no degree to be diminished, notwithstanding that immense numbers must be destroyed. They are considered a great delicacy, resembling the Smelt a good deal in flavour; and though certainly very palatable, the relish may be somewhat heightened by the difficulty of always procuring a supply. During the summer, fishing-parties are frequent, introducing some stranger-friend to this Lochmaben Whitebait; and a club, consisting of between twenty and thirty of the neighbouring gentry, possessing a private net, &c., meet annually in July, to enjoy the sport of fishing, and feasting upon this luxury."

The females of the Vendace are more numerous, as well as larger, than the males, and not uncommonly exceed 8 inches in length,—the males not measuring more than 7 inches, which was the length of the specimen here described, and they are stated to be seldom seen of larger size,—thus differing in a most important particular from the three other British species of *Coregonus*, which moreover in every case have the upper jaw longer than the under, whilst in the Vendace the lower jaw projects considerably beyond the upper. Its food consists of minute aquatic insects, distinguishable only under a powerful microscope, the magnified forms of the two most common of which, in two points of view, are shown in the vignette.

Characteristics of the Vendace.—Length of head compared to body as 2 to 7. Depth of body at commencement of back-fin nearly equal to one-fourth the length of body without reckoning tail. Lateral line straight along middle of side, with six rows of scales in an oblique line between it and back-fin, and the same number below between the line and the ventral axillary scale. Two back-fins; the first commencing halfway between nose and base of tail-fin, on upper side. All the fins large; tail deeply forked. Mouth small, with square opening. Under jaw slightly projecting. A few very minute teeth on tongue only. Colour: upper parts of body and back-fin a delicate greenish brown, shading gradually towards belly into a clear silver; lower fins all bluish white. Vertebræ 52.

Fin-rays: D. 11: P. 16: V. 11: A. 15: C. 19.

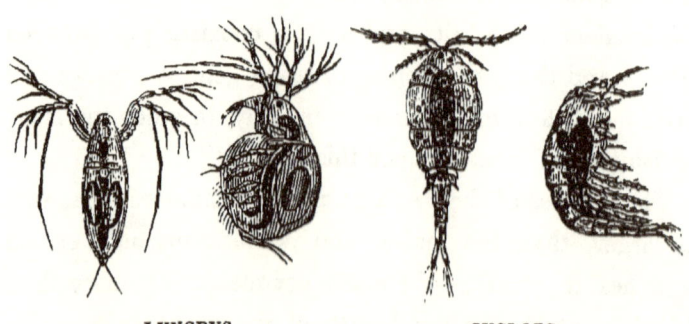

LYNCEUS.   CYCLOPS.

CHAPTER XI.

Series I. *BONY FISHES.*
Order III. *MALACOPTERYGII SUB-BRACHIATI* *.

Family *GADIDÆ* †.
Genus *LOTA* ‡.

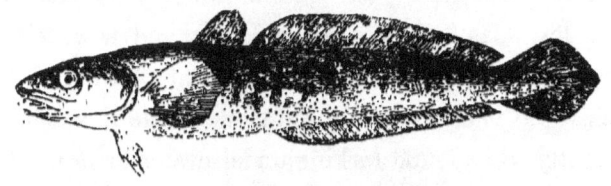

THE BURBOT or EEL-POUT.

(*Lota vulgaris* §.)

Characteristics common to all the species of the Cod-fish Family.—
Body more or less elongated, covered with small soft scales. Ventral
fins placed under the pectorals, or sub-brachial *. 1, 2, or 3 back-fins.
Anal fins 1 or 2. Jaws, front of vomer or central bone in roof of
mouth, and bones of palate armed with card-like patches of teeth.
Gill-rays 7. Air-bladder large.

IN all the fish of this genus (*Lota*) the form of the body
is very narrow and slender or elongated. They have two
back-fins and one anal fin, and one or more barbels or
beards on the chin.

Of the numerous and valuable family of the Cod, only
one British species, the Burbot—sometimes also called

---

* "Soft-finned Fish having lower arms." (See p. 37.)

† The Cod Family.

‡ *Lota*, generic name for this and several allied species;—§ *vulgaris*, common, Lat.

Burbolt—lives permanently in fresh water, and this fish is rather local than generally distributed, preferring oozy, slow-running rivers, and neither so much sought for nor appreciated as from its edible qualities it deserves. It is very tenacious of life, and has been known to attain the weight of 8 lbs., the usual growth, however, varying from 1 to 2 lbs. Its flesh is white and firm, and is considered by many to be superior in flavour to that of the Eel, with which it has many habits in common. Like this fish, it is constantly to be found lurking under drains or near eddies into which food is likely to be swept by the current, or concealing itself in holes with only its nose projected, watching for aquatic insects, fry, or other small animal matters. Its principal time for feeding is during the night, and it is seldom caught unless in eel-pots, or on trimmers or night-lines.

The Burbot is probably to be found in a good many rivers and streams of this country: amongst those in which it is known to exist may be mentioned the Cam, the Trent, and the Tame; the Ouse, the Esk, the Skern, and the Derwent in Yorkshire and Durham, and the Yare, the Bure, and the Waveny in Norfolk.

Principal Characteristics of the Burbot.—Length from 1 to 2 feet. Head depressed, smooth; jaws equal; chin with one barbel; mouth wide, studded with very numerous small sharp teeth above and below. Length of head compared to that of body only as 1 to 4. Form of body nearly round, flattened towards tail. First back-fin small and rounded; second reaching nearly to tail and occupying about half the length of body; both fins nearly equal in height. Ventral fins placed very forward, narrow and pointed. Pectoral fins large and rounded. Anal fin beginning behind commencement of second back-fin, ending opposite each other. Tail-fin oval and slightly pointed. Scales small. Colours: general hue of body yellowish brown, clouded and spotted with darker brown, and covered with a mucous secretion; under parts lighter; lateral line indistinct and straight. Fins nearly same colours as parts of body to which they are attached.

Fin-rays: D. 14—68: P. 20: V. 6: A. 67: C. 36.

CHAPTER XII.

Series I. *BONY FISHES.*   Family *MURÆNIDÆ* †.
Order IV. *MALACOPTERYGII APODES* *.   Genus *ANGUILLA* ‡.

THE SHARP-NOSED EEL.

(*Anguilla acutirostris* §.)

Characteristics common to all the Eel Family.—Body elongated into a serpent-like form.   Skin thick and soft; scales almost invisible, and very few bones.   They have no ventral fins and no pyloric cæca, but almost all have air-bladders.

THE special characteristics of the present genus, *Anguilla*, to which all our fresh-water Eels belong, are, that they have the body rounded, and covered with a thick mucus or slime; a row of teeth on each jaw and a few in front of the vomer or central bone in the roof of the mouth; the pectoral fins close to the openings of the gills, which are very small apertures; and the back-, anal, and tail-fins united.

* "Soft-finned Fish lacking ventral fins." (See p. 37.)
† *Muræna*, an eel-shaped fish, Lat.
‡ From *anguilla*, a little snake;—§ *acutus*, sharp, and *rostrum*, a nose or snout, Lat.

There are at least three distinct species of Eels in the fresh waters of Great Britain—

The Sharp-nosed Eel,

The Broad-nosed Eel, and

The Snig, or *Medium-nosed Eel,*

the first two of which are very common and pretty equally distributed throughout the three kingdoms, whilst the last, which is also yellower in colour than the others, appears to be peculiar to a few rivers, having been more particularly noticed in the Hampshire and Worcestershire Avons. The Snig is also in the habit of roving and feeding during the day, both the other species roaming and feeding principally by night. Further marks of distinction are to be found in the comparative sharpness or bluntness of the noses in the three fish—permanent peculiarities from which they derive their specific names,—the Snig being called *mediorostris* from its nose being intermediate in size between the Broad-nosed and Sharp-nosed Eels, as shown in the illustrative engravings. Should any doubt, however, still exist as to the identity of this species, an examination of the first five vertebræ will at once settle the point. It will be seen, by a reference to the woodcuts, that in the centre figure the vertebræ are smooth and round, and entirely destitute of the bony projections exhibited in the other two.

The following figures represent the relative size of the cranium in three individuals of exactly the same length ; and the immense difference between the head of the Broad- and that of the Sharp-nosed species makes any further distinguishing mark, so far as they are concerned, superfluous.

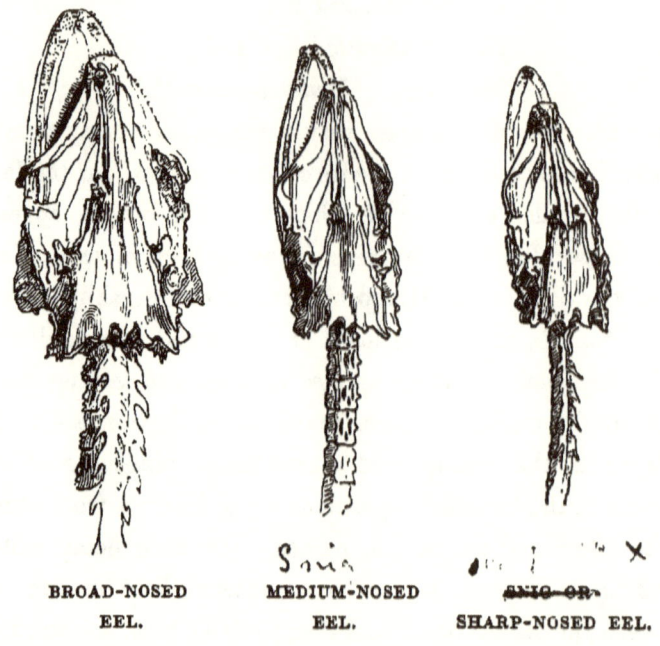

BROAD-NOSED   MEDIUM-NOSED   SHARP-NOSED EEL.
EEL.   EEL.

Eels form a very valuable staple of commerce both in England * and elsewhere, being exceedingly numerous, pro-

* Nigel, Bishop of Ely, in his charter to the monks of that place, granted about, 1133, included amongst other things 23,000 eels, to be taken in the marshes and waters of the manor of Stuntney, which he gave them, " and 6 fishermen with their dwelling-houses." The town of Ely has been said to be named from the rents having been formerly paid in eels, the lords of the manor being entitled to upwards of 100,000 eels annually. Elsmore, on the Severn, also obtained its name from the immense numbers of eels which were taken there. In the reign of Henry VII. the eel-fisheries of Sion Abbey (which are supposed to have included the well-known 'Eel-pie' Island) formed,

lific, and tenacious of life. Their consumption in some of our large cities is very great. The markets of London are supplied principally from Holland by two Dutch companies having a regular fleet of vessels expressly built for this traffic, and furnished with capacious wells in which vast quantities of eels can be preserved alive until required. One or more of these vessels may be seen at any time lying off Billingsgate fish-wharf, whilst the others ply backwards and forwards between England and Holland, each boat bringing over a cargo of from fifteen to twenty thousand pounds weight, upon which a duty of £13 per load is levied. These fish and Salmon are the only species sold by the pound weight in the London market.

During the winter months the Eels lie torpid or buried in the mud, at a depth usually of from 12 to 16 inches, affecting especially the soft and spongy soils of harbours

and river-beds from which the tide recedes daily. In Somersetshire the country people assert that they can trace the burying-places of Eels by the hoar frost not lying over such spots; and it is said that, following this clue, they dig them up in heaps. The mouths of drains or small streams, in front of which the mud is never without a

together with "the very superior breed of hogs" belonging to the abbess and her nuns, a principal part of the revenue of that establishment.

moist filtering current, are particularly favourite haunts of
the Eel; and in these situations they are frequently taken
in considerable quantities with eel-spears.

The following mode of Eel-fishing commends itself at
least by its novelty :—

"In the hard frosts of last year I saw," says a writer in
the 'Zoologist,' "a method of eel-catching practised which
was new to me, and would go far to prove that the hearing
of fish is nearly deadened by cold. The eels had come, as
they do in such cases, to the surface of the water, immediately below the ice, and, where it was clear, were easily
seen. About two or three inches off them, a hole was cut
through the ice large enough to admit a pair of nippers,
with which the eel was summarily pulled out. Where there
were reeds projecting through the ice, the concussion carried
downwards by any blow on them was sufficient to startle
the fish, but where the ice was uninterrupted they usually
lay quite still till extracted. I tried the plan myself after
watching it for some time, but did not calculate on the
difference of weight between myself and the boys, so that
though the hole I broke was large enough in all conscience,
it was in a fashion much more likely to give me as food for
the fishes than *vice versâ*; in fact, on the first blow I went
straight through up to my waist. I saw only Eels taken,
but was informed that Perch and Tench had also been
captured in this singular way." *

Perhaps equally curious is a method practised in some

* Zoologist, 1846, p. 1216.

parts of Lancashire. When a pond containing Eels is frozen over, a hole is made in the ice, and a small bundle of straw introduced into the water through the aperture, and there left for a day or two, when the Eels, which collect in great numbers round the hole for air, creep up into the straw and are drawn out with it.

During its state of torpidity, other enemies of the Eel, besides man, appear to be particularly active. Rats and Polecats are known to select this period for their attacks, and some of the accounts of their depredations are not a little singular. " In February last," says Mr. Hardy, " when walking by the side of the mill-race at Swalwell, near Newcastle-upon-Tyne, we noticed a common House-rat making its way close by the edge of the water, among the coarse stones that form the embankment. Curious to know what it could be doing there, we watched its progress downwards until it reached the outlet of a drain, into which it had just turned, when it gave a sudden plunge, and as quickly reappeared in the stream with a middling-sized eel in its mouth. It made for the edge, where it soon regained its footing; a matter, owing to the steepness of the bank, of some difficulty, increased by the struggles of the eel, which it had seized a little above the tail, and which was exerting itself vigorously to get free. The rat attempted to run forward and turn a corner, where, on a broader ledge, he might perhaps have had luck in his fishing; but the desperate efforts of the eel rendered his footing so precarious that, rather than have a second ducking, he was reluctantly obliged to drop it into the water. His first action afterwards was to give himself a good shake, both to revive his spirits and to rid his coat from the effects of his morning dip; and then, as before, he resumed his ' contemplative recreation.' As our paths lay differently, I have nothing further to report of his good or evil success."

In cutting recently through an embankment in a field adjoining the river Lune, for the formation of one of the culverts of the North-Western Railway, the labourers found a *collection* of between 15 or 20 lbs. weight of Eels, some quite fresh, and others in the last stage of putrefaction. They varied in size from a quarter to half a pound, and consisted of the common river-Eel and small specimens of the Conger. "As the marks of teeth," says a gentleman who was present, "were plainly visible on the heads of most of them, it was conjectured they had been destroyed by these weapons, and stored for winter provisions by some animal whose retreat was not far distant. This proved to be the case. On digging a little further, out bounded a matronly rat, with half-a-dozen young ones at her heels. The workmen gave chase, and ultimately succeeded in killing both mother and progeny, with a solitary exception, which took sanctuary in the trunk of a neighbouring tree. The embankment is about a hundred yards from the water's edge, so that it must have required considerable time and labour on the part of the old rat to have dragged the eels thither."

The fact of Eels having been discovered in the nest of the Polecat is mentioned by Bewick. The keeper of Mr. H. T. Frere, some years ago, when shooting in the Roydon Fen, near Aylsham, noticed the same thing. His attention was drawn to one of the pointers scratching vehemently at a burrow in the bank; he went to the spot and assisted the dog in turning out a Polecat's nest, in which lay a perfectly fresh Eel with its head bitten off. How the Polecat succeeded in catching it it is difficult to understand, unless, as the keeper suggested, "the Eel had been taking an evening stroll amongst the grass." In a letter in the 'Zoologist' for 1846 upon this subject, Mr. Banister says:—"We have Polecats abundant in Pilling during the whole year; and in the winter season, when the water in the ditches in the main drains is chiefly congealed, and more especially when the ice is covered with snow, the footprints of the Polecat may be traced on the ice, and the most indubitable evidence is thus afforded of its predilection for fish. Under such circumstances, I have repeatedly ascertained that this animal is a most expert fisherman; for in severe and long-continued frosts many Eels ascend our open drains, and as these water-courses are most slightly frozen over near the springs, the Polecats, either by instinct or experience, discover the retreat of the Eels. In tracing the footprints of the Polecat it will soon be ascertained that he halts at every hole or opening he meets with in the ice, and at once commences fishing by introducing a fore foot into the water, and no doubt groping all around under the ice as far as he can reach, in search of such Eels as may have come to the aperture for air. That he uses his fore paws in this manner is distinctly proved by his dirty footprints afterwards in the snow. It is also an admitted fact in the natural history of the Eel, that it cannot exist without air. The Polecats, then, aware, either from instinct or habit, of this propensity of the Eels to assemble round any aperture in the ice for the benefit of the air, invariably search for them at every opening they meet with ; and in tracing their footprints in the snow, as above described, it will frequently be discovered that Eels have been dragged from under the ice by these wily fishermen, and either devoured on the surface or carried to their dens to satisfy their hunger at some future opportunity. I may here also add that I have known a Polecat killed by a fisherman's dog on our extensive sands, nearly two miles below high-water mark ; and as herrings were taken at that very time in great numbers in nets suspended on stakes, it is very probable that this Polecat had been attracted to this distance by the strong smell of these fish."

It is a fact generally admitted by naturalists that cold is extremely inimical to Eels. There are no Eels in the Arctic regions, none in the rivers of Siberia, in the Volga, or even in many of the tributaries of the Danube, whilst the southern rivers of Europe produce four different species. It has been before observed that fishes in general, and Eels in particular, are able to detect very trifling variations in the temperature of the medium in which they exist; and this susceptibility may possibly account for their efforts to reach the warm, brackish water of the tideways before the colder months of the year, and also for the great numbers of the young of other fish usually found in the same situations. " It is a well-known law in chemistry that when two fluids of different densities come in contact, the temperature of the mixture is elevated for a time in proportion to the difference in the density of the two fluids, owing to the mutual penetration and condensation." Such a fusion is of course constantly going on at the mouths of rivers debouching into the sea, and the brackish mixture consequently maintains a temperature two degrees higher than either the pure salt or fresh water.

With the approach of winter (about October and November) the full-grown Eels descend the rivers in immense shoals in search of these warmer waters : whether because the process of spawning requires such a change, or simply because it is agreeable to themselves, does not appear quite certain. That they do descend, however, at least in the great majority of cases, at that period, there can be no doubt ; and that they will even overcome serious obstacles in their course is equally well known. As to whether they return to fresh waters again afterwards, authorities differ ; but from the great size at which river-Eels are often taken, one of three things is clear :—either they do not all migrate, or some of them (at least) return, or their growth-rate

s

whilst in fresh water is altogether much more rapid than that of any other fish.

It is asserted by some authors that this migration is confined entirely to the Sharp-nosed Eels. Mr. Pinkerton, who has given the subject much attention, is of that opinion. In an able letter on this subject he says :— " But the grand distinction between the two species (the Sharp-nosed and Broad-nosed Eel) is that the Sharp-nosed species is a migratory fish, while the Broad-nosed one is not. I admit that the latter has its summer and winter quarters—for Eels are very susceptible of the effects of cold and electricity—and it wanders about a good deal at night in search of prey ; but it does not migrate to the sea in large shoals as the Sharp-nosed species annually does. It is about this time of year that the annual migration commences, the Eels moving in the night, and always choosing a dark night for the purpose. A change of wind, a clap of thunder, a cloudy night becoming clear and starry, will at once stop the movement. I have frequently visited the great Eel-fishery at Toome, on the Lower Bann, where from fifty to sixty tons of Eels are annually caught in the migrating-season. As many as seventy thousand Eels have been taken at this place in one night, all of the Sharp-nosed species, with the slight exception of perhaps a dozen Broad-noses that have been accidentally mixed up with the shoal—the exception thus confirming the rule. On one night in 1842, when I visited the Toome fishery, there were caught, in round numbers, 11,000 Eels. Now, as the persons who purchase the produce of a season's fishing by contract expressly stipulate that they will not take a single Broad-nosed Eel, every eel—with a dexterity of eye and hand worthy of a Robin or a Frikel, and only acquired by long practice—is carefully counted, and all Broad-nosed ones thrown aside. And on this occasion there were only three Broad-noses in the whole number. What becomes of the immense quantities of Sharp-nosed Eels that descend to the sea every season? Do they remain in the brackish waters of the estuaries, or do they return in small detachments at various periods? This is a problem still to be solved."

These Eels are taken, during their descent, in wicker baskets, termed " Eel-bucks," of which the engraving represents the form.

The final destination of the parent fish, after spawning in the brackish water, we, as Mr. Pinkerton truly says, do

not know: they have never, so far as I am aware, been
observed to accompany the young Eels, or Elvers as they
are termed, on their ascent from the sea in March and
April.   This exodus of the fry has been observed in the
Thames, the Severn, the Jed, and many other rivers.
Countless thousands of young Eels from 3 to 4 inches in
length force their way up wherever a stream of fresh
water pours itself into the salt, and like an endless living
rope, deviously, but still keeping near the bank, twist and
twine along, surmounting all obstacles as instinct leads
them in their course towards the higher waters.   " I have
watched them," says Mr. Couch, " when their passage has
been obstructed by a waterfall 20 feet high, and yet, on
examining the wet moss over the verge, I have found them
tortuously winding their way to the stream above."

In the Thames and the Severn this migration is called
the *Eel-fare*, from the Saxon term 'fare,' signifying to
travel, as in ' wayfarer,' 'thoroughfare,' and other words
similarly compounded.   The Eel-fare continues for some
days at a time; and as it has been calculated that as
many as from 1600 to 1800 fry have passed a given spot in
the space of one minute, some estimate of their numbers
may be formed.   The term ' Elver ' is probably a corruption
of Eel-fare.   The young of the spring rapidly increase in
size, and acquire a greenish-brown colour by May and June.

The habits of the adult Eel when prevented from making
its autumnal migration to a warmer element are thus
described :—

" In a small pond in a walled garden at Craigo, the seat of David Cargegil, Esq., near Montrose, Eels have been kept for nine or ten years. They lie torpid during the whole winter unless the sun is shining brightly, when they will occasionally come out from their hiding-place under some loose stones and sprawl about the bottom of the pond, but refuse to take any food. They eat sparingly until the warm weather begins, when they become quite insatiable : one of them will then swallow twenty-seven large worms one after another. They generally lie quietly at the bottom of the pond, except when any of the family go and look into it, when they invariably rise to the surface, sometimes for food, and at others merely to play with the hand, or take the fingers into their mouths.

About the month of August they become very restless, and lose no opportunity of the pond overflowing to get out ; when sought for in the garden on these occasions they are invariably found travelling *eastwards* (the direction of the sea, which is about four miles from Craigo). Towards the end of August or beginning of September they retire to their winter retreat under the stones. Whether they breed in this pond or not is uncertain ; but on clearing it out last summer a few very small Eels were discovered ; and how else they could have found their way there it is not easy to conjecture, as there is a fine rose on the mouth of the pipe by which the water enters. From their rapacity, shown in devouring their companions (some Gold-fish), it is possible the Eels may eat the greater part of their own families." *

Tame Eels are known in various parts of the world. They are very common in Otaheite, where, according to Ellis†, they are domesticated and are fed until they attain an enormous size. These singular pets are kept in large half-filled holes 2 or 3 feet deep, on the sides of which they usually remain, unless called by the persons who feed them. Mr. Ellis was present on one of these occasions. The young Chief to whom the house belonged sat down by the hole and gave a shrill whistle, when an immense Eel instantly issued forth and moved about over the water, eating readily out of his hand.

If Eels are kept in confinement and not closely covered up, or shut in with smooth steep sides, they will almost certainly make their escape—generally in the night-time— and travel overland to any water which may be in their neighbourhood. The same thing occurs on a stream or pond being dried up in summer, when the Eels will quit it and wind through the wet grass in search of another. Occasionally they appear to migrate in this manner in pursuit of frogs and other suitable food, and at other times merely from a desire to change their residence.

There are some ponds that continually produce Eels, even where great efforts are made to get rid of them owing to their destructiveness to the spawn and fry of other fish ;

* Edinburgh New Phil. Journ. for April 1841.
† Polynesian Researches, vol. ii. p. 286.

whilst others again, which have been frequently and intentionally stocked with them, cannot be made to produce a single specimen : the quality of the water is obnoxious to them, or the food is not to their taste ; and they leave such pools during the night and seek fresh retreats, having been on several occasions actually caught *in transitu.* An instance of this is mentioned by Dr. Hastings *:—"A relative of the late Mr. Perrott was out in his park with his keeper, near a large piece of water, on a beautiful evening, when the keeper drew his attention to a fine Eel ascending the bank of the pool, and with an undulating motion making its way through the long grass : on further observation he perceived a considerable number of Eels quietly proceeding in the same manner to a range of stews nearly a quarter of a mile distant from the large piece of water whence they started. The stews were supplied by a rapid brook ; and in all probability the instinct of the fish led them in that direction as a means of finding their way to some large river, where their ultimate destination, the sea, might be obtained." This circumstance took place at Sandford Park, near Enstone.

The mode in which Eels effect their escape from a basin or other similar place of confinement is peculiar. They commence tail instead of head first, throwing the former over the edge of the vessel, and by this means gradually lifting themselves out. In all the Eels and other burrowing fish the tail is remarkably powerful and muscular.

* Illustrations of the Natural History of Worcestershire, p. 134.

That Eels breed in fresh as well as in salt water appears to be almost certain. A constant supply for the table is obtained all the year round from inland ponds whence there is no communication with the sea; and the following notes in a letter from Mr. Young apparently put the matter beyond doubt.

"The rivers in Scotland," he says, "were very low in the month of July, and I watched the motions of the Eels in swarms (as I thought spawning) on the sand and gravel banks in the river Shin. I should have mentioned this circumstance to you whilst here, had I not wished to be more certain; but in October last I got a few men and made them dig out one of the gravel banks where I had observed the Eels all together, and found it alive with young Eels, some of them scarcely hatched, at the depth of from 6 to 15 inches." The conclusion arrived at by Mr. Young from this circumstance is, that the river-Eel does not go down to the brackish waters to spawn at all, but deposits its spawn amongst the gravelly and sandy beds of the stream during the summer months,—the eggs hatching in the following September and October, but remaining concealed in the gravel until the succeeding April or May (according to the warmth of the season), when the young issue forth, the adult Eels, instead of migrating, hiding themselves upon the first cold weather in banks and under stones in the river, and there hibernating. This theory may probably be the true one in regard to many ponds (where, as observed, Eels certainly breed, and equally certainly remain all the winter), and possibly also in some rivers; but it appears also clear that in the great majority of rivers the Eels spawn in the brackish water, as before stated.

The most absurd ideas have prevailed at different times, amongst both ancients and moderns, as to the mode in which Eels are generated. Oppian believed that they were born of the slime with which their scales are covered; Aristotle that they sprang from the mud; Pliny that they were produced from particles separated from their bodies by friction against rocks and stones, and which, descending to the bed of the river, vivified and became a host of Eelets; and other authors, again, that they proceeded from the carcases of animals. Helmont assured his contemporaries that they were the birth of May-dew (as versified in the lines elsewhere quoted), and might be obtained by the following recipe:—"Cut up two turfs covered with May-dew, and lay one upon the other, the grassy sides inwards, and thus expose them to the heat of the sun; in a few hours there will spring from them an infinite quantity of Eels."

Another never-failing plan was to sow the river with chopped horsehair. In fact, the fallacies on this subject were endless, and it is difficult to award the palm of pre-eminence in absurdity. A far less unreasonable opinion was held until very late years, namely that Eels were viviparous. There seems now, however, to be no doubt that they are *oviparous*, although their habits, and circumstances connected with their structure, make it difficult to discover specimens containing the fully developed eggs. Of the fact of their being oviparous the immense number of young produced by them is a very fair negative proof,—viviparous fishes, such as the Sharks, Blennies, &c., producing but very few young at a time, and *those of considerable size when first born.* The eggs of the Eel are exceedingly minute, and the organs of reproduction differ somewhat from those of other fishes *.

The Eelets, or Elvers, are at first very small and transparent; gradually the skin becomes opaque, and finally black; in May and June they are of a greenish-brown colour, and from 4 to 7 or 8 inches long, attaining a length of not more than a foot during the first year, and maturing the roe only after the second or third year. They finally, however, acquire a large size. Yarrell mentions having seen the preserved skins of two of the Sharpnosed species which had together weighed 50 lbs., the heavier of the two having been 27 lbs.; these eels were taken in draining a fen-dyke at Wisbeach. No other fish of any sort were found in that dyke—a circumstance which is not very surprising considering the voracity of the species and the size of the individuals for whose appetite they had to cater. Failing a sufficient supply of fish, Eels will feed

---

* In some drawings in the Collection of John Hunter, published since his death, these peculiarities are beautifully exhibited; and Dr. Hornschuch, in an inaugural thesis dated 1842, has given very good figures and descriptions of the same parts.

greedily upon spawn, worms, larvæ, and in fact upon every
description of animal matter; and it is even said that they
have occasionally been seen swimming about on the surface of the water and cropping the leaves of small aquatic
plants. They have also been known to attack Carp and
other fish of large size, seizing them by the fins, though
apparently without the power of doing them any further
injury.

In the 'Practical Angler' (p. 13) it is stated that an Eel
has been seen to dart suddenly against a Trout, striking
it so forcibly in the eye with the protruding lower jaw that
the Trout was stunned, and floated insensible down the
stream. This it has somewhat fancifully been suggested
might have been an instinct on the part of the Eel, which
knew that it could not eat a fish of that size whilst alive,
but that it might easily pick its bones when dead.

The size attained by the Conger Eel is enormous. I have
in several instances seen it as thick round as a man's
thigh; and on one occasion a fish of this sort which was
pulled into my boat in a crab-net bit one of the sailors so
sharply through his thick wading-boots that he was lame
for some time afterwards. The singularity of this incident
is increased by the fact that the body of the Eel was divided
in two complete pieces when the head portion inflicted the
injury. This fish attains an immense size at St. Helena,
where more than one person has lost his life through
having become entangled in his line (a small rope) and
being dragged into the sea. It is not an uncommon prac-

Missing Page

Missing Page

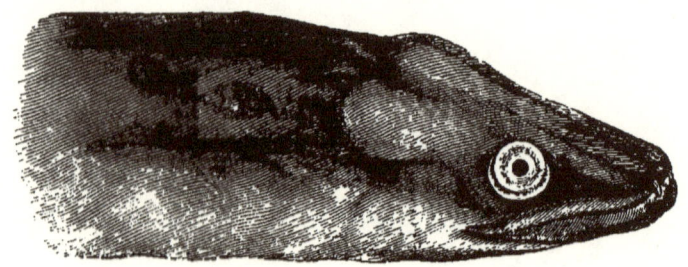

THE BROAD-NOSED EEL.

(*Anguilla latirostris* *.)

The points in which the Broad-nosed Eel differs from the Sharp- and Medium-nosed species are given at page 378. Beyond these, it is not distinguished by any peculiarities that I am aware of from the other common Eel, excepting in the nature of its food, which is filthy in the extreme, whilst the Sharp-nosed species is comparatively a cleanly feeder. The Broad-nosed Eel is moreover altogether a fiercer and more voracious fish, dashing at and seizing its prey much as a terrier does a rat. This Eel, which seldom exceeds 5 lbs. in weight, is the Grig or Glut Eel of Pennant, and it is probably also the " Frog-mouthed Eel " of the Severn referred to by Dr. Hastings †, and so called by the fishermen from its extraordinary width of mouth. It exists in many of the waters which produce the Sharp-nosed species.

* *Anguilla*, a little snake; *latus*, broad, and *rostrum*, a nose or snout, Lat.   † Natural History of Worcestershire, p. 135.

The term " Grig " is in the neighbourhood of the metropolis applied to a particular Eel of small size, of which the annexed figure represents the head. Grig is also a

name given by the Thames fishermen to any small Eel of not more than 9 or 10 inches in length.

In a Broad-nosed Eel of 22 inches in length, the three measurements given in the last species, p. 396, are respectively as 2 to 13, as 1 to 3, and as 10 to 22. Head very large, rounded at the back part and flattened from the eyes forward; gape large; both jaws broad and blunt, lower jaw widest and longest; lips fleshy. Teeth more numerous than in either of the other species, larger, stronger, and forming a broader band round each jaw. Gill-openings, pectoral fins, and dorsal fin placed further back than in Sharp-nosed Eel. Back- and anal fins also much thicker and deeper. Tail broad and rounded. Vertebræ 115. Colour: upper surface of body dark greenish brown, varying somewhat with locality and nature of water or soil.

THE SNIG, or MEDIUM-NOSED EEL.

(*Anguilla mediorostris* *.)

Besides the characteristics in which this Eel is distinguished from the other two species, as stated at p. 377, —including width of head, shape of vertebræ, habits, colour, and locality,—it may be mentioned that it never attains the same size as any of the other English Eels, to which, however, it is considered as superior in flavour. In weight it seldom exceeds half a pound.

When fishing for Snigs, the fishermen reverse the position of their eel-pots, having found by experience that this species get into such pots as are set in the opposite direction as regards the current to those in which the common Eels are taken. The term " Snig " is used in some counties to express any sort of small Eel.

Principal Characteristics of the Snig.—Head intermediate in size and shape between the Broad-nosed and Sharp-nosed Eels; slightly depressed or flattened over the eyes; openings for nostrils longer, and mucus-pores about the lips larger and more conspicuous. Both jaws rounded at the extremities; the lower one the longest. Teeth larger

---

* *Anguilla*, a little snake; *medius*, medium-sized; *rostrum*, a nose, Lat.

and straighter than in the Sharp-nosed species; gape large. Pectoral fins and origin of back-fin placed nearer the head than in any other of our fresh-water species. Colours : general colour above olive-green, passing into a lighter green, and thence into a yellowish white.

The vignette below gives a representation of a structural peculiarity noticed in the tail of the Eel. It consists of a pulsating organ, or "lymphatic heart" as it has been termed, which beats more rapidly than the proper heart of the animal, and the purposes of which have not hitherto been clearly recognized. A similar organ has been remarked in the Frog, the Toad, the Salamander, and the Green Lizard, and I have also observed it in the tail of the young fry of the Salmon when a few days old.

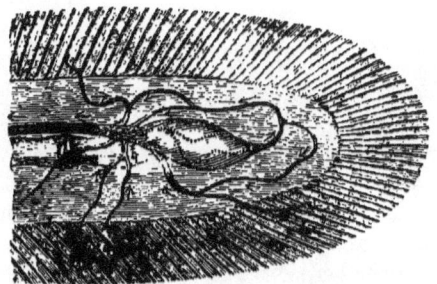

LYMPHATIC HEART IN THE TAIL OF AN EEL.

CHAPTER XIII.

Series II. *CARTILAGINOUS FISH**.
Order II. *CHONDROPTERYGII BRAN-
CHIIS FIXIS* †.

Family *CYCLOSTOMATA* ‡.
Genus *PETROMYZON* §.

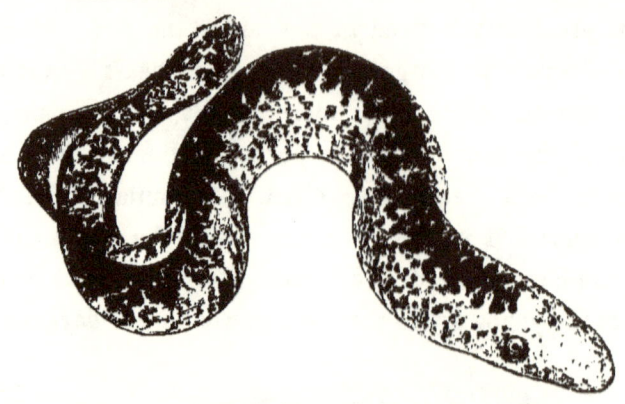

THE COMMON or SEA LAMPREY.

(*Petromyzon marinus* ‖.)

Characteristics common to the Family of " Round-mouthed" fish.—
No pectoral or ventral fins: body ending in a circular fleshy lip, with
a cartilaginous ring supporting it: no proper ribs or solid gill-arches,
and the vertebræ reduced to cartilaginous rays not readily distinguished from one another. Nostrils opened by a single orifice. In-
testine straight and narrow.

THE characteristics of the Lampreys as a genus are—

* *Chondropterygii,* from Gr. *chondros,* cartilage, and *pterygion,* a fin:
Fish without bones in their structure. (See p. 38.)

† "Cartilaginous fish with fixed gills." (See p. 38.)

‡ *Cyclostomata,* " Round- or Sucking-mouthed fish," from Gr. *cyclos,*
a circle, and *stoma,* a mouth.

§ *Petromyzon,* " Stone-sucker," from *petros,* a stone, and *myzo,* I
suck, Gr. ‖ *marinus,* Lat., of the sea.

body smooth and eel-like; head rounded; mouth circular, armed with hard tooth-like processes; tongue (which moves backwards and forwards like a piston, and causes the suction) with two longitudinal rows of small teeth; seven apertures on each side of neck, leading to seven branchial or gill-cells; the skin, towards the tail, extending in a fold above and below, forming the back-, anal-, and tail-fins, which are without rays.

The Eels are the last of the Bony Series of British fresh-water fish (in which are embraced all the species of which the sportsman takes cognizance); and we now commence the Cartilaginous Series, or those in which the skeleton is composed of gristle or cartilage. To the last family of this series belong the Lampreys, which, with one or two allied species, are, in reference to their skeleton and in some other respects, the lowest in the scale of creation amongst vertebrate animals, or animals possessing a ' back-bone.'

A few remarks here upon the habits of Lampreys and Lamperns generally, may prevent the necessity of repetition under each individual species.

In all these fish the swimming-bladder is absent; and as they are also without any pectoral fins, they usually swim at or very near the bottom of the water, where, in order to resist the current, they attach themselves by the mouth to stones or rocks, and have been consequently named *Petromyzonidæ* or " Stone-suckers."

The shape of this mouth or sucker will be best explained by a reference to the annexed engraving of the head of the common Lamprey (*Petromyzon marinus*), in which the left-hand figure represents the mouth of the fish when at rest, or closed, and that on the right the same organ when open, or in the act of suction—the point of view in both cases being from below. The small and numerous tubercular teeth are also shown in the right-hand engraving, and the central aperture leading by the throat to the stomach. The mouth is provided with a flexible lip, which effectually conceals its shape when closed. The organ of suction is the tongue.

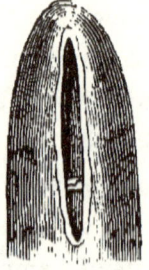   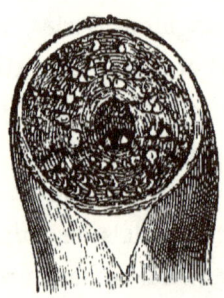

MOUTH WHEN SHUT.   MOUTH WHEN OPEN.

As it would obviously be impossible for these fish, when adhering to stones or other fixed objects (their natural position), to breathe through their mouths in the usual way, Nature has provided them with a breathing-apparatus differing from that of other species, and admirably adapted to their peculiar exigencies.

This consists of seven small apertures on each side of the neck leading to seven cells, in which are situated the

gills, and through these apertures the water obtains access
and egress, or by an aperture through the top of the head
communicating with the throat.   When the fish is swimming free, the water also reaches the gills by a peculiar
membranous canal, or trachea, placed under the gullet
and perforated with holes.   The position of the gill-cells
&c., is exhibited in the accompanying engraving of the
neck of the River-Lamprey, or Lampern as it is more
commonly called, a portion of the skin being removed to
show the arrangement beneath.

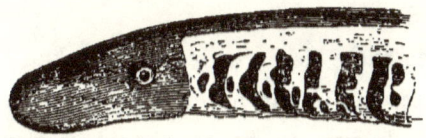

The Lampreys are all oviparous, and spawn late in the
spring.

To return to the common Lamprey (*Petromyzon marinus*).

This species appears to be generally diffused over most
of the rivers and seas of Europe and America, attaining,
however, a larger size in the southern than in the northern
latitudes—in the colder climates seldom exceeding from
17 to 20 inches.   During spring and summer they abound
to a considerable extent in some of the streams on the
southern coast of England, particularly in the Severn, and

to a lesser degree in several of the Scotch and Irish rivers at about the same period of the year.

They make their appearance in the fresh waters in England in April and May, and in Scotland in June, for the purpose of spawning, and are then considered to be in the most perfect condition. Pennant mentions that it is an ancient custom for the city of Gloucester annually to present the Sovereign with a Lamprey-pie covered with a large raised crust; and at Rodney, in Gloucester, a rent called "Pride Gavel" is paid by certain tenants to the lord of the manor for the liberty of fishing for Lampreys in the river Severn.

In the Lea these fish are frequently taken of from 1 to 3 lbs. weight; but in the Severn they attain a larger size, having been known to be caught more than 3 feet in length and 5 inches in diameter.

The food of the Lamprey consists generally of animal matter; and in the sea it will attack fish greatly superior to itself in size, fastening pertinaciously upon them, and gradually eating its way to the very bone. It is not unfrequently found in eel-pots and other similar receptacles, and is occasionally taken by anglers whilst fishing with a worm. Its motion when swimming is undulating and eel-like: where the current is rapid it moves by successive plunges, attaching itself instantaneously to the nearest fixed object that offers, so as to secure the advance gained.

In the "Treatyse of Fysshynge wyth an Angle" (included in the 'Boke of St. Albans,' 1496), the authoress, after prescribing a minnow and worm as appropriate baits for a March Trout, adds,—"In Aprill take the same baytes; and also Juneba, other wyse named VII. Eyes." 'Seven eyes' and 'Nine eyes,' in reference to the apertures about the head, are still common names for the Lamprey in this country and elsewhere. This fish is believed to deposit its spawn in holes in the sand or mud, where the eggs are soon hatched, and in three months the young attain a length of from 4 to 5 inches.

Characteristics of the Sea-Lamprey.—Ordinary length from 20 to 28 inches. Head rounded. Teeth small, numerous, and tubercular. Body long and cylindrical, slightly compressed towards the tail. An external aperture on top of the head, between eyes. Two distinct membranous back-fins. Colour of body olive-brown, very much mottled and spotted on back and sides with dark brown. By this mottled colouring alone the Sea-Lamprey may be at once distinguished from its congeners. Margin of fins inclining to reddish brown.

THE LAMPERN, or RIVER-LAMPREY.

(*Petromyzon fluviatilis* *.)

The River-Lamprey, or Lampern, is distinguished from the Sea-Lamprey more particularly by its size, colour, and arrangement of teeth. Its length is usually from 12 to 15 inches, whilst that of the Sea-Lamprey in England ranges from 20 to 28 inches; the colour of the latter is *mottled* and spotted with dark green and brown, and in the former is uniform blue on the back and sides, passing into silvery white underneath. The difference in the arrangement of the teeth will be observed by comparing the woodcut above with that at p. 404. In other respects its external characteristics closely resemble those of the Sea-Lamprey before described.

The Lampern is well known in English rivers, particularly in the Thames, the Severn, and the Dee, and also in many of the streams of Scotland and Ireland.

---

* *Petromyzon*, Stone-sucker, Gr.; *fluviatilis*, of the river, Lat.

Some authors have thought that this species, like that last described, visits the fresh waters in spring and early summer and returns to the sea after spawning; but the recorded opinions of others, including Yarrell, lead me to believe that it generally remains all the year in fresh water. "In the Thames," says the latter author, "I am certain it is to be obtained every month in the year; but it is considered in the best condition for the table from October to March, during which time it is permitted to be caught, according to the rules adopted for the conservation of the fishery."

The Lampern was formerly a fish of considerable importance in the neighbourhood of the Thames. It was taken in great quantities from Battersea to Taplow Mills, and sold to the Dutch as bait for Cod, Turbot, and other fish, 400,000 having been disposed of during one season in this manner at the rate of 40s. per 1000; a comparative scarcity of late years, however, has occasioned an increase in their price. Formerly the Thames alone supplied from 1,000,000 to 1,200,000 Lamperns annually.

The Lampern spawns in May, and its food consists of insects, worms, small live fish, and the flesh of dead ones.

TEETH OF PETROMYZON OMALII.

For a knowledge of this Lampern I am indebted to Sir John Richardson, who mentions that the species was discovered by M. P. J. Van Beneden. It is an inhabitant of the British Channel, but has hitherto been taken only on the Belgian coast, and by its discoverer alone. As it will very probably sooner or later be found in British waters, an illustration of the arrangement of its teeth (which is unique) is given, together with its principal characteristics * :—Length under 6 inches. Colour silvery white. Fins and external orifices like those of the Fringe-lipped Lampern. Mouth circular and symmetrical.

* From Bulletin de l'Acad. Roy. de Belgique, 2me série, xi. No. 7, 1857.

THE FRINGE-LIPPED LAMPERN.

(Petromyzon Planeri *.)

This Lampern, when full-grown, is easily to be distinguished from the River-Lamprey, or Lampern, by its much greater thickness as contrasted with its length. On comparison, it may also be recognized at all stages of growth by its having the broad edge of the circular lip furnished with a thickly-set fringe of papillæ, and by the depth and close connexion of the two dorsal fins: from the Sea-Lamprey it is distinguished by the mottled colouring of the latter. The arrangement of the teeth is shown in the engraving.

This species is found in the rivers of all parts of Ireland ; in the Forth, the Teith, the Allan, and the Tweed, in Scotland ; and, in England, in the streams of Surrey, Sussex, Lancashire, and Cornwall, and probably also in many others. In this country its length is usually about 8 inches in the males and 9 inches in the females. In food, habits, spawning-time, colouring, &c., the Fringe-lipped Lampern

* " Planer's Stone-sucker."

T 2

so closely resembles the common or River-Lampern as frequently to be mistaken for it ; and it is possible that at some period of the year both may migrate to salt or brackish water from that part of a river within tidal influence.

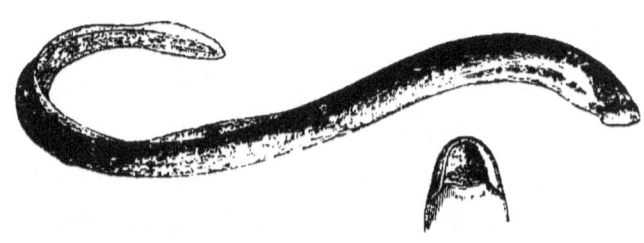

YOUNG OF FRINGE-LIPPED LAMPERN.

(Pride, Sandpride, Sandprey, Sand-lurker, Stone-Grig, and Mud-Lamprey.)

This small fish, which has until lately been considered as a separate species, has been discovered by Müller to be the young of the Fringe-lipped Lampern—although the differences in structure are so great, that the assumption of the adult form almost amounts to a transformation or metamorphosis, of a similar nature, though less in degree, to that which takes place in the tadpole on becoming a frog ; and there is every reason to believe that a somewhat similar change occurs in the case of the young of the other Lampreys, thus opening a new and interesting field to the researches of the naturalist.   In the adult Lampreys, the mouth, as already explained, performs the functions of a sucker; but in the young it has the form of a horse-shoe, the lower edge of the circle being not sufficiently developed for the purpose of suction; the teeth are unformed, and there are other remarkable structural differences.   It, therefore, has not the power of attaching itself to stones, &c., like the adult Lampreys, but usually buries itself in the mud or sand at the bottom of rivers and brooks, in most of which it will be discovered upon close search.   Its length seldom exceeds 6 or 7 inches, and its thickness is about equal to that of a large quill : the most common colour is yellowish brown, approaching somewhat to black on the top of the head and upper part of the back, getting much lighter underneath and on the fins.

These small Lampreys make excellent bait for eels and for some species of sea-fish.

The vignette shows the arrangement of the parts concerned in the respiration of the common or Sea-Lamprey, reduced from Plate 11, Philosophical Transactions, 1815.

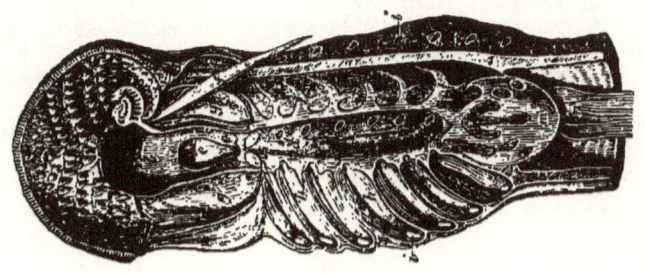

APPENDIX.

. . . .

DIRECTIONS FOR PRESERVING FISH.

First Method.—Wipe the fish dry; make a slit in the belly about half as long as the head, so that the preserving-fluid may reach the intestines, &c., and place it in a bottle containing any of the following mixtures—viz. common spirits of wine; methylated spirits of wine (a cheaper medium); carbolic acid (much cheaper than either), prepared according to the directions given below*; or, failing these, in any strong spirit that may be at hand: the bottle should be deep enough to hold the fish without bending it. As wide-mouthed bottles are rather expensive, pickle-bottles, or bottles used by pastry-cooks for keeping sweetmeats &c. in, will do as well, if large enough for the specimen. The bottle should be tightly corked, and, when sealed up *for permanent keeping*, a piece of wet bladder placed round the cork underneath, and another piece over it—the whole being covered with a layer of tin-foil, and afterwards varnished. To fix the fish in the bottle, suspend it from the cork, by a thread passed with a needle through one or both of its lips.

* *Carbolic acid.*—This is a recent invention for preserving fish, and will, I am assured by those who have tried it, be found to answer well. Its great advantage is that enough acid can be carried in a small bottle in the waistcoat-pocket to prepare 5 gallons of fluid. The acid, which is not otherwise soluble, is to be mixed in *boiling water* in the proportion of half an ounce (or two teaspoonsful) to a gallon, and used when cool. Carbolic acid can be procured, I believe, from most chemists; but that shown to me was obtained from Mr. Allgood, 14 Albany Street, London.

Second Method.—If no spirit of any kind can be procured, the fish may be preserved for a short period by first soaking them for a day or two in strong brine (salt and water), making a slit as before, and afterwards placing them, entirely covered and surrounded by salt, in a box or other receptacle. This may sometimes prove a convenience to sportsmen, as fish thus temporarily preserved are less easily destroyed in conveyance, or when travelling, than if preserved in fluid.

[It is earnestly hoped that in the event of any peculiar specimens of Trout, Charr, or other fish being met with, anglers will preserve them as suggested, and forward them for inspection, either to the Curator of the Ichthyological Gallery of the British Museum, or to some other competent naturalist for his examination and report.

Dr. Günther of the British Museum informs me that he is about to make a collection of the Trout (*Salmo fario*) of the British Islands, with a view to determining whether there are not, in fact, several distinct species at present included under this name; and he will, I am sure, be much obliged by any assistance which Anglers may give him in the task. In fact, it is only through the cooperation of fishermen that a comprehensive collection of these numerous fish can ever be practically made.]

To preserve heads of Fish.—Take out the eyes; place a piece of stick between the jaws to keep them wide open; wash the head thoroughly over with a solution of corrosive sublimate (four grains to the ounce of water), and hang it up, under cover, where it can swing in the wind; wash it a few times with the solution at intervals of two or three days; and when it is quite hard and dry, varnish it with shellac or copal varnish, inserting glass eyes in the sockets. If a difficulty is found in drying, place the head for a day or two in the kitchen fender.

Note.—In preserving in spirit it will usually be found

that the first bottle of fluid will become discoloured from the impurities of the fish. To provide for this, those who preserve largely often keep a jar of soiled spirit in which to place the fish before finally preserving them.

The best stuffer of fish is Mr. J. Cooper, Radnor Street, St. Luke's, London.

TAKING OF UNDERSIZED FISH IN THE THAMES.

Since the foregoing pages went to press, an excellent regulation has been issued by the Thames Angling Preservation Society for counteracting the wholesale destruction of small fish in their waters. The following is a copy of the notice issued by them on this subject :—

" *Undersized Fish.*—Anglers are requested to return to the waters all fish of less size than those authorized to be taken by the 24th item of the ' Rules, Orders, and Ordinances of the Fisheries in Thames and Medway,' or they render themselves liable to a penalty of £5 for every offence. The following are the weight and sizes of fish that are allowed to be taken :—Trout, not less than 1 lb. ; Pike, Jack, or Barbel, not less than 12 inches ; Chub, not less than 9 inches ; Perch or Roach, not less than 8 inches ; Flounders, not less than 7 inches ; Dace or Smelts, not less than 6 inches ; Gudgeon, not less than 5 inches. In each case measuring from the eye to the end of the tail. The assistant River-keepers have received orders to lay information in all cases where undersized fish are taken ; and they have power at all times to enter any punt, to examine the wells, and to seize all small fish that may have been taken of less size than those stated above.— W. H. BROUGHAM, Hon. Sec."

INDEX

(INCLUDING GLOSSARY OF TECHNICAL TERMS USED).

THE END.

PRINTED BY TAYLOR AND FRANCIS,
RED LION COURT, FLEET STREET.

WORKS BY THE SAME AUTHOR.

HOW TO SPIN FOR PIKE.

Second Edition, enlarged. Illustrated.

Field.—" Mr. Pennell's views in regard to spinning-tackle, as well as others connected with the art, certainly meet with our warm approbation. . . . His mode of employing flying-triangles is to us original."

" I tried to remedy these defects [in spinning-flights]; but my tackle, though a step in the right direction, was defective. Mr. Pennell's is, I am willing to admit, an improvement on it, and I am sure that no one who used his as I have ventured to modify it, will ever use mine again. I have, as a rival inventor, no jealousy whatever in the matter, being simply anxious to serve the angling world by finding the best tackle, and I am willing to own that I believe Mr. Pennell's to be so. I shall never use any other henceforth."—FRANCIS FRANCIS.

Sporting Life.—" The author's chief maxim, ' fish-fine,' is one which we have all along endeavoured to impress upon our piscatorial readers."

Sporting Gazette.—" Unlike the great majority of the lucubrations of the professors of the 'gentle art,' Mr. Pennell's volume is eminently practical, and is evidently the result of careful observation and long experience. Within the modest compass of something less than 30 pages he has contrived to compress, by some process of legerdemain best known to himself, a complete manual of the art of spinning, containing many invaluable hints, and a variety of information that will be novel even to the most experienced angler. . . Mr. Pennell is the first who has attempted to elucidate the causes of the loss of fish, 'kinking,' &c., on scientific principles. . . . His specific against kinking, the *bête noire* of the spinner, is alone worth ten times the price of the volume. . . A very few casts convinced us of the vast superiority of Mr. Pennell's tackle over any other description of spinning-tackle of which we have ever made trial."

PUCK ON PEGASUS.

Fourth Edition. Square 8vo, handsomely bound in cloth, gilt. Illustrated by upwards of 60 original Engravings, by Leech, Tenniel, " Phiz," Porch, and Geo. Cruikshank.

Saturday Review.—" Clever and amusing . . ."

Court Circular.—" One of the cleverest productions of the day, and gives the clearest evidence of the genius of its author in almost every page."

Press.—" We had occasion to speak highly of Mr. Pennell's powers when the first edition of this amusing *brochure* was published : it has now reached a fourth, at which we are not at all surprised. So facile is the rhyme, so natural the humour, that it is impossible not to be amused. . . . Mr. Pennell is a marvellous mimic—quite a Woodin amongst poets. Take, for example, a verse imitative of Tom Hood. . . . This is worthy of Hood himself. Still, excellent as is Mr. Pennell's mimicry, we prefer him in his own vein—the description of dashing and rapid movement. He is the poet of the railway and the racehorse. In such descriptions as these, his verse rises to poetry ; his words catch the rush of the steam-engine or the racer ; his metre seems to fly."

Examiner.—" Let Mr. Pennell trust to the original strength that is in him, and he may bestride his Pegasus without fear."

WORKS BY THE SAME AUTHOR.

Literary Budget.—"Mr. Pennell has caught the spirit, as well as the style, of the different poets he imitates, whilst his lines have an elegance, and a sly, bo-peep sort of beauty."

London Review.—"Humorous poetry of the genuine Ingoldsby or Bon Gaultier stamp is always welcomed by the reading public. . . . Few books of late years can boast such an array of comic talent. . . . The popularity this work has already attained serves to show that the author's desires have been crowned with success."

Frazer's Magazine.—"'Puck on Pegasus' is full of those eccentricities which make one laugh *with* oneself, or in spite of oneself, according as one takes it up in a grave or gay humour."

Morning Post.—"'Puck on Pegasus' is at the same time the handsomest and cheapest book of the kind that we have ever seen. . . . Puck, as he careers through the world on his mad horse, shoots arrows of the pleasantest raillery, dipped in *eau de Cologne* rather than gall, at the follies of the season, the artistic foibles of literary celebrities, and the affectations of all classes, high and low. Some of the youngster's capers are certainly unjustifiable ; but extravagant mirth is never severely judged when it expresses itself in easy running verses, the music of which is as sweet as their rhymes are ingenious and unexpected. Moreover, though Mr. Pennell's muse respects neither the age nor fame of those whom he satirises, he never forgets gentlemanly consideration for the feelings of his readers. A joke that would bring a blush to a maiden's cheek, or a sarcasm aimed at the inoffensive, are not to be found in his poems. Nor do we draw attention to the prevailing lightness of his muse in a spirit of condemnation, but rather of regret that the fine feeling and pathetic force manifested in the treatment of his two finest pieces, the ' Night Mail North,' and the ' Derby Day,' should have inspired him less frequently than mere gaiety of heart. . . . The rhythm and rugged swing of the ' Night Mail North ' will give the reader a taste of Mr. Pennell's higher qualities."

Literary Gazette.—"To be funny without being vulgar, to tell a story with gestures and yet not become a buffoon, to parody a poet and yet retain the flavour of his real poetry, to turn all the finest feelings of the heart into fun and yet not to be coarse or unfeeling, is not granted by Apollo to every writer of humorous poems. . . . Mr. Pennell is an excellent parodyist, an ingenious punster, a reviver and modifier of existing systems of fun, a vigorous worker of veins of humour not yet carried far enough. . . . Of all the poems we like best the ' Night Mail North,' which has a singular weird power about it that takes a hold on the imagination."

Athenæum.—"This volume has fared sumptuously at the Publisher's hands : inside, a creamy luxury ; outside, a glory of magenta and gold. . . . One or two illustrative faces and figures are of Mr. Leech's loveliest. . . . Cruikshank's frontispiece is a jewel."

Preparing for the Press,

THE BOOK OF THE PIKE:

Containing a Natural History of the fish, and a complete practical guide to Jack-fishing in all its branches, with diagrams of various improved tackles. Illustrated.

Catalogue of Books

PUBLISHED BY MR. VAN VOORST.

INDEX.

JOHN VAN VOORST, 1 PATERNOSTER ROW.

Students' Class-Books.

MANUAL OF CHEMICAL QUALITATIVE ANALYSIS. By A. B. Northcote, F.C.S., and Arthur H. Church, F.C.S. Post 8vo, 10s. 6d.

HANDBOOK OF CHEMICAL MANIPULATION. By C. Greville Williams. 15s.

ELEMENTARY COURSE OF GEOLOGY, MINERALOGY, AND PHYSICAL GEOGRAPHY. By Professor Ansted, M.A., &c. Second Edition, 12s.

ELEMENTARY COURSE OF BOTANY: Structural, Physiological, and Systematic. By Professor Henfrey. 12s. 6d.

MANUAL OF BRITISH BOTANY. By Professor Babington, M.A., &c. Fifth Edition, 10s. 6d.

GENERAL OUTLINE OF THE ORGANIZATION OF THE ANIMAL KINGDOM. By Professor T. Rymer Jones. 8vo, Third Edition, £1 11s. 6d.

JOHN VAN VOORST, 1 PATERNOSTER ROW.

ZOOLOGY.

MAMMALIA.

A GUIDE TO THE QUADRUPEDS AND REPTILES OF EUROPE, with Descriptions of all the Species. By Lord CLERMONT. Post 8vo, 7s.

HISTORY OF BRITISH QUADRUPEDS, INCLUDING THE CETACEA. By THOMAS BELL, F.R.S., P.LS., Professor of Zoology in King's College, London. Illustrated by nearly 200 Engravings, comprising portraits of the animals, and vignette tail-pieces, 8vo. New Edition, with the cooperation of Mr. TOMES, in preparation.

NATURAL HISTORY OF THE SPERM WHALE, and a Sketch of a South Sea Whaling Voyage. By THOMAS BEALE. Post 8vo, 12s. cloth.

BIRDS.

HISTORY OF BRITISH BIRDS. By WILLIAM YARRELL, V.P.L.S., F.Z.S., &c. This work contains a history and a picture portrait, engraved expressly for the work, of each species of the birds found in Britain. Three volumes, containing 550 Illustrations. Third Edition, demy 8vo, £4 14s. 6d.

COLOURED ILLUSTRATIONS OF THE EGGS OF BRITISH BIRDS, with Descriptions of their Nests and Nidification. By WILLIAM C. HEWITSON. Third Edition, 2 vols. 8vo, £4 14s. 6d. The figures and descriptions of the Eggs in this edition are from different specimens to those figured in the previous editions.

SYSTEMATIC CATALOGUE OF THE EGGS OF BRITISH BIRDS, arranged with a View to supersede the use of Labels for Eggs. By the Rev. S. C. MALAN, M.A., M.A.S. On writing-paper. 8vo, 8s. 6d.

ORNITHOLOGICAL RAMBLES IN SUSSEX. By A. E. KNOX, M.A., F.L.S. Third Edition. Post 8vo, with Four Illustrations by Wolf, 7s. 6d.

FALCONRY IN THE VALLEY OF THE INDUS. By R. F. BURTON, Author of 'Goa and the Blue Mountains,' &c. Post 8vo, with Four Illustrations, 6s.

MONOGRAPH OF THE BIRDS FORMING THE TANAGRINE GENUS CALLISTE; illustrated by Coloured Plates of all the known species. By P. L. SCLATER, M.A., Fellow of Corpus Christi College, Oxford, F.R.S., F.Z.S., &c. 8vo, £2 2s.

BIRDS OF JAMAICA. By P. H. GOSSE, F.R.S., Author of the 'Canadian Naturalist,' &c. Post 8vo, 10s.

GEOGRAPHICAL AND COMPARATIVE LIST OF THE BIRDS OF EUROPE AND NORTH AMERICA. By CHARLES LUCIEN BONAPARTE, Prince of Musignano. 8vo, 5s.

THE DODO AND ITS KINDRED; or, The History, Affinities and Osteology of the Dodo, Solitaire, and other Extinct Birds of the Islands Mauritius, Rodriguez, and Bourbon. By H. E. STRICKLAND, M.A., F.G.S., F.R.G.S., and R. G. MELVILLE, M.D. Edin., M.R.C.S. Royal 4to, with 18 Plates and other Illustrations, £1 1s.

JOHN VAN VOORST, 1 PATERNOSTER ROW.

ORNITHOLOGICAL SYNONYMS. By the late HUGH EDWIN STRICK-
LAND, M.A., F.R.S., &c. Edited by Mrs. HUGH EDWIN STRICKLAND
and SIR WILLIAM JARDINE, Bart., F.R.S.E., &c. 8vo, Vol. I. containing
the Order Accipitres, 12s. 6d. Vol. II. in the press.

REPTILES.

HISTORY OF BRITISH REPTILES. By THOMAS BELL, F.R.S., Presi-
dent of the Linnean Society, V.P.Z.S., &c., Professor of Zoology in King's College, London. Second Edition, with 50 Illustrations, 12s.

FISHES.

PRODUCTION AND MANAGEMENT OF FISH IN FRESH WATERS,
by Artificial Spawning, Breeding, and Rearing. By GOTTLIEB BOCCIUS.
8vo, 5s.

HISTORY OF BRITISH FISHES. By WILLIAM YARRELL, V.P.L.S.,
F.Z.S., &c. Third Edition. Edited by SIR JOHN RICHARDSON, M.D.
Two vols. demy 8vo, illustrated by more than 500 Engravings, £3 3s.

YARRELL.—GROWTH OF THE SALMON IN FRESH WATER. With
Six Coloured Illustrations of the Fish of the natural size, exhibiting its structure and exact appearance at various stages during the first two years. 12s.
sewed.

HERALDRY OF FISH. By THOMAS MOULE. Nearly six hundred fami-
lies are noticed in this work, and besides the several descriptions of fish, fishing-
nets, and boats, are included also mermaids, tritons, and shell-fish. Nearly
seventy ancient seals are described, and upwards of twenty subjects in stained
glass. The engravings, two hundred and five in number, are from stained
glass, tombs, sculpture and carving, medals and coins, rolls of arms, and pedigrees. 8vo, 21s.; a few on large paper (royal 8vo) for colouring, £2 2s.

FLY-FISHING IN SALT AND FRESH WATER. With Six Coloured
Plates, representing Artificial Flies, &c. 8vo, 7s. 6d.

AN ANGLER'S RAMBLES. By EDWARD JESSE, F.L.S., Author of
'Gleanings in Natural History.' Contents:—Thames Fishing—Trolling in
Staffordshire—Perch Fishing Club—Two Days' Fly-fishing on the Test—Luck-
ford Fishing Club—Grayling Fishing—A Visit to Oxford—The Country Clergyman. Post 8vo, 10s. 6d.

INVERTEBRATA.

HISTORY OF BRITISH SESSILE-EYED CRUSTACEA (Sand-hoppers,
&c.). By C. SPENCE BATE, F.R S., F.L.S., and Professor WESTWOOD,
F.L.S., &c. With figures of all the species, and tail-pieces. Uniform with the
Stalk-eyed Crustacea by Professor Bell. Parts 1 to 10, each 2s. 6d.

HISTORY OF BRITISH STALK-EYED CRUSTACEA (Lobsters, Crabs,
Prawns, Shrimps, &c.). By THOMAS BELL, President of the Linnean Society, F.G.S., F.Z.S., Professor of Zoology in King's College, London. The
volume is illustrated by 174 Engravings of Species and tail-pieces. 8vo, £1 5s.;
royal 8vo, £2 10s.

JOHN VAN VOORST, 1 PATERNOSTER ROW.

BRITISH CONCHOLOGY; or, an Account of the Mollusca which now inhabit the British Isles and the surrounding Seas; with particulars of their habits and distribution. By J. GWYN JEFFREYS, F.R.S., F.G.S., &c. Vol. I. containing the Land and Freshwater Shells, post 8vo, with Nine Plates, price 12s.

INTRODUCTION TO CONCHOLOGY; or, Elements of the Natural History of Molluscous Animals. By GEORGE JOHNSTON, M.D., LL.D., Fellow of the Royal College of Surgeons of Edinburgh, Author of 'A History of the British Zoophytes.' 8vo, 102 Illustrations, 21s.

HISTORY OF BRITISH MOLLUSCA AND THEIR SHELLS. By Professor ED. FORBES, F.R.S., &c. and SYLVANUS HANLEY, B.A., F.L.S. Illustrated by a figure of each known Animal and of all the Shells, engraved on 203 copper-plates. 4 vols. 8vo, £6 10s.; royal 8vo, with the plates coloured, £13.

SYNOPSIS OF THE MOLLUSCA OF GREAT BRITAIN. Arranged according to their Natural Affinities and Anatomical Structure. By W. A. LEACH, M.D., F.R.S., &c. &c. Post 8vo, with 13 Plates, 14s.

HISTORY OF THE BRITISH MARINE TESTACEOUS MOLLUSCA. By WILLIAM CLARK. 8vo, 15s.

GENERA OF RECENT MOLLUSCA; arranged according to their Organization. By HENRY AND ARTHUR ADAMS. This work contains a description and a figure engraved on steel of each genus, and an enumeration of the species. 3 vols. 8vo, £4 10s.; or royal 8vo, with the plates coloured, £9.

MALACOLOGIA MONENSIS. A Catalogue of the Molluscs inhabiting the Isle of Man and the neighbouring Sea. By EDWARD FORBES. Post 8vo, 3s. (Edinburgh, 1838.)

HISTORY OF BRITISH STAR-FISHES, AND OTHER ANIMALS OF THE CLASS ECHINODERMATA. By EDWARD FORBES, M.W.S., Professor of Botany in King's College, London. 8vo, with more than 120 Illustrations, 15s.; or royal 8vo, 30s.

ELEMENTS OF ENTOMOLOGY: an Outline of the Natural History and Classification of British Insects. By WILLIAM S. DALLAS, F.L.S. Post 8vo, 8s. 6d.

THE ENTOMOLOGIST'S ANNUAL FOR 1855 to 1863. 12mo, 2s. 6d. each.

HISTORY OF THE BRITISH ZOOPHYTES. By GEORGE JOHNSTON, M.D., LL.D. Second Edition, in 2 vols. 8vo, with an illustration of every species. £2 2s.; or on large paper, royal 8vo, £4 4s.

MANUAL OF THE SEA-ANEMONES COMMONLY FOUND ON THE ENGLISH COAST. By the Rev. GEORGE TUGWELL, Oriel College, Oxford. Post 8vo, with Coloured Illustrations, 7s. 6d.

NATURAL HISTORY OF ANIMALS. By Professor T. RYMER JONES. Vol. II. Insects, &c., with 104 Illustrations, post 8vo, 12s.

FAMILIAR INTRODUCTION TO THE HISTORY OF INSECTS; being a Second and greatly Improved Edition of the Grammar of Entomology. By EDWARD NEWMAN, F.L.S., Z.S., &c. With nearly 100 Illustrations, 8vo, 12s.

JOHN VAN VOORST, 1 PATERNOSTER ROW.

THE WORLD OF INSECTS: a Guide to its Wonders. By J. W. DOU-GLAS, Secretary to the Entomological Society of London. This work contains rambling observations on the more interesting members of the Insect World to be found in the House, the Garden, the Orchard, the Fields, the Hedges, on the Fences, the Heaths and Commons, the Downs, in the Woods, the Waters, or on the Sea Shore, or on Mountains. 12mo, stiff-paper wrapper, 3s. 6d.,

SIEBOLD ON TRUE PARTHENOGENESIS IN THE HONEY-BEE AND SILK-WORM MOTH. Translated from the German by W. S. DALLAS, F.L.S. 8vo, 5s.

PRACTICAL HINTS RESPECTING MOTHS AND BUTTERFLIES, with Notices of their Localities; forming a Calendar of Entomological Operations throughout the Year, in pursuit of Lepidoptera. By RICHARD SHIELD. 12mo, stiff-paper wrapper, 3s.

HEWITSON'S EXOTIC BUTTERFLIES. Vols. I. and II., containing 790 Coloured Figures of new or rare species, Five Guineas each volume.

Of Vol. III., Four Parts (41 to 44 of the entire work) are at this time published, 5s. each.

MANUAL OF BRITISH BUTTERFLIES AND MOTHS. By H. T. STAINTON. 2 vols. 12mo, 10s.

NATURAL HISTORY OF THE TINEINA. By H. T. STAINTON. Coloured Plates. Vol. I. to VII. 8vo, cloth, each 12s. 6d.

GEODEPHAGA BRITANNICA: a Monograph of the Carnivorous Ground-Beetles Indigenous to the British Isles. By J. F. DAWSON, LL.B. 8vo, without the Plates, 10s.

INSECTA MADERENSIA: being an Account of the Insects of the Islands of the Madeiran Group. By T. VERNON WOLLASTON, M.A., F.L.S. 4to, with Thirteen Coloured Plates of Beetles, £2 2s.

AN ACCENTUATED LIST OF THE BRITISH LEPIDOPTERA, with Hints on the Derivation of the Names. Published by the Entomological Societies of Oxford and Cambridge. 8vo, 5s.

BOTANY.

BRITISH WILD FLOWERS. Illustrated by JOHN E. SOWERBY. Described, with an Introduction and a Key to the Natural Orders, by C. PIERPOINT JOHNSON. Re-issue, to which is now added a Supplement containing 180 new figures, comprising lately discovered Flowering Plants, by JOHN W. SALTER, A.L.S., F.G.S.; and the Ferns, Horsetails and Club-Mosses, by JOHN E. SOWERBY. 8vo, with 1780 Coloured Figures, £3 3s.

BRITISH POISONOUS PLANTS. Illustrated by JOHN E. SOWERBY. Described by CHARLES JOHNSON, Botanical Lecturer at Guy's Hospital; and C. PIERPOINT JOHNSON. Second Edition, containing the principal Poisonous Fungi. Post 8vo, with 32 Coloured Plates, 9s. 6d.

JOHN VAN VOORST, 1 PATERNOSTER ROW.

THE BRITISH FERNS AT ONE VIEW. By BERTHOLD SEEMANN, Ph.D., F.L.S. An eight-page out-folding sheet, with descriptions of the Orders, Tribes, and Genera, and a Coloured figure of a portion of each species, 8vo, cloth, 6s.

FLORA OF CAMBRIDGESHIRE: or, A Catalogue of Plants found in the County of Cambridge, with References to former Catalogues, and the Localities of the Rarer Species. By C. C. BABINGTON, M.A., F.R.S., F.L.S., &c. 12mo, with a Map, 7s.

MANUAL OF BRITISH BOTANY; containing the Flowering Plants and Ferns, arranged according to their Natural Orders. By C. C. BABINGTON, M.A., F.R.S., F.L.S., &c., Professor of Botany in the University of Cambridge. 12mo, the Fifth Edition, with many additions and corrections, 10s. 6d., cloth.

WEEDS AND WILD FLOWERS. By LADY WILKINSON. Post 8vo, with Coloured Engravings and Woodcuts, 10s. 6d.

ELEMENTARY COURSE OF BOTANY; Structural, Physiological, and Systematic. With a brief Outline of the Geographical and Geological Distribution of Plants. By ARTHUR HENFREY, F.R.S., L.S., &c., Professor of Botany in King's College, London. Illustrated by upwards of 500 Woodcuts. Post 8vo, 12s. 6d.

VEGETATION OF EUROPE, ITS CONDITIONS AND CAUSES. By Professor HENFREY. Foolscap 8vo, 5s.

PRINCIPLES OF THE ANATOMY AND PHYSIOLOGY OF THE VEGETABLE CELL. By HUGO VON MOHL. Translated, with the author's permission, by Professor HENFREY. 8vo, with an Illustrative Plate and numerous Woodcuts, 7s. 6d.

RUDIMENTS OF BOTANY. A Familiar Introduction to the Study of Plants. By Professor HENFREY. With Illustrative Woodcuts. Second Edition, foolscap 8vo, 3s. 6d.

A SET OF SIX COLOURED DIAGRAMS; for Schools and Lectures. By Professor HENFREY. 15s.

THESAURUS CAPENSIS: or, Illustrations of the South African Flora; being Figures and brief descriptions of South African Plants, selected from the Dublin University Herbarium. By W. H. HARVEY, M.D., F.R.S., Professor of Botany in the University of Dublin, and Keeper of the Herbarium. 8vo, Vol. I., with 100 Plates, uncoloured, £1 1s.

FLORA CAPENSIS; being a Systematic Description of the Plants of the Cape Colony, Caffraria, and Port Natal. By Professor HARVEY and Dr. SONDER. 8vo, Vol. I. Ranunculaceæ to Connaraceæ. Vol. II. Leguminosæ to Loranthaceæ. Each 12s.

INDEX GENERUM ALGARUM: or, a Systematic Catalogue of the Genera of Algæ, Marine and Freshwater: with an Alphabetical Key to all the Names and Synonyms. By Professor HARVEY. 8vo, sewed, 2s. 6d.

MANUAL OF THE BRITISH MARINE ALGÆ, containing Generic and Specific Descriptions of all the known British Species of Sea-Weeds, with Plates to illustrate all the Genera. By Professor HARVEY. 8vo, £1 1s. Coloured Copies, £1 11s. 6d.

JOHN VAN VOORST, 1 PATERNOSTER ROW.

NEREIS BOREALI-AMERICANA; or, Contributions towards a History of the Marine Algæ of the Atlantic and Pacific Coasts of North America. By Professor HARVEY. Royal 4to, with 50 Coloured Plates, £3 3s.

HISTORY OF BRITISH FOREST-TREES. By PRIDEAUX JOHN SELBY, F.R.S.E., F.L.S., &c. Each species is illustrated by a portrait of some well-known or fine specimen, as a head-piece: the leaf, florification, seed-vessels, or other embellishments tending to make the volume ornamental or useful, are embodied in the text or inserted as tail-pieces. 8vo, with nearly 200 Illustrations, £1 8s.

MANUAL FLORA OF MADEIRA AND THE ADJACENT ISLANDS OF PORTO SANTO AND THE DEZERTAS. By R. T. LOWE, M.A. 12mo. Part I. Thalamifloræ. Part II. Calycifloræ. Each 3s. 6d.

PRIMITIÆ ET NOVITIÆ FAUNÆ ET FLORÆ MADERÆ ET PORTUS SANCTI. Two Memoirs on the Ferns, Flowering Plants, and Land Shells of Madeira and Porto Santo. By R. T. LOWE, M.A. 12mo, 6s. 6d., boards (150 copies printed).

WALKS AFTER WILD FLOWERS; or the Botany of the Bohereens. By RICHARD DOWDEN. Foolscap 8vo, 4s. 6d.

TERRA LINDISFARNENSIS. The Natural History of the Eastern Borders. By GEORGE JOHNSTON, M.D., &c., &c. This volume embraces the Topography and Botany; and gives the popular Names and Uses of the Plants, and the Customs and Beliefs which have been associated with them. The chapter on the Fossil Botany of the district is contributed by GEORGE TATE, F.G.S. Illustrated with a few Woodcuts and 15 Plates, 8vo, 10s. 6d.

HISTORY OF BRITISH FERNS. By EDWARD NEWMAN. Comprising, under each Species, Figures, detailed Descriptions, an ample List of Localities, and minute Instructions for Cultivating. 8vo, 18s.

SYNOPSIS OF THE BRITISH DIATOMACEÆ; with Remarks on their Structure, Functions, and Distribution; and Instructions for Collecting and Preserving Specimens. By the Rev. WILLIAM SMITH. The Plates by TUFFEN WEST. In 2 vols. royal 8vo. Vol. I. 21s.; Vol. II. 30s.

CHEMISTRY, MINERALOGY, GEOLOGY.

A MANUAL OF CHEMICAL ANALYSIS (Qualitative). By A. B. NORTHCOTE, F.C.S., and ARTHUR H. CHURCH, F.C.S. Post 8vo, 10s. 6d.

HANDBOOK OF CHEMICAL MANIPULATION. By C. GREVILLE WILLIAMS, late Principal Assistant in the Laboratories of the Universities of Edinburgh and Glasgow. Post 8vo, with very numerous Woodcut Illustrations, 15s.

JOHN VAN VOORST, 1 PATERNOSTER ROW.

ELEMENTARY COURSE OF GEOLOGY, MINERALOGY, AND PHY-
SICAL GEOGRAPHY. By DAVID T. ANSTED, M.A., F.R.S., F.G.S., &c.,
Consulting Mining Engineer, Honorary Fellow of King's College, London,
Lecturer on Mineralogy and Geology at the H.E.I.C. Mil. Sem. at Addiscombe,
late Fellow of Jesus College, Cambridge. A Second Edition, post 8vo, with
many Illustrations, 12s.

THE ANCIENT WORLD. By Professor ANSTED. Second Edition, post
8vo, 10s. 6d., with 149 Illustrations.

"The work may be described as an outline of the history of vegetable and
animal life upon the globe, from the early age when there were only sea-
weeds and marine invertebrates as yet in existence, down to the era when
the mammals received among them the king of species, Man. By his inti-
mate acquaintance with the subject, and power of arrangement and description, Professor Ansted succeeds in producing a narration, which tells
in its entire range like a romance."—*Manchester Examiner*.

GOLD-SEEKER'S MANUAL. By Professor ANSTED. Foolscap 8vo, 3s. 6d.

GEOLOGIST'S TEXT-BOOK. Chiefly intended as a Book of Reference for
the Geological Student. By Professor ANSTED. Foolscap 8vo, 3s. 6d.

THE GROUND BENEATH US; its Geological Phases and Changes. Three
Lectures on the Geology of Clapham and the neighbourhood of London generally. By JOSEPH PRESTWICH, F.R.S., F.G.S., &c. 8vo, 3s. 6d. sewed.

GEOLOGICAL INQUIRY RESPECTING THE WATER-BEARING
STRATA OF THE COUNTRY AROUND LONDON, with reference espe-
cially to the Water Supply of the Metropolis, and including some Remarks on
Springs. By JOSEPH PRESTWICH, F.G.S., &c. 8vo, with a Map and
Woodcuts, 8s. 6d.

MANUAL OF THE MINERALOGY OF GREAT BRITAIN AND IRE-
LAND. By ROBERT PHILIPS GREG, F.G.S., and WILLIAM G. LETT-
SOM. 8vo, with numerous Woodcuts, 15s.

HISTORY OF BRITISH FOSSIL MAMMALS AND BIRDS. By Professor
OWEN. This volume is designed as a companion to that by Professor Bell
on the (Recent Mammalia) 'British Quadrupeds and Cetacea.' 8vo, with 237
Illustrations, £1 11s. 6d., or large paper (royal 8vo), £3 3s.

DESCRIPTION OF THE SKELETON OF AN EXTINCT GIGANTIC
SLOTH (Mylodon robustus). With Observations on the Osteology, Natural
Affinities, and probable Habits of the Megatherioid Quadrupeds in general.
By RICHARD OWEN, F.R.S., &c. 4to, £1 12s. 6d.

MEMOIRS OF HUGH E. STRICKLAND, M.A., Deputy Reader of Geology
in the University of Oxford. By SIR WILLIAM JARDINE, Bart.; with a
selection from his Printed and other Scientific Papers. Royal 8vo, Illustrated
by Maps, Geological Sections, Plates and Woodcuts, 36s.

OMPHALOS. An Attempt to Untie the Geological Knot. By P. H. GOSSE,
F.R.S. The law of Prochronism in organic creation. Post 8vo, with 56 Illustrations on wood, 10s. 6d.

JOHN VAN VOORST, 1 PATERNOSTER ROW.

GENERAL NATURAL HISTORY, &c.

ESSAYS AND OBSERVATIONS ON NATURAL HISTORY, ANATOMY, PHYSIOLOGY, PSYCHOLOGY, AND GEOLOGY. By JOHN HUNTER, F.R.S. Being his Posthumous Papers on those subjects, arranged and revised, with Notes, by RICHARD OWEN, F.R.S., D.C.L., Superintendent of the Natural History Department, British Museum, &c. &c. 2 vols. 8vo, £1 11s. 6d.

THE NORTH-ATLANTIC SEA-BED; comprising a Diary of the Voyage on board H.M.S. 'Bulldog' in 1860, and Observations on the Presence of Animal Life, and the Formation and Nature of Organic Deposits, at great depths in the Ocean. By G. C. WALLICH, M.D., F.L.S., F.G.S. Published with the sanction of the Lords Commissioners of the Admiralty. 4to, Part I., with Map and 6 Plates, 15s. Part II., completing the work, will contain the remaining portion of the letter-press and Plates (7 to 20), and will be published shortly.

MEMOIR OF THE REV. J. S. HENSLOW, M.A., F.L.S., F.G.S., F.C.P.S., Rector of Hitcham, and Professor of Botany in the University of Cambridge. By the REV. LEONARD JENYNS, M.A., F.L.S., F.G.S., F.C.P.S. Post 8vo, with a Photographic Portrait, 7s. 6d.

THE HONEY-BEE; its Natural History, Habits, Anatomy, and Microscopical Beauties. With Eight Tinted Illustrative Plates. By JAMES SAMUELSON, assisted by Dr. J. BRAXTON HICKS. (Forming a Second Part of Humble Creatures.) Post 8vo, 6s.

HUMBLE CREATURES (Part I.): THE EARTHWORM AND THE COMMON HOUSEFLY. In Eight Letters. By JAMES SAMUELSON, assisted by J. B. HICKS, M.D. Lond., F.L.S. With Microscopic Illustrations by the Authors. Second Edition, post 8vo, 3s. 6d.

GATHERINGS OF A NATURALIST IN AUSTRALASIA; being Observations principally on the Animal and Vegetable Productions of New South Wales, New Zealand, and some of the Austral Islands. By GEORGE BENNETT, M.D., F.L.S., F.Z.S. 8vo, with 8 Coloured Plates and 24 Woodcuts, 21s.

THE MICROGRAPHIC DICTIONARY: a Guide to the Examination and Investigation of the Structure and Nature of Microscopic Objects. By Dr. GRIFFITH and Professor HENFREY. Second edition, with 2459 Figures (many coloured), in 45 Plates and 812 Woodcuts, 840 pp., 8vo, £2 5s.

OBSERVATIONS IN NATURAL HISTORY; with a Calendar of Periodic Phenomena. By the Rev. LEONARD JENYNS, M.A., F.L.S. Post 8vo, 10s. 6d.

OBSERVATIONS IN METEOROLOGY; relating to Temperature, the Winds, Atmospheric Pressure, the Aqueous Phenomena of the Atmosphere, Weather Changes, &c. By the Rev. LEONARD JENYNS, M.A., F.L.S., &c. Post 8vo, 10s. 6d.

PRACTICAL METEOROLOGY. By JOHN DREW, Ph.D., F.R.A.S., Corresponding Member of the Philosophical Institute of Bâle. Second Edition, foolscap 8vo, with 11 Illustrative Plates, 5s.

THE AQUARIAN NATURALIST: a Manual for the Sea-side. By Professor T. RYMER JONES, F.R.S. Post 8vo, 544 pp., with 8 Coloured Plates, 18s.

JOHN VAN VOORST, 1 PATERNOSTER ROW.

NATURAL HISTORY OF ANIMALS; being the Substance of Three Courses of Lectures delivered before the Royal Institution of Great Britain. By T. RYMER JONES, F.R.S., Professor of Zoology in King's College, London. Post 8vo, Vol. I. with 105 Illustrations; Vol. II. with 104 Illustrations, 12s. each.

GENERAL OUTLINE OF THE ORGANIZATION OF THE ANIMAL KINGDOM, AND MANUAL OF COMPARATIVE ANATOMY. By T. RYMER JONES, F.R.S., Professor of Comparative Anatomy in King's College, London; late Fullerian Professor of Physiology to the Royal Institution of Great Britain, &c. &c. Third Edition, 8vo, £1 11s. 6d.

FIRST STEPS TO ANATOMY. By JAMES L. DRUMMOND, M.D., Professor of Anatomy and Physiology in the Belfast Royal Institution. With 12 Illustrative Plates. 12mo, 5s.

GREAT ARTISTS AND GREAT ANATOMISTS: a Biographical and Philosophical Study. By R. KNOX, M.D., F.R.S.E. Post 8vo, 6s. 6d.

ILLUSTRATIONS OF INSTINCT, deduced from the Habits of British Animals. By JONATHAN COUCH, F.L.S., Member of the Royal Geological Society, and of the Royal Institution of Cornwall, &c. Post 8vo, 8s. 6d.

DESCRIPTIVE ETHNOLOGY. By ROBERT GORDON LATHAM, M.D., F.R.S., Fellow of King's College, Cambridge; Vice-President of the Ethnological Society of London; Corresponding Member of the Ethnological Society of New York. 2 vols. 8vo, £1 12s. The portion on Indian Ethnology, separate, 16s.

NATURAL HISTORY OF THE VARIETIES OF MAN. By Dr. LATHAM. 8vo, Illustrated, £1 1s.

ETHNOLOGY OF EUROPE. By Dr. LATHAM. Foolscap 8vo, 5s.

ETHNOLOGY OF THE BRITISH ISLANDS. By Dr. LATHAM. Foolscap 8vo, 5s.

ETHNOLOGY OF THE BRITISH COLONIES AND DEPENDENCIES. By Dr. LATHAM. Foolscap 8vo, 5s.

MAN AND HIS MIGRATIONS. By Dr. LATHAM. Foolscap 8vo, 5s.

ANATOMICAL MANIPULATION; or, The Methods of pursuing Practical Investigations in Comparative Anatomy and Physiology. Also an Introduction to the Use of the Microscope, &c. By ALFRED TULK, M.R.C.S., M.E.S.; and ARTHUR HENFREY, F.L.S., M.Micr.S. With Illustrative Diagrams. Foolscap 8vo, 9s.

ON THE VARIATION OF SPECIES, with especial reference to the Insects; followed by an Inquiry into the Nature of Genera. By T. VERNON WOLLASTON, M.A., F.L.S. Post 8vo, 5s.

MANUAL OF NATURAL HISTORY FOR THE USE OF TRAVELLERS; being a Description of the Families of the Animal and Vegetable Kingdoms, with Remarks on the Practical Study of Geology and Meteorology. To which are appended Directions for Collecting and Preserving. By ARTHUR ADAMS, M.R.C.S.; W. BALFOUR BAIKIE, M.D.; and CHARLES BARRON, Curator of the Royal Naval Museum at Haslar. Post 8vo, 12s.

JOHN VAN VOORST, 1 PATERNOSTER ROW.

LETTERS OF RUSTICUS ON NATURAL HISTORY. Edited by EDWARD NEWMAN, F.L.S., F.Z.S., &c. 8vo, 8s. 6d.

THE ZOOLOGIST; a Journal of Natural History. Nos. 1 to 251, 1s. each.

THE SEA-SIDE BOOK: an Introduction to the Natural History of the British Coasts. By W. H. HARVEY, M.D., M.R.I.A., &c. With a Chapter on Fish and Fish Diet, by YARRELL. Foolscap 8vo, with 83 Woodcut Illustrations, 4th Edition, 5s.

A HISTORY OF THE BRITISH SEA-ANEMONES AND MADREPORES. With Coloured Figures of all the Species. By PHILIP HENRY GOSSE, F.R.S. 8vo, £1 1s.

HANDBOOK OF THE MARINE AQUARIUM; containing Practical Instructions for Constructing, Stocking, and Maintaining a Tank, and for Collecting Plants and Animals. By P. H. GOSSE, F.R.S. Foolscap 8vo, Second Edition, 2s. 6d.

MANUAL OF MARINE ZOOLOGY OF THE BRITISH ISLES. By P. H. GOSSE, F.R.S. Parts I. and II., 7s. 6d. each.

A NATURALIST'S RAMBLES ON THE DEVONSHIRE COAST. By P. H. GOSSE, F.R.S. With 28 Lithographic Plates, some coloured, post 8vo, One Guinea.

THE AQUARIUM: an Unveiling of the Wonders of the Deep Sea. By P. H. GOSSE, F.R.S. Post 8vo, Illustrated, Second Edition, 17s.

THE CANADIAN NATURALIST. By P. H. GOSSE, F.R.S. With 44 Illustrations of the most remarkable Animal and Vegetable productions. Post 8vo, 12s.

TENBY: A SEASIDE HOLIDAY. By P. H. GOSSE, F.R.S. Post 8vo, with 24 Coloured Plates, 21s.

THE ISLE OF MAN; its History, Physical, Ecclesiastical, and Legendary. By J. G. CUMMING, M.A., F.G.S. Post 8vo, 12s. 6d.

NATURAL HISTORY OF THE COUNTY OF STAFFORD; comprising its Geology, Zoology, Botany, and Meteorology: also its Antiquities, Topography, Manufactures, &c. By ROBERT GARNER, F.L.S. With a Geological Map and other Illustrations, 8vo, with a Supplement, 10s. Price of the Supplement, 2s. 6d.

THE NATURAL HISTORY OF SELBORNE. By the late Rev. GILBERT WHITE, M.A. A New Edition, with Notes by the Rev. LEONARD JENYNS, M.A., F.L.S., &c.; with 26 Illustrations, foolscap 8vo, 7s. 6d.

TRAVELS IN LYCIA, MILYAS, AND THE CIBYRATIS, in company with the late Rev. E. T. Daniell. By Lieut. SPRATT, R.N., and Professor EDWARD FORBES. Two vols. 8vo, with numerous Illustrations, including Views of the Scenery, Plans of Ancient Cities and Buildings, Plates of Coins and Inscriptious, Cuts of Rock Tombs, Fossils, and Geological Sections, and an original Map of Lycia, 36s.

HEALTHY RESPIRATION. By STEPHEN H. WARD, M.D. Foolscap 8vo, 1s. 6d.

TOBACCO AND ITS ADULTERATIONS. By HENRY P. PRESCOTT, of the Inland Revenue Department. With upwards of 250 Illustrations drawn and engraved on Forty Steel Plates. 8vo, 12s. 6d.

JOHN VAN VOORST, 1 PATERNOSTER ROW.

A LIFE OF LINNÆUS. By Miss BRIGHTWELL of Norwich. Foolscap 8vo, 3s. 6d.

SCENERY, SCIENCE, AND ART; being Extracts from the Note-book of a Geologist and Mining Engineer. By Professor D. T. ANSTED, M.A., F.R.S., &c. 8vo, with Woodcuts and Four Views in tinted lithography, 10s. 6d.

ILLUSTRATIONS OF ARTS AND MANUFACTURES; being a Selection from a Series of Papers read before the Society for the Encouragement of Arts, Manufactures, and Commerce. By ARTHUR AIKIN, F.L.S., F.G.S., &c., late Secretary to that Institution. Foolscap 8vo, 8s.

THE POOR ARTIST; or, Seven Eye-Sights and One Object. "SCIENCE IN FABLE." Foolscap 8vo, with a Frontispiece, 5s.

SUNDAY BOOK FOR THE YOUNG; or, Habits of Patriarchal Times in the East. With Woodcuts, 2s. 6d. By ANNE BULLAR.

Other Books for Young Persons, by Miss Bullar.

DOMESTIC SCENES IN GREENLAND AND ICELAND. With Woodcuts, 2s. Second Edition.

ENGLAND BEFORE THE NORMAN CONQUEST. 2s. 6d.

ELEMENTS OF PRACTICAL KNOWLEDGE; or, The Young Inquirer Answered. Explaining in Question and Answer, and in familiar language, what most things daily used, seen, or talked of, are; what they are made of, where found, and to what uses applied. Including articles of food and aliment; miscellanies in common use; metals, gems, jewellery; and some account of the principal inventions and most interesting manufactures. Second Edition, 18mo, with Illustrations, 3s. cloth.

CUPS AND THEIR CUSTOMS. Post 8vo, 2s. 6d.

HOUSE DOGS AND SPORTING DOGS: their points, breeds, management, and diseases. By JOHN MEYRICK. Foolscap 8vo, 3s. 6d.

ARCHITECTURE AND THE FINE ARTS, &c.

INSTRUMENTA ECCLESIASTICA: a Series of Working Designs, engraved on 72 Plates, for the Furniture, Fittings, and Decorations of Churches and their Precincts. Edited by the Ecclesiological, late 'Cambridge Camden Society. 4to, £1 11s. 6d.

The Second Series contains a Cemetery Chapel, with Sick-house and Gateway Tower—A Wooden Church—A Chapel School—Schools and School-houses—A Village Hospital—An Iron Church—And Designs for Funeral Fittings, for Timber Belfries, and for a variety of Works in Metal, Wood, and Stone. Price also £1 11s. 6d.

BAPTISMAL FONTS. A Series of 125 Engravings, examples of the different Periods, accompanied with Descriptions. With an Introductory Essay by F. A. PALEY, M.A., Honorary Secretary of the Cambridge Camden Society. 8vo, One Guinea.

JOHN VAN VOORST, 1 PATERNOSTER ROW.

TREATISE ON THE RISE AND PROGRESS OF DECORATED WINDOW TRACERY IN ENGLAND. By EDMUND SHARPE, M.A., Architect. 8vo, Illustrated with 97 Woodcuts and Six Engravings on steel, 10s. 6d. And a

SERIES OF ILLUSTRATIONS OF THE WINDOW TRACERY OF THE DECORATED STYLE OF ECCLESIASTICAL ARCHITECTURE. Edited, with descriptions, by Mr. SHARPE. Sixty Engravings on steel, 8vo, 21s.

HERALDRY OF FISH. By THOMAS MOULE. The Engravings, 205 in number, are from Stained Glass, Tombs, Sculpture, and Carving, Medals and Coins, Rolls of Arms, and Pedigrees. 8vo, 21s. A few on large paper (royal 8vo), for colouring, £2 2s.

SHAKSPEARE'S SEVEN AGES OF MAN. Illustrated by WM. MUL-READY, R.A.; J. CONSTABLE, R.A.; SIR DAVID WILKIE, R.A.; W. COLLINS, R.A.; A. E. CHALON, R.A.; A. COOPER, R.A.; SIR A. W. CALLCOTT, R.A.; EDWIN LANDSEER, R.A.; W. HILTON, R.A. Post 8vo, 6s. A few copies of the First Edition in 4to remain for sale.

GRAY'S ELEGY IN A COUNTRY CHURCH-YARD. Each Stanza illustrated with an engraving on wood, from 33 original drawings. Elegantly printed, in post 8vo, 9s. cloth. (Small edition, 2s. 6d.)

A Polyglot Edition of this volume, with interpaged Translations in the Greek, Latin, German, Italian, and French languages. 12s.

GRAY'S BARD. With Illustrations by the Hon. Mrs. JOHN TALBOT. Post 8vo, 7s.

THE VICAR OF WAKEFIELD. With 32 Illustrations by WILLIAM MUL-READY, R.A.; engraved by JOHN THOMPSON. First reprint. Square 8vo, 10s. 6d.

"And there are some designs in the volume in which art may justly boast of having added something to even the exquisite fancy of Goldsmith."— *Examiner.*

MANUAL OF GOTHIC ARCHITECTURE. By F. A. PALEY, M.A. With a full Account of Monumental Brasses and Ecclesiastical Costume. Foolscap 8vo, with 70 Illustrations, 6s. 6d.

"To the student of the architecture of old English churches this beautiful little volume will prove a most acceptable manual."—*Spectator.*

MANUAL OF GOTHIC MOLDINGS. A Practical Treatise on their formations, gradual development, combinations, and varieties; with full directions for copying them, and for determining their dates. Illustrated by nearly 600 examples. By F. A. PALEY, M.A. Second Edition, 8vo, 7s. 6d.

"Mouldings are the scholarship of architecture."—*Christian Remembrancer.*

THE FARMER'S BOY AND OTHER RURAL TALES AND POEMS. By ROBERT BLOOMFIELD. Foolscap 8vo, 7s. 6d. With 13 Illustrations by Sidney Cooper, Horsley, Frederick Tayler, and Thomas Webster, A.R.A.

WATTS'S DIVINE AND MORAL SONGS. With 30 Illustrations by C. W. COPE, A.R.A.; engraved by JOHN THOMPSON. Square 8vo, 7s. 6d.; copies bound in morocco, One Guinea.

JOHN VAN VOORST, 1 PATERNOSTER ROW.

THE ECONOMY OF HUMAN LIFE. In Twelve Books. By R. DODSLEY. With Twelve Plates, engraved on steel, from original designs, by Frank Howard, Harvey, Williams, &c. 18mo, gilt edges, 5s.

BIBLIOGRAPHICAL CATALOGUE OF PRIVATELY PRINTED BOOKS. By JOHN MARTIN, F.S.A. Second Edition, 8vo, 21s.

THE CURRENCY UNDER THE ACT OF 1844; together with Observations on Joint Stock Banks, and the Causes and Results of Commercial Convulsions. From the City Articles of "The Times." 8vo, 6s.

NATURAL HISTORY OF THE BRITISH ISLES.

This Series of Works is Illustrated by many Hundred Engravings; every Species has been Drawn and Engraved under the immediate inspection of the Authors; the best Artists have been employed, and no care or expense has been spared.

A few Copies have been printed on Larger Paper.

SESSILE-EYED CRUSTACEA, by Mr. SPENCE BATE and Professor WESTWOOD. Part 1 to 10, price 2s. 6d. each.

QUADRUPEDS, by Professor BELL. A New Edition preparing.

BIRDS, by Mr. YARRELL. Third Edition, 3 vols. £4 14s. 6d.

COLOURED ILLUSTRATIONS OF THE EGGS OF BIRDS, by Mr. HEWITSON. Third Edition, 2 vols., £4 14s. 6d.

REPTILES, by Professor BELL. Second Edition, 12s.

FISHES, by Mr. YARRELL. Third Edition, edited by Sir JOHN RICHARDSON, 2 vols., £3 3s.

STALK-EYED CRUSTACEA, by Professor BELL. 8vo, £1 5s.

STAR-FISHES, by Professor EDWARD FORBES. 15s.

ZOOPHYTES, by Dr. JOHNSTON. Second Edition, 2 vols., £2 2s.

MOLLUSCOUS ANIMALS AND THEIR SHELLS, by Professor EDWARD FORBES and Mr. HANLEY. 4 vols. 8vo, £6 10s. Royal 8vo, Coloured, £13.

FOREST TREES, by Mr. SELBY. £1 8s.

FERNS, by Mr. NEWMAN. Third Edition, 18s.

FOSSIL MAMMALS AND BIRDS, by Professor OWEN. £1 11s. 6d.

JOHN VAN VOORST, 1 PATERNOSTER ROW.

Works in Preparation.

THE ANGLER NATURALIST.

BY H. CHOLMONDELEY-PENNELL, Author of "How to Spin for Pike."

HISTORY OF THE BRITISH HYDROID ZOOPHYTES.

BY THE REV. THOMAS HINCKS, B.A.

OOTHECA WOLLEYANA.

BY ALFRED NEWTON, M.A., F.L.S.

THE NATURAL HISTORY OF TUTBURY.

BY SIR OSWALD MOSLEY, BART., D.C.L., F.L.S., F.G.S.

FLORA OF MARLBOROUGH.

BY THE REV. T. A. PRESTON, M.A.

NOTES ON THE ARCHITECTURAL HISTORY OF ELY CATHEDRAL.

BY THE REV. D. J. STEWART, M.A.

JEFFREYS'S BRITISH CONCHOLOGY.

Vols. II., III., IV.—MARINE UNIVALVES, BIVALVES, AND NUDIBRANCHS.

JOHN VAN VOORST, 1 PATERNOSTER ROW.

www.ingramcontent.com/pod-product-compliance
Lightning Source LLC
Chambersburg PA
CBHW031055110726
47900CB00003B/933